JUGGLING

JUGGLING

Barbara Trapido

HAMISH HAMILTON · LONDON

For Annelise Schuddeboom.
And for Margaret Alice Stewart-Liberty

HAMISH HAMILTON LTD

Published by the Penguin Group
Penguin Books Ltd, 27 Wrights Lane, London w8 5TZ, England
Penguin Books USA Inc., 375 Hudson Street, New York, New York 10014, USA
Penguin Books Australia Ltd, Ringwood, Victoria, Australia
Penguin Books Canada Ltd, 10 Alcorn Avenue, Toronto, Ontario, Canada M4V 3B2
Penguin Books (NZ) Ltd, 182–190 Wairau Road, Auckland 10, New Zealand

Penguin Books Ltd, Registered Offices: Harmondsworth, Middlesex, England

First published 1994
1 3 5 7 9 10 8 6 4 2

Filmset by Datix International Limited, Bungay, Suffolk
Printed in England by Clays Ltd, St Ives plc
Set in 12/14½ pt Monophoto Garamond

A CIP catalogue record for this book is available from the British Library

ISBN 0–241–00218–4

PART I
Lying Down and Standing Up

Pam, Christina and the Nearly Father.
Intersecting Circles

When Christina was six, she went with her father to a museum. They stood for many minutes before a frieze depicting the Battle of the Greeks and the Amazons. The Greeks were all men and the Amazons were all women but Christina got it wrong. Since she had only recently learnt how to read, she thought that Amazon said 'Amazin'. It was perfectly obvious to her that the men were all amazing. The lines of their ranked bodies, veering just slightly from the perpendicular, made an impressive dense rhythm, something like tall, italic handwriting. The women were all lying on the ground. Their faces passive, their bodies displaying too much rounded curve for any such angular geometry, they lay listing elegantly from the horizontal in defeat. Heads thrown back, draped torsos arched, their recumbent bodies made a pliant counterpoint to the men.

'Who are the Amazins?' Christina said.

'The Amazons,' her father said. 'They were a race of mythical female warriors. They fought the Greeks in the streets of Athens. But Theseus defeated them.'

'Female?' Christina said. 'But they weren't female?'

'Sure,' he said. 'They cut off their right breasts in order to bear arms more effectively.'

'They didn't!' Christina said.

'The Greeks said they did,' her father said.

Christina paused. Then she giggled. She considered that, as usual, he was teasing her, but what he said reminded her of her paternal grandmother, who didn't like to wear her seat-belt because it got in the way of her breasts. She had bought a

T-shirt once in Naples with a fake seat-belt printed across it that was intended to outwit the traffic police, but unfortunately she didn't wear T-shirts much, precisely because she felt that her breasts were too big.

Christina stared at the recumbent Amazons. 'But what if they had twins?' she said. 'How could they feed both the babies?'

Her father laughed. 'I guess they weren't particularly maternal,' he said. The remark contained an unstated corollary which Christina clearly understood. Well, of course not – women like that – fighting in the street. 'Ice-cream, Chrissie?' he said.

'Maybe,' Christina said, not wishing to yield to him too readily, because her father, like the Greeks, was emphatically perpendicular, so that even there, in the museum, he seemed to her closer to the ceiling than to the floor. It brought to mind all those occasions on which she lost her temper with him and flew at him, fists drumming against his legs. He was always able to behave as if a little ant was tickling his knees. She marvelled that her sister Pam managed never to get so angry with him. How not?

'Chrissie?' he said. 'Ice-cream. Yes or no?'

Christina's mind ran along a rainbow line of frozen tubs. Pistachio, tequila, Dutch chocolate, banana, maple, strawberry, mint . . .

'I don't mind,' she said. 'Wouldn't you like an ice-cream?'

Her father knew this game of hers too well. 'Come on,' he said and he took her hand as they directed their steps towards the café.

Once she had succumbed to him, she struggled towards realignment. 'Papa,' she said, 'Pam isn't having an ice-cream, is she? It's only you and me.'

'Pam isn't here,' he said firmly. 'If she were, she'd be having one too.'

*

4

Pam and Christina were sisters. Pam was tall and black-haired with heavy dark brows and olive skin. Christina was small and fair. Since they were uncommonly different to look at and uncommonly close in age, people took them for best friends rather than sisters. And best friends, in the main, they were. Yes and no. There were problems, of course. Unstated problems. The girls never quarrelled, because it was not possible to quarrel with Pam whose sweetness neutralized discord. This was part of the problem.

Pam was adopted, but Christina was the natural-born child. No secret had ever been made of Pam's origins and the girls could see themselves in their parents' wedding photographs, in which Pam featured as a six-month-old baby, in Swiss cotton smock and buttoned kid baby shoes, while Christina was no more than a large bulge under the bias-cut satin of her mother's beautiful creamy dress. Their parents were called Alice and Joe. Alice was English while Joe was Italian-American.

Joe had chosen the dress which, in keeping with his extravagant celebratory nature, had been cut to reveal rather than obscure the fact of Alice's pregnancy. It caressed the undulation of her abdominal profile, giving it the look of a pale indolent sand dune tilted on its side. Alice was not in the least interested in clothes, so that, left to herself, as Joe had remarked to the girls, she would have married him in her sneakers and her sweatshirt.

He was much older than she. 'I was a child bride,' Alice would sometimes say, laughing, when people commented upon her youthful appearance in relation to the two little girls. She had more than once been mistaken for her own children's au pair.

Christina possessed a second confirmation of her status as the natural child of her parents. This had to do with a small birth defect on the lobe of her left ear – something to which

Christina had always referred as her 'Born Lump'. It was not much bigger than a mosquito bite, but evidence of it lay in a sheaf of birth photographs. Since Joe had taken so many of these, including some of her actually getting born, it was inevitable that the Born Lump was frequently apparent, glowing pinkly from her brand-new left lobe.

Sometimes, in her earliest years, Christina was wont to parade the birth process as a form of one-upmanship in front of her sister and, on these occasions, she would dive up her mother's skirt and issue Alice imperiously with her lines, her voice coming muffled through the cloth.

'Now you must say, "Whoops, I had better lie down, because my baby is going to be born."'

'Whoops,' Alice would say, obligingly. 'Gosh, Pam! I had really better lie down because my beautiful, adorable little baby is about to get born.'

Alice was always obliging. When Christina looked back on those infant days, she remembered her mother as being always in rosy mood. She was sweet-faced, blonde, and smiling. There was no sign as yet of the sarcastic edge. That came some years later. Right then she was so much enchanted by Joe that everyday life was like dancing. It was as though some superior force had come along and seized the reins of her life. Joe had appeared like a whirlwind and in doing so had blown away all her priorities – including, right then, a terrible and protracted grief. She had been grieving for the loss of her dearest friend – a girlfriend, Jem McCrail – and nobody else had managed to make any dent in her affections.

Then, almost at once, there was not only Joe, but the two little girls, so ridiculously close together in age. They were like a delightful new hobby; an entertaining extra – especially as Joe had immediately employed dear Elisabeth to help her with all the hard work.

She behaved as though her life were a new kind of game. It

had changed so suddenly that the novelty was still very much with her. One minute she had been a university student in England, an English girl, saving ten-pence pieces for the electricity meter and living on toast and Nescafé, and the next minute she was on Riverside Drive with Joe. One minute she had been wrapped in loss and struggling dutifully to feel something – something 'normal' – for both, or either, of the nice but irrelevant young men who sued insistently for her affections but for whom she cared, curiously, nothing. And in the next, Joe had appeared – all-star chef, bookman, lover and hound of hell – and had hijacked her whole existence.

It was a passion that at first both repelled and seduced her. She remembered once, early on, that she had watched, appalled, as he had taken a knife to a live lobster and had baked it, spliced open, its tail still feebly flicking, and thereafter had pounded its flesh into a sauce for her spaghetti.

'I want you to promise,' she said, 'never ever to do that again.' But his effectiveness, she realized even then, was all bound up with his genius for excess.

The apartment where they lived on the Upper West Side had pre-dated Alice's arrival but it delighted her along with everything else. She joked that it looked as though Bernini had worked on it as an interior design consultant. It gave off an overriding impression of tapestry and triptych and dark, ornate wood. A gilded Umbrian crucifix hung over her head in the bedroom and two fluttery stucco angels played block-flutes on the opposite wall. It was all a very far cry from her parents' determinedly secular and somewhat minimalist domicile in Surrey.

In consequence, Alice walked on air. This made for an exciting, if curiously intense domestic medium for the girls – more exciting than that in which other children were contained; the children whom Pam and Christina visited, whose mothers merely grumbled their ordinary suburban grumbles and yelled out their ordinary frustrations at the ends of long ordinary afternoons with perfectly ordinary children.

'I was not put on this earth to pick up your filthy wet clothes, Maria. Get back in that bathroom this minute!'

Sometimes, especially on their summer visits to England to stay with Alice's mother, whom they knew as Granny P, Pam and Christina had encountered people – ordinary people in shops or in trains – whose grudge vocabulary astonished them with its miserly unfamiliarity.

'I wants, never gets.' 'Just for that you'll 'ave no sweets till Friday, Jason.' Once, in their grandmother's local bakery, where they had gone to buy Pam a birthday cake, the sales person had said, 'And what are you having for your birthday, then?' And because Pam had been too shy to come forth with any answer, he had volunteered, 'Too much and that's for sure. Kids nowadays!'

So life for the girls had a great deal going for it. The spirit of it was expansive. By most people's standards it was like Christmas every day. But something in the air of it made Christina prickly. There was something that gave her an edge.

'You don't say "beautiful, adorable little baby",' she corrected sharply, still from inside Alice's skirt as she played at getting born. 'You say "I wonder if she'll get born with that Born Lump on her ear?"'

Pam did not have a Born Lump, nor did she play the getting-born game, because she had not got born that way. The truth of the matter, as Christina perceived it, was that Pam's origins were infinitely more exciting. Pam had been plucked from the body of her dying mother some weeks before full term. Joe had explained to the girls that the very same operation had been employed by the ancient Persians and also that it had been used at the birth of Julius Caesar.

Christina knew that, as Pam's mother lay dying, Pam had been lifted out and saved.

The effect of this had been to leave her feeling upstaged. She knew not only that Pam's mother had been a most dashing and brilliant creature, a young woman of great promise, who had been Alice's most adored, most dazzling and clever schoolfriend, but also that – because of their quite separate links with her – Pam's birth had brought her parents together. Without Pam they would never have met but, as it was, they had converged on the body of Pam's dying mother: Alice because she had been alerted by a heart-rending letter and Joe because he was the publisher of the dying woman's first novel.

Christina knew that, on first meeting, her parents had detested each other and had fought and quarrelled terribly – over the baby and everything else. For her, all reference to this phase of their acquaintance had got bound up with Joe's bedtime readings of *A Midsummer Night's Dream* from Lamb's *Tales from Shakespeare*. She knew that the fairy king and queen had fought and quarrelled bitterly over the beautiful dark boy and that the king had put a spell in Titania's eyes. And she knew that afterwards they had lain in a fairy bower in a dream that was always midsummer.

Sometimes the girls persuaded their mother to tell it them in place of a bedtime story. Alice would get a bit shy as she did so and make pretty, sideways eyes. Her voice was always full of laughter.

'Well,' she said, 'I thought your Papa was the most unpleasant man I'd ever met. I hated him with a passion.' She then explained how grossly unpleasant he had seemed to her at first; how pushy and manipulating. 'And I also hated his looks,' she said. 'But I was wrong, of course.' She described how he had come along, one day in late summer, bearing gifts and flowers, and had taken her on a picnic and had fed her in the New Forest near to her parents' home.

9

'The most delicious, mouth-watering food,' she said. 'And he'd cooked it all specially.'

'And then?' Christina said.

'Well,' Alice said, 'the next thing I knew, I was in love with him. He was the only person I'd ever met who was as dazzling as Pam's lovely mother. Suddenly I knew that I loved him more than anyone else in the world.'

'Except for Pam,' said Christina contentiously.

'Oh, of course,' Alice said, patting their quilts. 'Except for Pam.'

'He must have had a spell, Mama,' Christina said.

'Probably,' Alice said and she laughed.

'What did you have to eat?' the girls asked her, though they knew the answer already. Christina none the less liked to envisage ripe, oozing melons and buttered toast dripping from trees with gnarled human fingers.

'Squid,' Alice said. 'And the pancreas of calves.'

The girls screamed with laughter and squirmed under their quilts.

'Urgh!' they said. 'Yuk. Blergh. Squid! Not squiiid!'

Alice kissed the girls goodnight. Then she walked to the door and switched off the light.

'But you shouldn't have had squid,' Christina said severely. 'You should have had Kentucky Fried Chicken.'

Her mother blew her a kiss. 'Another time,' she said.

Christina blinked in the dark. *Another* time? But how could there possibly, ever, be another time? Perhaps it was then that some curious urge to preserve herself from the pull of that seductive, eat-me-drink-me texture, that extravagant, indulgent cradle – there on the seventh floor above Riverside Drive – took hold and stayed with Christina and became a part of her being. She had no awareness of its settling there within her, and she never really understood it. But among its other manifestations, it caused her to give up eating meat.

*

It seemed to Christina that her sister was a fairy child, a part of
the fairy dust, while she herself lived in the fall-out. There was
something disturbing to her about Pam's role in her parents'
affairs. Things were the wrong way round. It did not seem
appropriate for Pam to have preceded her parents' coming
together like that. There was something troubling about
the chronology. It was somewhat analogous to that which
troubled her about the chronology of God and His Blessed
Mother.

Christina could not easily accommodate the idea that God
had come before His Mother; that He should have planned for
her to be His Mother from before the world began. How
could anyone, she thought, even God, have come before his
own mother?

Mrs del Nevo was the first person to label Christina a
'sceptic'. She added, to sweeten the pill, that Our Lord had a
special role for sceptics and she pointed to the example of
Doubting Thomas. Mrs del Nevo withdrew the children from
the Mass every Sunday after the Gospel reading and gave out
pictures for them to colour. While these were usually of biblical
personages, one Sunday Mrs del Nevo had given out a pattern,
drawn with compasses and made up of three intersecting
circles. It represented the Trinity, she said, and the bit at the centre,
where all three circles overlapped, had to do with God as Three
and God as One. She had allowed Pam to use her special gold
fibre pen to colour this important central area, because Pam
could always be relied upon to be so careful and neat.

In later years Christina sometimes wondered whether she
had been born with a part of her brain missing, or whether it
had merely been the influence of Granny P's resolute material-
ism that had caused her, so early on in life, to have become the
Sunday School iconoclast. Right then, in the context, it had had
the effect of making her ears go fuzzy. She had endowed each
of her three cirles with brown eyes and yellow hair and she'd

thought of them as the Holy Family. Joseph, Mary and the baby.

'We're having a little difficulty,' Mrs del Nevo had said afterwards, addressing Joe and Alice in the forecourt.

There was no 'difficulty' at all as far as Granny P was concerned. It was all just a lot of mumbo-jumbo. She didn't understand, she said, how 'Mummy' could believe in so much nonsense. It evidently made her especially irritable to think of a man believing in it, though it was all right for 'old biddies', she said, who had nothing better to do. It was apparent that Granny P had always had plenty to do. For years she had run a thriving small business in her home town and she was especially indefatigable when it came to shopping and gardening.

Granny P lost few opportunities to vent her sarcasm upon her daughter and son-in-law. Once, Christina remembered, she had placed before them a photograph from her local newspaper showing a mother with her little triplets in matching, super-automated wheelchairs, alongside a prodigiously moustached civic dignitary who was holding up a gigantic cheque as big as a Monopoly box.

'And I suppose your Church,' Granny P said, 'can explain why God sees fit to land this poor wretched woman with three spastic children? Not one, mark you, but three?'

'Search me, Valerie,' Joe sniped back in kind. 'I guess it's all down to the Vatican's *in vitro* research capability.'

Granny P had ignored the remark and had gone on to tell a story about a beggar-man she had once seen, in Goa, in the precinct of the cathedral, who had been proof enough for anyone, she said, that there could not be any God. He had had no legs and no arms, it seemed, except for one ghastly little stump that he had made efforts to stretch out in supplication. Granny P had wanted to give him all her loose change, she said, but she had felt 'far too creepy' to go putting her money on the stump.

Alice, of all people, ought to know better, she said, because she was not 'some poor bog Irishwoman', but a graduate in Oxford Greats. Instead, she had simply espoused all the mumbo-jumbo along with her marriage to Mr Svengali. She had simply taken the whole package on board in a job lot, so to speak.

Not only did Granny P suspect her son-in-law of keeping prayer beads in his trouser pockets, but she tried intermittently to pick her daughter's brain on related matters pertaining to the maintenance of mumbo-jumbo rituals. She had tried, for example, to find out whether Alice gave any leisure hours to scraping wax from votive candles off old iron candelabras. Or did she darn and spray-starch altar cloths? Or what was that white nightdress thing that priests wore under their glad-rags?

'It's called an alb,' Alice said, but she never actually answered her mother's questions. She just sat there, smiling, like a person who had eaten enchanted mushrooms.

'It's the children I feel sorry for,' Granny P said. 'All that mumbo-jumbo.'

Pam did not enjoy these discussions. She usually climbed on to Joe's or Alice's knee and began to suck her thumb. Her heart exuded pity for the beggar-man who had no legs. She prayed for everyone to understand that he – along with the triplets in the wheelchairs, and all the maimed and all the festering, and all the abhorrent and abhorring; all the victims and all the perpetrators – that they, that he, that all of us are a part of the body of Christ.

Christina, who thrived on argument and was excited by rising tension, enjoyed any situation where she could take sides with her grandmother, because this so patently irritated her father, even though he pretended indifference.

Once, when she had wheedled two Polo mints from Granny

P's handbag in the moments before her parents had taken her off to Sunday Mass, she had succeeded – but only by sucking persistently – in getting him to lose his cool.

'Well, I must say,' Granny P observed, disdainfully. 'A grown man. All this palaver about a Polo mint. It's no bigger than a penny –'

'Mum,' Alice said, 'Joe's point is that Chrissie should abstain.'

'– it's even got a hole in the middle,' Granny P said.

'Terrific,' Joe said. 'Valerie, that's illuminating. Now you go devise some method whereby you can offer my daughter the hole without the substance and I'll be more than happy with that.'

'Joe –' Alice said.

'And in the meanwhile,' he said, 'I'd be even happier for you to stop corrupting my children.'

'Joe –' Alice said.

'*Your* children?' Granny P said pointedly. 'Corrupting?'

Afterwards – after Joe had given his mother-in-law a bunch of star-gazer lilies wrapped up with a cloud of feathery gypsophila – they had all sat down to an uneasy Sunday lunch during which he had laboured to praise the joint and the gravy and the potatoes and the beans and, most especially, Granny P's dessert.

'Oh my,' he said. 'Just look at that, girls. A chiffon pie. Isn't that just the most exquisite thing you ever saw?'

'Joe,' Alice said, once her mother had gone off to fetch the whipped cream, 'give it a rest, my love.'

'Give what a rest?' he said.

'You don't have to carry on as though the pudding was made in heaven,' she said.

The girls began to giggle. 'Papa's in love with the chiffon pie,' Christina said. 'He thinks the chiffon pie is his girlfriend. He wants to kiss it. Go on, Papa, don't be shy now.'

'And what have I done now?' Granny P said stiffly, upon her return. 'Or have I got egg on my face?' She seated herself with a pointed dignity and placed the cream jug before her on the table.

'Oh please Mum, it's nothing,' Alice said. 'It's Chrissie. She's being idiotic, that's all.'

'See, Papa wants to marry the chiffon pie,' Christina said. 'But he can't because he's already married to Mama.'

Granny P's state of mind was not improved by the contemplation of this particular intelligence. She sat in silence while the girls still giggled together.

'Chrissie does not deserve her dessert,' Joe said. Granny P promptly rose like a lioness to defend her younger granddaughter.

'Angelmouse!' she said. 'Pettikin-pie, *of course* you do! You come here to Granny-pegs, my precious, and help to serve the lovely pudding.'

'Oh, boy,' Joe said. But that was all he said as Christina minced smugly towards her grandmother and wriggled on to her lap. He watched her take up the large silver knife and the spatula. He was anxious, for Alice's sake, to keep the peace.

Let us offer each other the sign of peace.

Pam was not a Doubting Thomas. Her second name was Mary. Her names were Pamina Mary. She had been named after a person who was the female hero in an opera and she had been born on the Day of the Assumption. She could sing beautifully and had always sung perfectly in tune. Joe called this 'Pam's gift', and since he enjoyed extravagant gestures just as much as he enjoyed travelling, he had made a special point, one summer, when the family visited Venice, of taking the girls to a concert in the Ospedale della Pietà where Vivaldi had trained his choir of orphan girls.

The sisters had been captivated and afterwards it materialized that Pam could sing great chunks of the Vivaldi *Gloria* from the memory of having heard it just that once. Christina, as she heard Pam's voice steer its clear, melodious course through the repeating undulation of the phrase, *propter magnam gloriam tuam*, could not but once again consider how fortunate, how glamorous it might be to discover oneself an orphan; a six-year-old musical *orfana*.

The visit had closely preceded their annual July stop in England with Granny P, where, among Alice's extant children's books, Christina had fallen upon one about a little girl whom she at once took to be an orphan. The child was a French orphan, a Parisienne. This was obvious because in the pictures she walked past the Eiffel Tower and Notre-Dame and all along the Seine.

Christina fell easily into an identification with the fictional heroine since, like herself, the storybook child was not only small for her age and pert and possessed of two little braids, but she was sparky, conspicuous and accident-prone. She went to bed in a dormitory with eleven other little girls and they walked the streets two-by-two in the company of a kindly nun who made the gendarmerie stop the traffic for them.

'Ah,' said her grandmother in passing. 'You've found *Madeleine*. How nice. That was always one of Mummy's favourite books.'

'What's an orphan in French?' Christina said.

'Oh dear,' Granny P said. '*Orpheline*, I think.'

Christina was captivated – so much so that when Joe came in that evening, after his day visiting publishers in London, he found her still deep in the pages.

'Hi, Chrissie,' he said. 'How are you?'

'I'm not Chrissie,' she said. 'You have to call me Madeleine.'

'Madeleine,' Joe said. 'No problem. How are you, Madeleine?'

'You have to ask me in French,' Christina said, 'because I'm French.'

'Okay,' Joe said. 'French.'

Joe was fully aware that his younger daughter was throwing him a challenge. He was not that good at French and he knew that Christina knew this. She knew it from when they had gone to a restaurant in Paris and he had experienced a little difficulty in getting the waiter to understand him. He had wanted to tell the waiter that Christina did not eat meat.

'*Ma fille n'aime pas manger la carne,*' Joe said.

'*La viande,*' Alice said. '*Joe, he doesn't understand you.*'

'So what the hell's wrong with *carne?*' he said.

'Nothing,' Alice said. 'Except that it happens to mean tickets. You know. *Carnet.* A book of tickets for the métro. You're telling him your daughter doesn't eat tickets.'

It had been a perfectly logical error, he considered, especially for an Italian-speaker, but thanks to Alice, the girls had then got so tenaciously silly about it that he had had to come on heavy.

'Yummy yum,' Christina had persisted tediously, making gnawing gestures on her napkin. 'Mmm, yum-yum. Tickets, tickets.'

'From now on, Chrissie,' he said, 'you will eat what I put in front of you.' He had had no idea that her sudden mood of sobriety had been induced by a morbid contemplation of squid and the pancreas of calves.

'Madeleine only understands proper French,' Christina said to him. 'So you have to speak it properly.'

'Okay,' Joe said. 'Properly. *Comment ça va, ma petite Madeleine?*'

'Is that proper French?' Christina said.

'Sure as hell it's proper,' he said. 'Would you like me to spank you in French, Madeleine?'

'I'm an *orpheline*,' she said in reply. 'I live in Paris with a whole lot of other *orphelines*. I don't even live with you any more.'

'That's too bad,' Joe said. 'That's a real shame.'

'No, it isn't,' Christina said. 'It's nice. Look.'

Joe took up the book and volunteered himself to read her the story, during which it transpired that Madeleine was not in fact an *orpheline*. She was away at school, that was all. And the kindly nun was a certain Miss Clavel who merely looked like a nun because she wore a headdress in the manner of a World War I nursing sister, or an Edwardian nanny. And at the end of the story Madeleine's father turned up to visit her in hospital.

'See, she is not in an orphanage. She's in a boarding school,' Joe said. 'That's a school where you sleep over at night. You come home on the vacation.'

'Then I'll go to a boarding school,' Christina said. 'Like Madeleine.'

'Maybe,' Joe said. 'We'll see about that when you're older.'

Because Pam's interaction with adults was always less shot through with tension, Christina had made the deduction that grown-ups liked Pam better – even sensitive grown-ups, she thought, who affected impartiality. This was perfectly understandable because not only did Pam have exciting origins and obvious talents, but she was beautiful and kind and she was never any bother. She was thoughtful and compassionate towards every creature. In the country she rescued spiders from puddles of rainwater and petitioned her father, in the most reasonable tones, please not to poison the mice.

She read books on making splints for birds with broken legs, and one Christmas, when Joe's mother, Grandma Angie, came with gifts of dolls wrapped in tissue paper and a closet full of little clothes, Pam became the dolls' mother, not intermittently for minutes here and there, but for weeks and months and years. She sewed for the dolls and took them on outings and read them stories and gave them turns at sitting beside her at the dining-table.

Joe was especially charmed by these manifestations of Pam's femininity and when he did the cooking, as he always did on Saturdays and Sundays and holidays, it gave him enormous pleasure to produce exquisite culinary miniatures for the dolls. So that when the family sat down to their veal *scaloppine* – and Christina chose instead to fork half-heartedly at a half-dozen canned lima beans which she ate with a spoonful of green tomato relish – the dolls had their veal on the saucers from little espresso cups.

Occasionally Joe sought out miniature corn-cobs and zuc-chini for the dolls in the food markets and he served them their rum chocolate mousse with tiny swirls of whipped cream in crystal liqueur glasses on stems. Once, on Pam's birthday, and birthday breakfasts always came special, Christina could remember that her father had made everybody eggs *en cocotte*, only for the dolls he had cracked open two little quails' eggs while the family's eggs came from chickens; two exquisite miniature eggs, their yolks the size of buttons, blushing under a translucent veil of warmed cream.

The problem was that while the sight of them turned Christina's gastric juices all to bile, it did not make her wish to play with the dolls. And later that day, when Joe asked her to be his assistant and help him make pancakes, she refused, even though she loved it when he swathed her in a giant kitchen towel and stood her on a chair to pour the batter into the pan.

'Oh, come on,' Joe said. 'My best pancake assistant? I need your help. Say, are you sulking, Chrissie? What are you sulking about?'

'I don't seem to like your pancakes,' Christina said. 'That's all.'

19

'You don't "seem" to,' he said. 'What's that supposed to mean? You love pancakes.'

'Well, I don't seem to like your pancakes,' Christina said.

Joe emitted a knowing, sceptical laugh. 'Hey,' he said, 'what's the matter?'

'Nothing,' Christina said. 'Except that I don't seem to like your pancakes.'

'Uh-huh. So whose pancakes do you "seem" to like?' he said.

Christina gave the matter some thought. There was only one person upon whom she could bestow a preference in this respect, whose nomination would seriously wound him, and that was Granny P, who had passionately detested him from the beginning and who evidently found it difficult, even now, to hide her antipathy.

'I only like Granny P's pancakes,' she said. 'See, she doesn't put all that sloppy stuff in hers.'

She meant ricotta cheese. Her father was wont to fold his pancakes round little mounds of ricotta cheese, spiced with cinnamon and sugar.

'No problem,' Joe said between clenched teeth, and he looked close to committing assault upon her with the bowl of his wooden spoon. 'You go ahead and like whatever you need to like, Chrissie. That is really no problem for me at all.'

Christina did occasionally play dolls, but only on condition that Pam consented to play hospital or school. During these enactments she became wonderfully tyrannical with the dolls and fixed on one or other of them as subjects for sacrificial treatment.

While Pam manufactured little school books, or turned down the doll's bed sheets, Christina pronounced upon death and punishment.

'Suzanne's dead,' she announced decisively. 'She died of a fever.'

The morgue was behind the bookcase. When a doll died, Christina stuffed her behind the bookcase. When they played school, the same venue became the punishment block. When a doll misbehaved in school, Christina shook her and whacked her before stuffing her behind the bookcase.

'How does she come to be so dictatorial?' Joe said. 'Put her in charge and she behaves like a parade sergeant.'

'She's learnt it from you,' Alice said, and she kissed him.

'Say, Chrissie,' Joe said. 'Tell me. When one of your patients dies, you shove her behind the bookcase, right? The bookcase is the boneyard.'

'What if I do?' Christina said.

'And when one of your students shirks on her classwork, first you spank her and then you shove her behind the bookcase. Right again?'

'Anyway, it's none of your business,' Christina said.

'Sure,' he said. 'It's none of my business. I merely observe that it is evidently better to lose your life than to shirk on your classwork. I hope you will bear this in mind, Chrissie, now that you are yourself in school.'

'Don't tease her, Joe,' Alice said.

But he loved to tease her, because she would always bounce back so rewardingly. The name-saints had been just such a case in point.

The girls had recently entered first grade and one day their teacher sent them home to find out all they could about their name-saints. Joe had at once brushed aside their cloying and inadequate little tracts and had taken down his copy of Butler's *Lives*.

'Now, then,' he said, 'let us see what we can do with Christina.'

St Christina had materialized as a sort of twelfth-century bag-lady with powers of levitation since, during the *Agnus Dei* at her own Requiem Mass, she had suddenly risen from her coffin and had zoomed right up to the roof beam. There she had sat, refusing the parish priest's earnest exhortations to come down. She was 'escaping the stench of sinful humanity', she said.

After her resurrection, St Christina had always liked to say her prayers balancing on top of a farm gate, or curled up in a ball like a hedgehog. Since she was obviously as mad as a hatter, people had kept clapping her in leg-irons, but she was not only capable of defying gravity, she was an accomplished escapologist. She had lived to be a very old woman and even the king had come to pay her homage, as a very holy person.

'Oh, my,' Joe said, and he put the book down. 'I never knew that. Did you know that? She was an agile and resourceful woman.'

'Joe,' Alice said, 'don't tease her.'

'She doesn't mind,' Joe said. 'Isn't that right, Chrissie? You don't mind when I tease you?'

'Joe,' Alice said, 'she's just a baby.'

Christina had paused to gather her dignity. 'I don't pray in a ball,' she said. 'And I don't pray on a gate. And I'm not having that saint. I hate her.'

Joe loved it. 'But you can't hate a saint,' he said.

'I can,' Christina said. 'I can hate anyone. I can hate everybody if I like.'

Their teacher was Mrs Alfieri. While Alice and Joe considered her to be an incomparable first-grade teacher, Christina had found her something of a provocation from the start. She spent much of each morning before milk and cookies personifying the numbers and the letters.

'Our friend Mr Five cuts a very fine figure,' she said, her voice affecting jovial, baritone strut. 'His back is nice and straight and his tummy is b-i-i-i-g and round.' Here she paused to draw, first a near-vertical straight line on the chalk board

22

and then a clockwise, circular appendage dangling from it, that made the whole figure into an upside-down cup hook.

'Finally,' she said, with quite unnecessary enthusiasm, 'he has the neatest little hat on top.'

'But he has no head,' Christina said out loud.

The class was then required to draw rows of fine, fat-bellied Mr Fives marching identically from left to right. Sometimes Christina's fives marched unaccountably about-turn and faced their neighbours eye to eye, bellies touching. And when one of her own neighbours at the table joggled her by mistake, causing her pencil to slide in an arc across the page from the nether half of our friend Mr Five's spherical belly, Christina immediately made capital of it, playing to her youthful audience.

'My Mr Five has been to the bathroom in his pants,' she said. It caused a titter among her admirers.

Christina had acquired many admirers among her peers, where Pam had markedly few. In this respect going to school had altered the balance between them. At school Christina could pull in the crowd. She fell naturally into the role of rule-maker. Unless your shoes had buckles on them, you could not play in the sand. Unless you were wearing blue about your person, the easels were not for you. Great numbers of admiring little girls anxiously searched for blue flecks on their clothing, or they whined at home for new shoes. They jumped to meet her requirements and jostled to sit beside her at story-time.

None the less, it seemed that Mrs Alfieri was not altogether satisfied, since Christina had overheard her one afternoon in conference with Joe.

'She's a dear little girl,' the pedagogue ventured astutely. 'But I have always detected an edge. Christina has an edge, my dear sir. Is there anything at all about her background that you feel you would like to tell me?' They were seated, both of them, on little upright grade-one chairs. Joe found the question invasive. His reponse was to deflect it. And when Christina heard him, it gave her a certain thrill; a thrill to be in league with him against this homely promoter of fat-bellied Mr Five, this pedlar of blunt-ended paper-cutting scissors.

'I have an edge myself, Mrs Alfieri,' he said. 'I guess Christina takes after me.'

Pam was not a child's idea of heaven. That perception of her belonged to the adults. Indeed, she was so much favoured by adults that this worked, sometimes, to disadvantage her in the eyes of her peers.

'A remarkable child,' the school staff murmured each to each. 'An exceptional child. So poised. So gifted.' And it was left to the elder Sister Antony, a rare survivor from the old school in more ways than one, to cause the most distress.

'The child is full of God,' she said. 'She would make a beautiful nun.' It was a comment made to Mrs Alfieri, but it was none the less perfectly audible to at least one-third of the class.

That night, after dark, alone in the bedroom which the girls still chose to share, Christina was astonished to hear the sound of her sister's weeping.

'I don't want to be nun,' Pam said. 'I want to be mommy.'

Christina got into bed with her. 'Well, I want to be a juggler,' she said.

For Christina, the image of the juggler was one that recurred, always with clarity, but always with a clarity more luminous than real. In Christina's mind the juggler had grown glamorous with the passing of those summers now gone. He had grown taller than the distance between his naked feet and the pinnacle of his Hallowe'en hat. Taller and stranger, more deft and more radiant. He was perpendicular as a cathedral; as a castle in a dream.

24

He had been standing on the steps of the war memorial in Granny P's home town. Christina, at the time, was within weeks of turning four. He was making balls turn circles in the air so that they seemed to surround his head like the stars around the head of the Queen of Heaven.

'How does he do that?' Christina asked, but her grandmother merely tugged her on towards the car.

'But how does he do that?' Christina said again. 'What does he do with those balls?'

'Oh, he's a poor daft thing,' her grandmother said. She kissed Christina's cheek and buckled her into her seat-belt. 'Well, my lady. Who's got some fine new shoes, then?' she said.

Christina tapped together the toes of her new patent leather shoes. English Start-Rites with petal cut-outs and T-bars looped into ankle-straps.

'Thank you, Granny. I love my shoes,' she said.

Granny P kissed her again. She fastened her seat-belt. Then she took a bag of Devon toffees from the cubby-hole.

'Munchies, darling?' she said, and she tweaked Christina's cheek.

Christina began to suck and chew. It was not that Granny P was exciting company, as she realized even then, but it was fun to be so fawned on and so favoured. Her maternal grandmother was the only adult person, she thought, who blatantly preferred her to her sister; who invited her on outings while Alice and Pam stayed at home. Admittedly, Christina and Granny P shared a taste for consumerism which Pam and Alice did not, but her preference appeared to go deeper.

Granny P made a half-circle round the war memorial and stopped at the traffic lights. Then she headed on up the hill. At the top of the hill were some roadworks which caused her to take a brief detour through the suburbs.

'Now, there's a little house that your Grampy built,' she

said, suddenly and unexpectedly. 'Before he passed away.' Old Grampy P, Alice's father, had been a builder before he died. 'Mummy had a nice young man at that time,' Granny P continued. 'He lived in that little house. Your Grampy let him live in it because we were all so fond of him.'

Christina's mind, being engaged with the juggler, had little opportunity for involvement with the Nice Young Man of whom she had never previously heard.

'Of course, he lives in a much grander house nowadays,' Granny P said with approval. 'He's done very well for himself.' She pulled out the bag of toffees once more and offered it to her grand-daughter. Christina took not one, but two, since Granny P was so clearly in fond mood.

'Mummy nearly married him,' Granny P said. 'They were close as close for a while. Ah, well, it's a funny old life.'

Christina sank her teeth into the flesh of the toffees. She had put both of them into her mouth at once and had arranged them to left and right, like succulent lintels across her lower molars. She was in no position quite to appreciate what Granny P was telling her, and she allowed herself, instead, to imagine that it was the juggler whom her mother had nearly married. It thrilled her to reflect upon her closeness to the juggler's stunning talent.

Granny P shifted gear with a scarcely audible sigh. She was musing inwardly upon her own unreconciled regret. If only Alice had stayed in England, she thought. If only Alice had married her nice, familiar young man. If only that child's wretched mother had not so inconveniently seen fit to die and thereby precipitate Alice's rushing to the deathbed, there to embroil herself with an extravagant stranger. Granny P had never liked the child's mother, had never quite trusted her. And now, ever since, there had been 'that man'. He had risen up like the woman's spiritual heir. He was cast in much the same mould. Over the top, the pair of them. Neither of them ever quite straight. Both too full of fancy and fiction. Casting spells with words.

It was not altogether reasonable; it was not altogether kind, but Granny P could not quite forgive the dead woman's child – that dark-eyed orphaned child who had been so effective in cementing Alice's union. She turned for consolation to smile at dear little Chrissie who, in her appearance, so dimpled, so small, so blonde, was reassuringly like Alice. There were moments when it gave her considerable satisfaction to dwell on the fact that Christina had been born within seven months of Alice's meeting with 'that man'. It had always been patently obvious to her that Christina had not been premature. That was how Alice had explained it to her, but it was surely a funny sort of premature, she thought, that came weighing nearly seven pounds.

Later that day, when Christina walked back into town, she was surprised that it took her so long. She had never made the journey on foot before and in the car it took no time at all. Since she had not anticipated so epic a journey, she had simply slipped out through her grandmother's front door and had made her way beyond it, via the small front garden where, for both that summer and the previous one, she had so delighted in helping her grandmother to plant out beds of lupins and delphiniums.

Now, as she proceeded beyond the gate, she walked through streets of houses similar to her grandmother's and then through streets of closer-packed terraces that fronted on to the pavement.

When she got to the traffic lights, she stopped and waited for the bleeper. A red bus drew up and waited courteously for her to cross. Then she reached the widest street that led to the war memorial.

It was getting towards tea-time when she approached the

juggler. He had just decided to call it a day and had begun to count his money. Having done so, he shovelled all the coins into his coat pocket and he stuffed the balls in on top. They made a fat bulge, like a cheek, Christina thought, too greedily stuffed with cake.

'Excuse me,' she said, 'but how do you do that with all those balls?'

The juggler was extremely amiable. There was something unusual about his demeanour that brought to mind the inside of an old wind-up clock. He almost ticked and whirred.

'I'm just off to have a cup of tea now,' he said. 'I've got all this money, you see.'

'I'll come with you,' Christina said. 'If I am allowed.'

She scampered alongside him as he strode along, so lofty perpendicular, in his tall Hallowe'en hat. Now and then he stopped to look in the litter bins along the way and then Christina stopped too.

The café was in a side street. It was tiny, like a chapel, with high-backed seats like pews built out in rows at right angles to the central aisle. Its windows ran with steam.

At the counter, the juggler ordered two cups of tea and two plates of sausages, eggs and fries.

'But I don't like sausages,' Christina said. 'See, I don't like to eat meat.'

'All right,' said the juggler. 'We'll make it egg and fries twice. Help yourself to sugar. Have as much as you like. Go on.'

'Thank you,' Christina said. The sugar was in a large tin at the counter and the spoon was fixed to a string.

'I like it very sweet,' Christina said.

'Me too,' said the juggler. 'One, two, three and four for luck.'

They sat down and drank their tea. On the table there was a red plastic tomato and a brown plastic tomato, both rather sticky to the touch. In the next pew along was an old man with no teeth who was gnawing on the rim of his tea-cup. There were two wooden notices on the wall above the counter that Christina could not read, but she could see that both were made out of slices cut from tree trunks with the bark still on the outside.

'What do they say,' she said, 'those two notices?'

The juggler read them for her, one by one.

'"Patrons are requested not to consume their own food on the premises",' he said. 'That's what the first one says.'

'Who are the patrons?' Christina said.

'Well, that's us,' he said.

'Then why can't we eat our own food?' Christina said. 'Have we got to eat somebody else's food?'

'I'll tell you what,' said the juggler, 'when our food comes, we can swap plates.'

Christina giggled with pleasure at the idea, since they were both going to have the same. Egg and fries twice.

'Egg and fries twice,' called out the woman at the counter, and the juggler went to fetch the plates.

'Shall I tell you what the other notice says?' he said. He had paused to spread red and brown sauce with the back of his knife. 'It says, "Do not ask for credit as a refusal might offend".'

'That doesn't make any sense,' Christina said.

'No,' said the juggler. 'It doesn't.'

'But you didn't ask for credit, did you?' Christina said admiringly. 'I'm glad.' She envisaged that 'credit' was probably the local English for *crudités*, a thing that her father was wont to serve up occasionally, along with his homemade mayonnaise – the latter always so lamentably deficient in vinegar. The juggler, she considered, had excellent taste in food and had sensibly not asked for such a thing.

'You asked for egg and fries,' Christina said.

'Twice,' the juggler said proudly.

'Yes,' Christina said. 'Twice. You can be my Nearly Father if you like.' The juggler smiled his broad amiable smile. 'Pam has nearly two fathers,' she confided expansively, 'but she doesn't know who one of them is. That's because her mother died and she didn't really know either.'

The juggler pointed his knife hospitably at the plastic tomato. 'Have some more ketchup if you like,' he said. 'Go on, there's plenty of it.'

'Thank you,' Christina said. 'But can I please have some of those balls?'

'I'm sorry,' said the juggler, 'but I've lost some of them already. That's why I'm juggling with my socks.' He pulled out one of the balls and unravelled it, demonstrating that it was nothing but an artfully rolled-up sock and none too clean, come to that.

'But how do you do that?' Christina said. 'With all those balls?'

The juggler exhumed two of his balls and he placed them in her left hand. Then he balled up the sock once more and he placed it in the palm of her right. 'Always start with the hand with two,' he said. 'And always pass with the right.' He ran through the routine with her twice, moving her hands with the balls like a puppeteer. Then he took back the two balls and put them into his pocket.

'You can keep my sock,' he said. 'And I can roll both your socks into balls. How's that to be getting on with?'

Christina undid the buckles of her new shoes. She pulled off her socks and put them on the table. After that she did up her shoes again while the juggler made her socks into balls. Then she slipped off her seat and she kissed the juggler on the cheek.

'I think I have to go now,' she said. She walked down the aisle towards the door of the café. Then she turned.

'I'll come and see you tomorrow,' she said.

The last she saw of the juggler was the jaunty wave of his fork. She felt it was in her honour that he held it so high in the air.

When Christina walked in, weary and barefoot, all hell was breaking loose. Joe had just come in off his train from London and had found his wife and his mother-in-law beside themselves with worry. The women had explored all possible avenues but their efforts had come to nothing and dear little Chrissie was lost.

Joe was instantly suffused with terror. 'So call the police, in God's name,' he said angrily. 'What is the matter with you guys?'

And then, as Granny P turned to do so, the front door quietly opened and shut and the three of them breathed relief.

'Oh, my dearest darling,' Alice said. 'My baby. Oh, Chrissie, my sweet one!' She folded Christina in her comforting arms and dampened her head with a few unobtrusive tears.

'I had my tea with the juggler,' Christina said. 'So I don't need any supper.'

'Oh, my sainted aunt!' said Granny P in a shadowy, weak sort of voice. 'She means that half-wit by the memorial. She must have walked all the way back into town.' Granny P paused tenderly to survey the embracing figures before her. 'And where are your shoes, my little love?' she said, her voice all gentle solicitation.

'I took them off,' Christina said. 'But I couldn't carry them because I had to juggle. They hurt me because I couldn't wear my socks and I had to walk all the way home.'

'No socks?' Granny said.

'I had to juggle with my socks,' Christina said. 'But then it was too hard for me.'

'And where are your socks now, my angel-pie?' Granny P asked her. 'And weren't those your prettiest little lacy socks?'

Christina glanced up just in time to see that her father was staring at her intently.

'Valerie,' he said, 'if I might interrupt this affecting display of concern for my daughter's footwear –' He spoke in a tone just this side of rudeness. 'Chrissie, come here,' he said.

Christina left her mother and walked right to him. 'Granny P bought me new shoes,' she said. 'Can we go fetch them, please?'

'I have no interest whatever in your shoes,' Joe said, rather surprisingly, she thought, 'nor in your socks either. Am I to understand, Christina, that you left this house entirely on your own, without telling your mother or your grandmother?'

'Joe,' Alice said quickly. 'Please, love, she's terribly tired.'

He ignored her. 'Am I to understand,' he said, with rising menace in his voice, 'that you walked all on your own into town this afternoon, after which you took food from a stranger?'

It began to dawn on Christina that she had done something that her father did not like.

'But I crossed at the crossing,' she said.

Joe whacked her sharply across the back of her legs, which jolted tears to her eyes.

'Joe,' Alice said, 'she's exhausted.' But it only made him more angry. He was holding on to Christina by the wrist.

'Alice,' he said. 'You would be well advised not to provoke me. Thanks to your vigilance – and to that of your dear mother – I find that my daughter has been at liberty to wander unshod and unsupervised through the hazards of the town centre in the company of a crazed itinerant.'

'Oh come on,' Alice said, wishing to lower the temperature. 'She's shared a bun with dafty. He's as harmless as the day, that man. She's come back. She's safe and sound and she's exhausted. I'd really like to give her a bath.'

'Not so fast,' Joe said. 'It may be a paediatrician should take a look at her.'

Alice's mouth dropped open with disgust and disbelief. 'You have the foulest mind sometimes,' she said. 'Really. I dread to think what goes on inside your head.'

Christina could feel the tension rising, along with the pressure on her wrist.

'Chrissie,' her father said urgently. 'I have to know this, sweetheart. You have to tell me, okay? Did the man touch you at all?'

Christina began to cry. Her father was being so hateful, she thought, and everything had suddenly gone wrong. It was true that the juggler had touched her, since he had held on to her hands to help make the balls go round, but that had been a perfectly nice thing and nothing at all to get angry about.

'Chrissie,' Joe said. 'I'm waiting.'

She felt trapped and humiliated. She wiped snot from her dripline with the back of her free hand and hiccupped a staccato reply, feeling a precious instinct for defiance under scrutiny.

'Anyway,' she said, 'he was nice to me. And anyway . . . he showed me with his hands. And anyway . . . he said I could have just as much sugar as I liked. And anyway . . . he's got lots and lots of money. And anyway . . . I said that he could be my Nearly Father.'

Her utterance was followed by a painful breathing silence which Joe was the first to break.

'Say that again,' he said, but in a wholly different voice; a voice now devoid of anger but somehow pregnant with dread.

'I said that he could be my Nearly Father,' Christina said, sensing the need to capitulate. 'I only said my *Nearly* Father.'

'Chrissie,' Joe said, 'what is all this? The juggler said that he wanted to be your father?'

Christina felt the need of a little solidarity and she knew that the juggler wouldn't mind. She nodded her head, affirmative.

She heard her grandmother draw in breath. Then her father

released her wrist. He used his hand to wipe over his face. Then he let out a sigh like a whistle.

'Jesus Christ,' he said. 'Alice, I hope that you're satisfied.'

For a moment Christina thought her mother the only one of the three who was not behaving strangely.

'*Honi soit qui mal y pense*,' Alice said, sounding more than a little sarcastic, but that didn't make much sense either.

'Come on, my sweetie,' Alice said, and she got up and led her daughter towards the stairs. 'Let's get you into your bed,' she said. 'Pam's been waiting for you.'

'Valerie,' Christina heard her father say, as she got to the bend in the stairs. 'Valerie, I will need a detailed description of this man.'

'Oh, that's all right,' Granny P answered. 'The police all know him already. Just tell them it's that loony by the war memorial.'

It was something like the beginning of the end of childhood.

Jago, Peter and the Dog Star.
The Lost Boys

Peter had not always been Peter. Until the day that his mother had met the English schoolmaster on the beach in Lyme Regis, he had known himself to be Pietro, though his grandmother had always called him Pierre.

Until he was five, he had lived alone with his mother at the top of a tall grey apartment house in Paris, five minutes from the Luxembourg Gardens. When the change came, he had at first tried hard not to remember it, not because he had disliked his time there, but because it was necessary for him to strive assiduously to be English. In the language class at school, he spoke French competently but not so well that his peers would revert to calling him '*Grenouille*', or '*Mon-sewer Jérémie Pêche-à-ligne*'.

He remembered that he had slept in a sort of walk-in cupboard off his mother's attic bedroom – a triangular prism like a Toblerone box, so small that his mattress had covered all the floor space. At the weekends he had spread his toys over the floor of his mother's bedroom on a carpet that was pale grey. He remembered that his five cloth animals had lived on the sill of his mother's bedroom window, beyond which was a maze of grey slate roofs with leaded seams. Pigeons had strutted over the roof ridges and sometimes he had seen them stalked by a sure-footed, piebald cat.

He knew that his father, who was dead, had been a racing driver, but – as a person who related more to the sky than the ground – it had been a small step for his imagination to reconstruct the man as a pilot who would one night fly over the rooftops in a bi-plane and perch, like the pigeons, on one of the roof ridges. Peter trembled to think of his father proceeding inexorably towards the window in his great goggles and climbing in like Peter Pan.

He was afraid of Peter Pan. He was afraid that his father would come back. He was afraid that *le père Noël* would come down the chimney. He was afraid of almost everything except his own loneliness. He considered that the stars made satisfactory friends. Being an only child, an indoor child, a rooftop child, he interacted well with the stars. He knew that the nearest galaxy to our own was 1,600,000 light years away and that this could be written as 16×10^5. He knew that the Arabs had invented the astrolabe. He knew that the stars were great luminous balls of gases and that young stars evolved, over millions of years, into Red Giants and White Dwarfs. He knew the Twins and the Ram and the Great Bear and the Little Bear. He knew the story of Ariadne's Crown. He knew that Venus was the Morning and the Evening Star. He knew Syrius the Dog Star. He knew that their distances from each other were so great that these could be measured only in unimaginable waves of movement. He knew that isolation was benign.

On the April day that changed everything, Peter was on the beach in Lyme Regis, playing tennis with his mother. He had accompanied her there on a photographic assignment because his grandmother could not have him. She had recently acquired a hip replacement and was only two weeks out of hospital. They had travelled from Paris in an aeroplane reassuringly unlike the one that his father would land on the rooftops and had stayed in a hotel near the sea. Peter could remember how he had seen the plastic tennis set in a newsagent's window and had whined for it. Two yellow racquets and four cheap yellow balls made of sponge foam.

He was not an athletic child, but he had seen Bjorn Borg on his grandmother's television set and the bright yellow colour of the racquets and the balls had attracted him.

He could remember his disappointment and frustration at finding out how difficult the game was. When Maman served, the rubbishy, fake balls always blew on the wind and landed wide, which meant that he consumed his time in retrieving them. It was unpleasant to walk on the beach. It was like walking in lead boots and, whenever he himself tried to serve, the balls, after twirling in the air over his head, would evade the inept swipe of his racquet and fall immediately behind him.

As the hour got closer to lunch, Peter became intransigent and irritable. He whined that it was all not fair and that it was all Maman's fault. And Maman was wearing that familiar, half-concentrating look which meant that, while her body was with him, her mind was far away. Neither she nor his grandmother had ever been any good at playing.

Peter threw the ball up harder than ever and – having swiped the air once more, this time with angry vigour – he flung the racquet after it. It flew in an anti-clockwise arc and landed somewhere behind him.

'*Pietro!*' Maman said, and then she said, 'Oh, excuse me, sir,' and she sounded rather embarrassed. '*Pietro*,' she said. '*Va chercher la raquette et demande pardon au monsieur.*'

Peter turned to see that some distance behind him and seated on a deck-chair was an elderly man dressed in the collar of a *curé* and wearing an old straw hat. He was sitting alongside a younger man who had looked up from reading a newspaper. He saw that the old man had the plastic racquet in his hand.

'*Non!*' Peter said, his shyness sounding like bad manners. '*Non!*' But, to his horror, the old man then rose from his chair and walked purposefully towards him. Peter froze to the spot. It took him some moments to realize that the assailed person was advancing in a spirit of cordiality.

'My word, young man,' the old man said. 'This is really no way to play tennis.'

*

Gentille had been both charmed and diverted by the old man. So few people in this life conformed to type, she reflected, and here was a small, absurd slice of storybook England; an old cleric in a straw hat and rolled trousers who came forward on a beach to work at a small child's serve. To watch him with her son caused her a small glow of pleasure which enlivened her pale, impassive face. There was a quietness about Gentille, a complete absence of fuss and flap, that men often found appealing. Because of it they mistakenly assumed her to be vulnerable, but Gentille was completely sure of herself.

Meanwhile the old man had positioned the racquet in Peter's hand and, having gestured to indicate an invisible tennis net, had taken hold of the boy's right arm and shoulder. Gentille knew that Peter understood not a word of what the old man said, but he was responding readily to the spirit of the instruction.

'Now, then,' the old man was saying, 'right shoulder away from the net. That's the ticket! That is quite definitely one hundred per cent better!'

Gentille had not only taken to the old man. She had arrived with a predisposition towards certain things English. This was her way of being just slightly anti-French. While she seemed to people in England the very epitome of all things French, Gentille was an outsider by history and inclination. She came from a family of outsiders.

Her maternal grandmother had been a fair-skinned, blue-eyed Polish Jew who, being in the final stages of labour when the Gestapo had raided the hospital, had miraculously survived the fatal evacuation by crawling, mid-spasm, into a dark recess for fear of being trampled underfoot. An hour later she had given birth, all alone, in an unlit linen store, had wrapped her daughter in a towel and had licked the mucus from the baby's eyes. She knew that everything about her former life was over.

Young, recently married and very much in love, she knew that she no longer had a home or a family and that she would never again see her husband. Over the next few years, in a macabre and protracted odyssey to which she had never properly given voice, she had effectively walked to France. There she was taken in by an ailing, middle-aged storekeeper and put to work in the shop.

At some time thereafter she married the storekeeper. The arrangement was convenient to both. She was young and strong and the storekeeper needed her labour. He was possessed of an income and an identity which she and her small daughter lacked.

The daughter was Peter's grandmother. By the time she was eight years old, the storekeeper was a bed-ridden old man with ravaged lungs and rheumy eyes, a skeletal figure in an upstairs room. Then he was dead. She had nothing belonging to her real father; no photograph, no watch, no small book of verse awarded in school for good attendance, and her mother – who had learnt the wisdom of speaking as little as possible – had never been expansive in bequeathing to her the past. What she did bequeath was that quietude and muted emotional response which had been born out of her own ruptured life experience, and Peter's grandmother had bequeathed it, in turn, to Gentille – who bequeathed it to Peter.

Since Gentille's own father, aged twenty-six, had died within two hours in a freak attack of undiagnosed viral pneumonia, she too had come to maturity in the absence of a male parent. It seemed the natural state of things. She had grown up a bright, poised and diligent girl with a quiet, private manner and a fine, pale face. Having done very well at school, she had gone, young, to university in Paris, from which she had taken a step sideways into photo-journalism.

Soon afterwards, while on an assignment in Turin, she had

attracted the eye of one Aldo Rusconi, a racing driver. The marriage had been hasty, unsuitable and brief. Gentille's austerity had been ill-matched with her husband's dare-devil hedonism, and she had taken a prompt, uncompromising stand against his on-going sexual promiscuity. Within fourteen months she had returned to Paris with a very young baby and had taken a job, first in the picture department of a newspaper and then on a magazine. At the same time she had persuaded her mother to take an apartment nearby and to assume the day-care of the child.

By the time Peter was four years old, his mother was twenty-seven and his father, like all the fathers in his family, was dead. Gentille's first awareness of her estranged husband's death came when she saw the pictures of his burning vehicle in the offices of her workplace. She had subsequently inherited some money and, having no need of it herself, she had put it aside for Peter. She was a competent, hard-working professional woman and she earned a decent salary. Aldo's death in itself had had almost no effect on her. She already knew that nothing in this life was permanent; that change came, for good or ill, and that, when it came, one moved on. Aldo belonged to the past, and the past, by its very nature, was not there.

Now it was midday and she wanted to get on. 'You are very kind, sir,' she said, 'but Pietro keeps you from your lunch.'

The old man, preoccupied, merely gestured vaguely towards the deck-chairs. 'Take a seat, dear lady,' he said. 'My son will take care of you, I'm sure.'

Gentille was not accustomed to being patronized with male courtesies and was about to stand her ground when her eyes met those of the younger man. She saw that these were dark brown and sparkling and that they spoke ironic amusement at the old man's put-down. Her facial expression responded to this in kind. The young man removed his newspaper from the vacant chair beside him and rose politely as she approached.

'You mustn't let my father bully you,' he said. He was unaware that Gentille let nobody bully her.

'Your father is very kind,' she said.

'Yes,' said the younger man. 'Yes, he is.'

She offered him her hand. 'I am Gentille Rusconi,' she said.

'I'm Roland Dent,' he said.

It was clear from the vantage-point of the deck-chairs that Peter was having the time of his life. So was his companion. The old man had been feeling the lack of grandchildren. One of his daughters, who was in broadcasting, lived, childlessly, with a businessman in Dulwich, while the other, who was married with two small daughters, lived somewhat inaccessibly in Vancouver. As for dear Roland, he was thirty-one and unattached. Puzzling, that, the old man thought. His son was a thoroughly decent young man, capable, considerate and easy on the eye. Yet he had had – after a series of trifling youthful alliances – only one serious passion, some five years earlier, for a shy young student at Oxford called Alice. The affair had ended badly and the poor boy had been most terribly cut up. Still, five years was five years, after all, and the boy was distinctly eligible.

In the minutes that followed, Roland learnt that Gentille was a photo-journalist on a French magazine, and Gentille learnt that Roland was a schoolmaster who taught mathematics in a boys' boarding school in Worcestershire. She learnt that he was spending some days with his parents who had recently retired to a woodland cottage in the Dorset countryside some two miles from the sea and that the old man was a retired army chaplain who occasionally stood in for local clergymen when they were ill or taking a holiday.

Peter learnt that the old man's name was also Peter.

'So you're Pietro, eh?' the old man said. 'That's Peter. Like me. I'm Peter too. Peter Dent.' And they shook hands solemnly. 'Ever set a rabbit trap, old man?'

*

41

Peter went to tea at the cottage next day. He went with his mother. Roland drove out to fetch them from the hotel. The cottage was not visible until one came upon it because it lay in densely wooded terrain, down a winding half-mile lane and over a small bridge that forded a stream. The stream formed the boundary of the garden at the front and behind was a ring of old oak trees. Beyond these, and rising steeply, lay acres of mixed woodland. The old man, when he came out to greet them, had a jaunty little dog at his heels with a pirate-patch over one eye who wagged his tail and wiggled his back ecstatically.

'Hello, there,' said the old man. 'Syrius, meet Pietro.' Peter was already crouching to receive the canine kisses.

'*Alors, comme l'étoile?*' he said excitedly.

'Good man,' the old man said. 'Well done, Peter! Yes indeed. *Étoile*, just so. You have made the acquaintance of Syrius the Dog Star. The Star Dog, as he prefers to think of himself. I'm afraid that most people mistakenly believe his name to be "Serious". He's had to put up with the indignity.'

Inside the house, which they entered through the kitchen door, Peter and his mother met the old man's wife who was tall and grey-haired and beautiful. The kitchen had a wood-burning stove and flowery china displayed on shelves. The table was laid with a cloth and on it sat a fruit cake and a plate of scones along with little pots of jam and cream. The teapot wore a sleeveless silver jacket, hinged in the middle, over the orb of its fat body, but with its spout and its handle sticking out.

In the living-room there was a fireplace with what looked like a small iron cupboard on legs. It had red glass windows through which you could see the glow of burning wood, and beside it on the hearth-stone, judiciously placed, lay a pile of big, hard-covered books with pictures of moles and armadillos and aeroplanes and soldiers in uniform. Inside they all said 'Peter Dent' in a childish, pre-war hand.

Beyond the cottage, down a crunching gravel path, lay a well-house, like a glorified shed, full of choppers and hurricane lamps and pulleys and planks of wood. After tea, the old man took Peter, along with Serious Syrius the Star Dog, into a field to check rabbit traps. Peter was beside himself with joy and returned to the cottage armed with several straight sticks which he sharpened into spears. He did so with the active assistance of the old man who had proffered a bone-handled Bowie knife.

'*Fais attention, Pietro!*' Gentille said.

'Dear,' the old woman said solicitously, 'I really do not think that the boy has had much experience with knives.'

'Don't fuss, Heather,' the old man said. 'It's a funny thing,' he said to Peter, 'charming creatures, women, but they're always inclined to fuss.'

While Gentille talked to the old man's wife, Roland excused himself, saying that he had letters to post and would walk the mile into the village to do so. He longed for air and exercise since, damn it, the oldies couldn't be sweeter, but they would insist on a fire, even on a warm April evening. Furthermore, he felt the party to be perfectly balanced without him. His mother had taken to the Frenchwoman and his father to the Frenchwoman's boy. He spent all his working life with boys and right then he was on holiday. Plus it had to be admitted that the Frenchwoman's boy was more than a little bit wet, poor kiddo, doubtless through no fault of his own.

Yet on his return, Gentille had expressed such unequivocal enthusiasm for the local drama society's production of *The Provoked Husband* that he had found himself, graciously on cue, suggesting they attend it together and leave Pietro to spend the night with his parents.

The Frenchwoman had surprised him by turning out to be thoroughly clued up on Restoration Comedy – far more so than he – and he found her an agreeable companion, thought-ful, calm and unaffected.

And, next morning, after returning from an hour's ride, he had humoured his father by agreeing to trot tamely down a section of the lane and back, with the boy sitting in front of him on the saddle. Roland could feel the boy's terror against his own body but, once safely back on the ground, the child had turned it all into hostility.

'*Mon père n'aime pas les chevaux,*' he said. '*Il préfère aller par avion.*'

It was Gentille who made the first move. She had been thinking about Roland intermittently during certain evenings alone after work. A series of pleasurable images had lingered after her return to Paris; an image of Roland drinking beer with her in the churchyard during the interval of that ridiculous English play – all dolts and parsons and lechery; an image of Roland waxing his size forty-eight walking boots on the doorstep of his parents' charming kitchen. Then there had been all those photographs that had stood in frames on the piano – photographs of Roland almost invariably engaged in field sports, water sports and cook-outs. His evident sportiness entertained her with its novelty, since her own life was – had always been – conspicuously unathletic.

Roland was marking Sixth-Form maths books when the telephone rang. He picked it up immediately, sounding a little preoccupied.

'Gentille,' he said cordially, though he had not been thinking about her at all.

'You are well?' she said.

'Most certainly,' Roland said, who was never ill. 'Thank you. And you?'

'Oh, yes,' she said, dismissively, wishing to proceed to other business. 'And you are busy? But you will have a short holiday next week.'

Roland's laugh was like an admission. 'You're very well informed,' he said.

'Of course,' Gentille said. 'I am a journalist.'

Roland said nothing. He waited for her to go on.

'I invite you to spend your holiday with me in Paris,' she said.

He was startled and disarmed by her directness. 'Well –' he said.

'You know Paris, of course?' she said.

It came to him, suddenly, that he had never properly been there. Once, changing trains on his way to a climbing fortnight in the Alps. Once again, as a schoolboy, on a day trip during a memorably dreadful French 'exchange', throughout which the host family had alternated between ignoring him and watching him with interest as he struggled to consume jellied tripe – 'la treep', as he still thought of it with a shudder. He had subsequently gone on to acquire a perfectly decent pass in O-Level French, but he still, in his heart, associated the language not only with animal innards, but with the frightful Madame Lazarre, who had swept into his prep-school classroom once a week to fire incomprehensible questions. For many years, he had considered that her *Réponds en français!'* sounded suspiciously like 'Rapunzel!'

'No,' Roland said. 'No, hardly at all. I spent a little time just north of Paris once. It's going back a bit.'

'So you will come?' she said. Roland hesitated. 'Pietro goes to my mother,' she said. 'The time will be quite free.' After a pause, she said, 'I have the Musée d'Orsay here, just down the street . . . There are of course many little restaurants and bars . . .' Then she said, 'Or perhaps a trip to the country . . .'

Quite suddenly Roland thought, why not? Why not go? Open the mind. Breathe new air. A long weekend in a handsome foreign city not an hour away by plane – and in the company of a perfectly acceptable woman. After all, where's your spirit? He felt shamed by his habitual insularity which drove him to spend his half-term holidays walking the Pennines, or canoeing from Ross-on-Wye to Tintern. Once, admittedly, he had gone to see his sister in Vancouver.

'How very kind of you to ask me,' he said.

And so it was arranged between them.

Roland had the taxi drop him off at the corner near the man who sold oysters from a wooden counter in the street. He collected the key from the art dealer with the Dufy seascape in the window and he climbed the fifty-eight stairs to the apartment. Gentille's front door was painted pale matt grey. It opened on to a large, under-furnished room, the bare floorboards and walls of which had been painted pale matt grey. She had left coffee for him in a pale grey thermal jug and alongside the jug stood an outsize, pale grey cup and saucer, the cup shallow and bowl-shaped. A couple of *brioches* were evident, wrapped in a pale grey napkin. They sat – jug, cup and *brioches* – like a monochrome still-life, upon a matt grey trestle table which was otherwise bare, except that Gentille had wedged a sheet of pale grey Ingres paper under the saucer. On it she had written: '*Bon appétit!*'

The room possessed two tall, uncurtained windows fitted with grey-painted shutters, now fixed open. The windows overlooked similarly tall, grey apartment houses across the narrow street. Under the windows were two solid, pale grey armchairs of curving art deco design, separated by a pale, matt grey coffee table upon which stood a vase, stippled in tones of grey and containing a dozen matt grey tulips carved out of wood.

Otherwise, the room contained a single shelf of books, a small music centre and a chrome replica, the size of a shoe box, of a 1950s Citroën DS. This last startled him, being the very model of a car he had once possessed and cherished before his girlfriend – fiancée as he had then thought of her – had driven it into the Tees on what had turned out to be quite the most miserable day of his life.

He turned quickly from the model and looked around. The room was the only one on that level, except for a tiny kitchen that was wedged under a flight of turret-like, winding stairs. In the kitchen, Roland registered that Gentille possessed a small table-top fridge and a glazed sink in which there lay two pale, matt grey dinner plates and two wine glasses, unwashed but neatly stacked. He wondered idly who had dined with her the previous night, or had it been the boy? Various utensils and two small pans hung from a grey-painted, perforated board fixed to the wall above a small cooker on cabriole legs. A packet of Gitanes lay open on the workboard alongside a giant grey ashtray.

Roland returned to the living-room and poured himself some coffee. Gentille had made it fiercely strong and the establishment revealed no sign of sugar or milk. He gulped it, wincing, and then sat down on one of the armchairs to eat the *brioches*. As he adjusted to the spare, immaculate space, he began to imagine that Gentille was sitting in the other armchair, her long legs stretched out before her, her ankles crossed, her feet in those curious, medieval, velvety shoes that came up over her insteps. He felt the scrutiny of her shadowy grey eyes and began to feel out of place. Why the hell was it all so grey? He was not, in the main, a defiant person, but now he felt that all the colours about his person – his clothes, his hair, his skin, his travelling bag – were attributes constituted in defiance of an inviolable orthodoxy.

Gentille appeared in the lunch hour and walked with him to a bistro where they ate a few small clams and a salad made with dandelion leaves. After that she smoked her Gitanes and smiled and said very little and drank black coffee. Roland

47

drank beer and felt hungry and said less. Then they walked through the Luxembourg Gardens until they got to the Avenue de l'Observatoire, where Gentille explained that, since her office was within a stone's throw, he should return.

'Before you become lost,' she said.

'I don't "become lost",' Roland said, feeling an irritation which he had not yet diagnosed as proceeding from the inadequacy of his lunch. 'I am quite capable of taking bearings.'

'Ah,' Gentille said. 'Then you may walk with me a little further.'

That night she took him to a Japanese restaurant in the Rue Gregoire-de-Tour, where she taunted his stomach with dainty portions of bean-curd jelly and little parcels of raw fish. After that he slept on an air-bed on the floor of her living-room.

On Saturday morning, Gentille went in to work, but she returned at midday and walked out with him along the Quai de la Tournelle and on to the Ile St Louis, through a street of small exclusive clothing boutiques. One of these she suddenly, spontaneously entered and, once inside, obliged him to sit on a frail, bentwood chair, while both she and the sales assistant solicited his opinion of a pale, sack-like garment with far too many buttons in which Gentille had emerged from the changing room.

From the boutique they made their way, sans lunch and via two elderly churches rather too heavy with the trappings of idolatry, and two small bars, where Roland drank Belgian beer and Gentille drank Club Soda with a dash of what looked like liquid raspberry jam, to the Musée d'Orsay, where she stood, silent and reverent, for fully twelve minutes, before a small, severe wooden work-table designed by Philip Webb of Oxford in 1931.

She made supper for him in the apartment; a casual affair as it seemed to him, following upon several tots of Macallan's and consisting of two very small poached eggs smelling faintly of fish and served on fine-cut circles of fried bread the size of cross-sections through tennis balls. Intermittently, she filled their glasses with white wine. He was uncomfortably aware, throughout the meal, of an insistently mournful female voice emanating from the stereo.

Roland ate as slowly as he could and leaned back to watch Gentille smoke. As the hour for sleep became inevitable, Gentille, after a brief spell in the bathroom while he cleared away the plates, inquired, with that slightly taunting smile which had begun to get on his nerves, 'And you will be happy again to sleep here on the floor?'

'Perfectly happy, thank you,' Roland said, and then he lay awake, listening to the sound of her feet on the floor above as she crossed and re-crossed the room. He wondered what on earth it was like up there, since he had not ventured beyond her bathroom – a place which had struck him as being quite excessively cluttered with cosmetic jars and unguents, for a woman who appeared to wear no make-up.

On Sunday morning Gentille appeared barefoot from the turret, wearing a grey silk kimono. Roland woke to the aroma of her bath oil which had infused the apartment, cloyingly borne on steam. She brought two cups of coffee on a tray and four very small soldiers of toast with a measure of pink grapefruit marmalade. When she had placed the tray on the floor, she sat down beside it alongside the air-bed.

'*Voici ton petit déjeuner,*' she said. '*Tu as bien dormi?*

He sat up, shirtless, to lean his head uncomfortably against the wall, and took note, to his relief, that the coffee had been made with milk. He considered the possibility that she was addressing him in French in order to put him at a disadvantage. Rapunzel. Rapunzel. *Réponds en français.*

How cold she is, how snide, he thought, and his heart went out to the absent Pietro, whose stamp was nowhere to be seen in the apartment. Not that he was one to beatify the kiddie-winks – and, God only knew, he had had his fair share of dealings with the addle-brained, 'child-centred' parent – but where was there any evidence of the boy? Where were his toys, his drawings, his plastic soldiers? Where were all those bog-roll and cornflake-box constructions that his sister's kids bore home from playgroup? Where was the child's Peter Rabbit mug, so to speak? Or was the poor infant required to quaff his Ribena from one of those punitive matt grey coffee cups?

'*Alors*,' she said. '*Veux-tu aller à Versailles aujourd'hui? On pourrait faire un tour de bicyclette.*'

'Just out of interest,' he said. 'Why are you speaking to me in French?'

Gentille uttered a small, rippling laugh. '*Parce que nous sommes en France!*' she said.

She kept a grey 2CV in the garden of a friend's house in the suburbs. They went to fetch it on the métro. Then they drove to Versailles. Once there, they rented bicycles and cycled through the park. It was most invigorating, Roland thought, to have the wind in one's face, and the landscaping was exquisite. And then there was that absurd little Toytown milking shed where the queen had played dairymaid while her subjects groaned under their taxes and starved. Roland's stomach cried out in sympathy. He wondered, as they drove back in almost total silence, how it was that Gentille appeared to have no need to punctuate the hours with provender, or did she distil her nectar from the air?

Suddenly Gentille, without any visible reason, brought the car to a pointed halt along a quiet stretch of road. She sat for a while with her hands in her lap and said nothing.

'So,' she said eventually. 'Now you have seen Paris.'

'Yes,' he said.

'And you have seen Versailles,' she said.

'Yes,' Roland said.

'And you have seen the inside of my apartment and the inside of my car,' she said.

'Gentille –' Roland said.

She made a small, elegant, unfathomable gesture with her hands.

'Gentille –' he said again, and stopped. He thought, ought I to kiss her? But he merely sighed and did nothing. 'Gentille, I'm sorry,' he said, and they sat silent for a while longer.

'There is another woman,' she said eventually.

'No,' Roland said. 'As a matter of fact, no, there isn't.'

She turned her eyes on him, examining his face. 'But there was,' she said astutely.

'Oh, gosh,' Roland said. 'But so long ago. Really. Hardly even a woman. A girl, I suppose. What I mean is, the women I've met ever since – well – I haven't been able to persuade myself that any of them mattered, if you know what I mean.'

'And I?' Gentille said.

'I don't know,' Roland said. 'Forgive me, Gentille, but I can't say.'

After a long pause, she said, 'And the girl?'

'I believed that she cared for me,' Roland said reluctantly. 'I believed that she really cared for me, you see. She was very shy. Very undemonstrative – but she had given me to understand –' He stopped. 'I was wrong,' he said curtly. 'I'd misread her.' Then he was silent for so long that she thought he had given up his narrative. 'I propositioned her,' he said bluntly. 'I put my arm around her as she was driving my car over a bridge. I – well, we had been going out together for almost a year,' he said. 'She was so determined to avoid me that she drove my car into the river.'

'You *forced* her?' Gentille said in disbelief.

'Good Lord, no,' Roland said. 'I merely said, categorically, that I felt the time had come.'

'And for this she drive your car into the river?' Gentille said.

'Drove,' Roland said, correcting her involuntarily. 'Yes.' He was beginning to wish that he had never embarked on the disclosure.

'And you were *in* the car?' she said. 'Both you and this –?'

'Alice,' Roland said. 'She was called Alice. Yes. I shattered a window. I – she was concussed. She'd had a bad blow to the head.'

Gentille looked him over. Then she took up his right arm which was bare from the elbow and turned it over and stared at it closely, as if searching it for scars.

'This girl,' she said. 'This Alice. You saved her life.'

'Well,' Roland said, wishing to deflect tribute. 'End of car, however. Beautiful old Citroën. Just like the one in your living-room, actually. How do you come to have it?'

Gentille ignored the question. 'And now,' she said pointedly, never taking her eyes off his face, 'because of this . . . this ridiculous . . . this hysterical English virgin, you sleep in my apartment two nights on the floor and you are with me like a monk.'

'Good Lord,' Roland said. 'Gentille –'

'Though I feed you with *palourdes* and *salade angevin* in the Rue Jacob and I take you in the Musée d'Orsay to make homage to Mr Webb, your own countryman –'

'Gentille –' Roland said.

'– and I cook for you myself two beautiful eggs in the stock from mussels, and I play for you while you eat, Gluck's most exquisite *"J'ai perdu mon Eurydice"*. I wake you in my silk robe from the Kenzo house –'

'Gentille –' Roland said.

'I give you only my most precious Arabian coffee, ground with cardamom pods, and still you cannot climb the few small steps to where I sleep –'

'Good God,' Roland said, and winced. 'Gentille. What an idiot I've been. Hundred per cent brainless philistine. Dear girl, can you forgive me?'

In reply, Gentille leaned forward and kissed him on the mouth. As he gave himself up to the experience, he forgot completely that he was hungry. He was only aware of his thirst. The thirst was like that of a pilgrim in a desert place who has finally come upon a well. Then she drove him back in silence. In silence they parked the car and took the métro into the centre. In silence they climbed the turret stairs beyond the bathroom to where Gentille's bed lay under the exposed roof beam, like a tranquil grey island in the middle of the floor. To touch her was like putting on silk. Her cold, well-pumiced heels made shock waves judder through his abdomen. Roland had never before felt anything quite so extraordinary.

When he awoke it was the next morning. He saw that the light came in through a small dormer window that gave on to grey slate roofs and that five cloth animals sat in a line on the sill. He saw that the boy's Lego bricks were stacked in the corner in a wooden box with rope handles. Then he saw that Gentille was standing in the doorway holding that ominously small tray.

'*Bonjour,*' she said. '*Tu as bien dormi?*' This time it didn't get on his nerves, but the sight of the tray made him panic as his stomach cried out against its contents.

'Gentille,' he said. 'Tilly. Dear one. Can I tell you something? I'm starving. I've been starving ever since I got here. If you don't want me to expire, don't even think of offering me those little slivers of nursery toast with that pink marmalade. Don't even think of it.'

Gentille blinked. 'You may eat anything you like,' she said. 'If you will tell me what it is you like . . .'

Roland thought that maybe what he'd like was half a sheep

on a platter, dished up with a two-gallon bucketful of *pommes frites*. Or perhaps he'd like five *poulets*, roasted together on a spit.

'Tilly,' he said, 'I'll eat anything. Frankly, I'm so bloody hungry I could eat a horse.'

Gentille put down the tray and advanced upon the bed. 'Never,' she said and she began to draw down the sheet.

'Gentille,' he said. 'Please. Tilly, no. I'm too hungry. I need to pee. I beg you –'

'Horse?' she said. 'But I think an Englishman will never eat a horse.'

When Peter returned, Roland had already taken the métro for Charles de Gaulle. There was nothing observably different about the apartment, except that the chrome replica of the 1950s Citroën had gone. His mother's bed stood neatly made in the middle of the floor and his animals were waiting for him in a line along the window-sill. Through the window he saw that the piebald cat was once again stalking the pigeons. Everything was the same, except that everything had changed.

His mother faced the change, when it came, with a predictable absence of nostalgia. She moved on. For Peter, it was far more difficult – and no less so because he had initiated the change himself. He had been seduced from isolation by playing tennis on a beach in England. He had fallen in love with an old man and a well-house and a small dog named after the Dog Star. In doing so he had severed something; had left himself bereaved. He had lopped off the limb of his own infancy. But how was he to have anticipated that his mother would fall in love as well?

When Peter's mother got married again, they moved into a small country house in England, where Gentille took a break from her professional life to bear the schoolmaster's children.

Since she did not wish to extend this phase of her existence indefinitely, Gentille had both the babies within the first two years of her marriage and all those who met her were agreed that she organized her domestic affairs impeccably. With her marriage Gentille had taken on a new commitment and she managed it like a professional brief of a different but challenging kind.

Ellen and Lydia, Peter's half-sisters, were, in appearance, very like the schoolmaster. They were dark-eyed, brown-haired, robust little girls with nut-brown skins and broad, sturdy feet which they planted four-square on the ground. They were merry, outgoing girls, tailor-made to grow up good at tennis and flirting.

This phase of Peter's life – the phase that followed hard upon the stillness of his grey Parisian sky loft – was something he remembered as a hectic round of nappies and rumpus and bathtime and puréed vegetables, all of which made his head ache almost all of the time. And then there was the business of taking brisk walks in the cold, prefaced by the stuffing of pudgy infant hands into woollen mittens that hung from coat sleeves on strings and the stuffing of pudgy, infant feet into red waterproof boots so that Ellen and Lydia could stamp about in puddles of liquid mud, hyping each other with volleys of exuberant, hiccupping laughter.

For Peter, though he presumed neither to resent them, nor to question their right to exist, his sisters were alien creatures; strident cuckoos who had invaded his nest with squawks and scuffles; his nest which had once cradled him so quietly, so remotely, so high above the pavements of the Rue du Bac.

And then he was sent away to school.

It was true that the stars were still the same and they showed themselves very clear, some nights, from the windows of the dormitory, but it was difficult, in an English prep school, to recapture that benign communion. At school there was always somebody requiring that one buck-up, keep-it-up, shut-up, play-up, pull-one's-socks-up and, above all, be ready at any time, within the hours of daylight, to quote, with alacrity, the cube root of twenty-seven or the factors of sixty-four.

And in the French class, where there might have been respite, his own particular Madame Lazarre was called Madame Maloret. Peter did not consciously understand that she singled him out for the proficiency of his accent and his syntax, both of which constituted an affront to her pre-eminence, but he struggled instinctively to cultivate a protective mediocrity.

She had more than once demanded of him that he make public certain elements of his autobiography. Sacrificial offerings of himself, to be cast before his peers.

'I used to live in Paris,' Peter said at last, conceding the point reluctantly.

'*En français, s'il vous plaît!*' she said.

'*J'ai habité une fois à Paris,*' Peter said, struggling against his own facility.

'*Grenouille,*' hissed the voices behind him. 'Say, Ruskie's from "Gay Paree" did you know that? *Gay* Paree, d'you geddit?' 'D'you suppose his mother's a can-can dancer?' 'D'you suppose she's a warty old lesbian *grenouille-ess*?' 'But surely he can't be a Ruskie *and* a frog?'

And then, one day, as a follow-up, he heard the voice of Rutherford.

'Rack off, you morons,' Rutherford said. 'God, but aren't you lame!' Then he said, 'My mother's French too, by the way – if that's a problem for you.'

Rutherford – star of the house, star of the form – Rutherford, who could have chosen anybody had, for some reason, chosen Peter.

*

Jago Rutherford's early experience had been different from Peter's, though in some superficial respects it was comparable. His father was an English antiques dealer who had met his mother in the foothills of the Pyrenees. Jago's mother's family ran a small wine farm in the Carcassonne region of southern France. The antiques dealer's name was Charles Rutherford and he had met Jago's mother at a village fête one evening, while holidaying in the house of a friend. He had driven through the square in a small open car just in time to hear somebody singing 'Yes, Sir, She's My Baby' in a heavy regional accent from the back of a farmer's truck. The truck had accommodated the band and all its gear.

Charles Rutherford drew up to enjoy a cigarette and to observe the natives for a moment. It was then that he spotted Mireille in the crowd, among the dancers.

'Not bad,' he thought. 'Hey. Not half bad.' Being habitually predatory, he left the car immediately and, pausing only to drop his cigarette and grind it underfoot in the pinkish dust, he crossed the square and waited on the sidelines until the music stopped. Then, deftly aborting any possible advance from the quorum of village youth, he took possession of Mireille and led her by the hand on to the floor. A person in the band had begun, a little ironically, to address the keys of a clapped-out, lilac-painted piano.

They danced for an hour in the small, dusty square, under the strings of crudely rigged, many-coloured lights, which swung from the shutters of the rough, pink stone houses that bordered the square. Then they took a walk. For the remaining weeks of Charles's vacation, he and Mireille were inseparable. They touched and kissed on all the beaches around Béziers and Narbonne, and on all the banks of all the rocky inland pools. They kissed in the food markets before the varied rows of spiced, dried sausages, and in the cloisters of ruined abbeys and under the arches of the old bridge in Lagrasse. They dined out each night in one or other of the seemingly endless small fishbars and cafés round the coast.

Had he not got Mireille pregnant, Charles – his skin baked a few shades browner, his wild fair curls bleached lighter – would have closed the book on this agreeable interlude and returned unencumbered to his stalking-grounds off the Bayswater Road. As it was – and given that Mireille had lost no time in making the matter known both to him and to her entire family – Charles saw no good reason why he should not marry the girl. The long summer holiday had warmed his skin and the plates full of local fish stew and little spider crabs and fish striped pink and silver, and the glasses of pale rose and straw-coloured wine, had all left him rather more mellow than he normally found himself in his flat full of unwashed empties in the real world of his life. And one would, after all, get married to some girl or other some day, and this one, let's face it, was not only a great deal prettier than most of the spoilt, silly girls who pestered him back home, but – given that she didn't hang out with the gaggle – she made a hell of a lot less racket.

Charles Rutherford was clever, indolent and pleasure-seeking. He was also, when leaned on, rather a bully, but, with his golden curls, his Byronic looks and his dare-it-all way of proceeding, he had always been attractive to young women, many of whom were more than ready to leave their knickers on his bedroom floor.

They were married with little delay in the local church alongside the square where they had first met. This feat was made all the easier since through happy fluke Charles had been born to his C of E parents while they were holidaying in France and had been baptized there by the local Catholic priest.

Charles enjoyed his wedding. It was rather like being suddenly given the lead in a film by Claude Chabrol, and he played his part with gusto. He had already endeared himself to Mireille's family and he joined in the festivities with aplomb, laughing and joking with his many new brothers and cousins-in-law, one of whom, a young man he had previously observed returning with rugby boots tied around his neck, turned out to be the priest who had married them. He even took the trouble to cause little flutters of excitement in the bosom of Mireille's younger sister.

'You never told me you had all those names, Mireille,' he said. '"I, Charles, take thee, Mireille Aurélie Arianne Odile . . ." Whatever made you think I could pronounce them?'

After the wedding and the brief honeymoon, which the couple took in Cyprus, Charles swept Mireille off to London, where he ensconced her in his tiny, rather rough-and-ready flat. He continued to live as he had always done. That is, he proved quite incapable of spending a single evening at home and, if Mireille had no inclination to go out with him, he simply went out without her. It did not help that she felt sick for much of the pregnancy, and that her father-in-law took to coming round, rather too frequently, when Charles was not there.

Mr Rutherford senior had proposed within the month that they exchange apartments with him – since he was one, he said, and they would soon be three, or four if they decided to use the services of a nanny, as he had pressed them to – and the exchange was duly effected.

In spite of the obvious advantage of extra space, this measure was disadvantageous to Mireille in two ways. The first was that she did not like being indebted to her father-in-law, whose loud, pukkah-sahib voice and big red face alarmed her. The second was that she found the flat itself uncongenial.

It was on the top floor of a red-brick mansion block and as such, its hour had come again architecturally, but to Mireille the edifice, along with its wide, dark corridors, looked like nothing so much as a penal institution. And old Mr Rutherford's furnishings were uncomfortably foreign to her. After the warmth of the French farmhouse kitchen and the simple, shuttered rooms with their naked, tiled floors, Mireille now found herself in a living space that was furnished like a gentlemen's club.

Apart from the dark green walls and the oil paintings of military seascapes and fox hunts and jolly poachers in alehouses, and the buttoned leather chairs and inlaid ivory, it seemed to her that the place was far too dense with the relics of dead animals. The hide of a dead zebra was sprawled across the living-room floor with bits of its mane still attached at the centre fold. There was a dead swordfish in a long glass box over the fireplace and a glass urn full of dead humming-birds, wired into permanent hovering position. Umbrellas and walking-sticks were stored in the hall in a hollow, severed elephant's foot, complete with horny, discoloured toenails, each bigger than Mireille's fist.

Yet neither of the two gentlemen saw good reason why anything very much should be changed. Old Mr Rutherford because he liked it that way and Charles, not only because he was almost never at home, but also because he considered the flat's hideousness to be such terrifically good fun.

Because Charles despised the people who trooped through his shop and fell victim to his over-priced, polished-up treasures, he had cultivated a stylish indifference to the furnishings around his own home. Left to himself, he chose naked light bulbs and inverted packing-crates, but, if the old man's pad came complete with tally-ho place-mats and all that kitsch of Empire, so much the better. The best joke of all – and one that added considerably to his allure as raconteur in the pub – was that the flat boasted a king-size, circular, fur-covered bed.

'Dirty old bugger,' he said. 'It's round as a plate and covered all over in bunny pelts. God knows, he's been a widower these twenty-five years.' He paused to flick ash from his cigarette into a plastic ashtray. '*Et de plus*,' he said. 'He's got these *objets* in the bathroom, don't you know? Statuettes of darkies suffering perpetual engorgement of the phallus. Airport ethnic. Love it to death.'

The 'baby' materialized, not as one, but as two, since Mireille had been carrying twins. They were born over a Bank Holiday weekend, while Charles was off at the races, and in a grim, Victorian hospital where the medical personnel had kept on changing shift. Thanks to unscheduled bungle and routine staff shortage, only Mireille was on duty continuously, for something like ten hours. Eventually one of the doctors, taking over the evening shift, had declared the babies unacceptably fatigued, and had resorted at once to forceps.

Jago, who was in the vanguard of the process, was born weighing a good eight pounds. He was smooth-skinned and strong and it had taken a lot to fatigue him. Victor followed within ten minutes. He was smaller and not a little blue.

The babies had been sluiced and swaddled by the time Charles appeared. He had been celebrating his winnings and he came high on his luck and bearing flowers for Mireille, along with a bottle of Moët et Chandon. He was delighted by the sight of the two boy babies, but his inappropriately sanguine air and the shallowness of his tributes jarred with Mireille who had had a bad time in his absence. He had come too late and the damage was done. Her emotions had been irreparably bruised and she never really forgave him.

'Well done, well done, old bean,' he said. And he kissed her pale cheek, but she was hardly in celebratory mood.

It was at this point that Charles became aware that the obstetrics man was poised with needle and thread. He was positioned at the south end of Mireille, where Charles promptly hastened to place himself.

The obstetrics man had been making ready to stitch up an incision in Mireille's pelvic floor and Charles, coming unexpectedly upon the sight, pulled a ghastly face and winced.

'God Almighty,' he said. 'Is that normal?'

The obstetrics man had a soft spot for young men like Charles. He had been to school with them. He smiled indulgently, wishing to reassure with the implication that all such things were as mother's milk to him and well within his professional control.

'Perfectly,' he said. 'She'll bounce back in no time, I assure you.'

'But what is wrong with me?' Mireille asked, from the distant, north end of her own body.

'*Ma chérie*,' Charles said, baby-talking to blot out his own nausea and alarm, 'your poor little old wee-wee place is looking most horribly horrible.'

'But what is wrong with me?' Mireille said again.

Neither of them answered her. The obstetrics man had turned instead to address the disquiet of the husband. He felt it a kindness to jolly Charles along. 'Consider this the honeymoon stitch,' he said. 'You'd like it nice and tight, old man?'

'Oh, rath-*er*,' said Charles, covering for his own squeamishness and thinking, as he spoke, that the doctor must be mad – but seriously off his head – to be talking like this about a woman whose privates were currently looking like something in a butcher's shop, but the connivance was none the less gross.

Mireille was one of those women who is profoundly changed by childbirth – both by the birth and its aftermath. She was brought very low by it. The barriers of language and culture had prevented her from entering into the healing camaraderie of the other new mothers on the ward and she found the hospital regime inexplicable and mean-minded. She spent much of her time there in tears.

She had never in her life suffered inelegant complaints and there, imprisoned in the hospital ward, she had developed piles and constipation. Having no English words with which to describe these conditions, she felt herself all the more exposed and mortified. The nurses rationed the laxatives and engaged in jovial banter about her frequent crawlings to the lavatory.

'If you keep on pushing and straining, lovey,' said the ward sister, 'you'll find yourself bursting your stitches.'

She was perfectly right, because Mireille burst her stitches. It prolonged her incarceration by another three days during which time the curtains were drawn around her bed so that she could cry without upsetting all the others.

Once she was home, it was feeding the babies that proved to be the biggest nightmare, since Jago yelled for food incessantly and Victor fell asleep at the nipple. Furthermore, he vomited with alarming frequency. The doctors weighed him and prescribed supplementary bottle feeds which only made him vomit all the more. Great splats of curdled milk would project themselves from Victor's throat as Mireille raised him to her shoulder. They would land in the hairs of the zebra-skin rug, some five metres from where she stood, or they would hurl themselves against the bottle-green walls, between the ugly pictures.

In consequence, the doctors decided to operate on Victor's stomach. Then, in the aftermath – his nether body afflicted, like his mother's, with coarse black surgeon's tacks – he became a victim of constipation. For Mireille, this proved to be a powerful bonding experience. It was one which necessarily excluded her husband and her more robust baby son, whose digestive process could always be relied upon to manage itself with regularity.

Charles had not expected his marriage to become so heavy so quickly. For all that his experience of dating, charming and seducing women was extensive, he had grown up in the absence of a mother, and his resources for coping emotionally with women in distress were very limited indeed. The glow had vanished almost immediately upon his return from southern France, since Mireille, lifted from context, stubbornly ceased to shine. It came to Charles that she was rather like an item of holiday clothing bought looking exquisite on home ground, but showing up strangely dull in the place of its destination. He knew so well that the interaction of colour and unaccustomed light could play havoc with the charm of any item and yet he had failed – damn and blast it – to bear the matter in mind.

Mireille was lonely. In her rare moments of pleasure she walked the babies along Kensington High Street in their wide, well-sprung pram and she bought them new clothes and fortified herself on the benign glances and admiring comments that the babies provoked in Barker's. But the twins grew fast and they did so without harmony. They fought like cat and dog. They pulled out bunches of each other's hair, and stole the food off each other's plates. Whenever they fought, Jago won. Jago was bigger and better coordinated, and it was not surprising that, in response, his mother became protective of Victor. Victor was Jago's victim, just as she herself was a victim. She identified strongly with him. Victor was Mummy's boy, Cry Baby Bunting. Jago was Daddy's boy, bold as brass; ready well before his time to go a-hunting. He was on course from the outset to break the hearts of women.

Jago's handsome, easy-going father managed a certain resilience in the face of parenthood. He showed no sign of allowing it to modify his way of life. He enjoyed the babies for ten to fifteen minutes each day, during which time he threw them in the air and provoked attractive chortles of infant laughter. He seemed not to appreciate that for his wife the experience of motherhood was proving to be an ever-descending spiral. True, the internal stitching and abdominal complaints had drained her of sexual appetite, and even Charles, who intermittently coaxed her into action, could not quite forget the bleeding mess that had so recently transformed her pelvic floor.

His response was to party incessantly and to dine out more than ever – and it wasn't long before the nightly return to Mireille's kill-joy presence in the apartment began to get on his nerves. He felt it as a reproach which, briefly, provoked his guilt, and then, more forcefully, his resentment. His appetite for pretty women had not abated upon marriage and – since his wife was now paler and thinner and less sexually responsive and wholly unwilling ever to go out with him – he felt all the more licence to enjoy himself without her. His solution to Mireille's problems was to acquire for her a French au pair. Sod it, he thought, the thing was a matter for one of these rent-a-bimbette agencies. That's what these bloody places were for, *n'est-ce pas?* And they were two-a-penny round Bayswater.

For the two summers after the birth of the babies, Mireille took long reviving holidays with the little boys in France. There they were immediately absorbed into her large, extended family, which provided a welcome for the babies and diluted their squabblings until these appeared fairly minimal. Motherhood in this context ceased to be a problem. The babies toddled about half-naked and piddled merrily into the thirsty pink dust. Their laundry was dry within the hour and their daily routine fitted in easily enough with everybody's work. Even Mireille's cousin the rugby priest had been known to lend a hand in the fields, wearing one or other of the babies in a sling across his chest.

Yet each time she returned to London, the inertia and the heaviness came back. Charles, who had wholly lost the power to charm her, now appeared to sit like an incubus on her chest. He had become a shallow, contemptible nothing with his nose in the *Sporting Life*; a stupid, selfish Englishman with unmanly yellow hair that grew from his head in ridiculous corkscrews. In short, she found him physically repulsive. Too much contact with Mr Rutherford senior had given her the means to extract, from Charles's handsome young man's face, the beginnings of that jowly, bulldog blubber that had claimed the physiognomy of the older man.

By the time Jago and Victor were two years old, their parents were hardly speaking. Charles and Mireille broke their silences only occasionally and then usually at night when they did so for the purpose of quarrelling. Quarrels occurred whenever Charles made the mistake of returning home not quite late enough to ensure that Mireille was asleep, since her wakeful, hang-dog body language was irresistible to his bullying inclinations. And if the bloody woman was so hell-bent on presenting herself as a victim, he thought, well then, he'd do her a favour and victimize her, okay?

On the day that Charles first hit her, though he accomplished the assault as to the manner born, it was in fact the first time in his life he had ever done such a thing. True, he was not altogether sober at the time – he was not altogether 'himself' as he said afterwards – but he was certainly not fall-down drunk. His aim was true and the blow was not slight. It propelled her against the wall and cracked an upper incisor. After that, though the tooth was duly filed and capped, Charles habitually shunned the king-size, fur-covered bed and slept on the chesterfield. And Mireille made a careful point of being asleep when Charles came home. Indeed, she was usually asleep by nine with little Victor fast asleep beside her.

Jago was nearly three when his mother went to France for the third time. But this time she took only Victor with her and she had no intention of returning. The division of the children was strictly equitable and designed to ensure that Charles would not pursue her. Daddy's boy. Mummy's boy.

Oddly enough, it had not occurred to Mireille, in her severely reduced condition, how easily she could have walked out on Charles and taken both her children. Charles was rather fond of them, particularly of Jago. And he had simply bawled at her recently, with the meaningless but flamboyant rhetoric of his rage, that she could go if she bloody well wanted to, and she might as well take 'lover boy' along with her, since she so obviously got her rocks off on sleeping with him in her bed. Just try taking his little Jamie, however, and she'd have to kill him first.

For a week or two after this outburst, Mireille had focused quite seriously on Charles's proposition as she brooded over ways of effecting his death. She could wait until he fell into a drunken sleep on the sofa – and then? Then what? Could she pulverize his skull with the elephant's foot? Pour a solution of caustic soda down his gaping mouth? Wrap him in petrol-soaked rabbit pelts and set him alight?

It was all wholly beyond her. Besides, she was not quite that far gone as to wish the exchange of one form of imprisonment for another. Instinct impelled her to eschew the courts and to have no truck with any system that would embroil her, even minimally, in negotiations with Charles. No custody arrangements, no visiting rights, no alimony payments, no telephone calls over the collection and return of children. She wanted only to cut her losses, to return to France and to take up her life as though Charles Rutherford had never existed on earth.

Charles was out when she made her escape, but she left him a brief leave-taking letter. She also left him Jago.

'Coming-coming too!' Jago screamed, panicking too late as he smelled a rat, because, although he had no idea that his brother had been settled in a waiting cab along with his mother's bags and boxes, Victor's absence in the apartment had suddenly triggered a red alert within his conscious mind. And his mother was hugging and kissing him with an intensity ill-matched with the careful carelessness of her voice.

'Next time. Next time, Jerome,' she said, but Jago clutched so determinedly at her clothes that she was obliged to wrench herself free.

'This time, *this* time!' Jago screamed and he ripped and kicked at the French au pair who had moved forward to peel him off his mother. He tore two buttons off her fine lawn shirt and bruised the girl's pubic bone.

'But you must look after Daddy, Jerome,' the au pair said. Jago saw his mother run from him like the wind and then he heard the front door slam behind her. He threw himself to the ground in rage and yelled until, completely hoarse and caked in snot and zebra hairs, he fell into a wretched sleep.

It took Jago quite a while to sort out what had happened. His mother had not taken Victor out to tea, or to the swings, or to the seaside. She had not gone down to the end of the town. She had gone. And she had taken Victor with her. She had left him behind as compensation for Daddy. He was second-best in her eyes. She had passed him over for Victor, who had always cried more and still wore nappies at night.

'I think Victor need her more,' the au pair said, who was a brick in the circumstances, but Jago spat sucked biscuit into her face and hurled his Tonka truck at her head. She did well to last nine weeks. Her charge was a major pain in the rear end, and being alone in the flat with her employer was potentially awkward for her.

When the au pair left, the agency sent another and then they sent another. The turnover was rapid and the girls were always young. They were scarcely out of school and they were very new to England. They were homesick and easy to bully – especially for Jago who, like his father, was something of a natural in this area.

For quite a while after his mother left, Jago refused to eat anything but chocolate and highly sugared breakfast cereal. He refused point-blank to feed himself or to see to his own personal hygiene. Jago spat out mouthfuls of half-chewed food right into the au pairs' faces and he attacked them with table forks if he saw them touch Mireille's umbrella, or Mireille's pinafore. He dropped his turds on the floor of the shower and he reverted to peeing in his underpants. He wet his bed until the year he started school. He was a nightmare in the supermarket, where he squirmed out of his child-seat and ran amok, screaming his lungs out and writhing on the floor if he was not given *carte blanche* to fill the trolley with anything that happened to take his fancy.

At three and a half he was entered at a playgroup, where he hogged the toddle trikes, committed assaults upon other children which more than once drew blood, and used the plastic play shovels to throw sand into little girls' eyes. He moved on from there two years later, and raged through the infant class of a small, private day school where, notwithstanding his turbulent and wearing behaviour, he was found to be uncommonly bright.

One of the au pairs had already taught him to read from a copy of *La Belle et la Bête*, and he had discovered for himself the logic of hundreds, tens and units from the door numbers he encountered daily on his way to and from Holland Park. He had also discovered the concept of negative numbers through a chance altercation with an au pair so new that she had not yet taken on board her employer's apartment number.

'We rest at sixty-two, it is not so?' she said, as she made her way with Jago along the polished chevron wood floor of the mansion block's wide corridors.

69

'You don't say "rest". You say "live", dumbo,' Jago said. 'And, anyway, it's number sixty-eight.'

'Ah,' said the au pair, determinedly sweet. 'So. It is six more 'owses, yes?'

'Six less "'owses", turd brain,' Jago said. 'Because sixty-eight "'owses" from sixty-two makes six "'owses" less than nothing. Anyway, it's a flat.' Then he launched his schoolbag at her boobs. The satisfaction was short-lived, since the au pair deserted him that day. She returned weeping to the agency and implored them to place her elsewhere. But the arithmetical concept which her query had inspired remained with Jago who, that weekend, happened to put it to his father.

Jago had always engaged with numbers; always liked the patterns that they made. A teacher in the infant class had gone so far as to explain to him Pascal's Triangle. She had done so because he had told her, quite truthfully, that one hundred and twenty-one was the number that he 'liked best'. And he had often played around in his head with the number on his own apartment door. He knew that seven came between six and eight and that twice seven made fourteen. And that six and eight made fourteen as well – if you added them together. So that when schoolteachers came along and gave him terms like 'mean' and 'median', and talked about numbers as 'rational' or 'directed', these were not new concepts for Jago. They were merely new labels to be appended to existing ideas.

'Daddy,' Jago said that Sunday. 'I'm sad.'

'Why are you sad?' Charles said.

'I'm sad,' Jago said, 'because I don't know what to call a number when it's less than nothing.'

'Say that again, Jamie-boy?' Charles said. He was very proud of Jago, who had always behaved well for him. Charles had never patronized the boy with special care and attention and he was very seldom around. He had never removed his son's soiled underpants, or pushed a swing, or scraped squashed infant foodstuffs from off the kitchen floor. But whenever they were together, Jago had always responded to Charles's careless, mannish style in a manner that made it difficult for Charles to believe that his son was so much trouble.

He was dismissive of all the school reports and all the weeping schoolteachers; even more of all the weeping au pairs. The accumulated evidence of their ineffectuality made him, as he advanced in age, more contemptuous than he had been of women. They were simply not capable human beings. They belonged to some other, half-way species, not quite properly evolved. Some of the younger ones – before the *derrière* began to sag – could be a lot of fun in bed. That was all you could say for them. Half-wits, most of them. Heads full of straw. Incapable of exercising authority, even over a five-year-old boy.

So that when the au pairs wept and told tales at the end of the day, his response was always sanguine. He was very much inclined to pat his knee and offer his dimpled smile.

'Come and sit on my knee, young woman,' Charles would say, 'and tell me all about it.'

These were attitudes that were not lost on Jago as he watched the female of the species come and go. Sometimes it was au pairs and cleaning women. Sometimes it was the shiny, feathered creatures whose giggles he occasionally overheard emanating from the circular, fur-covered bed.

When enough of the au pairs had left or succumbed, or both, Charles, who had not much alternative, hired a full-time, live-in nanny of the old school. A formidable old bat, who looked like a man in a pin-striped skirt. She sat with her knees apart and threatened to warm Jago's backside with a bone-backed hairbrush. Jago responded to her with spirit. He pushed her dentures down the waste disposal unit and activated the grinder. He made her cups of tea using piddle water from the lavatory bowl. He peed into her bedroom

71

slippers and he drew indelible black moustaches on the photographs she kept at her bedside of her deceased parents and sister.

By the time she finally tendered her resignation, Jago was ready to be sent away to school. He became a boarder at the age of eight. By that time he had long forgotten the reality of his mother, so that when he said, 'My mother's French', as he had done in his sudden defence of Peter Rusconi, he conjured up no faint but lingering image of her, no tone of voice. He had never been taken to see her and he never expected it. The severance was complete.

Once at school, Jago ceased to be Jerome, or even James or Jamie. He became Rutherford. 'Jago' was his own latter-day construct and dated from a time when he had happened upon a book about Miguel de Cervantes. He had opted for the name because he liked to imagine for himself a bright congregation of maternal antecedents who, prior to crossing the Pyrenees into France, had fought at the Battle of Lepanto and had been held captive by Moorish slavemasters until they had escaped with valour and guile. He envisaged them as resplendent, armoured pilgrims on the road to Santiago de Compostela. Santiago. Iago. Jago. James.

> James James
> Morrison Morrison
> Weatherby George Dupree.

Jago took to boarding school like a duck to water. He thrived on it and shone there like a rising star. He had, by this time, become socialized. His cleverness had brought him to the realization that intellectual rigour provided more long-term satisfaction than a blow to a serving-maid's shin. And, unlike so many of the children, he felt no need to cry himself to sleep after the lights went out in the dormitory, or to wet the bed, or clutch at mementoes from home under the duvet. He had been through the fire already.

So Jago was in the happy position of being able to despise and patronize the weakness of his peers – although, by then, his experience had taught him to do so with considerable subtlety. Jago could now despise and patronize in a manner which charmed and menaced in just such proportions as to make him terrifically popular.

Jago was much sought after and much admired. There was status to be gained from proximity to him. He was tall, strong, handsome, highly intelligent and commanding. His academic work was consistently way out in front. He always excelled at games. More than anyone, he was in a position to pick and choose his company. And it wasn't long before, to the surprise of all and the disappointment of many, Jago made his choice. He chose Peter Rusconi. Weedy little Ruskie, with his funny accent and his froggy mother.

Jago, of course, had no idea what had drawn him towards Peter, other than the pleasure it gave him to confound the expectations of more credible contenders. He could not possibly have understood the nature of his own blurred yearning; his wish to reach out and touch something smaller and paler and softer than himself; some comforting, shadowy memory of little Victor – that more reticent and less viable half of himself. Victor, his womb companion, the occupant of his cradle; the owner of the other heartbeat that had drummed alongside his own in a time before either of their eyes had let in light. Victor, who had been both victim and victorious.

Now that he was friends with Rutherford and sat beside him in the French class, Peter took note of something that could not but intrigue him. It was apparent that Jago never strove towards a protective mediocrity. He had no need of it. Jago was permitted always to speak his French lines with a proficiency and panache that never got him teased, only admired. Or, conversely, when Jago chose to play entertainer, as he did, occasionally, in the presence of a student teacher, or a temporary member of staff, then he would translate in off-the-cuff, dead-pan *franglais* which always brought the house down. If a sentence requiring translation asked, for example, whether Pierre would go jogging at a quarter to six, then Jago had only to render it as, 'Is it that Pierre goes to make the jogging at six hours less the quarter?' for him to reap quite unwarranted explosions of mirth.

Or if one were walking through the school grounds with Jago, boys would call to him from ten and twenty metres off. 'Hello, Rutherford', 'Hi, Rutherford', 'See you in Science, Rutherford'. It carried on well into their teens, when first names had, once again, become acceptable currency. 'Hello, Jago', 'Hi there, Jay-Jay', 'How's it going, Jay-Jay?', 'Jaggs, hi'. Peter occasionally felt himself to be invisible alongside his friend. It was a feeling he had experienced, from time to time, with his half-sisters.

There was, of course, his appearance to explain it – his size and his fine blond hair; his pale, translucent skin; his feathery blond eyelashes and pale blue eyes – but the thing went further than that. And then there were those occasional, weird moments – there had been that moment, the previous Christmas, as he posed with his sisters for a photograph. He had happened on some impulse to glance down at Lydia's feet and, in doing so, had noticed that his own feet beside hers were raised two centimetres off the ground.

For fear of ever having this happen to him again, Peter had gone about with stones in his pockets and had urged himself to cultivate an interest in geology. He had never really engaged much with rocks and stones, even though he knew about them in relation to his own name. 'Thou art Pierre. And upon this *pierre* I will build my church,' as the old man, his dear step-grandfather, was all too fond of remarking. He knew that his name meant 'stone'. He had no interest in stone. Stone bronze stone steel. Those were things for Jago and Roland. He was far more attracted to the sky.

It was not long into the friendship before Jago came to spend all his holidays at Peter's house. Jago's father was often preoccupied during vacations and he travelled a lot in Europe and the Far East, gathering items for his business. The flat in London was no fun for a child, left alone with an agency minder and the wherewithal to buy fast foods. Peter's father, on the other hand, had recently become the headmaster of a public school. His holidays conveniently coincided with those of the boys and he lived, with his wife and his family, within the beautiful grounds of the school.

As a result, the children had all the access they could wish for to tennis courts, swimming pools and cricket nets. In the holidays, the school and its marvellous facilities belonged almost exclusively to Jago and Peter. They could hang upside-down on the wall bars of the gym, and borrow books from the school library. They could improvise dramas from the imposing heights of a real stage in a theatre complete with orchestra pit. They could bang the kettle-drums in the music rooms and write on all the blackboards. They were allowed to do almost anything, it seemed, so long as they were not destructive and left things as they had found them.

Since there were already three children in the family, one more didn't make that much difference. Besides, both Peter's parents were fond of Jago. For Jago the house was redolent of all the homey images he knew only from books and the television. He loved the simple ritual of sitting down to family meals, which Gentille brought from the Aga to the kitchen table. Pyrex dishes with *pommes dauphinoise* and pots of carrot soup sprinkled with chopped coriander.

He liked the jostling of the two little sisters who made eyes at him and teased him and fought each other for the privilege of sitting next to him. He particularly liked and respected Peter's step-father, who, in turn, found him congenial. Jago, inevitably, was Roland's sort of man, he was physical and brave and sporty. He was well-coordinated and manifestly talented with any sort of ball. He was interested in maths. Jago shared Roland's enthusiasm for pushing out in canoes and investigating underground limestone caverns. Peter saw this and understood completely. He did not consider it at all unfair that Roland should find Jago admirable. Peter admired Jago too much himself for that.

And so the friendship went on. It worked well until the boys were twelve. It survived uneasily through the following school year and some way into the long holidays. It came to pieces at the end of the summer. That was the summer during which the boys had met Pam and Christina.

Adolescence had begun to accentuate their differences. Jago's voice had already deepened and he began to chat up girls. Not as he had always chatted with Peter's younger sisters, but in a special sort of voice that Peter noticed and found disconcerting. He noticed, too, that intermittently Jago was to be found in a huddled foursome with Marty and Pongo and Stet – three awesomely streetwise characters already oozing testosterone and biceps, who had appeared with the move to Roland's public school. Their names were Martin Hanbury-Wells, Ned Portius and Stetson Gregory. Their discourse always died when Peter approached, and he began to sense the unmistakable politics of exclusion.

Furthermore, Jago's domicile, the ugly flat in London, with its vulgar, fur-clad bed, had suddenly ceased to be a thing to be eschewed in favour of weekends at Peter's place. It became a feather in Jago's cap. A flat in central London, with a well-stocked booze cupboard and a frequently absent single parent, gave scope for adolescent revels and made Jago the envy of his peers.

A group of social activists began to gather around Jago of which Peter was not, and could not be, a part. There was no way – even for Jago – that Peter could chat up women, and, in any case, Jago never asked him. Once or twice he had approached Jago out of old habit, only to catch the tail-end of some exploit which had reputedly been enacted by one of the elect on the circular king-size bed. All Jago's body language towards Peter on such occasions said, 'Not in front of the children.' Peter understood that he was damaging to Jago's street-cred and he tried not to embarrass him. For Peter, adolescence had as yet done little, other than to increase the frequency with which he felt his feet take leave of the floor.

Jago, meanwhile, was too high on success to notice Peter's wretchedness. He was himself a victim, since his hormones told him to chase after women and his instincts told him to lead the pack. His senses dominated his life, which became a tightrope of excitement and danger. All through that first summer term, and in homage to Jago, 'the group' – Jago's group – proved their worth by knocking off bottles of hard liquor from the local off-licence and drinking it until they threw up. School life became a matter of hiding one's cigarettes from the masters and endeavouring to ensure that one did not reek of Dubonnet.

Home weekends and holidays were given over to groping young women in dark, smoke-filled rooms. The women wore heavy make-up and short black skirts with black tights. Their faces were made up white. Some of them pierced their nostrils and poured chlorinated lav cleaner over their heads of razored hair. The style was modified prostitute. As the boldest and wittiest of them had recently bragged to Jago, 'Even a prostitute mistook me for a prostitute.' They were all of them the daughters of affluent London professionals and they all attended expensive private schools. Their names were abbreviated versions of those appearing regularly in the *Times* Births and Marriages columns. They were Tori and Toni and Suki and Tatti and Chessi. They kept their dope in elegant little silver boxes and for all of them social success meant visibly scoring with Jago.

For a while the friendship with Peter maintained itself in spite of these preoccupying diversions. It sustained itself uneasily through a technique of rigorous occupational segregation. Jago still visited Peter's house where he swam and hiked and messed about much as he had always done. Both the boys enjoyed it, especially Jago, to whom it gave respite and relief from the pressures of his more competitive social life, but it was destined not to last. The problem was to be that final week of the forthcoming summer holiday.

Jago and Peter had always gone boating together in the last week of the summer. Boating and camping. When they were younger, Peter's step-father had accompanied them, but, for years now, they had managed it on their own. This week had always been nothing short of idyllic. They had paddled downstream and pitched camp at night on river-banks. They had made cooking fires over which they had singed sausages and heated packet soup or spaghetti hoops. They had fished and set rabbit traps and messed about in the water. Then, after seven days, Roland had come to collect them.

This summer, as the holidays drew to a close, Jago was seriously torn.

'About the trip,' he said. 'How about if Stet comes too?'

Peter hated the idea. 'All right, then,' he said.

'Just the three of us,' Jago said, knowing full well that Stet had already asked Pongo and that Pongo knew these women

78

who were hatching to camp a few yards downstream with a ghetto-blaster and a stack of cassettes and two massive coolbags filled with Stella Artois.

In the event the women cried off, but Stet and Pongo and Marty needed no back-up to prove themselves effective saboteurs. Having no outdoor equipment of their own, they colonized Peter's three-man tent and slept every day until noon. They smoked through the night and burnt cigarette holes in the floor and threw their empty beer cans into the river. Since such money as they had brought along with them had quickly been spent on alcohol and cigarettes, they were wholly parasitical on Peter's food supplies and blamed him when these ran out.

Finally, bored rigid without their urban props, they commandeered the remains of Peter's money while Jago was taking a swim. Then, hailing Jago from the shore to clothe himself and join them on a foray into the village, the four of them set out to fill their stomachs at the local doner kebab van, after which they spent the balance in the pub before returning at some point around midnight.

Peter was already asleep when Pongo and Stet conceived the idea of setting the tent alight with him still inside it. But, since the exercise proved to be rather more difficult than they had anticipated, Peter awoke, not to find himself surrounded by flames and noxious fumes, but to the smell of sulphur and the sound of the clumsy drunken duo singeing their fingers on ignited matches which they were dropping frequently, amid loud expletives and guffaws.

Jago had taken no part in this scheme, just as he had taken no part in the commandeering of Peter's money. But, though he was considerably less affected by the evening's drinking spree than the others, he had certainly imbibed enough to take a fairly sanguine view. He had seated himself at a little distance and had begun to take off his shoes.

79

Peter was both angered and wounded by his friend's neutrality. He felt that matters had come to a head and he got up and confronted him.

'You've got to choose,' Peter said. 'Jago, you've got to choose. It's either them or it's me.' Anger and sleep and fear and hurt had caused his still unbroken voice to rise and rise in the night air.

'"You've got to choose, Jago",' Pongo parodied in a pantomime treble. '"Jago, please choose me".'

Jago laughed. Given an ultimatum like that, he really had no alternative. In truth, he had made his choice already.

The pain of severance was terrible for Peter and difficult to assuage. It signified another landmark in the taking leave of childhood. It felt, once again, like a limb lopped off. Naturally, it was also painful for Jago, though he had been the one who had made the choice; the one who had brought down the axe.

The camp was abandoned next morning. Though Stet and Pongo and Marty had barely noticed, it was glaringly apparent both to Jago and to Peter that the thing had become dangerously redolent of *Lord of the Flies*.

Christina had been reading *Lord of the Flies* some two months earlier. She had been lounging in a swimsuit on a small wooden pier built out into the waters of Lake Sanopee in New Hampshire. She was in the company of her recently widowed paternal grandmother.

'This is crap,' she said. 'Have you ever tried to read this, Grandma Anj?'

Grandma Angie smiled at her. 'Your grandpa liked it a lot,' she said. 'Me, I couldn't get along with all those little hobbits and elves.'

'That's *Lord of the Rings*,' Christina said. 'This one's about a bunch of boys that hunt and fish and have cookouts and then they go to war with each other.'

'Same thing,' Grandma Angie said. 'For myself, Chrissie, I like to read a book that provides a little female company.'

Christina laughed. 'These kids,' she said. 'They're English schoolboys, right? They dress up and they start doing all this ritual sacrifice and stuff. Well, I just can't get myself to believe those kids would behave like that.'

That was the summer before she chose to attend Roland's boarding school in England.

PART II
Leaning Forward

The Fat Priest, the Nice Young Man and the Beautiful Dark Boy

During Christina's thirteenth year, Joe's father died. He was known to the girls as Grandpa Bernardo and his mistress was one of the many people who turned up at the funeral. She was quite a shock for everyone except for Grandma Angie who had been aware of her existence for almost twenty years. The mistress was a good deal younger than Grandma Angie and she looked very pretty in her size ten, black crêpe sheath dress and her small, black, pillbox hat which was veiled with black tulle and daintily trellis-patterned with a host of tiny black beads. Her grief, like Grandma Angie's, was patently genuine, and it was difficult not to notice that, of the two bereaved women, she made much the more picturesque widow.

Afterwards, alone with his wife and his mother, Joe had declared himself outraged. He had fumed and stormed and advocated the stripping of any assets that had accrued to the mistress over the past two decades and any that might possibly accrue to her in the future. Pam and Christina had heard it all through the wall, though every now and again their father lowered his voice in a spirit of *pas devant les enfants*. Alice said straight out that secrecy was idiotic and that the girls were not babies any longer, in case he had not noticed. Certainly, neither girl was a baby and both were using tampons.

Grandma Angie made soothing noises while Alice grasped the issue more contentiously.

'You've got to respect your father's wishes,' she said. 'All this fuss and bother. What's the point? We all know the man was an absolute sweetie. I know he was always lovely to me.'

This was true. He had always been lovely to her. He had never forgotten that, because of her, he and Grandma Angie had at last acquired two grandchildren. He had determinedly considered her every action as evidence of peculiar ability and peculiar virtue. He had showered her with tokens of his affection and had fallen upon her with praise. Once he had come upon her as she was guiding Pam through her piano practice. 'A perfect wife, a perfect mother *and a musician*,' he said.

'Well,' Alice said, made weary now by her husband's judgmental wrath in the aftermath of the funeral, 'what I say is hats off to Bernardo for "keeping" the woman. Most kept women nowadays are required to keep themselves.'

'Alice,' Joe said stiffly, 'your terminology is insensitive.'

'Oh, excuse me,' Alice said. 'Dear, dear. Mr Purity himself. And I don't suppose the tiniest little transgression has ever crossed your mind?'

The pause that followed this throwaway taunt was just a little too long for comfort.

'I don't stoop to answer such a question,' he said.

'Well, I wonder why not,' Alice said.

They had got to England late that summer. Weeks later than usual. They had been pampering Grandma Angie. And then, having been no more than three days at Granny P's, Christina's father had telephoned from his hotel room in Russell Square, to announce a wholly unscheduled meeting with his wife and daughters on a railway station platform somewhere in Worcestershire.

He would catch the train direct from London, Paddington, he said, while the three of them would leave by train from Surrey. They were to spend the weekend in the Malvern Hills and they would put up at an old coaching inn.

It was evident that he had chanced to read, in one of his most recently acquired travel and food guides, that this idyllically portrayed establishment served the best of traditional English food and kept its cellar stocked with English wines. Christina's father had immediately become curious to taste its pink-fleshed lamb and its West Country goat cheese rolled in wood ash. Furthermore, he was entertained by the notion of Chiltern hock.

Alice had not responded to the project in quite the right spirit, both because she feared that her mother would be displeased and because her husband had made the arrangement without consulting her. She had, during the course of that year, developed a distinctly sharper edge. Alice had brought to the surface a latent talent for put-down and was wont to spike her marital interaction with compulsive barbs of irony.

'Irony,' Christina had recently observed to her sister, 'is the refuge of the impotent.' She had borrowed this assertion from the introduction to an eighteenth-century novel, but it seemed to her that it met her mother's case.

'She always ends up caving in to him,' she said. 'So why does she bother with all the sniping?'

Right then, as she lent an ear to her mother's proceedings on the telephone, Christina pulled a face at Pam, rather sour, drawing down the corners of her mouth.

'Bor-ing,' she said, sing-song-wise, because that was what it was. Boring so you wanted to scream. Boring and irritating. Could anyone else's parents possibly be that irritating? Take her mother. There she was, embarked upon a pointless repeating ritual, like a dance. The intention was not to move on and get somewhere different, but always merely to return to the starting position. A lobster quadrille in which she and Pam were somehow impelled to take up horribly predictable positions. Pam would always be pleasing and appeasing. She, Christina, always stoking and provoking. But nothing would ever change. And, if the man irritated the hell out of her mother – as assuredly he had to – then why didn't she for God's sake just spit on his face and quit?

'Joe,' Alice was saying, 'but we've only just got here. It's absurd. And frankly, I'd rather day-trip into London and eat moussaka in Greek Street. Why this sudden passion for hunting down toad-in-the-hole and spotted dog?'

'Pardon me?' he said.

'It's food,' she said. 'You know. Brit food. Traditional. Like what you're suddenly so keen to have us eat.'

'Alice,' he said, 'you'll love it. This place. It's beautiful. The countryside is beautiful. It's Piers Plowman country.'

'Oh, but that's gross!' she said. '"Piers Plowman country". That's some cruddy little enticement from the heritage industry. How can you? Really. I wonder they're not claiming it as the "home of the plowman's lunch".'

'Alice,' he said, 'you'll love it.'

And then he detailed the travel itinerary. 'Take care now,' he said, after he had given her the departure times and had impressed upon her the need to change trains at Reading. 'That's Great Malvern, okay? That's not Malvern Link.'

'So whose country is this, anyway?' she said.

'Listen,' he said, 'it's possible I'll be a little delayed. There's a restaurant right there on the platform. I'd guess it's pretty nice. The girls will like it. It's an old railway tea-room. It's been renovated.'

'Ah,' Alice said. 'The "Romance of Steam". And meanwhile the British Government is murdering the railways.'

'Oh, well. Now we'll definitely go,' Christina said to her sister. 'You can always tell when she's capitulated. It's when she decides to stop sniping at him and she starts to snipe about politics. What's the matter with her? Do you suppose there's something wrong with her sex life?'

'I expect it's very beautiful,' Pam said.

'Not her sex life, I hope?' Christina said.

'Chrissie,' Pam said. 'I mean this place. You know. This place up in the hills that Papa wants us to see.'

And they went – of course – though Granny P took umbrage at their going, just as Christina ground her teeth. She had come to regard these family excursions as inexcusable exercises in pseudo-togetherness; tyrannical demonstrations of coercive cohesion scarcely to be endured. There were times when she dreamed of running away. Would she survive 'out there'? Would she make out? She envisaged herself as one of those forlorn little faces that stared out from occasional milk cartons back home, or from the posters in Grand Central Station.

Have you seen this child?
Christina Rosalia Angeletti.
Twelve years, eleven months.
Last seen changing trains in Reading, UK
Eyes: blue. Hair: blonde.
Bermudas and sneakers screaming green.
(Purchased with satisfaction in defiance of parental taste.)
Small gristly lump on left earlobe.
Parents: irritating.
Mother: ineffectual.
Father: culture-fiend.
Also, Professional Guardian of Traditional Family Values.

Yet, in the event, there was something unexpected about the Renovated Railway Tea-room. It was offering an unscheduled extra. Something was there, along with the pretty iron chairs and tables that had spilled out on to the platform in the July sunshine. Something marvellous was there along with the big brass bell over the doorway and the rows of cakes on the counter sitting fatly under their glass domes. Something uplifting and beautiful was there and it was making the dark oak varnish of the wainscoting take on colour and sing to her.

The beautiful thing was Jago.

Jago Rutherford
Iago
Jago
Jerome
James George Rutherford
James the Son of Zebedee
James the Son of Thunder
James James
Morrison Morrison
Weatherby George Dupree.

Jago Rutherford, thirteen the previous day, had not yet fallen out with Peter. He had spent the few days since school had broken up in Peter's parents' house. He was, without doubt, a beautiful dark boy. He was the most beautiful boy in the world. He was tall, slim and olive-skinned – an exquisite schoolboy with white teeth and hazel eyes fringed with thick, dark lashes. His hair, which was raven-black and curly, had been cut severely in the style of the 14–18 War, but was struggling to get out of line. His features were not only bold and striking in themselves. They were much enhanced by the ease with which top-doggery had chosen to sit on him.

Christina found something Moorish in his looks – something that allowed her at once to transpose him to a scene in which, turbaned in bright silk, his djellaba doused in the sea-spray, he was managing wild, white stallions on a beach somewhere in North Africa. And as her adoring eye travelled from the perfect arc of his brow, to the wing shape of his shoulder-blade, to the jut of his exquisite, angular hip, she was struck by an unfamiliar but none the less powerful emotion whose cause was instantly definable as the piercing dart of love.

I am in love, Christina sang to the inside of her head. I am in love. I am in love. I am nearly thirteen and I am in love.

Forever.
Like Clara Schumann.

There were in fact two boys in front of her and both were dressed for cricket. The smaller boy had at first been invisible to her, both because Jago had so captured her attention and because the boy himself was somehow curiously insubstantial. He was blond and not quite opaque. The only colour about him was in the two bright green grass-stains that besmirched both knees of his white flannels. These, as if by compensation, were peculiarly vivid. They were not so much the colour of moss; more the colour of crystallized angelica – but then, English grass, after a rainy July, could be very green indeed. And he stood there beside the beautiful dark boy, his mouth slightly ajar, insubstantial as an elf, or as a small, androgynous angel beside a Barbary pirate.

The beautiful dark boy did not have grass-stains on his knees. What he had, instead, was an intriguing streak of wine-red dye that ran along the top of his right thigh from a source so close to his crotch that it was difficult for Christina to examine it without self-consciousness.

The boys were in the company of an amiable, middle-aged adult whose large, loose frame had been bundled into a comfortably old, flecked hiking jumper and faded corduroy bags. It was apparent that he had begun to stare hard at the girls' mother.

'Good Lord!' he said. 'No, it can't be!'

'I don't believe this!' said the girls' mother, colouring

slightly. They followed up these exclamations with short bursts of laughter and long embraces and kisses.

'But what on earth are you doing here?' she said. 'This is completely ridiculous. Gosh ... well, now ... it must be thirteen years.'

'I'm afraid so,' he said. He had smiling brown eyes that were at that moment beaming pleasure down on to her face. 'As a matter of fact, I live here,' he said. 'Fifteen miles as the crow flies. We're in town because the boys have been lending their services to the local Under-Sixteens.'

His eyes then ranged over the whole of her person, after which he glanced with interest at the two girls.

'But what about you, Alice?' he said. 'You are the one of us who is out of context, my dear.'

'Yes,' she said.

'Still living in America?' he said.

'Yes,' she said. 'We're here on holiday. I am waiting for my husband.'

'Ah,' he said.

In the pause that followed, Alice took stock of the boys. They were just as different to look at as her own two girls. One so tall and dark; one so small and fair. Strangely, even the colours of their clothing correlated after a fashion. The green grass-stains with Chrissie's ferocious green shorts; the wine-red dye stain with the deep burgundy lamb's-wool of Pam's new sweater.

'And these are your boys?' she said.

'One of them,' he said. 'Peter here is my step-son.' He indicated the small blond boy. 'James is his great friend.'

'Ah,' she said.

'And one of these young ladies,' he said, 'would be the infant I once encountered in a rush basket?'

'Why, so you did,' Alice said. 'Yes. And that was Pam. And now you must meet Christina, who is my younger daughter.

92

Girls,' she said, 'this is my dear friend Mr Dent, from long ago, before either of you was born.'

Christina shook hands with the stranger and surprised herself by assessing him as inescapably nice. But then this ought not to have surprised her, since here was no ordinary adult. It came to her in a moment that she was shaking hands with none other than Mummy's Nice Young Man.

Having been so suddenly wooed from adolescent ill-humour by the unexpected appearance of Jago, Christina was disposed, now, to exercise benign judgment upon the Nice Young Man. It seemed to her that her mother's friend was far more nice than merely 'nice'. There was something about him that she could savour and relish; something avuncular and reassuring. It was as if he had come trailing a bag of blessings from a calmer, kinder world. A world of wood fires and skillet bread and lilac trees. A world in which men would knock out pipes on the soles of their boots and put their feet on the fender.

She observed, thereafter, with a glow of pleasure, how courteously he bestirred himself for them and with so much easy, unofficious aptitude, gathering extra chairs around a table for their comfort, insisting firmly on the need for some refreshment while they waited for her father's train.

And there was the sun, shining so brilliantly, slanting across the platform and catching the polished brass of the bell. And there was the beautiful dark boy, who had seated himself beside her, just as she knew it was ordained that he should.

'Pimms, Alice?' her mother's friend said, addressing her as though he were involving her, lightly, in some nostalgic reference to their own past. 'Now, how does that strike you?'

It seemed to Christina that her mother's layers of barbed irony had suddenly fallen away.

'As heaven itself, Roland,' she said. 'Oh, I say. What fun this is! What a coincidence. What luck!'

*

93

The children drank ginger beer and ate hot chicken sandwiches – all except Christina, who picked happily at the soft, sweet inside of a large, vanilla-flavoured cup-cake that the management had been pleased to call a 'muffin', but who cared? Everything was so perfect. Her mother's drink came clinking with ice cubes and coloured like amber; floating with mint leaves and wedges of citrus fruit and apple. It was a drink like a distilled orchard. It was the summer contained in a goblet. And then there was her mother, prettily flushed with surprise, as she sat beside her charming, well-mannered man friend from all those years long ago.

'And then there is my father,' Christina thought. 'Who is blissfully not here.'

For Christina to be wooed by an adult that year, and an adult who was in any way associated with her parents, was really most unusual. She had been finding her parents and all their acquaintances increasingly difficult to stomach. In the case of her father, these negative feelings had come accompanied by a particularly strong sense of physical revulsion.

Her antipathy had struck with the onset of puberty and had been exacerbated by events surrounding Grandpa Bernardo's death. It was, at times, so profound that she found it necessary to leave a room if either of her parents entered it. Mealtimes had become a penance; an unavoidable and protracted source of contact. The style of her parents' interaction made her want to scream. Their voices drove her mad. The manner in which they forked up their food, or smiled, or sniffed, induced murderous intent. She could not but squirm uncomfortably if either one of them touched her and, while her mother seemed half-way sensitive to this particular new difficulty, her father patently was not.

Her first essential act of severance was a decisive break with God. This had become not only rational but imperative, given her need to avoid all possible occasions for touch. It was

94

absolutely necessary to ensure that she would not find herself alongside her parents during the iniquitous 'sign of peace'. She knew that, inexorably, there would come that point where the priest would say, 'Let us offer each other the sign of peace', and her parents – both of them, one after the other – would take her hand in theirs. Or her father, God forbid – but all things were possible to him who had no inhibition at such times about crossing the aisle to embrace Pam's antique, retired piano teacher – her father would clasp his daughters, one by one, in a brief embrace and plant affectionate kisses on their cheeks.

Peace be with you.

Her diaphragm had begun to tense against the prospect from the start of the Lord's Prayer.

Now she had shaken the whole thing off with a most surprising ease. Because to lose what you have never properly possessed, she realized, is no real loss at all. Merely a burden lifted. The only noticeable effect upon her was the absence of fuzziness in the channels of the ears. The messages, she realized, had been reaching her since before Mrs del Nevo's intersecting circles, or the Sunday Polo mints.

Her lapse was the only feature of her present life that had occurred like a stepping out of grave clothes. Yet it had done very little to relieve the bugbear of parental contact.

Christina could not have explained these feelings to her parents any more than she could have given coherent account of them to herself. All she knew was that, in order to breathe and to hold on to her own self, it had become imperative for her to despise her father and, more than ever, to hold contrary opinions and contrary tastes. And it was equally necessary, in lesser degree, to despise and pity her mother, who was his helpmate and collaborator.

Christina found that she could no longer call her parents by the names she had always used. She resolved this difficulty by ceasing to call them anything at all when addressing them face to face, and by avoiding almost all situations where reference in the third person might possibly have become necessary. Where it was unavoidable, they became 'he' and 'she' – pronouns which she endowed with so peculiarly disdainful an emphasis as to make their application to specific persons unambiguously clear.

Family holidays had become events to be avoided whenever possible. This one, to Granny P's, while unavoidable, was definitely less appalling than most. She had retained a qualified fondness for her grandmother and, added to that, her father habitually spent the weekdays working in London where he put up in a hotel. None the less, the eight hours trapped on the plane that summer had been little short of agonizing. Christina had breathed relief when at last the Fasten Seat-belt and the No Smoking signs had come on and the plane had begun its slow descent upon London.

It made her sad to realize that a fortnight in the company of her maternal grandmother was no longer, to be honest, her idea of heaven. She had reluctantly come to the conclusion that Granny P could be a little stultifying. She was a predictable and limited woman, whose persistently partisan indulgence towards Christina – and equally persistent coolness towards Pam – was an embarrassment rather than a triumph. Moreover, there was not the previous thrill to be got from shopping trips alone with Granny P, since the two of them no longer shared a passion for shiny shoes. Christina's father, with his own wholehearted and conspicuous enthusiasm for stylish personal adornment, had had the effect of driving his younger daughter towards intransigent indifference.

It was also no longer appropriate or rewarding for Christina to exercise her talent for raising the temperature among uneasy in-laws. Her need was now to escape them all, not to become the focus of their intensified attention.

There was one thing and one only, one pleasure that had remained with her through all those summers past, and that was the pleasure she had always taken in tending her grandmother's garden. Even now, as the aircraft began its descent, she applied her mind determinedly to aphids and apple trees and manure on spiraea. She wondered, would the sweet williams and the foxgloves have finished their flowering? Would she be in time to see the last of the roses that rambled so profusely over the roof of her grandmother's porch? And then there was that scent that she, in childhood, had attributed to her grandmother's own person. She knew it now as a benign accessory of jasmine flowers in July.

'But the sign's come on,' Pam was saying. 'One of us ought to go get Papa.'

Christina wished that her sister would not behave quite so much like little Beth March where their father was concerned. She had more than once reminded Pam of that sacrificial creature's remarkably swift dispatch.

'Don't worry, Pam,' their mother said. 'He'll come. The steward will make him.'

'But he's *smoking*,' Pam said anxiously.

Alice sighed. 'Don't worry, Pam,' she said again. 'He's over twenty-one. He'll stop. The steward will make him.'

When Christina glanced down towards the end of the aisle, she saw that, sure enough, her father and some newly acquired companion, were drawing on the weed. They were also evidently sharing a joke. There was something irritatingly schoolboyish, she considered, about two grown men snatching a hurried smoke alongside the airplane toilets. But then, her

97

father, having opted as usual for the non-smoking section of the aircraft – 'for the girls' health', as he put it so piously – had been up and down like a yo-yo during the flight to indulge his nicotine habit.

All the same, there was something in the gracefulness of the smokers' gestures – the cupped palms around the flame, the languid positioning of the hands, the forms that it gave to the mouth – that Christina always found unsettling, even as it irritated the hell out of her. And to be sure, right then, it irritated her still further that her father, as the world would persist in judging these matters, was inclined to look imposing.

He was not only possessed of a tall, powerful body which, thanks to his repellent ego-mania, he had kept impeccably in shape, but he had always had that happy knack with his clothes. Right then he wore a loose, petrol-green, chenille sweater pulled over his shirtless brown torso and his pale cotton bags hung elegantly loose around his hips and thighs.

And – given that the man was almost completely bald – he had had the good fortune to have been endowed with a shapely, bump-free cranium, the skin on which tanned evenly. He had also always had the sense to keep such hair as he had clipped short. Preening as he was, Christina had grudgingly to admit, he was not the man to delude himself with a few glued strands across his pate. He had never been a member of the Brotherhood of Silly Hair.

These things could not have been said about his smoking partner, whose outward appearance, in most respects, was something reminiscent of Mrs Alfieri's fat-bellied Mr Five. He was overweight, flight-rumpled and sweaty-looking. His coal-black hair, ineptly layered and straggling limply downwards on to his collar, had managed to recede in a manner unconducive to personal dignity. It had accomplished its retreat to the apex of the crown, while leaving a small, tufted island on the brow as witness to the site of the original hairline. Christina could only glimpse, partially, the upper half of his person, but he wore what appeared to be a tent-like black shirt over an immoderate spread of chest and belly, and his black-framed, bottle-glass spectacles, bound at the hinge with electrician's tape, were far too small for his face. They had that look of a wedding ring, adopted in youth, on a bloated, middle-aged finger.

'I'll go,' Pam said, and she moved to undo her seat-belt, but just then, as if telepathically impelled to it by the quality of her concern, the men broke up and stubbed out their cigarettes, and gestured hurried partings before returning to their seats.

Her father fastened his seat-belt with a brisk click. Then he smiled at his wife and his daughters.

'Looks like nice weather down there,' he said. 'You'll have a good time, I think.'

'But I wish you could stay with us for more of it,' Pam said. 'I really wish you didn't always have to work so hard.'

Their father beamed his pleasure upon her. 'Adorable girl,' he said.

He is always happy, Christina reflected, to accept homage for the value of his presence.

'So who is your fat friend?' she said, wishing to erase the smile. 'Does he have a glandular disorder, or does he snack too much?'

'He's Father Zachary Levine,' her father said.

'Who?' she said.

'Father Zachary Levine,' he said. 'He's a Jesuit who works with cut-throats in the ghettos of Jamaica. He's visiting with his parents who keep a delicatessen in Finsbury Park.'

'Oh yeah,' Christina said, wishing she hadn't asked. And wouldn't he be, she thought. Wouldn't the bloated creature just *have* to be Father Levity Whatsit SJ? And wouldn't her father just *have* to be in possession of some morally rank-pulling little scenario like that? Some hyper little slice of somebody else's biography to offer in return for an honest put-down? He was like a jack-in-the-box, her father. Squash him and he would leap up shouting, 'Look at me. I'm jumping.' Furthermore, he was like a witch-detector who could sniff out wacky types.

Christina began at once to choreograph in her mind the fat Jesuit's context. The aged parents, she decided, would be small and frail as birds. They would be worn with toil, like two little hedge sparrows who have expended their resources on a cuckoo. She envisaged them pausing to dab at rheumy eyes as they bottled sour dill pickles and sliced up kosher pastrami. All the while they would be grieving for the defection of their boy; their clever only son, who had always brought home such golden reports from grade school.

Before long, she had thoroughly satisfied herself with the intensity of her loathing for the fat Jesuit. She despised him. And she despised her father too, for that easy, promiscuous way in which he struck up friendships with strangers. With people like Father Thingummy Whatsit with his outsize shirt and his silly hair and his bag of one-upmanship with regard to his doings in 'the ghettos of Jamaica'. How come he was a Jesuit, anyway? Had he come to the Spiritual Exercises via the rabbinical school?

Her father would be glad about this, Christina reflected. That's why he had sounded so jaunty in reply to her. He would be rejoicing in the man's defection. If you were a serious Catholic, then that was what you were supposed to be glad about. If people forsook their fathers and mothers and defected to the Cross, then you were supposed to consider this a sign of special grace, when really it was just a piece of ordinary treachery. Like in *The Merchant of Venice* when Shylock's daughter defected to the courtly dandy and gave her dead mother's beautiful ring to a monkey.

Christina began, in her imagination, to accuse the fat Jesuit of stealing his mother's jewellery and flogging it in order to swell the coffers of the Priests' Training Fund. Or maybe merely in order to acquire for himself one hundred sacks of bagels?

By the time she was disposed to respond to her father, her voice was carefully loaded with disdain.

'I read about this army officer in a magazine,' she said. 'He joined the Jesuits for the discipline. But then he left because all they do these days is watch TV.'

Her father laughed. As he did so, he placed a hand lightly on her upper arm. It produced a sensation which Christina imagined to be something like lockjaw in the ball joint of her shoulder.

'You have an edge, Chrissie,' he said. 'You have your knives out. I guess we are getting closer to your grand-mother.'

'As a matter of fact,' said her mother's old friend, as they sat in the Renovated Railway Tea-room, 'I too am waiting for somebody. I am waiting for Tilly.'

'Tilly?' said Alice.

'My wife,' he said. 'She's shopping for ballet shoes with the girls. We have two little daughters aged seven and six.' He smiled at Pam and Christina as they sipped at their ginger beer and then again at their mother. 'But you will know all about little girls and their shoes,' he said. 'And the time it can take. Dear me.'

And then the train roared in and got between the tea-room and the sunlight and it screeched and stopped. And Christina saw her father leap nimbly on to the platform, with his leather valise over his shoulder. He was wearing shades, but, even so, she observed, just before he composed his features to engage with the company, a glance so sharp, so intense, it was like the quick unsheathing of knives.

'Joe!' Alice said, sounding surprised, because the time had passed so quickly and there he was standing behind her. She offered him her cheek as she spoke, but he pointedly tipped her head back and kissed her on the mouth. Christina was all too painfully conscious, through the duration of the kiss, that the beautiful dark boy was watching intently, while the small blond boy kept his eyes to the floor.

'I see that you are enjoying yourself, Alice,' her father said at last. 'Just as I predicted that you would.'

'Joe,' her mother said, 'yes, but Joe. *So* exciting! *Such* a thing! You will remember Roland? Dear Roland. My teacher friend from Oxford? Well. Here he is!'

The two men promptly shook hands and said that they remembered each other, from a brief meeting, just once, in Oxford, when Pam was a brand-new baby. A baby whose birth had caused her parents so precipitously to fall in love and forsake all other, greatly to the detriment of the Nice Young Man of whom everyone had been so fond.

'He's a headmaster,' Alice said. She was evidently entertained by the idea. 'And his school is terrifically okay,' she said. 'Absolutely *crème de la crème*. And it's round the corner. Eight miles as the crow flies.'

Roland smiled. 'I'd call it fifteen, Alice,' he said.

'Congratulations, Roland,' the girls' father said, finding it a little difficult to enter into his wife's rush of girlish enthusiasm.

'But the *most* important thing,' Alice said, 'the best bit is that we are all going to see it! All of us. Roland has asked us all to tea. Don't look at your watch like that, Joe. So kill-joy. He doesn't mean today. He means tomorrow. Today we are having tea in this idiotic little station caff. Hey, but this was a good idea, Joe. So clever of you to have thought to bring us here.'

'Now, please,' Roland said, attempting a little diplomacy. 'About tomorrow. Absolutely only if it suits. You may well find that you've plenty to do.'

'But *of course* we're coming!' Alice said. 'Aren't we, Joe? *Of course* we're coming! We wouldn't miss it for the world.'

'Alice,' Roland said, and he couldn't help laughing, 'if you will excuse me for just a moment, your husband needs a drink.' He turned to Joe. 'What can I get you?' he said.

'Absolutely not,' Joe said, and he made a move from the table towards the counter. 'I'll get it myself. Please sit down.'

Christina watched, enjoying the edge of tension. She understood that, in refusing Mr Dent the right to give, her father was passing a message. And the message was not quite friendly. For what can be less friendly than one person's refusal to place himself in the debt of another?

And then came Tilly, accompanied. She was slim, pale, translucent and gliding, whereas the two little girls were stocky, robust, corporeal and chattering. They had ruddy cheeks and dark brown eyes and chunky little brown legs. Tilly wore a narrow, grey linen skirt with a long slit up the back. She wore a plaited leather belt and similarly narrow, grey leather shoes with peep-toes and sling-backs. She carried the little girls' cardigans over her arm, while the girls were busy pulling from carrier-bags pastel-pink knit cross-over tops and pairs of pale pink ballet slippers bound with elastic bands.

'My dear,' Roland said, and he rose politely, as did all the males among the party. Joe, who had just returned from the bar, regarded the newcomer with interest.

'I ran into some friends,' Roland said. 'You'll have heard me mention Alice?'

103

'Ah,' Tilly said, with the slightest hint of meaning. 'Ah, yes. And I am Gentille.' She spoke a beautifully modulated English, her voice soft and low.

For Alice, the meeting was evidently pure pleasure. It delighted and entertained her that Roland, who was as English as the West Somerset Steam Railway, should somehow have acquired for himself a French wife whose elegance and hauteur he probably did not notice and whose name he had so absurdly and conveniently anglicized. It also allowed her to exorcize guilt, since, of the two young men who had presented themselves to her before Joe's coming, Roland had been distinctly the more worthy and the one whom she had the more dramatically short-changed.

Gentille, meanwhile, unlike Alice, was sparing in her smiles. She had heavy-lidded, somewhat Garbo-esque eyes, and a manner sufficiently muted and aloof for Christina to decide that she was cold. She is cold-blooded, like a mermaid doing time on earth, Christina thought. And she has her nice, solid, earthling husband and her two solid little earthling daughters.

But then she has that other child from before; that weird, transparent boy from another element who seems, if anything, more air than water. And he is best friends with exquisite James whom I will love until I die. And her eyes crept again to that object of her desire, the beautiful dark boy, who was so close that it was scarcely to be borne.

Roland's two little girls, meanwhile, excited by the unexpected company and sensing Joe's strong predilection for young children, attached themselves to him at once, like two steel pins to a magnet. They put on their ballet shoes for him and chattered excitedly in unison. They turned pirouettes for him on the platform, while he admired them and egged them on. It gave Alice time to observe the little girls and, having done so, she turned to address Roland.

'Looking at your daughters,' she said, 'it's clear that you have quite absurdly dominant genes.'

She could not help laughing at the ebullient little girls, who were dancing about her husband, colliding merrily, like heated molecules in a pot.

'See how my skirt goes twirly when I turn round,' Ellen said.

'Mine too. Look at me,' Lydia said.

'This is called arabesque.'

'This is called fifth position.'

'Oh, my,' Joe said. 'What exquisite ballerinas.'

Christina noticed that Roland was not a man for feminine display.

'Ellen. Lydia,' he said abruptly. 'Sit down and be quiet. That is quite enough for the time being. Thank you.'

The ballerinas stopped. They wriggled undaunted on to their chairs and contented themselves, instead, with crazy eye-rolling to prompt little bursts of half-smothered giggles.

Next day, Roland came for them at three. He collected them from the old coaching inn where, on the previous evening, Christina had been sufficiently mellowed by love to have succumbed at dinner to a platter of skate in black butter and a measure of puréed parsnip.

The following morning, however, she had refused enticements to participate in family walks and had consumed the time in her bedroom reading back numbers of *The Field*. In between, she had counted the hours until three. Her anxiety hovered around the question of Jago Rutherford's whereabouts. Would he or would he not be at Peter's house that afternoon? The school year, she knew, was over. She had heard the boys say as much. So might he not have packed for home and left?

Roland, regrettably, came alone, so this did not help to

enlighten her. She had noticed his arrival at once, because her window overlooked the car park and she leaned out of the window to watch him crunch over the gravel towards the hotel reception. He was wearing the exact same clothes as he had worn the previous day – the identical flecked jumper and faded old beige cords. It gave her pleasure to contemplate the comfortable nature of Roland's clothing along with the comfortable doggie-largeness of his hands and feet. She liked him for being so comfortable with himself. She knew that, unlike her father, he would never show off; never preen. He would have no need for those things. She thought how fortunate were Peter and those funny, bouncy little girls, to have a person so straight, so unaffected for their male parent.

Christina, at thirteen, had long ago relinquished any serious fantasy that she, like Pam, had been born in enviable and mysterious circumstances – an *orfana*; a foundling; a changeling; a melodious inmate of the Ospedale della Pietà; a Parisienne protégée of the kindly Miss Clavel. She knew now, beyond all doubting, that she was her mother's daughter and her father's also. She therefore did not seriously consider the possibility that the man crunching the gravel underfoot as he passed beneath her window could have been her natural father. It was simply as a sort of tribute; as a parody of her own infant self; a mere involuntary throw-back, that she found herself murmuring to the top of Roland's head:

'You can be my Nearly Father if you like.'

The Stolen Boy and the Idea of the Objective Correlative

Tea was a disappointment, though its preamble was definitely seductive and its corollary dramatic. The party, coming upon the school by road, wound through dense, light-stippled woods until the foliage gave way to parkland and the great brick structure appeared, clear on a low hillside, its charming conical turrets and tall chimneys throwing a pattern on to the sky.

The main building dated from the first decade of the nineteenth century and had been erected to replace a smaller, Elizabethan structure which, before being gutted by fire, had nestled at the foot of the hill.

Roland and Gentille occupied stately quarters to the right of the house, where their two ground-floor living-rooms, each with wide, low bays, gave on to a formal garden cut into symmetrical quarters by paths. Beyond this were views over parkland, farm and woods. At the back, to Christina's delight, a pergola ran from the kitchen door to the apple orchard, making a canopy of vine leaves from which hung bunches of tiny, unripe grapes.

'Tea,' Roland said hospitably. 'Come along in.'

For Alice, disappointment lay in the increasing realization that she could not warm to Roland's wife. She wanted so much to rejoice in her dear friend's marital circumstances, but Gentille was by nature distancing and seemed to grow more so with the passing of the afternoon.

For Joe, too, Gentille was a source of disappointment. On the previous day he had been very much struck by her. His irritation at finding Alice accompanied had melted upon

Gentille's arrival. He had been attracted to her by precisely those attributes that Christina had taken against. He had admired her stylish cool and her pale, understated sexiness. He had been charmed, and a little provoked, by the whiff of superciliousness implied in the arch of her eyebrows and by the careful rationing of her smiles. He appreciated – as only he among the party could – the exquisite cut of her subtle, cloud-grey clothes.

Joe was not a devotee of afternoon tea which, in general, he considered a somewhat tedious, Anglo-Saxon plate-balancing ceremony epitomizing the mores of his mother-in-law. He had assumed that Gentille would bring to it a little touch of Paris; that her catering would be in conformity with the nature of her appearance. So it jarred with him when, in place of the *petits fours* and the *tarte aux fraises* ("It is a French recipe of my grandmother's," said Mrs Ramsay'), there appeared a plate-ful of fan-shaped, shop-bought, sawdust cookies of the kind that Alice's mother referred to as 'petticoat tails' and an item to which Roland now referred as 'Mother's Victoria Sponge'.

For Roland's mother, wife of a clergyman, this confection had been the mainstay of all her parish fund-raising activities, but to Alice's husband it appeared as two hefty, aerated discs, coarse-textured and wedged together with a layer of violent red jam.

'The parents left just yesterday,' Roland said, issuing slices of the item on small, square plates, along with napkins and little silver forks. 'What a pity they missed you, Alice.'

'Yes,' Alice said. 'That *is* a shame.'

More shame, her husband thought, unreasonably, to leave behind them a cake such as this, bearing witness to the hazards of excess baking soda and showing a terrible want of eggs. The sponge, he decided, was certainly spongy. It was like chewing on cheap cushion filling.

*

'More cake there, Christina?' Roland said.

'Oh, please,' Christina said eagerly, and she offered him her plate with a smile. 'Oh, please. This really is the *most* delicious cake, Mr Dent,' she said.

Dutifully, Joe forked up a second mouthful of Roland's mother's cake, but the sponge, with its too liberal outer dusting of confectioner's sugar, had made a trap for his unsuspecting larynx. He was seized with a fit of coughing and he reached at once for his tea-cup. The action succeeded in causing a beige puddle to appear in his saucer – a puddle that he knew was designed to drip all over his clothes.

Goddamnit, he thought, what was he doing there? And where the hell was his hostess?

Gentille had early on been called away to the telephone and now he became aware that his daughters were being swept away upstairs by the wiles and persistence of little Ellen and Lydia. He was left undiverted to observe his wife who was like a person regressing in reunion with a childhood favourite. Reference to the shared past had made Alice livelier. It had raised her spirits and enhanced her looks. How pretty she was, he thought. Her eyes so blue and sparkling. The colour in her cheeks.

But then, to pit against these advantages, was the disconcerting fact of Alice's diction. Something had happened to Alice's speech. She was talking very fast and had commandeered Roland's attention in order to indulge in a form of culturally specific bubble-talk, that excluded him. He found it boring and irritating. Much of it, as it struck his ear, had to do with Oxford place-names. It required frequent reference to one or other of that city's streets and these, he considered, were being uttered as if in sacred mantra. Averagely boring names, as they seemed to him. He observed that the suffix 'street' was generally being substituted by the prefix definite article. Thus, 'Turl Street' had become 'The Turl' and 'Broad Street' had become 'The Broad'. Alice made reference, now, to New College

Lane – new, as he guessed, because it *had* been new somewhere round 1103. Goddamnit, so what? How about the Pyramids? How about the Pantheon? He wanted suddenly to rub her little parochial nose in the dust around the Temple of Queen Hatshepsut.

Alice's talk was suddenly littered with examples of alien terminology. She made reference to 'wellington boots' and to 'Marmite' and to 'Morris Minors'. She relayed an anecdote requiring verbal recourse to hot water bottles which she had taken to calling 'hotties'. She had adopted silly, dated adjectives like 'grotty' and 'scrotty', which all appeared to be interchangeable. Joe slumped pointedly in his chair and sighed and cast his eyes to the ceiling.

And there, suddenly, to lift his spirits beyond piffling national proscription, he saw something beautiful. Depicted naked and in delicate bas-relief, was the fleeing figure of Venus worked in stucco. She was just beyond the range of Cupid who, with the assistance of a flock of dimpled putti in mid-flight, was carrying her billowing nuptial cloak. The groom, he observed, was biding his time as he leaned prettily against a broad, knotty oak. He was wearing nothing but his martial boots and a graceful Athenian helmet.

Joe got up. Goddamnit, he thought, the time was pushing on. He needed a drink and, more than that, he needed Alice, naked and white and silent as stucco, in that charming, low-beamed bedroom back at the old coaching inn. That was what he was paying for and the hotel didn't come cheap.

'Let's take a walk,' he said abruptly. 'Let's go check out the park. Come on. It's getting late, isn't it?'

Christina's disappointment with the afternoon had come in phases one and two. The beautiful dark boy was indeed a guest of the family, but both boys had gone out. They had undertaken to be back for tea but in the event they had returned late, bearing a tale of a punctured inner tube and a repair kit missing its rubber solution. They had come just in time to be co-opted on to a walk where the alignments had not gone as Christina might have hoped. The line-up here was sabotaged by the intervention of her father and by the weediness of that unlikeable Mrs Dent.

Christina had expected that her mother would walk beside her dear old friend and that her father would accompany the Mermaid Woman. Either that, or he would give his attention to the two ebullient little girls. But no. Instead, the Mermaid Woman had excused herself and cried off. She would use the time to supervise the children's bathing, she said.

'Tilly is not a great walker,' Roland said. 'Her ankles don't bear up awfully well.'

And what would one expect, Christina mused with venom. The Mermaid Woman could only glide. She could not walk. Of course!

In the vacuum, then, the beautiful dark boy had appended himself with unerring instinct to the person of Christina's father. He had done so, in truth, because the girls themselves – with their Pollyanna looks and their orthodontally orthodox teeth – held no interest for him, while in the father he perceived something of a kindred spirit. He appreciated there a degree of egotistical power. Jago was not unattracted by power. He had always held so much of it himself.

Christina was therefore obliged to adopt the galling role of spectator as she watched another example of her father's instant bonding. The two of them had claimed each other in spirit. Released, respectively, from the tedium of the tea-cups and from the frustrations of an inadequately equipped puncture repair kit, each grew in humour and high spirits. They walked on ahead in the bracing air, not only through the park and round the lake and over the playing-fields but, thereafter, through the music rooms and through the chapel and through the centre for computer studies. They walked through the theatre and through the physics laboratories and, as they did so, they bounced off each other, talking with animation and cracking the air with their bursts of laughter.

They talked of weights and folios. They talked of bytes and scores. They talked of balanced forces and of circuits and of volts. And then, finally, when they lingered in the theatre, amid the props of last term's *Hamlet*, Christina heard that they talked about the idea of the Objective Correlative.

Passed over and bruised by the fact of her own relative ignorance, Christina was obliged to walk behind with her sister who accompanied the small blond boy. Both were almost completely silent, but she sensed, in spite of this, that a sort of communion had grown up between Pam and Peter. Immediately ahead of them, Alice walked with Roland.

'He knows nothing at all about volts and circuits,' Alice was saying, with a slightly brittle volubility. 'And as to English field sports – well – ' She paused and laughed. 'He's a genius at bullshit, actually. Inspired crap artist and that's the truth.'

Roland was finding Alice's manner increasingly disconcerting. He was not quite reading her correctly. He recognized that somewhere inside the person who walked beside him, with her fluent but compulsive retro-speak and her edgy, barbed merriment, was the same shy, stammering girl who had once been the love of his life. He thought it possible that she was making a play for him, and his sense of propriety told him to discourage it. He found himself disappointed in her. He found her changed, even though her appearance was almost completely the same. To allow her to continue would merely be to become her victim all over again. And had she not already once driven his beautiful old Citroën into the Tees?

Thirteen years ago, Roland reflected, Joe Angeletti had

come along and won this woman with the extravagant landscapes of his mind; had drawn her into antres vast and deserts idle and into rough quarries and hills. Roland had known in a moment that his chance with her was history. For what power, he thought, the romance of the familiar in competition with the romance of the strange?

He turned to her and spoke pointedly. 'I think,' he said, 'that in these matters, loyalty is the watchword.' Alice was shaken by the put-down and startled by what she read as Roland's sudden, schoolmasterish pomposity. She could think of nothing further to say.

Christina, who could not hear the words that he spoke, observed that Alice's nape took colour, and that – while her father and the beautiful dark boy talked on – a silence had finally fallen upon her mother.

And then the afternoon turned. Something happened. It could so easily not have happened and, having happened, it changed the sisters' lives. Joe, having learnt from his thirteen-year-old interlocutor that the school in recent years had opened its doors to girls, had immediately conceived the idea that his daughters should join the school's ranks. He had conceived it, on the spur of the moment, for a bundle of reasons, both legitimate and otherwise, and, having done so, he stuck to it with all the force of his dominating personality.

First, there were the public reasons. He knew that Christina had always been attracted to the idea of boarding school and longed to breathe new air. The school's situation was lovely and the education, on the evidence of his own eyes, was indisputably first-rate. For all the school was some distance from home – and he would, admittedly, have to write frequent airfares into his costs – the family travelled a good bit anyway and the fees for Roland's school, he estimated, would be as chicken-feed when compared with the price of such a school back home.

And, again, why should his daughters not spend some time in an English school? They had an English mother and travel was broadening to the mind. Cultural diversity in a person's background was an excellent thing, he considered. It was for this reason, was it not, that both his girls spoke passable Italian. Furthermore, now that Pam and Chrissie were of an age where certain forms of parental supervision were no longer appropriate, the girls, he hazarded, would be generally less at risk from psychotics, muggers and drug pedlars – both within school gates and without.

His other reasons were either those he chose to keep to himself, or those of which he himself was unaware. There was Gentille's absence from the afternoon, which had insulted his sense of propriety and had put him out of humour. In consequence of it he had been left to feel like an appendage as the schoolmaster had become the focus of Alice's best attention. What more satisfactory way to redress the balance, he thought, than to delegate to the schoolmaster the care of his two daughters and to keep his wife for himself?

That idea was suddenly most alluring. Things had not of late been terribly good between himself and Alice. He sensed that she had begun to drift away. And now here was his chance. He at once began to envisage a succession of nightly candle-lit dinners, and evenings at the theatre and the opera house, while the girls would be advantageously contained within the bounds of Roland's school. The way was clear. No problem. Educationally. Pam would thrive almost anywhere, while Chrissie, whose dealings with teachers had more often been fraught with storms, had got on with Roland from the first as though they were made for each other.

And then there was the boy. That marvellous, brilliant boy. Some men care about having male children and other men do not. Joe adored his daughters, would have laid down his life for either one of them, but deep down, buried where he was altogether unaware of it, was a force impelling him to annex the beautiful dark boy.

He began to quiz Roland almost as soon as they returned to the house.

'But Joe,' Alice said, who, coming new to the idea, had an instinct to hang on to her children. 'This is a highly selective school, you know. It's not like entering the supermarket. Parents will be beating down the doors to get their kids in here.'

'So what are you saying?' her husband replied. 'Are you saying our girls aren't bright? Or are you saying they are under-educated?'

'Neither,' Alice said. 'Only that the system here is quite different and the girls are unprepared.'

'So what?' her husband said. 'I defy any school to find a better student than Pam. She's always been a straight-A student. Besides, she's musically gifted. Any school would be lucky to get her.'

Roland waited politely for them to finish. He wondered if they were always like this. From what he had seen of Alice's daughters, they struck him as perfectly acceptable girls and refreshingly old-fashioned in their style. The younger one he liked particularly, and not only because she looked so very much like her mother. She was sparkier, he thought, and less brooding than her sister. Less earnest. He found her a particularly bright and appealing child. His only slight sense of misgiving came from a hunch that Alice's husband could spell trouble.

'Well,' he said, 'we normally admit on the basis of heads and housemasters' – or housemistresses' – report and performance in the twelve-plus examination. In a case such as your daughters', we would require applicants to sit some basic tests in English, French and mathematics.'

'There you are!' Alice said. 'The girls don't know any French.'

'Not yet,' her husband said. 'So what? They're fluent in Italian. Plus they know a little Spanish. What's so special about French?'

'Merely that it isn't Italian,' Alice said.

'In point of fact,' Roland said, feeling like an umpire at a tennis match, 'Italian – or Spanish – either will do very well. Both have become increasingly popular. We no longer insist upon French.'

'And Latin?' Alice said hopefully.

Roland spoke with caution. He remembered that Classical languages were Alice's area of expertise. 'Latin –' he said, but Alice's husband immediately interrupted him.

'The girls know quite a bit of Latin,' he said. 'What's the matter with you, Alice? Why are you running down your daughters?'

'Because you're selling them,' she said. 'You'll be showing off their teeth to Roland next. They know prayer-book Latin. I don't call that "knowing Latin".'

Roland coughed, wishing to pull her up. 'You'll not like to hear this, Alice,' he said, 'but Latin is not really at issue. Time and tide, you know. We have declining numbers wishing to take that option.'

Alice retreated into aggrieved silence as she envisaged her subject trampled underfoot. She gave up. She heard her husband inquire about the scope for his girls to fulfil their Sunday obligation and then he appeared wholly satisfied. She did not rise to make the point that one of his girls had not fulfilled her 'obligation' for almost four whole months.

And so the idea, which had arisen so arbitrarily, took root and became a fact. For Christina, though she suspected her acceptance would be on the back of her sister's merit, the prospect was one of earthly paradise. She envisaged that, at the end of two months, the beautiful dark boy would rise before her, just as dark and as beautiful as ever. And that this time her father would not be there to get in the way.

Only the talk of *Hamlet* had given some cause for misgiving and she acknowledged, soberly, the need for certain extended libations of self-improvement.

'What's the "Objective Correlative"?' she said.

Her father looked up in surprise. He was not accustomed to have Christina sue for information. 'It's a notion of Eliot's, used in connection with *Hamlet*,' he said. 'It asserts that the objective facts of the plot don't correlate with the enormity of Hamlet's emotion. So the play, he asserts, is a failure.'

Christina pulled a face. 'That's crap,' she said. 'Because maybe there's something else about Hamlet's life that's helping to screw him up. Maybe there's something that just never made it on to the page.'

The sound of her father's laughter threatened to bring her out in spots.

PART III

Tumbling

The Groupies, the Smart-Arse and the Werewolf

Boarding school. It was a shock. It was not as it had been for Madeleine. This was only in part because the school was so terrifically male. Admittedly, there were always too many persons with too much colt energy, forever sliding down bannisters, or jumping over lighted firecrackers, or crashing through swing-doors *en route* to the playing-fields when adult eyes were averted. In the classroom, there was always a person on crutches, or a person wearing head bandages. Sometimes there was a person with an eye-patch. There was almost always a male person who had recently been anointed with antiseptic.

Then there was the business of being constantly appraised as sex object. About that, one had on the whole tried hard not to care. Except about Jago. His indifference. For Christina, the real shock had all to do with Jago.

At boarding school, there had been Jago's group. The in-group. There had been the in-group and the out-group. It was Jago who always acted as arbiter of inclusion and exclusion. Naturally he did not do so in any formal way, but power always lay with him. Judgment was in his hands.

The nuance of Jago's disapproval was enough to cause the average schoolboy to abandon a girlfriend, or a friend, or even a pair of shoes. Conversely, Jago's approval could cause a person to be suddenly in favour, when yesterday that person had been overlooked. Jago's thumbs-down was almost always conclusive.

In this way, Jago's group dictated fashion, not only in social acceptability, but in dress, in music, in habits of work and leisure and in permissible cross-gender alliance. It was seldom necessary for Jago to assert himself. His aura – or indeed his minions – were there to do the work for him.

If Jago returned from a half-term at home, having taken to wearing a ravelled fisherman's knit exhumed from the bottom of his father's cupboard, then all other forms of knitwear would become obsolete overnight. Or perhaps not quite overnight, since felicitous timing was of the essence in cases of imitation.

Imitation, if exhibited with too great an eagerness, could smack of sycophancy. And sycophancy was inclined to bore Jago. He had an active mind and had always been easily bored. Thus, imitation could cause even those among the favoured few to fall. Imitation from members of the out-group meant that Jago took no prisoners.

Jago maintained a form of control whose tenets were sufficiently unstated and shifting for its nature to be unfathomable even to fine-tuned initiates.

None the less, for Christina, Jago's top-doggery employed techniques with which she herself was already a little bit familiar. She had had her own earlier experience of becoming big smell of the classroom. Yet her methods had seemed less devastating. Not only had she escaped Jago's damaging early life experience, but the nature of her cosy little school had more effectively kept her in check.

In the context of a small, North American day school, with its emphasis on mutual support and its vigilant, nurturing tradition, Christina's tendency to play martinet had been far more constrained by adult intrusion.

'In this class, we have no vulturing,' Mrs Alfieri had intoned benignly. 'Isn't that right, children?' And the class had dutifully taken this assertion on board as holy writ. Here, in England, not only were the pupils older, but the attitude was one that made a virtue of *laissez-faire* in matters of social shake-down. The lesson quickly learnt at boarding school was toughen up, or die.

In the context, Christina had committed some initial errors of strategy. The first of these had been to take the initiative in approaching Jago Rutherford. The second had had more to do with unacceptable dress.

She had duly appeared kitted out in a range of wholesome, brand-new garments, which were similar to those appearing on the pages of *Seventeen* magazine. It was therefore quite impossible that she could have passed into Jago's elect. To be wholesome was not, right then, in fashion. It gained a person no credit within the sub-culture. At the moment of Christina's arrival, tack was more zealously striven for. And her fine blonde hair was not a feature with which to chalk up credit. Blonde hair was acceptable, but only if it came brutally cropped. Christina's hair was neatly french-plaited and fixed with an elastic band. Neither was natural hair colour an asset, where dark roots were a fashion accessory and split ends an advantage.

Christina's hair had been enough in itself to define her as a kid from Coke-ad Country. For Jago, she was no more relevant to his life than Little Polly Flinders. And Christina – even once the cues had become familiar – was far too stubborn simply to fall in with the dogma of another person's aesthetic.

Gradually, as her senses adjusted themselves; as her eyes developed another way of seeing, she came in the main to prefer the local look and she began to make it her own.

She razored her hair and painted her eyes and acquired a small, glittering nose-stud. She wore heavy laced shoes with tiny skirts and opaque, black tights, or rumpled black hiking socks. With her pale pointed face and narrow thighs, the style was one that became her. Yet it had been a long time in evolving and, worse still, when it came, it was too much stamped with her own, perverse originality. All unwittingly, she had rendered herself not so much Jago's acolyte as his rival. And it was not long before she had acquired several acolytes of her own.

Yet, in her heart, Christina continued to yearn for Jago. Two years on, she still ached for that beautiful dark boy whom she had met in the Renovated Railway Tea-room, but who would not and could not care for her.

Pam had none of these problems. She possessed no power to change herself and no awareness of any need to do so. She continued to wear her thick, dark hair either plaited, or tied in a ponytail. Or she wore it loose to her shoulders and fixed with two grips at the temples. She saw no reason to abandon her clothes, which were expensive, elegant and bought to last. She wore mid-calf length skirts and fine tailored shirts and a well-cut cashmere jacket. She was the only girl amongst the school's female intake who had ever been observed using shoe trees and it was rumoured that she ironed her underwear.

She continued, throughout, to commit the offence of carrying school books in a calfskin knapsack when the method of transport then in favour was to carry all equipment loose in a pile from place to place. In this way, pad, pencils, mathematical instruments and the contents of clipback files could cascade to the ground with a clatter or fly away in the wind – but better, surely, to lose a whole year's coursework than to contain it in a receptacle and risk the scorn of the in-group.

Then there was Pam's uncompromising interest in scholarship; her apparent inability to score less than brilliantly in all academic assignments. In this she posed far more of a threat to Jago than Christina ever could. Jago had never in his life before been beaten in tests by anyone. He had never been confronted with a person who was able to get higher marks for essays. As a result, he had had little alternative but to allow his minions the opinion that Pam was a pathetic, slavish swot; a learner by rote; a teacher's pet, who compensated for inferior ability by burning the midnight oil.

While Pam's friendship with Peter Rusconi was doomed to

dictate against her – as was her physiognomy, since she had matured early into a large, unfashionable Renaissance beauty with sizeable breasts and hips – there was, more specifically, the telling matter of her eyebrows. Pam had always left her prominent, dark eyebrows unplucked, even where these encroached a little on to the bridge of her nose. It meant that, among the in-group, her nickname had become 'the Werewolf'. Her presence in any company could be signalled by a canine howl. Jago, naturally, had never stooped to such childish and conspicuous silliness. He had had no need to compromise his demeanour when others were so willing to do so on his behalf.

In the first term of the Upper Fifth, mock exams were looming. Before them, came Hallowe'en. It was a festival that, until very recently, had gone uncelebrated. The body of the school was still more able to identify that time of year by the Vaughan Williams hymn for All Saints' Day than by pumpkin lanterns and ghoulish pranks. Tricking and treating in spooky costumes was a still uncommon phenomenon.

Jago, naturally, despised it as having to do with infants begging, door-to-door, for sweets. With the cultural arrogance of his carefully constructed European identity, he resented Hallowe'en as a blatant intrusion of American custom upon his more venerable traditions. It was a form of Big Mac imperialism and he had no interest in it.

What caused him to alter his opinion was that he noticed on his radio that Saturday morning an evangelical clergyman who was banging on about Hallowe'en's dangers. The inadvisability of any dabbling with the occult was being vehemently laid out before him. The clergyman was imploring his listeners to risk no truck with Satan.

Jago sat bolt upright in bed. 'Christ,' he said – and he laughed out loud and reached to turn up the volume. 'Who the fuck is this clown?'

As he got up to take his morning shower, Jago's thoughts were all with the occult. He began to formulate a plan for coaxing some of the inner circle into ghoul costume. It would provide relief from boredom. He was sixteen and even the in-group had begun to bore him intolerably. He had begun, recently, to think of its members as the 'groupies' more often than the group.

With the weekend, many of the Upper Fifth pupils had got permission to attend a party. It was to take place at the house of one Henry Beasley, whose parents lived in the vicinity. There would be time, Jago reflected, between school supper and Henry's party, to get the groupies up like agents of darkness and set them loose to knock at householders' doors. He envisaged that, robed in dog-collar and cassock – and brandishing the weighty Bible he planned to borrow from the chapel lectern – he would present an impressive figure as he brought up the rear, exhorting the public to eschew all contact with the Evil One and his mighty servants of darkness.

Jago contemplated the fun of all the blood-and-bluster rhetoric with which he would up-stage and sabotage the groupies in their pursuit of treats and tricks. He raised his voice for comic effect as he sluiced himself under the shower.

'For Behold, My Dear Brethren, it is the Policy of Satan,' he pronounced loudly in his best, mad preacher voice – and he drew heavily, for effect, upon the lingering, sibilant S – 'to Send Temptations for to Snare Us through all Unsuspecting Means.'

'What?' Marty said from the row of sinks beyond. Jago emerged, naked and gleaming, his genitalia bobbing slightly as he paused to rub with a towel at his exquisite left haunch.

'Yea, through the Innocent Hands of Children,' he intoned. He bound the towel round his loins and proceeded to the shaving mirrors.

'What the fuck are you on about?' Marty said, tight-mouthing to the glass as he squeezed purposefully at a pimple maturing on his chin.

'Tremble as You Stand, My Merry Pustule,' Jago said. 'For, Verily, the Hour Cometh by Stealth and the Wiles of the Evil One are Many, for to Draw Us into His Realms of Darkness. Yea, for He would Devour Us with Our Own Compliance, Brother.'

Stet, at this point, farted loudly. Pongo's and Marty's resultant guffaws were not particularly well timed.

'What the fuck's he on about?' Marty said to Stet.

'Hallowe'en,' Jago said, reverting easily to his ordinary voice. 'Communing with Satan, comrades.' Then he detailed for the faithful his intentions for the evening's entertainment.

'You mean us to go off and scare the town virgins?' Pongo said and he and Marty began, at once, to enact a comic turn. It was loosely based on a television commercial for vaginal sanitary protection and it had to do with dampness in female undergarments.

Jago winced. He began to address himself to the business of lathering his face. The trouble with bloody Marty and Pongo, he considered, was that they had never bloody known when to stop. They had insufficient discretion. How had he managed not to notice this until so very recently? And Jesus, they couldn't half flog one's own bloody japes to bloody death.

Yet, for all his irritation with them, he had recently begun to find himself more browned off with Stetson Gregory. Marty and Pongo were jocks, after all – handsome, creditable specimens, though, admittedly, their physical energy was still so much in thrall to their testosterone imbalance, that it was increasingly difficult to get any word of sense out of either.

Stetson Gregory was different. Stet was clever. All right, he could be gross, but that was merely a cover for what Jago perceived as Stet's more deep and brooding personality. Stet was complicated. He had a real brain. In the classroom he could always acquit himself quite well, even though he treated lessons as a doss. It had seemed to Jago, recently, that Stet was bent on working himself up to some sort of challenge; that Stet was aiming to usurp him.

'Cut it out,' Jago said sharply, turning on Marty and Pongo. 'You're boring.'

They paused and looked at him in surprise. 'What?' Marty said.

'Boring,' Jago repeated. 'I said boring. As in that which is tedious and dull. *Ennuyant.*' Christ, he thought, but life could be so fucking bloody boring. It could make you want to commit a violence. Everything – everyone – was so fucking boring and irritating. It went beyond endurance. And the groupies, they were all a monumental yawn.

He wondered, as he drew his razor over his jaw, whether women – proper women – were ever half-way less bloody boring. Not those scrawny, fuck-wit women that he'd worked over on his father's fur-covered bed. He meant women of stature. Were there any? God only knew. Women like Maud Gonne? Lucrezia Borgia? Even Cordelia? Or maybe some lovely, pale-faced, female chemist in a lab coat, on her way to the Nobel Prize. Would you want to take off her glasses and her lab coat and bend your knee to her and say, 'My God, but you're divinely beautiful. Oh, Letitia, I love you. Your body and your mind'?

And then, if you met her, would you ever, in honesty, want to screw her? Jago doubted it. It was contempt that made you want to screw them. If ever you found one that wasn't contemptible, then she bloody well wouldn't turn you on. Or would she? And, even if she did, it wouldn't last. Or would it?

Then, to his own extreme discomfort, Jago found that his mind had begun to dwell upon the Werewolf.

'Shit,' he said, as he snicked his chin. It occurred to him that, more than once in recent days, Pam's image had floated into his mind. More than once, he had found himself staring at her in the classroom. And, on one occasion, when their eyes had actually met, she had turned away immediately. She had fixed her eyes on her textbook and had refused to look up after that. So why the fuck could she not so much as look him in the eye?

And why did she never bloody speak up in class? Quiet as a bloody mouse in lessons and then, off she'd go, to write better essays than his on the poetry of William Blake. Or on Disraeli's foreign policy. Or – damnit – on the difference between Speed and Velocity. Mr bloody Ballantyne had seen fit to read her answer out loud. And, all the while he was reading it, Jago had had fucking Marty sitting there beside him. Marty, who had thought it clever to observe that you couldn't 'get high on Velocity'.

So. Sod the girl. She was a pain. She had hidden depths. Why did she never sodding talk? Strut her stuff? Like her sister? Smart-arse Chris. Jago was quite certain that Pam had hidden depths. He had never himself bought his own propaganda about her slavish rote learning. His role had merely been to invent the idea and then to sit back and watch it propagated.

Fucking women, the pair of them, he thought. What the fuck had they come to the school for in the first place? They were American for Christ's sake. And why did they not even look like each other?

He remembered the day on which he had met them. The sisters. Station platform. Great Malvern. He'd just won a cricket match that afternoon on the last ball of the final over. Won the day for the local town team. What a hoot – to have won the match for the very same snot-nosed oiks whose sisters he was now planning to have the groupies go off and harass. Trick or treat. Hah!

The girls had been in Bermuda shorts and flat, matching

tennis shoes. Strictly off. Christina had been head-to-toe in traffic-light green as he recollected, but then it could never be said that dress was a big talent that side of the Atlantic. He could not help remembering, however, that the girls' father had appeared and had livened things up no end.

Fun bloke, as it had turned out. Great talker. Great to bounce off. So how the fuck had he come to produce these two bloody weirdo girls? One was a brainy wimp who was seldom known to open her mouth. Bum too big and walked around like the fucking Sistine Madonna in Classic Co-ordinates. Did she buy her clothes by mail through the ads in the *New Yorker*?

The other was a talkie little know-it-all, who had tried to gatecrash his affections. Always too obtrusive by half. Pushy, like one-of-the-boys. Sexless, like one of those scrawny old women one encountered occasionally in the lift of the mansion block. Usually called Daphne, or Ethne, or Xanthe. Big doe eyes and smoking through a cigarette holder. Thinking it was witty to go round pinching young men's bums.

Jago had had a curious experience some three days before Hallowe'en. It had happened to him in the art room. His artwork had always been very good indeed, but his talent in this area was one for which he had no use. Being academically ambitious for himself, he saw it as an irrelevance; an extraneous, so-what practical skill, appended to himself for no reason.

Among the raw materials in the art room were portfolios full of colour reproductions cut from catalogues and magazines. These were, some of them, of various works of art, classified chronologically into different historical periods. Jago had found himself gazing upon a batch of Renaissance Madonnas with Child. Most of them were enthroned with various saints, angels and donors. The earlier ones sat impassively against walls of flat gold leaf, while the later ones sat, smiling decorously, against Tuscan trees and river valleys, or against pink and gold palazzi.

Having suddenly before him the holy face so endlessly, hypnotically duplicated, Jago had been overcome by an inexplicable wave of anger. The upshot was that he had seized the scissors and begun to mutilate the figures. He embarked, then, on a harsh collage whose well-spring was little more than rage against the female sex.

Jago, with the aid of acrylic paint, fragments and paper glue, had created a Massacre of the Innocents; a Waste Land, in which eyeless Madonnas smiled sweetly from pike-staffs, or trampled the Holy Infant impassively underfoot, as He still reached out for trinkets and pomegranates and grapes. All around them, palazzi smoked and tumbled, and Tuscan trees became stumps.

He could not remember when last he had found any project so intensely involving. And, as he'd worked, two meaningless lines of verse had gone round and round in his head. Round and round, like being trapped inside a revolving door. He could not bring to mind quite where the lines had come from, but for quite a while they would not go away.

> That the topless towers be burnt
> And men recall that face –

Now where the hell was that from? God only knew, but Mr Cassidy, the art master, had been crazy about his picture. Jago shook off the praise as coming from a pretty indifferent source. Distinctly un-cool type, Mr Cassidy. Liked to wear fisherman's smocks. So who gave a fucking toss for his opinion? Wheezy old mediocrity. Watery eyes. Facial hair. One of those all-time losers who imagine that a beard is a badge of masculinity.

Now, as he made his way, sluiced and dressed, across the courtyard, two things dawned upon Jago. The first was that

131

what he had been doing in the art room, was cutting up Pam's face. The recognition sobered him and left him half afraid of himself. He wondered, suddenly, if he was going insane. Where had all that anger come from? And could anything ever assuage it?

The second alarmed him even more and hit him like a cold wind. He was aware that something had happened to him that had never happened before.

'Christ Almighty!' Jago said. He was aware that he had fallen in love with the Werewolf.

At that very moment, he saw Christina. She was some ten yards from where he was walking and she was on her knees, groping on the ground. Her books and papers had fallen from her grasp and had dispersed themselves on a slight breeze.

Jago promptly pursued them and, having gathered them up, returned them to her. His manner with her was unusually subdued and courteous. The gesture had been one of atonement to the sister of the violated girl.

'Here you are,' he said. 'They've got a little bit damp, I'm afraid.'

'Thank you,' Christina said. She stood up and, for the first time since she had come to the school, Jago hesitated beside her. Then they walked, side by side, and entered the building together.

'I must go,' she said uncertainly.

'No –' Jago said. He caused her to hover in parting. She sensed that he was stalling. 'This party of Henry's tomorrow,' he said, 'are you planning to go, by any chance?'

'Well –' Christina said, and she stopped, feeling herself thrown into confusion. 'Maybe. I don't know –'

'Come,' Jago said. 'Come with me.' He hardly knew what he was saying. 'Come,' he said again. 'And bring your sister. That's if you'd like to.'

Christina was aware that a weakness at the knees had followed Jago's invitation. 'I can't speak for my sister,' she said. 'I think she's rehearsing tomorrow night. She's got this concert. You know. Or maybe you don't? It's for that church. The one that's having a birthday.'

'Well,' Jago said, not knowing what Christina was talking about and hardly hearing the words. He was feeling, at once, frustrated and relieved that Pam, whom he wanted so urgently – so suddenly – was somehow protecting him by her benign absence for just a little bit longer; protecting him from himself, with her mysterious, divine remoteness.

'Whatever,' he said, affecting a composed semblance of normality. 'Thing is, I'm "tricking and treating" tomorrow. I and a group of us.' He smiled at her, the sister of the beloved; an engaging, satirical smile. 'I and the groupies,' he said, and he laughed. 'But we'll be all done by eight.'

Christina smiled back at him. 'The "groupies"?' she said.

Jago wondered again whether he was mad. What was he doing? Was he dating Pam's sister, or what?

'Diminutive of group,' he said. 'Hence, "groupie".'

'You?' Christina said, incredulous. 'Tricking and treating?'

'Big fun,' Jago said, bluffing it out. 'Big, bigger, biggest. Chris, it's going to be good.'

Jago, Christina thought admiringly, had always possessed that flair for turning the tables on relative value. She appreciated a person with the authority to do that. She knew that one word from Jago could change the winds of fashion.

'I've a plan to transform the groupies into a clutch of mental cases,' he said. 'Just you wait. They'll be unrecognizable.'

'I doubt it,' Christina said, and she wished, even as she heard herself speak the words, that she could have bitten her tongue. 'Not if you're getting them up as mental cases.'

Again, Jago laughed. He was being inexplicably charming. 'Ah,' he said. 'But will you recognize me?'

To her annoyance Christina blushed. She was thinking shakily to herself that she didn't recognize him already.

'I'll see you, then,' Jago said. 'Dog and Duck, okay? Eight o'clock. Be there.'

'Yes,' Christina said. 'I'll be there.' And then they parted.

The Ghouls, the Beata Beatrix and the Sister-Sprite

Jago, by early afternoon, was in ever filthier mood. He was angry at himself and he had duly modified his Hallowe'en plans to make them less benign. It was his intention, by then, to induce fear in the populace, not to make people laugh. A fire-and-brimstone cleric would be bound to provoke simple mirth. So he would not go as a clergyman. No. He would go as a Nazi brain surgeon. And the groupies would be the gruesome products of his surgical experiments.

It did not take much to inspire him, once he had come upon a crutch in a skip at the back of the boiler-house. And the Lost Property had, predictably, yielded up a number of old white towels and incidentals. Nor had it been a problem to persuade Marty to prove his daring by stealing a couple of kidney dishes from the medical store, along with something like fifty metres of crêpe bandage.

It was delightful for Jago to witness how willingly the groupies collaborated in their own discomfort and belittlement. And he accomplished his effects so cheaply. A little joke-shop latex and a tube of fake blood.

Only Stet had ventured to produce a sneer or two, and had duly been punished by the nature of his costume. True, it was less outspokenly grotesque than the others, but it was certainly destined to be the least user-friendly. Jago – having reduced Pongo to a one-eyed, gap-toothed cripple, with a crutch and an artificial hump, and Marty to a maimed, legless imbecile – felt Stet to be his masterpiece. Stet was a Mummy Man, a cloth-bound cadaver, among mere Breughel outcasts.

His concession to Stet had been to allow him free use of his limbs, but this had merely been in order that Stet could push Marty in the wheelbarrow. This last had been Pongo's spontaneous contribution. He had found the wheelbarrow, new and gleaming, with the toolshed door's chain and padlock slung carelessly over one of its hand-grips. A small key was fitted into the padlock itself, while a second key dangled invitingly from a little metal ring attached to the first. The head gardener, being a security freak, had always been perceived by schoolboys as constituting a challenge, and the theft was accomplished forthwith. Marty would be in the wheelbarrow, with his legs cobbled up in a sack.

Stet was stripped to his underpants and T-shirt. He was then wound, head to toe, in crêpe bandages. No inch of him was left uncovered, though, with Jago's artful readjustment, Stet could see out through tiny apertures in the gauzy film that all but covered his eyes. And Stet himself had managed to work a small, reptilian suck-hole in the latticework around his mouth.

Jago's disguise consisted almost entirely in altered speech and body language. He wore steel-framed spectacles from the Oxfam shop and he affected a slight but chilling facial twitch. He wore a white lab coat with steel implements protruding from the breast pocket. His hair and eyebrows were dusted lightly with grey powder. Yet, for all his minimal modifications, Jago had, unquestionably, taken on a new and sinister identity.

Jago carried a list, fixed to a clipboard, upon which he had entered a few bogus names of 'patients'. He consulted it before he spoke, icily quiet, as doors were opened to them. His voice was a triumph of understated mimicry; his persona that of a mirthless, teutonic scalpel man. Out in the dark streets, even Stet was intermittently unnerved by him.

Certainly, the householders were made uneasy by his presence. Any Hallowe'en jollity faded promptly, as doors were opened to them. Residents found that their smiles quickly died on confrontation with that steely gaze. Younger women looked haunted as Jago, with the merest hint of Prussian heel-clicking, reported – impressively deadpan, in his Nazi-butcher accents – that the householder was down on his list of candidates for exploratory surgery.

'Please to schtep ziss vay,' Jago said briskly. 'Vee are finding zat procrastinazion *ist immer* ze sieff of time.' And he offered an arm as escort.

The groupies, meanwhile, had had their instructions. Stet was to remain completely silent, while the other two were permitted the faintest, demented moan. Marty and Pongo were softly unintelligible, their mooning, cleft-palate voices producing a sad, unearthly disharmony.

'Some of my previouz patientz,' Jago remarked crisply. 'Unfortunate. Most unfortunate. Ze brain, *gnädiche Fräulein*. *Es ist ein* complex organ, *nicht wahr*? I vould like to assure you, *Fräulein*, that I am having alvayz ninety-zeven per zent succezz. Zis vay, please, *Fräulein*! Ze vaiting list is long, *wissen Sie*? Ze Nazional Heltz – *ach jah*!'

Then, abandoning the bedside manner, Jago turned, suddenly tyrannical, upon Marty in the wheelbarrow. 'Ze kidney dish, *Dummkopf! Einz, Zwei, Drei*.' And, just as the householders had begun to recollect themselves and to shrink into their doorways, one or other of the Breughel outcasts swiftly held out a kidney dish containing a few pathetic pennies and one boiled sweet.

'Trick or treat!' drooled the maimed ones.

'Trick or treat!' Jago yelled, suddenly maniac loud, the accent slicing sharply through the cold night air.

Then there were the occasional, spontaneous variations. In one hallway, for example, where Jago spotted the souvenir tack of the Vatican, he explained to the female householder that the groupies had been the unfortunate victims of one-time abortion attempts and that he, personally, had rescued them, in the eleventh hour, from the sluice.

'Vee are needing a little money for ziss valuable vurk!' he said and, again, the cripples held forth the kidney dish, as the door was shut in their faces.

The kidney dish was better received by the local publicans and their clientele, who were not only more robust about the Hallowe'en party's bad taste, but buoyed up by their awareness of safety in numbers. As a result, they readily forked out and drinks were not infrequently offered on the house.

This meant that the groupies were something under the influence by the time they reached the Dog and Duck. Jago, naturally, was as sober as a judge, but Stet – whose unconducive costume had made him, in especial, an eager target for free drinks – had developed an unsightly, beery stain around the suck-hole in the bandages. Once or twice, *en route*, Stet's burping had induced in Jago a silent, murderous inclination.

Jago did not at first recognize Christina. She sat, all alone, waiting for him on the wall of the pub forecourt. What Jago saw was a slight, pastel-clad Pierrot figure, who wore a curious, delicate mask made of wire mesh. It was like a moulded, white-painted sieve, touched lightly with angel features. The mask did not so much block out the wearer's face as transform it and enhance it. She stood up when she saw him and came forward. An insubstantial, dreamlike, androgynous figure. A visitation. For a moment Jago took her for Peter – but not so much for Peter at sixteen, as the spirit and essence of Peter from five or six years back. And then the figure spoke.

'Hello, Jago,' she said.

Jago took off the Oxfam glasses and put them in the pocket of the lab coat. He handed the clipboard to Pongo and dusted the powder from his hair.

'God Almighty,' he said. 'It's you. But Chris – that mask. You look extraordinary.'

'It's a Nicaraguan carnival mask,' she said. The mask had once been a present from one of her father's Latin American authors.

'Are you all on your own out here?' Jago said.

The mask face nodded at him, hauntingly. 'My sister's rehearsing with Peter,' she said. 'He's playing the organ for her.' For a moment, Jago's anger almost rose to destroy the enchantment.

Music was not one of Jago's subjects. He had never learnt to play a musical instrument. Had he tried it, he might well have found that it came quite easily to him. As it was, he had never given himself the chance. He had sealed his own musical fate many years before when, upon befriending Peter Rusconi, he had discovered that Peter, at the age of eight, could already do two hands together on the piano. It was necessary, at once, for Jago to affect no interest in acquiring such a skill.

His resolution had been reinforced, shortly thereafter, during a prep school clapping exercise. Peter, on that occasion, had had cause to explain to Jago that different pauses were necessary for minim and semibreve rests. Jago's musical indifference had thereby been firmly cemented. He had never been comfortable, anywhere, in the role of second fiddle.

Now, for a moment, he cursed his own shortsightedness, which had allowed Peter Rusconi this additional source of access to the Beata Beatrix. Here he was – he, Jago – with the wrong sister in a pub car park, attended by three drunken idiots, while Peter, with his two-year bloody head-start on the woman, was off somewhere in bloody church, playing the organ for her, as she rehearsed her sacred arias. *Exultate Jubilate*. Fat bloody chance of that for him.

He was flooded with zeal to seek Pam out, but he didn't even know which church. Would it be the school chapel?

Definitely not. He'd have known, in that case, about the 'birthday'. Was it the parish church? The Catholic church? Could it be that she and Peter were rehearsing together in that hideous Roman pile – that Victorian brick and concrete eyesore in the urban back-street? Now that he thought about it, Ms Angeletti must surely, habitually, frequent the eyesore – as did all the school's Catholic contingent – for her weekly genuflections.

Jago tried his damndest, then, to summon scorn. Would Daddy Roland be stretching his ecumenical tolerance so far? he considered. Would he be sanctioning little Peterkin's entrance there? But of course he would, for Christ's sake. This was art, after all. This was a concert. This was music. Sacred music.

Jago was aware of his own violent contradictoriness in wishing at once to pour ridicule upon Roland for his decent, Protestant persona and, at the same time, in wishing to take out for himself letters patent on Pam's Catholicism. Religion, after all, meant nothing to him. Nothing, except for that childhood vision of his shining, maternal antecedents, lining the road to the shrine of Santiago de Compostela.

Instead, he smiled gracefully at the dainty sister-sprite before him. He told himself to calm down; that this time everything would be different; that Pam would be forever; that Pam would wait and so would he. And that time no longer had meaning. For Pam, he was willing to go forever in and out of his days, seeking to capture dragon-fire with swords of ice from unknown frozen wastelands.

'So you recognized me,' he said.

Christina laughed behind the mask. 'I recognized the groupies,' she said.

The groupies, by then, were acting drunk. Stet had tipped Marty out of the barrow, and Marty, who had succeeded in freeing his legs from sackcloth, was charging it at Stet. Pongo, with his hump still firmly in position, was whirling his crutch somewhat hazardously about his head until Stet snatched it from him.

Stet had clearly had enough. He was tired of taking orders from Jago and – unlike Marty and Pongo – was conscious of having been duped. Henry Beasley's party would be getting underway and he wasn't bloody well going along there wrapped in Matron's bandages. He needed to get back and change. Meanwhile, here they were, hovering in a bloody car park while Jago – the only one of them who was looking his usual, gorgeous self – was scoring, as always, with a woman.

'Sod this,' he said suddenly. 'I'm off. Anyone coming with me?' Jago took no notice. He was tracing the outline of Christina's mask with his right index finger. Then, in a tender, brotherly gesture, he took both her hands in his own for a moment and smiled at her before he let them drop.

Stet had begun to cross the road. The pub was opposite the south end of the wood that bordered the school on its east side. There was a sloping bank between the road and the woodland which Stet looked about to scale. He turned before he did so.

'Anyone coming?' he said. There was a sound of screaming brakes as a car veered round Marty who had stepped promptly into the road, pushing the wheelbarrow before him. Pongo laughed delightedly and dashed to join him . . . They clung to each other, laughing raucously. Neither was particularly steady.

'Leave the fucking wheelbarrow, you morons,' Stet yelled, in a voice not unlike Jago's. 'And hurry up! I'm going.' Marty gave the barrow a shove, which sent it crashing back towards the verge. It landed upside-down, throwing the gardener's lock and keys into the gutter. The three reviving ghouls then whooped drunkenly as they scrambled up the bank, which was knarled with the roots of trees.

'Idiots,' Jago said dismissively, his eyes on Christina's face.

'You ought to move that wheelbarrow,' she said. 'It's dangerous lying there.'

When Jago addressed himself to do so, the groupies had already managed to grope and scramble their way almost to the top of the bank. The Mummy Man got there first. He was using Pongo's crutch to assist his cripple comrades in their conquest of the summit. Then all three of them made it to the top and were swallowed up by the darkness.

Jago moved the barrow. Then he returned, with relief, to Christina. He was enjoying the groupies' absence.

'You look so amazingly pretty,' he said. His sincerity quite surprised him. 'You look so dreamy. Sort of like a mirage. Do you know that?' Then he went on. 'What a strange pair of girls you are,' he said. 'You and your sister. Really.'

'Strange?' Christina said.

'Yes,' Jago said. 'I don't know. Just strange. And how is it you come to look so different?'

Christina laughed. She shrugged. 'Papa's Girl. Mama's Girl,' she said, tongue in cheek. 'Virgin Birth, maybe? How should I know.' She did not say that her sister had been adopted. She was wishing then to have Jago concentrate entirely upon herself. Enjoying the balm of their benign aloneness there in the car park, she felt enclosed by the faint hum of traffic and by the rustle of trees from the wood.

'Do you have any brothers or sisters?' she said.

Jago avoided the question. It was not one that, at any time, he felt equipped to answer. Did he have a brother? Yes, he had. He had had a twin brother about whom he fancied that he retained some shadowy memory. Or had it merely been that the first of the au pairs – that young Frenchwoman, who had wrenched him free from his mother – had undertaken, artificially, to reconstruct his recollections in those first, early months?

When Jago thought about his brother, it was all to do with presence; nothing to do with physiognomy. Nothing tangible. A silhouette; a dream-time *doppelgänger*; a sense of movement caught at the corner of the eye when the head turned suddenly; an occasional, curious apprehension of altered smell and light that always faded within the moment.

The same was true for his mother. She was a presence without definition. Once, long ago, he had had a mother and a brother. They had gone. Back to France. The south of France. Somewhere near the Spanish border. How was it he knew that? Because, other than that, he knew nothing. No detail. His father had simply erased the subject. It wasn't on the menu. Charles Rutherford – with whom Jago continued to have a perfectly easy, chappish sort of communion – had so effectively wound a bramble hedge around the question, that it had become impossible for Jago to think of asking.

And then, as he struggled to blot out Christina's question, something else of greater immediacy flashed upon the inward eye. The clipboard. Shit! He had handed Pongo the clipboard just as he'd met Christina. And the clipboard had his name on it. Plus his handwriting, of course. And the ghouls would – of course – whoop and shriek their way drunkenly through the wood. And get caught – of course.

The bloody wood was private property, was it not? Seriously out of bounds. It belonged to old Sir Peregrine. Sir P had been known to get pretty shirty if boys were found trespassing there. So had the housemaster. And, even if they didn't get caught, Pongo would, in all likelihood, abandon the bloody clipboard with its list of bogus names. It would be returned to the school and its purpose duly investigated.

In the cold night air, Jago began to realize that he had probably gone over the top. His crazy, driving anger had got the better of him that evening. He had invaded householders' privacy and had given offence to the citizenry. Especially to a number of apprehensive younger women. And definitely to that Catholic party with the papal tack in the hall.

Oh, Jesus, and he had even gone so far as to offer his arm here and there. Could this be interpreted as molestation? Attempted assault? It was certainly possible that the Catholic party might guess at their schoolboy status and lodge a complaint with the Head. Might somebody even go so far as to contact the police?

God in heaven, but the barrow had better find its way back, pronto, to its position alongside the gardener's toolshed from whence Pongo had been moron enough to take it. Yet the first priority just had to be to get the clipboard back from said moron. He would have to abandon Christina for the moment and get the groupies to return by road. Then, with luck, she'd have no objection to returning the wheelbarrow with him before they went on to Henry's party.

Jago, unlike the groupies, was completely serious about his future. He fully intended to go far. He had always been élitist and open-eyed about his abilities, particularly in maths. Then again, the groupies' parents were all backed by huge amounts of money – far more money than his own father could ever begin to dream of. Their post-school role in life would be to fart around and play the stock market and fly small, private aircraft, etcetera, until they stepped into directorships and married vacuous, tittering women who would then give birth to the groupies of the twenty-first century.

Jago had always taken it as read that he would get into Cambridge. Brilliant exam performance coupled with glowing reports from his Head and housemaster would be his open sesame. And, right now, he was fucked if bloody Ned Portius and Co. – if one indiscreet but unimpressive prank – was going to snatch all that from him.

'Chris,' he said. 'Will you excuse me? But only for a moment. Look. I'll have to go after them. They'll end up breaking their legs, you know – falling into rabbit holes and Christ knows what. They'll certainly call out Sir Whatshisname. Say. You will wait for me, won't you? Wait inside, Chris. It's warmer. I'll pull them out in a flash, I promise, and make them go by road.'

Jago took off the white coat. He handed it to her and then he turned to go. 'Wait for me,' he said.

'I'll wait,' Christina said. His concern for the unworthy revellers was, in a way, rather impressive, she considered. And what the hell. Had she not waited for him two whole years already?

Shortly thereafter, Jago found himself fuming as he stumbled, through the uncompromising dark, on the roots of Sir Peregrine's oak trees. He caught his clothes on brambles. And where the fuck had the groupies got to, that they had managed to outpace him so quickly? Christina, he fretted, would be beginning to wonder where on earth he was.

Pam, meanwhile, was all alone in the tiny, ancient church in the wood, appointed for her rehearsal. It was a thousand years old that year. She had come to the conclusion, earlier, that Peter had been held up and that she ought to proceed there ahead of him. She could accompany herself as she sang.

She knew that Peter had been visiting Roland's parents near Lyme Regis and that the two elderlies were due to deliver him back in time for this extra, last-minute run-through. She knew, also, that Roland's parents were planning to stay over and attend St Elfreda's birthday concert which was to happen in two days' time.

Music was just one of the things that Pam and Peter shared. Both of them had piano lessons and Peter had, in addition, become quite accomplished as an organist. He loved to play and, because of his special access to the school chapel during the holidays, he had had ample opportunity to practise.

Pam took voice lessons. She had a beautiful soprano voice and Lady Vanessa, her teacher, was as anxious as Pam's parents to see that it was properly nurtured.

Lady Vanessa was Sir Peregrine's wife. The elderly couple lived quietly in a pretty little gamekeeper's cottage within the wood that adjoined the school. The school had acquired its present premises, shortly after World War I, when the encumbent nobleman – Sir Peregrine's late uncle – his four sons killed in the war, had decided to sell up and retreat to smaller quarters.

After dismissing the servants and shipping the last of the ancestral portraits off to the auction house, he had retired gratefully to the gamekeeper's cottage, along with a pair of guns, a half-dozen pipes, and two devoted labradors. Then the school had moved into the big house.

Upon the old man's death, Sir Peregrine had inherited the cottage along with the wood. He and Lady Vanessa, a one-time concert soprano, were a devoted, childless couple. They had decided, some eight years previously, to give up their lives in Chelsea and retire to the cottage. Ever since, they had had excellent relations with the school and had become particular friends of Roland and Gentille. Lady Vanessa was godmother to Roland's younger daughter Lydia.

In addition, she had come to consider Pam and Peter as her 'special' young people. She was charmed by their decorous friendship and found them most adorably old-fashioned. Besides, Pam's voice was a responsibility and a challenge. She felt that the project kept her young.

Peter frequently accompanied Pam when she walked the five hundred metres into the wood for her singing lessons. These took place in Lady Vanessa's sitting-room which was only just big enough to accommodate her two young guests along with herself and her upright piano. The rest of the space was taken up with Lady Vanessa's collection of antique dolls' houses and with a small musical curiosity. This was a portable, seventeenth-century reed organ, which Lady Vanessa had acquired along the way and which she was delighted to have Peter play.

Among a multitude of laudable projects, all of which kept her young, Lady Vanessa had championed the restoration of the tiny, tenth-century church of St Elfreda's. It had stood, neglected and half derelict, in the wood near her home. Public subscription, charity concerts and all manner of local and metropolitan effort had gone into its restoration, until St Elfreda's, complete with new roof, new bell rope, anti-damp treatment, wall-mounted oil lamps and well-tended churchyard, was once again a functioning church. It was visited, occasionally, by a local vicar and had become a popular venue for weddings and memorial services.

Lady Vanessa's assiduous local researches, including her perusal of the Domesday Book, had satisfied her that this was the year of St Elfreda's thousandth birthday, and it was to mark this occasion that she had arranged a special concert during which Pam would sing a variety of sacred songs, accompanied by Peter on the reed organ.

For this purpose – although there was a perfectly usable piano in there already – she had had the reed organ transferred to the church which, for the duration, was to be kept locked. Pam and Peter had been issued with one precious key to share in case of impromptu rehearsals. The key was an enormous black iron item and Lady Vanessa had impressed upon them that to replace it, should it be lost, would cost her two hundred pounds.

Lady Vanessa had also undertaken to see that Pam and Peter were given special dispensation to go to the church whenever they were free. To exercise this recent and temporary privilege had given both young people particular delight and they had planned to spend the early part of Saturday evening there together, running through the programme. The final rehearsal was to be with Lady Vanessa the next day and they wanted to do her proud.

Pam had never been afraid of being alone in the dark. Nor was she ever afraid of being alone in old churches. She felt their aura of sanctity. And, besides, St Elfreda's had become a very familiar edifice. Armed with a torch, she had walked the short distance through the wood and, having turned the huge key in the lock, she had entered and set about lighting the lamps in the front half of the church. After that, she had opened the piano and had begun to warm up.

Then she worked at the Purcell *Te Deum for St Cecilia's Day*. Pam was especially fond of the *Te Deum*. She had told Peter, just the previous week, that St Ambrose and St Augustine had sung it together at the baptism of St Augustine. The anecdote had charmed Peter, who – not knowing, then, that St Augustine had been a black man; an African – had seen, in his mind's eye, the two tall saints as blond, long-haired Duccio figures in pale, flat gold haloes, their mouths making shapes like smoke rings.

Pam's voice conveyed a peculiarly appealing combination of personal humility and spiritual certainty as it rose to the wooden roof beam of the little church with its rush mat floor-covering and scrubbed wooden chairs. When she stopped, the silence hummed at her strangely.

She looked at her watch. 'Oh, come on, Petie,' she said. She sat for a moment taking in the smell of recent washing soda along with the ancient smell of stone until she became aware, suddenly, that the silence had developed a kind of rhythm and that the rhythm was the sound of someone breathing. It was coming from the back of the church.

Pam made her way up the aisle, keeping the beam of her torch low on the ground. She saw then that an old man lay, dead to the world, on the floor between the two back pews. He was wrapped in a ragged overcoat and had an empty vodka bottle beside him.

It was extraordinary to Pam how he had got there, though the truth was he had entered that afternoon, while Lady Vanessa's cleaner had been busy at the east end with her ears plugged blissfully into James Last and his Orchestra on her Sony personal headset.

Suddenly Pam knew that she ought not to be in there; that she ought to leave at once. Suddenly she knew that Peter was not coming. She turned quickly to go. She closed the instrument and gathered up her sheet music. It gave her a moment's uncertainty, not knowing quite what to do about locking up, but she was, after all, only four minutes' walk from Lady Vanessa's house. For this reason, she left the oil lamps burning and locked the church door quickly behind her.

It was just as the groupies were entering the churchyard. Marty and Pongo had come through the trees together, guffawing and falling about. This was because Stet – drink having provoked in him the urge to urinate – was some few yards behind them, struggling to free his penis from the latticework of bandages under which his underpants, along with his nether anatomy, had been trapped.

'Shit!' he said. 'Oh, Jesus, I'm about to piss down my leg.' Having succeeded at last in freeing himself, Stet peed in profusion, churning up a muddy froth at the root of an old yew tree.

'Christ!' he said. 'That's better.' And he tucked himself back into the loosened grave clothes. He grinned at Marty and Pongo through the beery, discoloured suck-hole, just as Pam emerged, illumined, from the porch.

Pam did not at first recognize Marty and Pongo, but she could see that they were Hallowe'en revellers and, as such, they gave her no fear. Quite the opposite. They brought to her a touch of home. And it occurred to her at once that she could enlist their aid in rousing the old man.

'Pardon me,' she said into the darkness. 'But I have a little problem.'

The pair stopped dead in their tracks and stared at her. Then they looked at each other, grinning stupidly. Pongo threw down the clipboard, ready for action. In that moment, two things came to Pam at once. One was that the revellers were drunk and the other was that they had been joined by a third who had the unmistakable gait of Stet Gregory. He had stepped from the more opaque darkness beyond, with his grave clothes gleaming white in the dull glow thrown by the oil lamps.

Pam's eyes darted quickly from one to the other as they advanced, within that second, to close her in because, with the appearance of Stet, the groupies had at once seemed to take on the nature of a posse. Their every gesture spoke menace. Pongo's face was shining, idiot-like, with latex puckering and blacked-out teeth. Marty had a trickle of blood dribbling from a hairline crack. But it was Stet who most alarmed her. Stet, who was almost eyeless – almost faceless – except for that ugly, reptilian suck-hole. And the tongue within, like a darting snake.

Pam's first thought was to make a dash for the church and take her chance with the old man, but to unlock the door would take precious seconds. And then her shaking hand, as she assessed her chances, betrayed her and let the key drop. When Stet stepped forward and stood on it and breathed into her face, that was when she made her mistake and turned on her heels to run.

Stet, who was still in possession of the crutch, extended it and tripped her, so that she fell hard and ignominiously, on to her left hip and elbow. Then she turned and raised herself with intent, at least, to face him. She opened her mouth to speak, but Stet prodded her downwards with the cane. He planted it across her chest and held it there with his foot.

'Is it a worm or is it a Werewolf?' he said, as she tried to writhe free.

For that instant, Stet felt terrific. He felt heroic. A conqueror posed with planted flag. He felt like Jago, as he loomed over the girl with the crutch pinning her to the ground. He was aware that his two companions had become transfixed by him.

'Leave her to me,' he said, though neither Marty nor Pongo had moved. He bent to take the torch from the ground beside her right hand. Then, using it first to throw back her skirt, he flicked the switch and beamed the thing crudely between her legs, where Pam's wide, loose-fit silk underpants made possible for him a glimpse of her vaginal lobes and a section of dark pubic hair.

When Stet began to press his mouth insistently down on to hers, Pam found not only that the suck-hole stank, but that it was bordered with the stiff, rasping fabric of the crêpe bandage which had by then been formidably starched with dried beer. It eroded the skin around her mouth. A sensation of oral violation invaded her mind so profoundly, that she was hardly aware that Stet was wrenching at the grave clothes around his pelvic region. He found access to himself much easier this time, since his peeing had conveniently loosened the bandages.

As an act of rape, the episode was not of the most dramatic, since Stet, having made his entry, had almost immediately lost his nerve. Though he had always been big enough and handsome enough, and quick-witted enough to pass muster with the in-group by miming the right degree of nonchalant credibility, Stet's was by no means a sanguine character. He had always been a more complex, more sardonic, more brooding proposition than either Marty or Pongo. And, unlike them, he had not as yet made it all the way with a person of the female sex. What was driving him to it now, along with drunken bravado, was his long habit of ascendancy in the business of hounding the Werewolf.

What was putting him off, however, was disgust – not for himself, but for the girl. It had been that unfortunate, injudicious glimpse, which he had afforded himself in the beam of the torch, of Pam's pubic region.

Stet was of course acquainted with the photographs in girlie magazines. It had seemed to him, from a perusal of these, that what women harboured between their thighs was not an attractive item. It had struck him as an unpleasant sort of mutation; a kind of hirsute clam. Now that he was actually confronting the thing, it had become, in addition, a sly, concealed weapon; a bearded malformation of dark, bruise-coloured flesh, designed precisely to lie in wait and to lure. It was like one of those spooky, insect-eating plants. Unnatural. Treacherous. Neither fish nor fowl. And actually being there felt to him like playing Dead Man's Eye. Murder in the Dark. Stet shrank inside her and was at once overcome by nausea.

As a small child, Stet, on his very first fishing trip, could remember having caught a fish right away. He had hooked it in the hard palate and had screamed and screamed to have the slimy, scaly thing taken from him. 'Beginner's luck,' his father had said in cheery commendation. 'Hey, what a big one.' But for Stet, that fish, so slippery, so twitching, had become the enemy by dint of being the victim. The moment of Stet's victory had become the moment of his defeat. He had been cheated of the conqueror's joy.

Now, as he loathed and feared the girl for the alien apparatus into which he had coerced himself, he began, without warning, to throw up.

For Marty and Pongo the spell was broken. Humorously, Marty groaned out his disgust. He thumped Pongo on the shoulder.

'Urgh,' he said. 'The bugger's puking. Come on!'

When Stet heard the footsteps of his comrades retreating from the churchyard, he knew that he would have to go at once. He could not be there alone with Pam, who was now all the more disgusting for having been the recipient of his malodorous, oral emission. He rose unsteadily, stumbling over her, like a person rising from bed. He wiped his mouth on his bandaged arm and tucked away his penis as he loped along anxiously behind his two friends.

'Wait for me,' he called like a plaintive child. It made Marty and Pongo want to tease him. 'Hold on,' Stet called. 'Shit, you guys, wait. I need to pee again.' In response, the fleeing pair gave out a penetrating wolf call. They were wishing to goad their adventurous but laggard friend with the Werewolf's menacing proximity. Then, magnanimously, they paused and allowed him to catch up. They were all three of them still drunk enough to think the thing rather a prank.

Pam's only conscious emotion was relief. Her only thought was not to breathe, not to inhale, not to swallow, until she had wiped the filth from off her face. Stet's vomit, issuing as it had done, through the rasping, discoloured suck-hole, had loomed so much larger in her mind than the bungle of his entry between her thighs, that she still felt predominantly abused by mouth.

She did not attempt to rise until she heard the sound of the revellers retreating well beyond the boundary of the churchyard. When she heard the Werewolf howl, it was with relief as a measure of their considerable distance from her. Then she sat up and used the hem of her skirt to wipe her face and neck. She dampened sections of hemline with spittle and wiped again and again. All over her shirt front, and beside her on the ground, lay a mess of food clods and enzymes in a foul, beery wetness.

Pam took off her shirt, opening the buttons with difficulty. She took off her camisole. She balled the garments together and tied them in a bundle by the shirt-sleeves. Then she took off her underpants. She used them to wipe between her breasts. Having done so, she buttoned her jacket over her naked torso, shivering as the chill of the lining made contact with her skin. She got up and gathered her things.

Two items still evaded her. The church key had resolutely obscured itself and the torch had disappeared with Stet. But never mind, she thought. She'd find her way to the cottage all right and the key would turn up quickly enough, in the light of Sir Peregrine's hurricane lamp.

Pam, unlike her sister, had taken on board the ideology of Christian forgiveness. She was infused with its demanding tenets and was formed by its powerful symbolism. She knew that if her enemy took her coat she was to give him her cloak also. She knew that it was not enough merely to love her friend. She was required to love her enemy. The stripped garments and the crown of thorns were a part of her visual baggage. And, right then, a recurring phrase had begun to invade the blank space that her mind had, for the moment, protectively made of itself. Its monotonous, humdrum rhythms beat out the pace of her stride.

'Marty and Pongo and Stet,' intoned the phrase, 'are all part of the body of Christ.'

Once Pam had made it to her singing teacher's house, she knew that she did not want to see anyone. Most of all, she did not want to speak. Could not. If Lady Vanessa were to come to the door, then no words would come out of her mouth. She would need to bathe and gargle and scrub and soak before her speech would issue forth.

So she could not knock on the cottage door. Instead, she sat down and opened her music bag. In the light of the porch lamp, she took out a pencil and the score of the Purcell *Te Deum*. On the back of the score, she wrote a message.

'Dear Vanessa,' she wrote, and then – as she thought – she went on to explain about the old man asleep in the church and about the oil lamps and the key, which she had regrettably, but only temporarily, mislaid. She signed the letter and pushed the score through the flap. When she heard it fall into the letter-box, she rang the bell and ran off swiftly into the covering darkness.

She paused for a moment, and turned to see that the door was opened and the letter recovered. She saw that Sir Peregrine peered out briefly, holding the score in his hand. Then the door was closed again and, with relief, she went on. Even in the considerable darkness, it took her no more than a few minutes to span the distance between the cottage and the school. Once there, she took a long, hot bath and washed Stet's vomit from her chest and out of her mouth and out of her hair.

Sir Peregrine, together with his wife, had been lingering over his supper when he heard the sound of the letter-box flap followed by the sound of the bell. He made his way into the hall where he picked up the Purcell *Te Deum* and noticed that Pam's writing was on the back of it.

'Something for you, Vanessa,' he said, and he handed it to his wife.

Lady Vanessa glanced it over. 'Good gracious,' she said. 'It's from Pam. But it's really very odd.' She gave it back to her husband who began to read the letter out loud. '"Dear Vanessa,"' he read, '"Marty and Pongo and Stet are all part of the body of Christ. Marty and Pongo and Stet –"' He stopped and looked up.

'She's written it over and over,' Lady Vanessa said.

Sir Peregrine sniffed the air twice. Then he put the score to his nose. 'Pah,' he said. 'It stinks, Vanessa. Reeks of stale beer and God knows what. I am, of course, aware that there has been some junketing in the vicinity. Sounds of youthful merriment. Do you suppose – it is possible – that your two young friends have been imbibing?'

Lady Vanessa enjoyed the idea. She smiled at him. 'Could be,' she said. 'Oh, I do hope so. It really is about time that the dear things began to let their hair down.' Then they washed their supper plates and dried them and listened to the radio news before retiring to bed.

When Jago approached the churchyard he could not believe what he saw. He paused on the verge and trained his eyes with some difficulty upon the figure of Stet. Could it really be that Stet was doing the business, right there, with a female person? There, in the light of the church porch? And that Marty and Pongo were actually standing by and watching? What bloody next! And who, he wondered, was the itinerant tart in question? Where on earth had they picked her up?

Jago found himself in that moment disinclined to intervene. His sense of privacy prevented it and forced him into the uncomfortable role of voyeur. He resented it; found it gross.

Christ, he thought, what made it worse was that Stet appeared to be pumping his stuff through the bloody bandages and all. Oddly enough, it was this small detail that caused him his most fastidious recoil. To be doing it in your clothes, he thought, it was so bloody low; so bloody rank. It was like that oafish gardener in *Lady Chatterley's Lover*. Forever unbuckling his trouser belt and then buckling it up straight afterwards. With half of himself, Jago wanted not to watch and with the other half he could not stop. He could see the whiteness of the mummy cloth unmistakably in the dull glow. He could also see the whiteness of the woman's exposed left thigh.

And then, before he could dwell upon the matter, bloody

Stet had actually begun to throw up. The sound of his retching was unmistakable. Stet, Jago reckoned, incredulous, must be hurling his vomit right into the poor tart's face. Christ, but it was the foulest thing. Gross, but to a degree. Jago found that his whole body tensed and cringed against the sound of it. And why, in fuck's name, was Stet behaving like that? Why was he not even trying to lean sideways and chuck the vomit clear?

Then, just like that, the episode was over. Marty and Pongo had gone prancing off and then the trio of drunken ghouls was whooping it up, merry as you please, through the woodland and back towards school. Stet had simply climbed off the woman and left her there, lying on the ground. What the fuck was going on inside his head? Why hadn't he waited for her? Why had they all just run off like that, like kids playing Postman's Knock?

Jago, to his own annoyance, found that he was shaking. He was longing for a smoke. A coldness was spreading over the surface of his skin. Could it be – oh, Jesus Christ, please not – that Stet had actually been *coercing* this wretched female person who had, it seemed, made no sound of protest at being so disgustingly abused? The woman's silence unnerved him. And Stet – was he completely off his head to be doing such an appalling bloody thing?

At that instant, Jago's speculations were interrupted by the Werewolf howl. His sense of shock was something akin to an arrow shot through the shoulder. For some moments he felt dizzy.

'Oh, no,' he said, though his voice made no sound. 'Oh, please God, no.' And he gnawed at a shaking index finger.

Shortly thereafter, Pam sat up and Jago drew in his breath. The sound he made was mingled with the quiet suspiration of surrounding trees. He watched, appalled, as the girl began, carefully, purposefully, to wipe Stet's vomit from her face. He saw Pam remove her shirt and her camisole. He saw her wipe the gunge from off her chest. He saw her get up and put on her coat and shiver.

Jago, as he watched her, was overcome with wonder. More than that, he was overcome with a wild, extravagant conviction. He was suddenly, completely sure that there, in Pam, in the violated girl, reposed the guardian and stronghold of all his better self. Yet, at the same time, he was quite certain that she had become, through this foul act of Stet's, unreachable. The groupies were – had been – God damn them, his friends. That very night they had positively been his zombies. He, Jago, was rooted there, hopelessly, within the enemy camp. To approach Pam, even in her hour of greatest need, was altogether unthinkable. Between the topless towers and the enemy encampment; between herself and himself, lay the widest darkest plain. And the plain had become unbridgeable.

For the first time in his life, Jago found himself on the edge of selflessness. He was also very much on the edge of tears. Yet still he held himself back. He would not reveal himself to the girl and risk implication in Stet's assault. Too much was at stake here and not only with regard to the girl's response to him.

Jago felt that here could be the end of his reputation; the end of his glittering future. And as he became increasingly transfused with unease at his own unworthiness; his own inability to stride forth and play the rescuing knight, Jago began to focus angrily upon Peter. It was Peter who had let the girl down. Where the fuck was he? He'd been rehearsing with her, had he not? In the church. This church. The one church that had not come to mind. So had Peter simply abandoned her? Had he run off, just like that, when Stet had come breezing along? How pathetic!

All the while, Jago ached with concern for Pam. Beautiful Pam. He wondered, was she all right? He wondered, could she walk? Was she weeping? But Pam seemed to him quite remarkably composed. He saw her gather together her sheet music. He saw her begin to walk the short distance towards her singing teacher's house.

Jago conceived the idea that he would follow her at a distance. He needed to make sure that she was all right. He saw her stop at the cottage and sit down to write her letter. He saw her post the score and then walk on. He followed until he saw her pass through the small, eastern gate of the school, after which he saw her take the path for the Girls' House and go in.

Then he turned back and retraced his steps until he was once again in the churchyard. There, by extraordinary good luck – if any luck there was on such a night as this – he almost fell over his clipboard which had been abandoned on the outermost edge of the church lamps' dull glow of light. He continued his journey until he had reached the lower road. On the verge, in the light of the car-park lamps, he paused to pick up one of the keys to the school gardener's padlock. Then, having torn up and pocketed the list of bogus patients on the clipboard, he went off to find Christina.

She was not the sister that he longed for. She was not the object of his profound, extraordinary love. But he needed her, then, rather badly. He found that he was fond of her for the first time in his life. He valued her, with the utmost sincerity, for her nearness to the beloved and for the power she possessed, thereby, to anoint his multiple wounds.

Christina was sitting in the window-seat of the pub when Jago finally came back. She had taken off the mask which now lay beside her on the table, along with an empty lemonade bottle and a glass. She was wearing the wheelbarrow chain and padlock like an ornament around her neck.

'You were ages,' she said, when Jago appeared. She spoke

in sympathy, not in reproach. 'And did you find your groupies?'

Jago avoided the question. 'They were pretty quick,' he said. 'It was dark.' He stopped. He saw that Christina was carefully studying his face. 'God knows,' he said, and he sat down.

He was looking dreadfully sad, Christina thought. Really sad. Wistful. Alone. She had never before seen Jago look anything like that.

'They're not worth it,' she said. 'That's if you want my opinion.'

'Right,' Jago said. 'Quite right. Listen. How keen are you on going to this party? What I mean is, would you really mind if we just gave it a miss? What I mean is —' He stopped.

'What?' she said.

'Chris,' Jago said, 'how would you feel if I offered you a lift back to school in a wheelbarrow?

The Floating Boy and the Falling Star

It was difficult to know who had had the worst time of it, Pam or Peter. Peter had gone that day, before lunch, to visit Roland's parents – his dear, adopted grandparents whom he knew as Grandfather and Grandmother. He had gone by train and then by bus. After that, as he always did, he had walked the quarter-mile from the little sub-post office, passing a rural intersection where, on this particular occasion, he had happened unexpectedly upon Grandfather who was out walking with Serious Syrius the Star Dog.

Syrius was, as usual, off his lead. Grandfather, who was wont to vouch for his reliability with a most loyal and enduring intransigence, was inclined to walk the dog without putting him on the lead – though this had always been against Grandmother's better advice. And he was indeed a most excellent, obedient little dog, except that he adored his master's grandson and had not expected to come upon Peter, so suddenly there, in the wrong place.

Syrius was doubly unlucky that day in that not only had he recently begun to lose his hearing but, in the main, there were very few vehicles passing that way. When one did, at that moment, Syrius was hurled, yelping and twitching, into the air. Then he fell, inanimate, on to the road.

The driver stopped some ten metres away and got out and retraced the distance, as Peter bore the little creature gently to the hedge. Then he turned to make contact with his grandfather.

Peter noticed right away that something unpleasant was happening to Grandfather. All in a moment, the old man

161

grimaced and tried to mouth words. He was clutching at his shoulder and staggering to his knees. Then, almost immediately, he collapsed into the road.

The driver had broken into a run. 'For God's sake, boy, leave the dog,' he yelled. 'And help me get the man into my car.'

Peter left Serious Syrius lying on the grass verge. Though he felt very foolish in doing so, he struggled, quick as lightning, out of his sweater and threw it over the dog. Then he dashed to where Grandfather was lying.

He sat in the back of the driver's car with Grandfather's head in his lap. The driver was possessed of a carphone which had proved most useful for making contact, both with the ambulance service and with Grandmother, who was to meet them at an appointed local hospital. The ambulance driver, who would liaise with them along the way, had already alerted the medical staff.

The afternoon was a most gruelling affair, as he and Grandmother waited anxiously for nurses to bring news of Grandfather's condition. Roland was summoned, and Gentille too. They drove down as soon as they could manage it. And all the while, as Peter worried for Grandfather and fetched his grandmother plastic cups of tea, he was grieving in duplicate, remembering the little dead dog so precipitously abandoned on the verge.

Grandfather's heart attack had unfortunately been followed by a stroke, which had taken away his powers of speech and had left him completely paralysed down one side of his body. The decision, as the evening wore on, was that Grandmother and Roland would stay on at the hospital and that Peter would accompany his mother on the arduous drive home to Ellen and Lydia.

It is probable that, had Peter been travelling with Roland,

he would have felt quite able to explain his need to return via the intersection where Serious Syrius lay on the verge. As it was, he knew that he could not possibly do so. His mother was not an 'animal person'. She never would have understood. To have mentioned the dog at all, in the circumstances, would have been perceived by Gentille as a serious affront, both to the old man and to the family's anxiety

So Peter allowed himself, lamely, to be driven back to school. As he did so, he grieved, not only for the dog; not only for the sick old man, both of whom he loved, but also for himself. He grieved for his own apparent lack of clout; for his reprehensible ineffectuality. He grieved for his weightlessness and for his inclination towards invisibility.

It was only Pam, he reflected gratefully, whose timely, lovely friendship had saved him from floating away altogether; from vanishing into cloud vapour. In the circumstances he yearned for Pam's company. He was sorry so to have stood her up that evening but, really, it was a very minor transgression in the context. And Pam would certainly understand. Pam was always understanding. And, given that she had not freaked when his feet left the floor without warning, she was hardly likely to freak at a single missed rehearsal. Pam was his dearest friend. Come to think, now that Serious Syrius was dead and Grandfather was fading, she would soon be his only friend.

The next day was not a comfortable one. Not for Pam, nor for Peter. Peter rose early to discover that Grandfather was dead and that Pam – far from being supportive to him – had become silent and remote. Neither was it a comfortable one for poor Lady Vanessa, who approached St Elfreda's towards midday to encounter, lying in a spread of dried vomit near the porch, the precious iron key with which she had entrusted Pam and Peter.

And worse awaited her within. Not only did St Elfreda's

163

reek of stale urine and burnt-out oil wicks, but the old man was, by then, not in the best of moods.

Though the day was Sunday, Lady Vanessa took it upon herself to call upon Pam and Peter. It was clear to her at once that poor bereaved Peter had had no hand in the matter, but she could not fail to indicate how disappointed she was in Pam – Pam who had nothing to say for herself and simply sat there, silent and unyielding.

'Partying is all very well,' Lady Vanessa prompted gently. 'But betraying a trust is a serious matter.'

When Pam did not reply to her, she went on, 'You wrote me a very odd letter. I could make no sense of it at all.'

Pam said nothing for ages. She looked withdrawn; hostile, Lady Vanessa thought. She had never anticipated that Pam would be so disobliging.

'Maybe I was drunk,' Pam said.

Lady Vanessa got up. 'Well,' she said, 'I hope we can forget all about it.' She looked with concern at Peter. 'We won't even think of rehearsing today,' she said. She suggested they try the following morning.

'I can't sing,' Pam said abruptly to her teacher's departing back. Lady Vanessa turned.

'I beg your pardon?' she said.

'I said that I can't sing,' Pam said. 'I just can't, Vanessa. I can't and I'm afraid I won't.' And, with that, she got up and left.

Most of the teaching staff were entertained by the change in Jago Rutherford. It was bandied about the staff room during coffee breaks that Jago, the invincible, had fallen victim to the smallest member of the Upper Fifth. Christina, it was agreed, was small, but she was none the less perceived as being a formidable young woman who would constitute a suitably worthy challenge. What pleased the staff most was the effect that this new alliance was having on Christina. The pair were working well together and had been observed by all to be spending long, quiet hours together in the library.

'It's a pleasure to see Christina take herself seriously at last,' said Miss Barnes, her English teacher. 'I have always believed about that girl that there is more there than meets the eye. It's been her bad luck to be so close in age to her sister. She's been reluctant to compete.'

Jago, it was generally noted, had seemed to lose his arrogance. His body language was less imperious, he had ceased to be a little Caesar, and all his eager acolytes had suddenly been forsaken, as he now accompanied Christina almost everywhere; a faithful devotee. One of the masters observed that Christina now wore Jago's sweatband wound twice around her wrist.

For Christina it was in many ways quite the best time she could remember. Jago, heartless, ruthless Jago, about whose sexual exploits the school mythology hummed, was now all hers. And the stories about him were nonsense, since Jago was gentle, courteous and reticent in the matter of physical approach. Admittedly he was a little more reticent than Christina sometimes wished. She had found herself, occasionally, much provoked by Jago's nearness; by the tantalizing proximity of his exquisite brown forearm as they worked together in the library; by her desire to have him kiss her on the mouth, where he chose, instead, always, to kiss her on the cheek. But that would come in time. And it was nice, she reflected, that Jago, in the newness of his altered self, was asserting, by wordless implication, that theirs was a marriage of true minds.

It was no surprise to anyone, least of all to himself, that Jago, in the mock exams, had done brilliantly well. Christina's results, however, were very pleasing to all and represented considerable advance. She had done especially well in maths, which was gratifying to her headmaster, since maths was also his subject.

Roland had never ceased to have a small soft spot for Alice's younger daughter. It was always startling for him to encounter those uncannily familiar blue eyes, now bequeathed to a person of such wholly different temperament; a person who stared out of them so boldly and had no problem with eye contact as she came forth and spoke her mind, whereas her mother had always been given to blinking and stammering and shyly averting her gaze. He admired Christina for her spirit and hoped that she would go far.

Pam had not done all that well in the exams. She had done well, of course, but not as well as usual. In short, she had done just well enough for her results to pass without appearing to provoke undue concern. And she had certainly done well enough to stay ahead of Stetson Gregory.

The Gynae Bloke and the Hell Hound

At this time there was not much to intrude upon Christina's happiness. The prize of Jago's devotion, coupled with the novelty of her recent academic success, had rendered her almost wholly self-absorbed. She was taken up entirely with thoughts of herself and Jago.

Her very creditable performance in maths meant that she now found herself promoted to membership of Roland's additional maths group – a small class of mathematical hopefuls of which Pam and Jago were already members. Christina found that she looked forward to the class and progressed in noticeable leaps. She especially enjoyed being taught by Roland who was one of those benignly endowed teachers for whom all pupils, no matter how wayward, will put their best foot forward. She liked the shapes of his neat, lucid sentences and the patterns of his tall, jagged writing as he wrote up examples on the blackboard.

'He has beautiful hands,' she whispered one morning to Jago who sat beside her. 'Don't you think he has beautiful hands?'

Jago did not hear her. He was watching Pam across the room. Intermittently, throughout the lesson, Christina's sister had been doodling slow, spiral ellipses into being on the back of a wallet file. She always began these at the centre, he noticed, and she spiralled slowly outwards until each elliptical shape had assumed a diameter through its wider axis of something like five centimetres. Then she began again. The action impressed Jago as one of absolute futility. He loathed himself, as he watched her, for his inability to intervene.

Sometimes he felt as though his brain was going to explode.

There were occasions, such as these, when the buoyancy of Christina's spirit was difficult for Jago to handle. Though he had become so genuinely fond of her – devoted to her; indebted to her – he was, right then, truly thankful that the lesson was almost at an end. It was getting on towards ten-thirty and, within the hour, he, along with Christina and certain members of the drama society, were due to leave for London on a visit to the Barbican Theatre.

Roland wiped the blackboard clean and put away his papers. The class rose and began, slowly, to move out. Yet Christina, in her enthusiasm, lingered after the rest. Jago suffered himself, mutely, to linger beside her. She chatted to Roland with a brightness that always embarrassed him slightly.

'I really like those matrices,' she said. 'The way they come together. Horizontals to verticals. They're so elegant.' She made Insey Winsey Spider movements with the fingers of her small white hands. 'They're sort of like dancing the galliard,' she said. 'Sort of like writing a sonnet. Has anyone ever thought of trying to construct a sonnet matrix?'

Jago cringed. Roland laughed. 'Would that be Shakespearean?' he said. 'Or Petrarchan, Christina?'

'Oh,' Christina said, disarmed. 'I suppose I mean the kind that comes in groups of four with a rhyming couplet at the end. I guess the rhyming couplet could cause a bit of trouble.'

'Ouch,' Jago said, hoping to stop her. 'Don't be so girlie, Chris.'

Roland laughed again. He moved off towards the classroom door, wanting his morning coffee.

'Enjoy the theatre,' he said. Then he left.

Jago had noted, as Christina talked, that Pam was waiting around outside. She was hesitating. He saw that she tensed and lowered her eyes as Roland emerged from the classroom. Jago deduced that Pam was waiting for her sister. He considered that she looked particularly burdened. Evidently so did Roland, who paused and looked at her carefully, searching her face for clues.

'Tell me,' he said, 'is everything all right?'

'Yes, sir,' Pam said, rather too promptly. 'Perfectly all right. Thank you.' And, though he continued to stand and search her face, she yielded absolutely nothing.

Reluctantly, Roland gave up. 'Come and see me,' he said, and then he moved off.

Inside the classroom, Jago was glancing uneasily at his watch. 'Chris,' he said, 'I have things to do before we go for the train. Listen, I'll meet you in the library. Ten minutes, okay?' He passed Pam in the corridor without acknowledging her presence. Then he proceeded to the dormitory, where he snatched a few moments' indulgent, solitary misery.

To have Pam there, in place of Jago, caused Christina's feet to touch the ground with a bump. Of late, she realized, there had been something less than exhilarating about her sister's presence. It seemed to her – now that she gave the matter thought – that her sister had, for the last few weeks, been devoid of Peter's company. And why had Pam cried off the concert like that? Hadn't that been rather weird?

'Chrissie,' Pam said, 'look. I'm sorry to intrude on you.' Then she stood there, saying nothing. Nothing at all. Christina became a little agitated as she waited for Pam to speak.

'Pam,' she began. She stood, on the edge of impatience, worrying that the time was passing and that she needed to head out for London.

'You're not to tell this to anybody,' Pam said. 'This thing that I'm about to say. Please, Chrissie. Nobody. That's including Jago.'

'Tell what?' Christina said.

'I need you to promise me,' Pam said. 'I need you not to repeat it.'

'All right,' Christina said. 'I promise.' But then Pam, once again, said nothing. She was silent for so long that Christina began to think she had given up all intention of speech.

'I'm probably pregnant,' she said at last.

For quite a while, Christina could only stare. Then she leaned against the classroom wall and closed her eyes for a moment. When she looked up, it seemed to her that Pam had not moved an inch; had not moved a muscle.

'Those kits,' Christina said, inadequately, having no experience in these matters. 'Those tests. You haven't used one, have you?'

Pam's shrug surprised her with its air of apparent indifference. 'Not yet,' she said. 'But all I know is I'm nearly four weeks late.'

They lapsed once more into silence.

'Who?' Christina said. She added, without much hope, 'Not Peter, I suppose?'

'Of course not, Peter,' Pam said. 'Don't be ridiculous, Chrissie.' Then she said, 'I don't know who, as a matter of fact. Isn't it irrelevant?'

Christina could not but fail to be astonished by this remark. It seemed to her so wholly out of character. 'Jesus, Pam,' she said. 'But how can you not know?' She was exasperated by her sister's total lack of oomph. Why was Pam so hell-bent on behaving like a victim? Why was she allowing time to pass and doing nothing to help herself? Why was she apparently so incapable of seizing the reins of her own life? And why, in heaven's name, had she − she, of all people − abandoned herself so prematurely to the act of procreation without so much as a thought for the consequences?

'Pam,' Christina said, 'look. I'm about to leave for London but I'll come back this evening with one of those testing kits.

It'll be okay, I assure you. It'll be negative. It's anxiety. It's hormones. Dearest Pam, don't worry. Promise me that you won't worry. Not until I get back.'

When Pam neither budged nor responded to her, Christina, mistakenly, awkwardly, talked on. 'Pam,' she said, 'about contraceptives –'

'Don't,' was all Pam said.

'Well, about the "Holy Father" and all that,' Christina said. 'Encyclicals and that. All that's meant as a counsel of perfection. Only crazies would ever begin to take that stuff seriously. People don't. People like our parents –'

'I was raped,' Pam said. She said it so undemonstratively that Christina, bent upon making her point, did not at first register the utterance.

'All those years,' Christina said. 'And our mother's been pregnant once –'

'I was raped,' Pam said again. 'Chrissie, please. Somebody held me down. He was drunk. He spewed into my mouth.'

Christina was stunned into silence. She felt a shiver, as if in response to cold, unearthly fingers taking hold of the back of her neck – the more so because her sister's delivery had been so unnervingly without emotion.

'It's the reason I reneged on that concert,' Pam said. 'I can't sing right now. It feels as if, every time I open my mouth to try, I'm choking on someone's vomit.'

They stood, after that, facing each other, stiffly, like two blocks of wood. Christina sensed that, had she reached out to her sister; had she tried to embrace her, Pam would have edged away; would have avoided her touch. She became aware that, while moisture had started to blur her own eyes, Pam's eyes, by contrast, were unencumbered.

In response to Pam's passivity, Christina was all at once flooded with resolution. She knew, as she stood there, that her sister needed her and that she, personally, would move heaven and earth in the matter. She would nail whichever slimy bastard it was that had so horribly abused her sister. And neither would her sister find herself a martyr to the creature's alien sperm. Not if she could help it.

'Pam,' she said. 'You must have *some* idea who it was who did this thing to you.'

Pam threw off the question. 'It was dark,' she said. 'Chrissie, forget it. I didn't mean to tell you. I don't know what possessed me. I was lonely. I'm sorry.'

But Christina was all resolve. 'We're going to tell Roland,' she said. 'We're going to tell him this minute.'

Pam shook her head. 'Chrissie, *think*,' she said. 'Just imagine if it was you.'

Christina thought. Imagine if it were she. Would she want it told? Would she want to risk the leaks; the raised eyebrows; the smirks on the faces of the likes of Stetson Gregory; the murmurs that she must have had it coming to her? No. Pam was right. She would not want it told.

'Okay,' she said. 'All right. Listen, I'm going to put off Jago.'

'No,' Pam said. 'Please don't. That's really the last thing that I want.'

Christina had no idea, as she conceded to Pam, reluctantly, how near the London theatre visit would bring her to finding the answer to her sister's needs. The answer came in the unlikely person of one Dulcie Jackson.

She met Dulcie that afternoon in the ladies' lavatory at the Barbican. It was during the interval at a schools' matinée performance of Shakespeare's *The Winter's Tale*.

Since Jago had so recently come good, that day Christina was, as usual, marking this minor miracle by wearing Jago's overcoat – a voluminous article made of cashmere that Jago had bought from the Imperial Cancer Research Fund Shop during a weekend at home. He had found it lying in a large cardboard box under a pair of cretonne curtains. When Jago wore it, it hung to mid-calf, making him look like a handsome officer *en route* to the Eastern Front. On Christina the coat skimmed the ground, obscuring her feet that were shod in Jago's outgrown walking boots. Jago's feet had outgrown the boots just after his ninth birthday.

Dulcie's companion in the ladies' lavatory was an ample blonde classmate who was teasing her hair ferociously with a fine-toothed metal comb. Both girls were wearing new high-street clothes; flash get-up for a school outing. Dulcie was tall and lean and strong. Atalanta in Calydon. Her skin, which was darkish Afro, had been highlighted at the cheekbones with a purple-tinted face gel embedded with tiny, luminous particles. Her hair had been dragged back severely from her brow into a short, high, plaited ponytail.

She wore her favourite skin-fit, dark indigo jeans that hugged her tight, shapely buttocks and long lean shanks in a manner that daily threatened to induce orgasm in young male commuters with whom she shared the Northern Line to Finsbury Park. On her upper body she wore a bright yellow, short-waisted stretch-lycra bust bodice that fitted taut over her high, conical breasts and left a span of her midriff exposed. Dulcie toted a short, lime green teddy bear jacket spattered with black dalmatian blobs hanging from one shoulder. Brass fans dangled from her ears. On her elongated, size eight feet, she wore backless, fake snakeskin stilettos. Since, at the moment of Christina's entry, she was being reflected full-length in the glass, it was possible for anyone coming into the room to register, at once, the dual charms of her lumbar vertebrae and of her deeply concave umbilicus.

'Fuckinell,' she said to the Teaser, staring rudely, as Christina

173

made her entrance. 'Look what the cat dragged in. Where the fuck d'you reckon she buys 'er clothes? Fuckin Tramps' Outfitters?'

'Yeah,' said the Teaser, and she went on teasing. 'Fuckin freak, I reckon.'

Christina crossed in haste to the lavatories and bolted herself into the furthest cubicle. She hardly dared pee for fear of provoking further volleys in the class war. Yet, even on so brief an exposure, she had been shaken by Dulcie's looks.

'Hey, Dulce?' the Teaser was saying. 'What the fuck's going on then, in this fuckin play? You're the fuckin brainbox, then. Fuckinell, I reckon it's fuckin stupid. Fuckin load of double fuckin Dutch.'

'You fuckin serious?' Dulcie said. 'Don't you even fuckin know what the fuck it's on about?'

'Fuck,' the Teaser said. 'It don't make no fuckin sense, that's all.'

'Fuckinell,' Dulcie said. 'Right. So there's this woman, then, right? And she's the queen. And her husband's fuckin slung her in prison, all right? And it's because she's got fuckin pregnant and he reckons the kid ain't his. So when it's born he fuckin takes it, right? And he gets this geezer to dump it in the forest to get fuckin ate by wild bears and that, all right?'

'Fuckinell,' said the Teaser. 'Fuckin bears? Get fuckin real, all right, Dulce?'

'Fuck,' Dulcie said. 'It's like up my cousin's last week. Fuckin Michelle. She's thirteen and she's fuckin pregnant and she reckons she wants to keep it, right? But her dad – that's me mum's bruvver – he reckons he'll fuckin sling her out by the neck, so she fuckin comes crying to me mum.'

'Fuckinell,' said the Teaser. 'So what's your mum supposed to fuckin do about it?'

'So me mum she gets this gynae bloke from up the hospital

174

where she works, right? He has a look at her and he goes' –
here, Dulcie assumed the gynae bloke's Mister Posh voice –
"No, no, the girl's not pregnant! Good Lord, no! She appears
to have something of a polyp in the uterine wall. A small
irregularity. Perfectly harmless, but I'm afraid it will necessitate
an immediate douche and curettage."'

'Fuckinell,' said the Teaser, after a pause, and she sounded a
little perplexed. 'So what the fuck was the matter wiv her?'

'Well, it's a scrape, you moron,' Dulcie said, somewhat
heavy on innuendo. 'He give her a fuckin scrape. So what
d'you fuckin reckon was the fuckin matter wiv her, then?'

'Fuckinell,' said the Teaser. 'I dunno. But what he give her
a fuckin scrape for, if she weren't fuckin pregnant?'

'Fuck!' Dulcie said. 'Forget it, all right? Just fuckin forget
it. And there's the fuckin bell. Fuck. And now I need to have
a wee. Go on. I'll see you inside.'

Christina found this conversation so pertinent to her present
needs that the skin on her arms had come out all over in
goosebumps. On each goosebump a hair was standing up at a
right angle to her skin. She emerged cautiously from the
cubicle into the vacated sink area and waited, trembling
slightly, for Dulcie to come out. They washed their hands
together, side by side. Their eyes met in the glass and each
stared, unblinking for a moment, into the reflected eyes of the
other. Then they turned and made the contact direct.

'Excuse me,' Christina said. 'You don't even know me –'

'You're American,' Dulcie said.

'Well,' Christina said, 'sort of. I was. I don't know. Listen.
There's really no reason why you should want to do me a favour –'

'What favour?' Dulcie said.

'That gynae person,' Christina said. 'Do you think I could
possibly arrange to have an appointment with him?'

'Fuck,' Dulcie said, and she sighed deeply. 'Me and my big
fuckin mouth.'

*

And that was how it began. And, while everything else in the immediate aftermath had seemed to misfire most terribly, the friendship with Dulcie had flourished and prospered. The friendship with Dulcie was heaven.

'I'm really sorry,' Christina said, once the theatre attendant had denied them access to their seats on grounds of lateness. 'Now I've made you miss the second half.'

'I don't reckon you want to see it,' Dulcie said. Her voice sounded sagely for her years. 'It's all about that baby, isn't it? The one that was supposed to have been got rid of. It's all about how she grows up beautiful and marries the prince and all that.'

Christina sighed. 'Would you like something to eat?' she said. 'We might as well go somewhere comfortable.'

They sneaked out, like conspirators, into the London City streets and found a small pub, squeezed between high-rise office blocks. It served them with waffles and Cokes.

' "Exit pursued by a bear",' Dulcie said wittily, and she drank her Coke through three straws.

'This is about my sister,' Christina said. 'It's not actually me who's pregnant.'

'Oh yeah?' Dulcie said, sceptical.

'No, really,' Christina said. 'It's my sister. She's sixteen and she got raped. The thing is, I'd need to lie to her. That routine about the polyps and all that. Like you were saying about your cousin.' She stopped abruptly. 'Look,' she said, 'I'm sorry. As I said, you don't even know me.'

'Well, I do now,' Dulcie said. 'You're Chris the Angelfoodcakemix and I'm Dulce the Jackpot. Would you like us to shake hands?'

Christina looked at her gratefully. Dulcie was so radiant, she thought; so beautiful; so incredibly strong and sure. However had she got like that? They were both the same age, after all.

'She's very brainy, my sister,' Christina said. 'And she's got this fantastic voice. People expect her to do great things. Go to music school. Something like that. Get into Cambridge, maybe. Go to Harvard.'

'*Cambridge?*' Dulcie said. She spoke as though Christina had just told her that her sister was destined for planet Mars. She took a large mouthful of waffle. 'Blimey,' she said, once she had swallowed it. 'If it was me I reckon I'd probably have it. Have the kid, I mean. But *Cambridge*. Fuck. I dunno. Listen. My mum will probably go ape-shit, but I'll find out that gynae bloke's name if you like.'

The whole thing, Christina had assured her new friend, would be as easy as blowing soap bubbles. The plan could not fail to run smoothly. Pam was currently so vague and undirected that it would be the simplest matter to arrange all things around her.

The sisters were to go to Granny P's for the first two days of the Christmas holidays and, after that, their parents were to join them. The whole family, including Alice's mother, on this occasion, were to join Grandma Angie for a rural Christmas in Tuscany.

The posh-voiced gynae bloke had duly undertaken to see Pam during those two days. He had required no small sum of money in advance, and Christina, in order to oblige him, had cleaned out almost all the savings that Granny P had accumulated for her in the Bristol and West Building Society. It would all be completely worth it, however, since the gynae bloke would make an examination and pronounce Pam to be not pregnant. He would then follow up with an immediate D and C.

Since Christina had returned from London offering the gynae bloke as an alternative to a pregnancy testing kit, she saw no reason why Pam should discover the man was not altogether upfront. No. Pam would surely be happy to believe him – especially since she habitually imputed to others her own high standards of integrity and truth. Then, within two hours, she would be discharged and unencumbered. She would be ready to live again, all over. She would cease to be that pale, silent shadow.

Granny P, too, had been easily duped and was all too happy to release the girls for what she imagined to be a shopping spree in the jollier parts of the metropolis. She had even pressed two twenty-pound notes into the palm of each girl's right hand.

'Come along, dears,' she said. 'I'll drive you to the station. Now, where did I put those car keys?'

And then the worst thing happened. Alice and Joe came early – two days early and unannounced. Pam had just gone to pay a last-minute visit to the bathroom. 'Frequency' was an ominous sign, according to the manuals and booklets that Christina had begun to thumb through, somewhat furtively, in bookshops. Granny P was still casting about for her car keys when there came an assertive knocking. Christina, who responded to it, was confronted by a sight that was to her as bizarre as it was unwelcome. Although the month was December, her father stood towering before her in skinfit shiny black lycra. He wore long cycling shorts and a cycling jersey with a logo that said 'Giordana'. In his hand he was holding a black cycling helmet.

Alongside him, looking slight and girlish, stood her mother, not dissimilarly attired. Alice was shivering slightly and had pulled a short, polypropylene fleece about her narrow shoulders. In the background, dressed in outsize brushed-jersey shorts and looking quite a lot like Captain Pugwash encased in a barrel, was none other than Father Zachary Levine, whom Christina had last seen at thirteen, fleetingly, on an aeroplane. He was busy locking a mint-green road bike to two similar vehicles that leaned against Granny P's garden wall. All of the party, she noted, were wearing cycling shoes.

'Hi, sweetheart,' Joe said effusively, his voice filling the porch, his elongated, sinewy body showing up splendidly in the black, skinfit lycra. Christina felt dwarfed beside him. She suffered his wholehearted embrace, tense with unexpressed panic. Then, releasing her, Joe moved on into the room.

'Valerie,' he said, and he strode forth, hands outstretched.

'Dearest,' Alice said quietly, giving Christina a hug in her turn. 'We're rather ahead of schedule. I hope that's not a nuisance for you. Your Papa has had us bicycling through the length and breadth of the British Isles.'

Joe had turned jovially to his daughter. 'I guess you're really surprised to see us?' he said.

Christina paused and swallowed, endeavouring to digest his unacceptable good humour. 'I'm really surprised to see you,' she said. Sarcasm was gnawing at the edges of her voice.

Then Zachary Levine made his entry and introductions became a necessity. Granny P blinked in surprise at the fat priest, who had stepped forward and taken her proffered hand in not one, but both of his own. She had some idea that men of the cloth were never parted from their cassocks, rather in the way that children assume kings always sleep in their crowns.

And then it was that Pam entered the room.

'Pam and I are going to London,' Christina said, rather too quickly perhaps. 'You've caught us at a bad time. Say, we'll see you guys this evening.'

'Hey,' Joe said, 'hold it, Chrissie. Now wait a bit. What's the rush?'

'The rush,' Christina said, gritting her teeth, 'is that we have a train to catch. It leaves in ten minutes and we don't intend to miss it.'

But something was happening to her sister that Christina was powerless to subvert. Pam made a rush upon her father

179

and clutched at him now, as if she were drowning. All the emotion that she had not seemed to possess, was issuing from her person in gigantic sobs and tears.

'Oh, Papa,' she said. 'Oh, Papa. I'm so relieved to see you. Oh, Papa, hold me, please. Oh, Papa, something so *awful*.'

'Pam!' Christina said in horror. 'Stop it and come away! Come *now*!' She made an attempt upon her sister's sleeve, but it was altogether ineffectual. Pam seemed not to be aware of her. Instead, Christina tried bashing at her father's upper arm. 'Let her go, you manipulating bastard!' she said. 'Just look at what you've gone and done to her!'

Joe paid no attention. He was far too busy stroking Pam's hair and holding her head against his chest. 'It's okay, sweetheart,' he was intoning quietly. 'Sweetie-pie, it's going to be all right.'

Christina aimed a kick at his shin. She felt once more like that cross little ant that had once used to tickle his knees. 'Pam!' she yelled. 'If you don't come now I swear I'm going without you! I'm going and I'm never coming back!'

Joe looked up at her over Pam's head. Then he chose to address his mother-in-law.

'What the hell is going on around here?' he said.

Poor Granny P looked astonished. 'The girls were going to do a little shopping,' she said. 'In London.'

'*Shopping?*' Joe said.

She nodded. 'Christmas shopping.'

Pam looked up and sniffed and wiped her eyes. 'Oh, Mama,' she said. 'Oh, Granny P. Oh, dear Father Zachary, please. Forgive me, but there is something that I've really got to tell you.'

It was then that Christina accepted that she had lost her sister. The acceptance endowed her with greater clarity and self-control. She strode in silence to her grandmother's front door. Then she wrenched it open.

'Chrissie!' Alice cried, noticing too late. 'Dearest Chrissie, wait!' But Christina had crashed the door shut behind her. She ran through the small front garden with its dead brown hydrangea heads and its little wintry spears of bulb shoots. She passed through the gate and out into the street where, with extraordinary good luck, she noticed that a taxi was pulling away from a house some five doors down. She called out wildly and gesticulated, and succeeded in flagging it down. The driver zoomed into reverse and stopped alongside to receive her. It was just as Alice, having taken possession of her mother's car keys, had made it as far as the gate. Then the taxi bore Christina to the station.

Once she had arrived at Waterloo, she took the precaution of removing her jacket and stuffing it into a plastic bag. She pulled her beret low over her telling blonde hair and left the station, head down, walking briskly. She had the idea that her father would, by then, have brought on his heavy guns and that several uniformed police officers would be there at the turnstile to greet her.

From the safety of a phone box out in the street, she called the gynae person and cancelled Pam's appointment. Then she made her way to Dulcie's house.

Dulcie got her a cup of tea and listened to her story.

'I'm not going back,' Christina said. 'I swear it, Dulce. I'd rather beg and steal. I'm telling you. I've run away from home.'

'Give me a break,' Dulcie said, refusing to get too excited. 'Running away in a taxi? Fuckinell, but it's all right for some.'

The commotion of Christina's arrival had roused Dulcie's mother from her bed. She had been resting after a night shift at the hospital, where she worked as a geriatric nurse.

'You go call your folks directly,' she said, her Caribbean speech rhythms in marked contrast to those of her daughter. 'Come on now, dearie. You give me your gran's phone number. Chrissie girl, I tell you, you've got to speak to your da.'

'No,' Christina said. 'Excuse me, Mrs Jackson, but you don't understand. See, I don't want him to find me, that's the whole point. Pam doesn't know about Dulcie. She doesn't know about either of you. And if I were to tell my father – well, you don't know him, that's the problem. He's sort of the Demon Ego on legs. Sort of number one hell hound. And he's angry with me. He'll barge in here and throw his weight around. He'll probably end up dragging me out by the hair. He's six foot six and he keeps himself in shape –'

Mrs Jackson laughed. Then she cast her eyes to heaven. She had the air of one who could grapple any person into a straitjacket.

'You pick up that phone right now,' she said.

But the fact of the matter was that, when Christina finally did so, there was nobody available to answer. Could it really be, she thought, that they had all run away from home?

Alice, having narrowly failed to intercept her daughter's flight to the railway station, had watched the train gather speed with no small degree of anxiety. She had no idea where Christina was heading, nor whether she meant to return. Alice had been unable to make herself hurry back to the house where, whatever the cause of poor Pam's distress, the matter had already been effectively co-opted by Joe. That was usually the pattern whenever it came to things concerning Pam. Papa's girl; Mama's girl. Curious how Pam had always been more of a stranger to her, Alice thought sadly, given that it was she who had been so close to Pam's wonderful mother.

She bought herself a cup of railway coffee and drank it slowly in the car park. Then she returned reluctantly to the house, where she felt herself every bit as irrelevant as she had anticipated. Joe and Pam sat cosily together, drinking coffee and talking. Pam appeared quite composed. She rose and kissed her mother and offered her a cup of coffee.

'How are you feeling, my darling?' Alice said.

'Oh, *so* much better,' Pam said. 'Really *so* much better.' She and Joe exchanged glances. 'Would you, Papa?' she said. 'Please. I can't. Not all over again.' She was ceding to her father the obligation of telling her story to Alice.

Pam, it materialized, was pregnant as a consequence of rape.

Alice gasped, horrified. '*Rape?*' she said her voice emerging as a shriek.

'Keep your voice down, Alice,' Joe said. 'Your mother is at last getting some rest. She has been in quite a state, I assure you.'

'Sorry,' Alice said. 'A state. Yes. Rape. Please go on.'

'Drunken schoolboys,' Joe said. 'Probably. It was too dark for Pam to be quite certain.'

'*Boys?*' Alice said. '*Plural?* But God in heaven, my dearest! Pammie, how appalling! Pam, my baby. My angel one, why didn't any of us know about this? Tell me, does Roland know about this?'

'He will do before too long,' Joe said grimly. 'I just fixed up to hire a car. Pam and I are driving down there. We ought to be there by two o'clock.'

'This is dreadful,' Alice said. 'And Chrissie? What was all that about Chrissie?'

Pam then came to her enlightenment, in a muddling sort of fashion. 'Mama, Chrissie really meant well,' she said. 'She'd arranged for me to see a doctor. A private doctor in London. Look, Mama, I'm really sorry. I didn't mean to upset her. I was too upset myself. It was just that when I saw Papa – well – everything fell into place. I sort of knew what I needed to do. I knew what Chrissie had been getting at. I've been acting weird lately, Mama. I've been a real drag on Chrissie. She's kept on doing her best for me. She's kept on trying to persuade me that I'm most probably not really pregnant. But all along I've sort of known that I was. She was only trying to help me.'

Pam looked up and smiled faintly at her mother. 'Where *is* Chrissie, by the way?' she said. 'She didn't really take off, did she? She didn't really go for that train?'

When Alice left the room, it was so that Pam should not see the fall of her tears. She ran into Father Zak, however, who was crossing the hall, having just come from upstairs. He had assisted Alice's mother to bed, as he explained, but she had found it hard to settle. He had been out to buy her a particular brand of favoured headache pills and he had filled a hot water bottle for her. Finally, he had taken her a nice cup of tea which he had expediently laced with a hefty slosh of Glenlivet. He now recommended the same for Alice and he offered to make it for her.

Alice observed that, at some time since she had last been in his company, Father Zak had enveloped his girth in a shirt and a pair of trousers which he must have taken from his saddlebag. After he had made her tea, she saw him glance a little anxiously at his watch.

'Alice,' he said, 'would you mind? I ought to call my sister. She's expecting me for lunch in Cambridge.'

'*Cambridge?*' Alice said, thinking it rather a distance in view of the advancing hour.

'Yes, Cambridge,' said Father Zak mildly. 'Newnham Croft. Do you happen to know Cambridge, Alice?'

Father Zak's sister had a telephone voice so piercingly confrontational that Alice could hear the woman clearly from over five yards off. Intermittently Father Zak would say, 'Jude . . . but Jude . . . say, Jude . . .' But the sibling voice rolled right on over him. Alice discovered herself glad of the entertainment. She went through to the kitchen and picked up the extension.

'Hello?' said Father Zak's sister, sounding extremely piqued. 'Do I detect the telltale echo? And who the hell are you, then? The resident heavy breather?'

'I'm Alice Angeletti,' Alice said. 'I'm a friend in need, I suppose. I want you to please stop bullying your brother who has been indispensable round here. He has nurtured the fallen. He has found headache pills and laced people's tea with whisky.'

'What whisky?' said Father Zak's sister.

'Glenlivet, I believe,' said Alice, wondering why she wanted so much to find favour with Father Zak's sister. 'Duty-free. You know.'

'You swine, Zakky,' said Father Zak's sister, reverting to her brother. 'And all the time it's me that's needing the bloody Glenlivet, as you know. You get your fat rump over here and bring that bottle with you.'

'Jude . . .' said Father Zak. 'Say, Jude . . .'

'And bring that friend of yours as well,' said the sibling. 'I really like the sound of her.'

And so it was that, when Christina called from Dulcie's house, Joe and Pam were on their way to Roland and Alice was on her way to Cambridge. Granny P, who was sound asleep, was in no position to pick up the phone.

Joe turned up the following day. He was not accompanied by Alice, who had stayed over, unexpectedly, at the house of Father Zak's sister, but she had now returned to her mother's house to keep Pam company. It was Granny P who had come with Joe. Unbeknown to Christina, Alice was, for the moment, feeling so distanced from her husband – both by virtue of his overbearing role in Pam's affairs and by the new strength that had been lent her by Father Zak's bossy sister – that she had preferred not to travel with him in the same car. Her plan was to make the contact later, when Chrissie, she imagined, would be better disposed to receive her.

Mrs Jackson greeted her visitors warmly and asked them into the front room. Then she went to make a pot of tea and to summon both the girls from Dulcie's bedroom. Christina entered reluctantly and sat, sullen and hostile, at the furthest point from her father. Dulcie was bubbly and charming and showed up rather well.

Granny P, like Christina, was guarded and uncomfortable. She perched stiffly, clutching at her handbag, her knees neatly together. Alice's mother found that drinking her tea was more difficult than she had hoped. She knew that her son-in-law despised her for it, but the barrier in her case was one of relative ethnic naivety. She had nothing against 'them', as she had been known to remark in the past. Far from it. Yet the drinking of tea now gave her a feeling of slight unease – not unlike the feeling one got upon occupying an empty seat on a bus and finding it still warm from an unknown posterior.

Joe and Mrs Jackson talked easily together, mainly about Mrs Jackson's job, in a sparky, unserious sort of way. It was evident, much to Christina's annoyance, that an element of sexual chemistry was oiling the wheels of their discourse.

'Come now, girl,' Mrs Jackson said suddenly, beginning to gather up tea-cups. 'Your da come to take you home for Christmas. Lucky girl, you.' With that she left to carry out the tea things and gave her visitor the floor.

Joe got up. 'Come on, sweetheart,' he said. 'Go get your stuff. Mrs Jackson has been very kind.'

Christina, who had not thus far uttered a word, now paused before she did so, for fear of choking on indignation. She remained pointedly glued to her chair.

'What have you done with my sister?' she said, her words coming slowly, like little vials of poison.

Joe sighed heavily. 'Chrissie,' he said, 'don't be childish. Your sister, as you very well know, is pregnant. It must be self-evident, even to you, surely, that she is having a difficult

186

time. It would be enormously helpful to her if you – if all of us – could sink our differences and give her our best support.'

'Just so long as we all of us fall in with your agenda,' she said. 'No, thanks. Count me out. If you call that support what I saw you doing to her yesterday, well, I want nothing to do with it. I want nothing to do with any of you. Frankly, I've had it up to the neck. I want you all to get out of my life and leave me alone from now on. If you think that I'll come back and be a part of your little fan club; if you think I'll come back so you can screw up my sister and have me for an audience –'

Joe winced slightly. 'Oh, Chrissie,' he said. 'Come on now. Pam's life is entirely her own.'

'Oh yeah?' Christina mumbled, but he ignored it.

'I intend that you will come back with me now,' he said. 'And also that you will conduct yourself civilly through Christmas. After that, I'm perfectly willing for you to return to your school here in England – if that's what you really want. If you feel that a certain distance from the rest of us would be helpful to you through all of this. I must tell you, however, that I have already withdrawn your sister. I really had no alternative.'

'Great,' Christina said. 'Terrific. Just pull her out of school before her exams.' She got up suddenly and moved towards the door. 'So long,' she said. 'I need a walk.'

She left the house and crossed Seven Sisters Road. She entered the local branch of Tesco's, directly across from Dulcie's house. There she began to fill a shopping trolley with items chosen at random. Tamarind sauce and bargain biscuits. Tuna fish in brine. Long-life batteries, size AA. A litre bottle of lime juice. A bag of King Edward potatoes. Six free-range eggs, class A, size 2. Extra-length Luxury Paper Towel. A bag of Pedigree Chum Small Bite Mixer, chain-stitched across the top with coarse brown string. She had an idea that her father, were he to try coming after her, would not think to look inside a supermarket.

After a while she began to experiment. She tossed in throwaway nappies and two bottles of baby oil. She chose four jars of Gerber baby food and a box of Farley's rusks. She tried to imagine that she was Pam. She began to walk with her stomach stuck out in front and her back severely arched. She splayed her feet as best she could and adopted a penguin waddle. It felt disgusting, she decided. As she walked, she mumbled to herself. Damn them. Damn them all. Damn my father. Damn my sister. Most especially damn my mother. Why is she letting this happen? Remind me not to become a wimp when I grow up. Better to sell double glazing.

After a while, she noticed that other shoppers were giving her funny looks. A grey-suited floor manager had got her under surveillance. Then suddenly she was crying. Tears were running down her face. The floor manager hailed a female attendant who drew her aside and stuffed the pocket of her jeans with wads of Kleenex. She was encouraged to abandon her trolley as she was shepherded through to the back, past disassembled cartons and a row of friendly butchers making up polystyrene parcels of meat.

Then they came upon a tea-making region where several women in identical smocks offered comfort and hot drinks. It was all a bit like Being Saved, Christina thought. She'd seen it on the television. Born Again Clappies. If you stood up in the marquee to Be Saved, then a lady ushered you through to the back and you got to see what it looked like. Mostly, after that, you just returned to your seat in the auditorium and you sang stuff like 'I met Jesus at the Crossroads' instead of 'Mary Immaculate, Star of the Morning'. So what?

The ladies had all by then benevolently agreed that the shopper must recently have lost her baby.

When she finally got back to Dulcie's house, darkness had overtaken the world. Her father and her grandmother were gone. It was evident from Dulcie's spirited report that – after waiting a whole hour at the house – Joe had finally admitted defeat and had left in a condition of ill-concealed fury. He was angry as much with himself for having been patient and reasonable with his daughter, when what he ought to have done, Goddamnit, was heave her bodily out of the house and bundle her into the car.

As things stood, he had achieved absolutely nothing except the prospect of Alice's sarcastic recriminations and the more immediate prospect of a stony drive back in the company of his damp-eyed mother-in-law. Alice's mother was, in truth, always uneasy when left alone with him, so she desisted, *en route*, from offering any opinion, except to venture – timorously and once only – that she did not like to think of little Chrissie sleeping another night with 'those' people.

'"Those" are perfectly delightful people,' Joe snapped irritably. 'And far better than Chrissie deserves. My concern is merely that they may tire of her by bedtime and turn her out to spend the night in a doorway.' After that they maintained a judicious silence.

When Joe called Mrs Jackson from a mobile phone in the car, Christina had returned, she said, but was refusing to come to the telephone. All the same, he found Dulcie's mother so warm and unfussed about the business of billeting his daughter, that he was not only reassured, but much revived.

'I'm indebted to you, Mrs Jackson,' he said. 'Beat the girl for me, won't you? Lock her up at once on bread and water.'

Mrs Jackson laughed heartily. 'Don't you worry there, honey child,' she said. 'Anything to oblige you.'

That evening, after supper, Christina was telephoned twice. Once by her grandmother and once by her mother.

Granny P assured her that she understood completely just exactly how Christina felt. The whole thing with Pam had been absolutely dreadful and her father had obviously steamrollered the girl, but what else had one come to expect?

189

Chrissie's problem, however, was easily resolved. First of all, Granny P said, they would stay at home for Christmas. Just the two of them. Then, after that, since Chrissie meant to finish her education in England, there was no reason why she should return to her boarding school. She would live at Granny P's house and attend Mummy's old day school. Mummy's name was up there in gold letters in the Assembly Hall and the current Head would, sans doubt, be overjoyed to accommodate Mummy's progeny.

Alice, too, assured her daughter that she understood completely just exactly how Chrissie felt. The whole thing with Pam had been too dreadful – but what else had one come to expect?

'Now, Chrissie,' Alice said, 'what about you and me? Just the two of us. Why don't we change the plan for Christmas? Perhaps you would like the island of Sark? Perhaps you would like the Mull of Kintyre? Somewhere utterly, wonderfully alone. Or perhaps you would like my new chum to come along? She's terrific fun, Chrissie. She's a whirlwind. And she is truly formidable in the presence of Glenlivet. We could have the most adorable, girlie time together.'

Alice waited for Christina to reply, but a reply was not forthcoming. 'Then afterwards, my sweetie,' she said, 'of *course* you can stay at school in England, but maybe you'd prefer a nice quiet girls' school? Say, what about that Quaker school in York?'

Christina swallowed hard. 'I've decided I don't want to see you,' she said. 'I don't want to see any of you. I'm sorry, but I really need you all to leave me alone.'

For the second night running, Christina and Dulcie shared Dulcie's thirty-inch bed. They had learnt the art of sleeping stretched out, flat and straight. No bumps or curves. In the morning, Dulcie got ready for school. She wore her jeans with the yellow stretch bust bodice and the backless high-heeled shoes. The terms were longer in the state schools and Dulcie hadn't yet broken up for Christmas.

'You might as well come to school wiv me, Chris,' she said. 'It's no good you skiving here indoors.'

PART IV
Balancing

Judith and Dulcie. Late and Early Perpendicular

Judith was definitely perpendicular. That was the first thing
Christina noticed about her. She saw Judith for the first time
on the evening of her first day. Everything was just beginning,
yet everything, until that moment, had seemed so dull. Then
suddenly there was Judith, at the far end of the room, standing
where she had not been before.

Judith was dark-haired and beautiful and six foot tall. She
was wearing a scarlet raw silk party dress which, being ruched,
wrapped her briefly from cleavage to crotch like tissue paper
round a bunch of St Valentine's Day roses.

Christina was eighteen. Almost three years had passed since
the day she had first set off to school with her friend Dulcie
Jackson. She was attending a party given for new undergraduates by the college secretary. She had been standing near the
door, attempting a little interaction with a group of cowed
newcomers. The women among the undergraduates – with the
exception of the one glowering metal exponent – were dressed
either in drooping pastel or, like Christina, in sweatshirts and
jeans. The men – with the exception of those who had done 'a
year out' in India – were short-haired and either blazered or
tweedy.

Since the secretary's manner was one of conspicuous and
guilt-inducing bustle, the youthful guests had become increasingly timid and apologetic, as though they felt their presence
there to be a nuisance to her. The only ice-breaker, Christina
noticed, had been the secretary's cat – a rotund, beige eunuch
with a startling raven's croak.

Christina, just as the vision of Judith had intruded to

195

distract her, had been endeavouring to determine what the party was all about. Was it a mechanism through which the secretary, by getting in first and chalking up Brownie points, could annex the loyalty of all incoming undergraduates against other, rival claimants? If not, where were the college dons? Or was the party merely a condition of the unfortunate woman's employment? Written into her contract? Something like the charters of those medieval grammar schools that made it obligatory to provision each impecunious scholar with a measure of small beer at breakfast? Thou shalt feed Warm Sherry and Pretzel-Flavoured Bread Sticks to all Newly Entered Scholars on the Fourth Day of October.

In this perceptibly damp context Judith looked electric. Christina thought she looked as if she had just leapt from a millionaire's cake.

The college secretary was suddenly at her elbow. She topped up Christina's glass before she spoke.

'There is somebody here who wants to meet you,' she said. 'If you will come this way.'

Christina followed the ball-bearing action of her hostess's busy rump. The woman, being not only purposeful but stocky and wide around the hips, was making an effective pathway through the throng. She was wearing a scratchy-looking, knee-length kilt made of heavy wool and finished with leather straps and buckles – the real McCoy, this kilt, Christina thought – no fashion item, this. The secretary's legs were clothed in opaque, white tights and, like a highwayman, she wore a bunch of lace at her throat.

'Judy,' said the college secretary. 'This is Christina. Christina – Judy.'

'"Judy",' Judith said promptly, 'is the abused wife of a misogynist in a seaside pantomime. Nobody calls me Judy.'

'Nobody?' said the secretary, her manner touched, just perceptibly, with a hint of unpleasant innuendo. She left, at once, to play busy hostess elsewhere.

'My name,' Judith said, 'is Judith.' She paused and looked rather fiercely at Christina. '"Judith",' she said, 'drove a tent peg through the head of a Babylonian general. In one temple and out the other. Bingo. She nailed him to the floor.' Judith accompanied this intelligence with a small, satisfying gesture, tapping with the knuckles of her right hand upon those of her left. 'I was named, you see, after one of the Great Redeemers of Israel.'

'Me too,' Christina said.

Judith blinked. Then she laughed. When Judith laughed, she revealed that her wide, red mouth was crowded with small, slightly overlapping white teeth. 'True,' she said. 'That's true. Still, if we are talking female role models here –' She broke off and took possession of Christina's glass.

'If we are talking female role models here,' Christina said quickly, 'then my name-saint could break through leg-irons and sing plainchant while doing headstands on a gate.'

Judith laughed again, showing her pretty, criss-cross teeth. 'Hey,' she said. 'Chrissie. It's great to meet you. I mean really. Follow me.'

In the kitchen, Judith surprised Christina by extracting a silver hip flask from her clutch-bag. Then, from a cupboard, she took down two gargantuan green tumblers with tiny bubbles set into the glass. They looked like stage props from the giant's table in the pantomime *Jack and the Beanstalk*.

'Forewarned is forearmed,' Judith said. 'A precaution against Fiona's drinking habits. She gets in the twice annual bulk-buy for occasions such as this.'

She banged an ice-tray forcefully on the drainer, making the ice cubes jump. Then, having allotted the tumblers a good five ice cubes each, she doused them from the hip-flask and she placed a glass in Christina's hand.

'So,' she said, after the first savouring drink, 'Christina. Quiz time. Who was the Babylonian general?'

Christina sipped at the glass. Then she put it down. She hesitated, toying as she did so with one of the beige feline's high-class foil tubs of catfood that sat upon the workboard. It looked like *pâté de foie gras*.

'I have no idea,' she said at last. 'Sorry. Anything to do with Delilah?'

'Wrong!' Judith cried gleefully. 'So, you're obviously not here as a student of English literature?'

'Well, as a matter of fact –' Christina began.

'Nor theology either,' Judith said. 'I suppose that goes without saying. Nor ancient history, of course. Nor history of art. How is it that your mind is so delightfully under-furnished?'

'Well,' Christina said, rising to the provocation. 'There's a lot more to reading than the Bible. Anyway, the Old Testament is a Protestant's book.'

'Wrong again,' Judith said, sounding something like the Red Queen. 'Major hijack there. The Old Testament is a Jewish book, from Genesis right through to Zachariah. I think, by the way, that you will find it on your syllabus and that you ought to have read it in advance of coming up.'

'Are you an English fellow?' Christina asked, suddenly suspicious. 'Or are you trying to wind me up?' Judith did not seem to her at all like the other undergraduates.

'I'm a doctor,' Judith said. 'Medical doctor. I've got myself a little niche here in neonatal research.' Then she said, 'My husband is an English fellow. I pick up these little snippets vicariously.'

'Well, if he's a fellow, why isn't he here, mingling with his new students?' Christina said. She felt her impertinence justified in view of Judith's confrontational style.

'"Mingling"?' Judith said. 'Ah, well. He doesn't "mingle".
And he certainly doesn't attend functions.'

'Why doesn't he?' Christina said.

By way of reply, Judith topped up Christina's glass. 'Drink,'
she said. 'It's free. Free to you, that is. Not to me.'

It was embarrassing to Christina thereafter that she could not
be sure how she had behaved. It seemed to her quite unthinkable that Judith had set out to get her drunk. Judith, so
striking, so beautiful, so dynamic, had singled her out, had
chosen her from among the entire undergraduate assembly,
and she, Christina, had very probably, ungratefully, blown it.

The whisky on her empty stomach had certainly gone to
her head but, even though she felt hazy, Judith's company
was a sort of compliment and a challenge which she was
reluctant to relinquish. For want of a chair in the secretary's
kitchen, Christina sat cross-legged on the floor with her back
up against the fridge, so that the shapely columns of Judith's
long legs in their sheer black tights rose before her. Her
brain, lumbering towards connections, connected in
consequence with legs; with the secretary's legs in white
tights.

'So why does our hostess dress like Bonnie Prince Charlie?'
she said.

'"She"?' Judith said. 'The cat's mother? Her name is Fiona
Campbell.'

'Why is she wearing that kilt?' Christina said.

'Why not?' Judith said. 'She's a Scot.'

Something was stirring clumsily in Christina's memory.
'The Campbells,' she said, 'they were all traitors, you know. I
expect she's a traitor.'

'What exactly are we talking about here?' Judith said. 'If it
isn't too much to ask.'

'We are talking,' Christina said, 'about the Battle of Glencoe.

I did it in history.' She paused, trying to get her mind back on the rails, just as she heard Judith's guffaw.

'*Glencoe?*' Judith said. '*Glencoe?* Could you be drunk already by any chance? And what's your usual tipple, then, little Chrissie? Dr Pepper's Sarsaparilla?'

'I know a song about the Campbells,' Christina said. 'But I always used to think it was about camels.' She paused. Then she sang the first two lines and followed these with the refrain:

> The Camels are coming. Aho! Aho!
> The Camels are coming. Aho! Aho!
> The Camels are coming to bonnie Lochalin,
> The Camels are coming. Aho! Aho!

Her diction had become so slurred, that Judith appeared to have misheard her.

'Loch Levin?' she said. 'But that's my name. Judith Levin. Just fancy all those camels coming to liaise at my loch.'

Christina began carefully to rearrange her mind. It felt like a heap of bent forks. The effort of doing so felt tangentially like arranging old forks into one of those baize-lined boxes with an interior labyrinth of purpose-built grooves. She dwelt for a moment upon Granny P's cutlery box which had had little ivory labels telling you which fork and spoon went into which groove. Dessert Forks. Dessert Spoons.

Granny P had told her that 'Mummy', as a small child, had thought the spoons were for using in the desert. That was because in England dessert was called pudding. And in *Alice in Wonderland*, the pudding had had little legs and shoes, and Alice was not permitted to eat the pudding, because it had already been introduced to her. There was a picture of the pudding making a bow. Rotund like fine Mr Five; like the fat Jesuit; like the secretary's croaky beige raven–cat. 'Alice, pudding. Pudding, Alice.' 'Christina does not deserve her dessert.'

*

Camels lived in the desert, she reflected, but how was it that everything had suddenly to do with camels? She had once gone with her father and her sister to the zoo on one of those afternoons – always far too many of them – in the aftermath of her school report card. The camels had been out walking with their minder as the girls watched. They had ambled by, slowly, slowly, looking disdainfully at Pam and Christina, eyes popping from their silly little tortoise heads.

And, as they walked, they had kept on dropping their turds; huge, steaming turds. There were so many of these and so big, that the camels had had to have a special boy whose job it was to walk behind and shovel the droppings into a cart. It had given the girls a fit of the giggles.

'I guess that'll be the job for you, Chrissie,' her father had said. He had been lecturing her, just previously, on 'Achievement' and 'Application'. 'That's if you should ever get tired of washing the floors in McDonald's.' Christina could remember that she had stuck her fingers in her ears, but it was a fallacy that this expedient ever blocked out what people said.

'Dung Person,' her father had said. Then he had indulged himself in a spot of alliteration. 'Dung Person to the Dromedaries,' he had said. 'How about it, Chrissie?'

'Anyway,' Christina said out loud from her position on Fiona Campbell's floor, 'they were camels. Who says they were dromedaries?'

'Chrissie?' Judith said. She was kneeling beside her. 'Chrissie, can I get you some black coffee?'

Christina yawned. 'Hey,' she said, 'you keep on calling me Chrissie. Do you know that? Why do you keep on calling me Chrissie?'

'Is she all right?' somebody said, and the room was suddenly full of blurred legs. Even the secretary's legs were there, in their unbecoming white tights.

'If you're a beggar-man in Goa,' Christina said, 'then you most probably haven't even got any legs.' She uttered a heavy sigh which she directed towards the assorted knees. 'There isn't any God as a matter of fact,' she said. 'That's all a lot of mumbo-jumbo.'

'Chrissie,' Judith said again, 'get up. Don't do this to me.'

'There were these people that used to call me Chrissie,' she said. 'But that was quite a long time ago. Before I ran away.' She smiled sleepily at all the knees. 'I ran away in a taxi,' she said. 'And then I refused to go back.'

'Who is she?' said one of the pairs of legs.

'I'm Christina,' she said. 'I was named after one of the Great Redeemers of Israel. First you draw three circles and then you have to colour them in. Then it's called the Trinity.'

'Chrissie,' Judith said. 'Hey, sweetie. This is getting embarrassing.'

'But they have to intersect,' Christina said. 'The circles. They have to intersect. And the bit in the middle – the gold bit – that's really important.' Then she slid gently sideways and fell asleep on Fiona Campbell's floor.

Christina had got into Cambridge. Cambridge *University* – as Dulcie wisecracked – not the Cambridge branch of Spud-U-Like. She had got there, not from Roland's boarding school, but from Dulcie's inner city comprehensive. Christina liked to think that she had got there on her own – but with a lot of help from Dulcie.

Initially, after walking out on her family and abandoning her place at Roland's school, Christina had succeeded in getting her parents to accept that she would live and go to school with Dulcie. She had done this using Mrs Jackson and Father Zak as intermediaries, and her parents had eventually agreed to the idea as an alternative to having Christina abandon school altogether.

In the event, it had not been difficult for her to make herself eligible for a place in an English state school, since, for the two-year period of the girls' sojourn in Roland's boarding establishment, she and Pam had been registered as 'resident' at her grandmother's house. This had been an expedient piece of dishonesty to which her father had subscribed in order to allow for the possibility that the girls – who might wish, at some point, to study at British universities – would then be eligible for Local Authority grants.

Then there had been that extraordinary willingness of Dulcie's prodigious mother – a single parent who laboured most nights in the geriatric ward. Dear Mrs Jackson, who had so hospitably accommodated her for the duration of her A-Levels. The whole thing had been quite a lesson in the school of life. It had been the best thing in the world.

Dulcie's house grew plastic dustbin bags and dog turds in the front garden. Since it was *en route* to the White Hart Lane football ground, it sometimes also grew crushed lager cans and styrofoam burger boxes. The dogs were two in number and their job was to keep intruders at bay. They approximated to German Shepherds and were kept permanently tethered to a large, plyboard kennel. Once a day, Dulcie's brother Wayne laid out two battered enamel pie dishes in which the dogs rooted greedily until their muzzles had worked the dishes beyond the locus of their tethers.

Inside, the house was immaculately clean. It was ruled on sound matriarchal principles by Dulcie's mother and, in her absence, by Dulcie who showed every sign of donning the mantle triumphantly.

'Me mum reckons she don't really mind,' Dulcie had said one day – once the protracted negotiations had seemed finally concluded. 'You can doss in my room wiv me. It don't matter to her.'

'Fuckin lezzies,' said Dulcie's brother, who wore his hair

cut square and upright, like a box of sprouted mustard cress under a carmine red designer baseball cap.

'Knock it off, derk,' Dulcie said. 'Go give your fuckin brains a blow job.'

School was a breezeblock and aluminium structure, built over a sort of minefield that Dulcie helped her negotiate. But being in the Sixth Form had helped quite a bit, so long as one visited the loo only in packs and avoided the smokers' dugouts. It was not half so much like *Lord of the Flies*. It was more like adult education classes undertaken in a discontinued warehouse visited by swirls of urban litter. The teachers and her classmates were all fairly pleasant, especially given that Dulcie's former henchman, Tracey, had by then left.

In the beginning, Christina's life had been dominated by the tremulous expectation that Jago would make contact. She had written to him, almost daily at first, but Jago had never replied. This had been extremely difficult for Christina, especially as it had not been possible for her to cry herself to sleep at night – not in a shared bedroom containing a single two-foot-six divan and a limited area of floorspace.

Yet somehow, somewhere around Easter – somewhere between her mastery of Standard Deviation and her assignment on the Albigensian Crusade – Jago had suddenly ceased to impinge in quite the same raw and piercing way. While his silence and his betrayal and his absence still caused heartache, the ache was more like scar tissue; less like an open wound.

She had agreed to submit, for her parents and her sister, the briefest two-monthly bulletins pertaining to her state of health and welfare – but only on condition that they made no attempt to write to her, to telephone her, or to pay her any visits. She also declined money from them. Her food, clothes and incidental expenses, she paid for herself, out of her earnings from part-time jobs.

*

Dulcie was a miracle. She offered faith in the human species. In a post-literate world, where the TV screen came four foot square and existed, for her brother Wayne, as a daily sixteen-hour opiate, Dulcie read books. She had been turned on to books in the junior school by a young Australian supply teacher who had admired the enormous ribbon bows in her hair and had taken her class to the local library, where the librarian had issued the children with readers' tickets.

Very soon Dulcie's greatest source of annoyance was that the librarian restricted her to three books at a borrowing and would not allow her to change the books more than once a day. Occasionally there had been those dreadful days when, having walked the lengthy distance between the library and the house, she found that she had forgotten herself and had already finished all three of her books before she had got them home. As she grew older, she read voraciously and widely, having no snobberies, no preconceived hierarchies, nor any notion that the books she read were, somewhere, received with accolades or brickbats by literary critics.

Until she had met Christina, it had not occurred to Dulcie that books were a pleasure one could share. Being a bright and popular girl with a great well-spring of *joie de vivre*, she had always had so much else to share without needing that as well. But, having discovered Christina as a kindred spirit in this area, she brought to bear on the shared, literary experience, a brilliant, satirical edge. Revelling, as they did, in each other's company, the girls together tapped a nerve; mined a seam. They moved together through classroom, corridor and playground, quoting, laughing, improvising and wisecracking. They enacted spontaneous comic sketches in a hundred different voices.

Sometimes – especially when they were juggling – they communicated entirely in literary quotations. Dulcie had at last taught Christina how to juggle and they had devised a system of juggling in tandem. It had something of the quality of playground skipping routines that younger girls perform to popular nonsense rhymes. The trick was to juggle in sync with the rhythms of one's favourite quotations, which were, in themselves, being used as code and shorthand for sparky social comment.

Dulcie had some unexpected literary favourites. Beatrix Potter had always offered a world of unfamiliar, ironic gentility and also, occasionally – as with the starvation coma of the Tailor of Gloucester, or the bankruptcy and dispossession of Ginger and Pickles – one of harsh, capitalist realism. And her 'Alack, I am worn to a ravelling' was a quotation as much in use as James Joyce's Mother Grogan. So, also, was 'Indeed, indeed, you will stick fast, Mr Jackson,' which became a routine put-down for her brother, as he grew into the sofa, in front of the television screen.

T. S. Eliot was another favourite, whose exquisitely turned, Edwardian snobberies were lent an unintended edge by the force of Dulcie's accent. She was addicted to Eliot's 'young man carbuncular' who was pressed into service, once again, for the purpose of undermining her brother. Social climbing, or any hint of pretension, in a schoolteacher or a politician, would instantly have the victim categorized as 'one of the low on whom assurance sits as a silk hat on a Bradford millionaire'.

Dulcie had a particular soft spot for sloppy plotting and could bring the house down in class over Shakespeare's nonchalant inconsistencies. She adored the 'second son' of old Sir Rowland de Boys – and for no other reason than that Shakespeare had catapulted him into the cast at three minutes to closing time.

Sir Andrew Aguecheek and the Lure of Logic Lane

And then, one day, a Cambridge don had come to address the Lower Sixth. A talent scout, he, in bifocals and open-toe sandals.

The college, of which the don was a distinguished fellow, had been anxious to reform itself. It had come to be troubled by the nature of its undergraduate intake which was predominantly male and white, and privately educated in prestigious boarding schools with long traditions of academic excellence.

In its attempt to cast the net more widely, the college had embarked upon a campaign of talent-spotting by setting up liaisons with the heads of urban state secondary schools and sending out some of its fellows as ambassadors and missionaries.

In the case of Dulcie and Christina's school, the college had possibly boobed in the nature of the ambassador it had, so defencelessly, sent forth. The man had watery, pale blue eyes and white, floor-mop hair. He had a squeaky, high-pitched, class-bound voice, and his complexion was pale as unfired China clay. He was beanpole-thin and he wore his sandals with grey wool socks. Furthermore, he had evidently bicycled to the railway station, because he had forgotten to take off his cycle clips.

'What a Charley,' Dulcie said. 'Fuckinell, Chris.' It amazed her to the point of incredulity that the Cambridge don wore a plain gold ring as evidence of the married state.

The headmistress, none the less, had had no hesitation in recommending to him four of her Sixth Form pupils. All of them, on this occasion, happened to be girls. It was apparent to her that all four were in possession of intellectual gifts that set them well above their peers. They were all of them poised, confident and articulate girls and all of them had performed consistently well.

Christina Angeletti was among them. The Head had been delighted with Christina, a newcomer to the school; a sudden and unexpected arrival, but for all that, Christina had settled extremely well and had proved to be a valuable addition. She was a strong, bright, independent girl, and it did not concern the Head in any way that she was hardly the product of the humbler sort of background that the more egalitarian collegiate members had had in mind. With the notable exception of Dulcie Jackson, neither were any of the others. They were splendid girls, the lot of them, and that was the end of the matter.

In this way, the college embarked upon a policy that gradually succeeded in replacing its traditional élite with a newer élite which, for all it was more lively and independent-minded, was less inducted into the rigours of communal collegiate living, less tutored to sing in the college choir, less equipped to play rugby, and certainly – in the case of its female intake – less capable of dragging its heavy, book-bound luggage up the onerous three flights of uneven old stone stairs.

It was an ebullient, girlish foursome, then, that boarded the Cambridge train from Liverpool Street on the morning of the college Open Day. The girls had not much notion that they were being cast as torch-bearers in the vanguard of the levellers. One of the four was Christina, the daughter of a New York publisher and a graduate in Oxford Greats. Another was Julia, daughter of a defected Czech violinist who had fallen on hard times. A third was Trinh, a fostered Vietnamese refugee from a family of medical research scientists long presumed dead. The only indigenous high-flyer among them; the only one humbly born; the only one not trailing residual assumptions of privilege and expectation, was Dulcie.

It ought not to have been surprising, then, that Dulcie was the first to retreat from certain implications of academe. Nor that her retreat took place that very same day. The girls were on their way from the railway station when it happened. They had chanced to pass a college lodge gate through which, unluckily, at that moment, six pre-pubertal choristers were emerging, dressed in top hats and pin-striped trousers. Dulcie immediately stopped in her tracks.

'Fuckinell,' she said. 'Look at that! I don't believe it. It's fuckin child bridegrooms. Come on, then, Chris. We're not fuckin staying around here!'

'Yes we are,' Christina said. 'We haven't even got to the college yet. Look, Dulce. They're choirboys. Pipsqueaks in fancy dress. They've got nothing to do with us. Come on.'

But Dulcie, now filled with misgiving, had eyes for everything that threatened. She found menace in the number of signs that exhorted her, as she put it, to 'Keep Off of the Grass'. She found menace in the prevalence of mullioned windows.

'The whole sodding town looks like churches,' she said. 'Everything looks like Westminster Abbey.'

'Don't be so silly,' Christina said. 'I don't know what's got into you. All these buildings – they're just old, that's all. Old buildings look like that. Like my old school in the country. It sort of looked a bit churchy. Once you've got past all those gargoyles and things, well, they'll be full of old sinks and gas leaks. Honest to God, they'll be done up with those scratchy Dutch carpet tiles. You know. There'll be Harpic behind all the toilets.'

But Dulcie was intransigent. 'Well, I've never seen a fuckin school that looked like a church,' she said. 'My schools've always looked more like Cell Block H. Anyway, me mum reckons it's time I got a job.'

'Dulce,' Christina said. 'Please. Don't. I need you. Have you any idea how much?'

'Chris,' Dulcie said firmly. 'I'll see you later at home.'

She returned at once to the railway station and set her sights elsewhere.

The remaining three made it through the Open Day and even through the weeks beyond it, but the drop-out rate was impressive. The Czech violinist returned suddenly to the newly declared Czech Republic and took her daughter with her. There they were received with roses and accolades and the return of the family home.

The Vietnamese orphan was fortuitously contacted by a missing cousin who had turned up at the University of Toronto and, within the month, she had flown over to join him in a transport of delight. Dulcie stayed to finish her A-Levels, but she had lost something of her zest. The Cambridge trip had bruised it. And she refused, thereafter, to engage her mind upon what the brochures around the Sixth Form room were calling 'opportunities in tertiary education'.

'So that leaves me,' Christina reflected, morosely, from the isolation of her unfamiliar college room. 'I am a survivor from three sets of four.'

Because first there had been her family – her parents and Pam and herself. Then – before Dulcie and Julia and Trinh who, along with her, had made up that apparently unstoppable quartet of bright, high-achieving girls – there had been that other foursome that had begun in the Renovated Railway Tea-room and had ended in a mess of ruined hopes. There had been Jago and Peter and Christina and Pam.

And what had happened to them? Mostly she had tried not

to think about them. It had helped that she had had to work so hard – and she *had* worked incredibly hard for all the time she had lived at Dulcie's house. She had got calluses from digging people's gardens for money over weekends. She had got tired feet doing an evening job with Dulcie in a Greek-Cypriot café that was not unlike the juggler's greasy spoon. Bacon, sausage, egg, chips twice. She still didn't like to eat meat. And what had become of him, she occasionally wondered – her juggler; her kindly, lofty, barefoot myth-man in his tall, pinnacle hat?

Yes, all the time that she had been with Dulcie, she had worked really hard – not only at the gardening and at the café, but also at the school books. Partly, she had perhaps done so because she no longer had Pam around to whom all responsibility for virtue and diligence could be delegated. Partly, she had done so because she had had to grow up fast and had discovered genuine interests. But partly, too, it was because the academic work had functioned as a block-out, since even the balm of Dulcie's company and the force of Dulcie's example had never been altogether enough to stop her getting sad. The tears she had wept in the supermarket on Seven Sisters Road had somehow managed to linger there, beyond the backs of her eyes.

She wondered, would Pam be stagnating, thanks to Mr Svengali? And Peter? She had some idea that Peter had gathered up his unhappiness and had gone somewhere abroad, but she had no idea where. And Jago? He was probably around – probably right there in Cambridge – given that, unlike Dulcie, he was one of those who had always imagined the ancient university to be, automatically, a part of his birthright. Yet she was absolutely confident, by then, that he would not be in touch with her. And it was certainly easier that way.

And yet, and yet . . . there had seemed to be such prospects for them; such a perfect and propitious symmetry. Two of them dark; two of them fair. Two short; two tall. Two of them ebullient and two of them grave. Like the stuff of Shakespeare Comedy. Like *Twelfth Night*; like *All's Well*. Wine-red trunk-hose with wine-red farthingale. Green silk breeches with green jewelled overgown. Dramatis personae.

It equipped her, now, to think about the Comedies. How terrible they were, how raw, how wild, how red in tooth and claw. All that tempest and treachery. All that torture and prison. And how bravely the characters wisecracked as they waited to fall through the air.

Hugo Campbell Recumbent. The Green Man by Water

'Comedy,' said Hugo Campbell. 'Shakespeare Comedy. Go away and write me an essay about the Comedies.' Hugo Campbell was one of her supervisors and this was the first time they had met.

'But I've only just got here,' Christina thought. 'Is he turning me out already?'

It was clear to her, however, that poor Dr Campbell, invalid that he evidently was, had a need to conserve such energy as he possessed. She had entered his room, via an unlit flagstone corridor, to find him unambiguously horizontal, bathed in a watery green light from a trio of leaded windows that gave on to the river. He was reclining upon a moss-green sofa. He wore dark green corduroy trousers and a paler green lamb's-wool pullover. The fine, taut skin of his handsome, bony face was freckled and pale to greenish. His hair, which was bronze and thinning at the temples, appeared to her, at that moment, to be overlaid with a patina of green light.

It had been a little embarrassing to discover that Hugo Campbell was Judith Levin's husband – embarrassing and difficult to credit. They were like the Greeks and the Amazons in reverse. Horizontal and perpendicular.

Though Hugo's desk was dominated by up-market word-processing machinery, he appeared to have been processing his words in a wire-backed A4 notebook on his knee. The notebook was balanced on a large pastry-board and his mottled green fountain pen was poised, uncapped, in his hand. Under his head, in the hollow of his nape, he had a small, green kneeler cushion worked in needlepoint.

213

'Excuse me,' Christina said, before she took her leave, 'but is that all?'

'All?' he said. 'There are eleven of them, you know.'

'Eleven?' Christina said.

'Comedies,' he said.

'Yes. I know that,' Christina said. 'But what I mean is – well – shall I go now? Is that the end of my supervision?'

'What's the problem?' he said. 'I expect that you have read the plays, haven't you?'

'Yes,' she said. 'I've read the plays. I've even acted in some of them.' A pageant flitted briefly across her mind of herself and Peter at thirteen. Identical twins, Viola and Sebastian. Jago as Count Orsino, drunk with love for somebody else. Alas. Ouch. Our frailty is the cause . . .

'Good,' Hugo said. 'Then go away and write about them.' He moved his head very slightly to indicate that she was dismissed. The movement caused the cushion to tumble from behind his head into a collection of crumpled paper that lay around the sofa. Christina, fearing that he might risk injury in trying to retrieve it, lunged for it with alacrity and gave it into his hands. She noticed, as she did so, that, at some time in the past, the fingers of one of the faithful had worked the letters 'XP' into its underside.

'Thank you,' he said.

' "Peace be with you," ' she said.

'What's that?' he said.

'Your cushion,' she said. 'It's Greek. Those are the first two letters of Christ's name.'

Hugo Campbell glanced at the cushion as though he were looking straight through it. He turned it over once in his hands.

'Never noticed,' he said. 'It was here when I came.'

'Must have been filched from a church,' Christina said, and she watched him stuff it back behind his head.

'You will be aware,' he said, 'that the college acquired all its property by filching it from churches. We are cushioned, here, by the Acts of Dissolution.'

Christina gulped. 'Well, then,' she said. 'I suppose it's no wonder that the whole sodding place looks like churches.'

Hugo Campbell looked at her for a moment with something half like interest. Then, with a sigh, he returned his gaze to the pastry-board.

'Consider Shakespeare's aunt,' he said. He made a vague, dismissing gesture. 'One of a thousand suppressed nuns. Only think how easily one might have found oneself with a nun for one's mother.'

'Yes,' Christina said.

'Consider,' Hugo said, '*The Comedy of Errors.*'

'Yes,' Christina said. And then she took her leave.

After that, she made copious notes. She drafted the essay repeatedly. It got longer and longer as the subject got further away. Finally, she threw away the essay drafts along with all the notes. She walked the country path from Newnham Croft to Grantchester and asked herself why it was that she liked the Comedies so much, while the Tragedies failed to touch her. That was, except for *Hamlet*. Oh, Hamlet! How she longed to elbow that poor, pliable Ophelia out of his reading path and have the prince to herself. And why, incidentally, did all these four-star men so invariably fall for shrinking violets? What was the matter with them?

'Testosterone,' she said out loud. A cow stared at her as she passed, needling her with what she considered to be an excess of bovine placidity.

'Well, don't just stand there,' she said. 'There is supposed to be more to life than saggy boobs, you know. I mean, just because we're both vegetarian –' She stopped. 'Concentrate,' she said firmly. Comedy. Why was it so funny? Why was it so sad? All those brilliant people – had they survived the plague and the Protestants and the Catholics and the executioner's axe, just so that now syphilis could get them? Rampage through their flesh? It put a new complexion on the idea of dying for love. Risk all. Dare all. Crack jokes in the prison cell. Make us laugh. Ejaculate. They had called it 'dying' to ejaculate. No wonder, then, that the Comedies were a better sort of Tragedy.

When she got back, she began all over again. She tried for a while a technique of talking aloud, imagining that Dulcie was there with her in the room. Then she wrote very fast, off the top of her head. First she gave her essay a title:

'Shakespeare Comedy – a Better Sort of Tragedy'.

Then she underlined it. She omitted the next line and wrote, under the title a phrase remembered from Charles and Mary Lamb:

'They laughed at the lady Olivia for the pleasant mistake she had made in falling in love with a woman.'

Then, omitting another line, she wrote:

'And what about the youngest son of old Sir Rowland de Boys?'

Then she wrote her essay.

The Tragedies [she wrote] are Tragedies and the Comedies are Tragedies. The Comedies are a better sort of tragedy because they make us laugh and because the characters stay alive. Survival is admirable. It is more difficult than death, since it takes more energy and guile. The Comedies send us home feeling happy, because we believe that we have witnessed happy endings. What we have really witnessed are sexy endings; visionary endings; endings frozen in a moment of precarious, brilliant symmetry, like a rain of fireworks in a prison yard. The Comedies climax on a moment of upbeat that is balanced between all time and no time. Their reality is forever and never. In between the tortures and the banishment, the leg irons and the threats of execution, the Comedies operate like Comp-U-Date, hell-bent on making matches. Everyone is paired off two-by-two like animals going into the Ark. Every Jack must have his Jill. 'An ill-favoured thing, sir, but mine own.' And 'you and you are sure together as winter to foul weather.' Symmetry is all. And if you've got to the end of Act V and still there are threads untied – a woman as yet un-husbanded; a dukedom in the wrong hands – don't worry about it, because Shakespeare will always intervene and resolve it. He will reach into the pool of unemployed actors hanging about in the wings and he will shove one of them on to the stage, already colour-coordinated in two-tone slashed trunk-hose.

'I am the second son of old Sir Rowland,' says Mister Mystery Man, breaking through the undergrowth into the clearing. And, 'Oh yeah?' you think – you the audience – 'Oh yeah? And where have you been hiding yourself, Mr Second Son, for the preceding four and a half acts of this play, that none of the other characters has made any reference to your existence?' But he has been on hold for the duration of his whole life, precisely so that he can appear like this, brazenly, in the eleventh hour and taunt you with your own humdrum incredulity.

So the Comedies end juggling; holding a balance in the air which dares us to disbelief. The characters are like a troupe of Chinese acrobats balanced on a pyramid of chairs. The act would fail to uplift us if it ceased to be precarious. It would not excite our optimism if the chairs were all nailed to the floor.

The Comedies are a better sort of Tragedy [she continued], with the glaring exception of *Hamlet*. This is because while the Tragedies are concerned with Establishment people, straight people, married people, people bothered about ambition, status, power and reputation, the Comedies are about the you-and-me people; the young people, single people, street people, people with free spirits to celebrate and wild oats to sow. Of course we know that the Wild Oats people will eventually turn into the Establishment people but in the Comedies we are living for the brilliance of the moment. If Shakespeare had given us the sequels, we would see at once that all those brilliant, bantering Beatrices, having become the wives to all those brilliant, bantering Benedicks, will be whining in back bedrooms that they are neglected, while their husbands chase the maids.

She sighed. She omitted the next line. She wrote, on the following line, one word:

Testosterone.

Then she wrote on:

The Comedies take on as their subject what people seem to care about most. That is the business of getting it together with a member of the opposite sex. In this they are just as abrasive and cruel as life. The sexes are matched in a constant state of war. The war is represented by the words. The quick-fire banter between men and women is a mating dance and a metaphor for the act between the sheets, in all its violence and joy.

At this point she narrowly stopped herself putting on the page what she had on the tip of her tongue:

Dear Dr Campbell,
    I know precious little about the act between the sheets, though this has not been for want of trying. It is a fallacy that men go after women like Beatrice. They don't find talkie women sexy. That is to say, while gabbling is acceptable, wit is beyond the pale.
    Yours sincerely,
    Christina.

What she did write went on as follows.

In the conflict of gender, the women win the war of words, but the men will win the battle. The women win on points, but the men are the people who have the points. They have the last weapon against the last word. They have kisses and penetration.

'Peace! I will stop your mouth.'
'Women are made to bear, and so are you.'

The tragedy of the Comedies is that while sex draws men and women together, gender draws them apart. This is the terrible contradiction. Contradiction makes friction. Friction makes heat. Heat makes energy. Energy makes electricity. The Comedies are electric and it is not by accident, then, that their sparks fly against some X-rated scenarios:

Comedy A – has a faithful manservant manacled in a dark dungeon while the cast gets on with the business of rampaging through the wine cellar.

Comedy B – has a young man broken up in a wrestling match, after which a banished duke's daughter flees for her life into a forest inhabited by lions.

Comedy C – has a woman framed and near to death, after which, as a prelude to a wedding feast, we are offered the promise of brave tortures.

Comedy D – has a sexually blackmailed nun whose brother is thrown into prison.

Comedy E – takes place in a space of contracted time between sunrise and sundown, when an old man, searching for his lost son is condemned to execution.

Comedy F – the most putrid with the smell of sinful humanity, offers us a *leitmotif* of Jew-baiting, while we wait to have the flesh ripped out from around the heart of a bankrupt merchant.

Christina paused here. She omitted a line and, on the next, she wrote:

Funny peculiar, or funny ha ha?

She omitted another line, after which she went on:

And another thing. The Comedies are much more okay these days than the Tragedies, because they are much more okay about women. They appreciate that women make up half the human race. There are more women among the dramatis personae and the women are allowed to speak. Not just to speak, but to contradict, initiate and utter smutty wisecracks in the presence of the male sex. Some of them are even blatantly otherwise, such as the beautiful Olivia.

At school, you get told that Olivia falls in love with Viola by mistake. But the more you look at the play the more you know it's not a mistake. Viola may be dressed up like George Sand at the time, but all her body language is screaming XX chromosomes. And wouldn't you be a lesbian if you were the beautiful Olivia? If your brother and your father had gone and died on you and left you to the mercies of your only surviving male relation? Sir Toby Belch. All fart and beer belly and hands on your maid's tits and drinking your wine cellar dry, while he's trying to fix you up with his sidekick. Mr Worzel Gummidge of the dish-mop hair and wrinkled tights. And your only suitor is the indolent Count Poove, forever horizontal on the chaise longue, sniffing the odour of violets and experiencing heightened states of consciousness. Can it really be *violets* that the exquisite Count is sniffing? He's probably got platinum linings in both of his exquisite nostrils.

The Comedies [she wrote] are terrifically unfussed about cross-dressing and homo-stuff. In this the page boy is extremely useful. He is like a junior in an English boys' public school. The universal Cherubino. He is someone for people to practise on:

Olivia falls in love with Viola, who is pretending to be a page boy.

Phebe falls in love with Rosalind, who is pretending to be a page boy.

Orlando makes love to Ganymede, who is pretending to be a page boy.

Count Orsino proposes marriage to his page boy, who is Viola pretending to be a page boy.

Then she wrote:

There is a serious shortage of page boys these days. People don't have them any more, except at royal weddings when they wear kilts, which is another form of cross-dressing.

In conclusion, Christina became lightheaded:

You would have to go to Amsterdam to marry your page boy today, but Count Orsino does it in Albania. Shakespeare calls Albania 'Illyria'. And he calls Bohemia 'a desert country near the sea'. For us it is in the Czech Republic, but this has to do with continental drift. Continental drift is beyond the scope of this essay.

She put down her pen and read the essay through. She picked up her stapler and she stapled the pages together. She wrote her name with a flourish across the top of page one. Out loud, she said, 'Hey, Dulce. Do you know something? I'm really pleased with this essay.' Then she got up to deposit the essay in Dr Campbell's pigeonhole. On the way she stopped at the library to check on the Old Testament. Genesis was the first book, but Zachariah was not the last. The last book was Malachi. Judith had got it wrong.

The Green Man sur l'Herbe

Within the week it was clear to Christina that someone had begun to use her bicycle. Afterwards he always left her chocolate bars and pencils in the cycle basket. Twice recently, when she had needed the bike in a hurry – to get to her lunchtime job in the Fish Bar – the thing had not been there. The first time she had found it locked up round the corner. There had been a box of Staedtler pencils along with a small Cadbury's Flake. The next time she had found it leaning up against a telephone box in the market place. The wheel rim had been buckled slightly, but two milk chocolate Bounty bars were gleaming at her from the basket in their enticing pale blue wrappers. It was obvious to her that the phantom bike sharer was adept at cracking open padlocks.

She had written him a letter after the Bounty bars. In it, her annoyance had been somewhat modified by her admiration for his dexterity – and by the softening effect of his gifts.

'Fix my wheel,' she wrote. 'Or there'll be hell to pay.' She signed it, 'love Christina.' Then she wrote, 'P.S. I'd prefer plain chocolate Bounty bars, if it's all the same to you.'

Now, as she hurried to check on the bicycle, just prior to her supervision, she found that it had been locked to a railing opposite Barclays Bank. The wheel was gleaming with a brand-new rim and spokes and there was a letter for her in the basket. It had been wrapped around a small Toblerone box and fixed with an elastic band. Christina removed the elastic band with a flutter of expectation.

The phantom bike sharer had terrible handwriting. Quite the worst she had ever seen.

'You suggest that I "love Christina",' he had written. 'And I only wish I could. I must tell you, now, with my hand on my heart, that I am committed to another.'

Christina laughed as she made her way to Hugo Campbell's rooms. She munched the Toblerone as she went, enjoying the intrigue of the business. The bike sharer was fun, she thought. He was more fun, certainly, than the mass of undergraduates whom she had encountered thus far. And was he trying to make her jealous?

Then she arrived at the watery green rooms at the end of the flagstone corridor.

Hugo, too, had left her a message, but his was less appealing. It was inscribed on a yellow Post-It — one of the more objectionable Post-Its, she considered. It had the silhouette of a small black telephone at the top and was marked out, officiously, with little lines and spaces for recipient and sender, date and time. The message had evidently been dictated over the telephone to Fiona Campbell, whose neat, backward-sloping hand was there — as always, Christina reflected — to interpose itself between one party and another in any matter of college business. The Post-It ran as follows:

> To: Christina
> From: Hugo
> Message: Go away.

Under this, perhaps by accident of layout, the rest ran as if by afterthought.

> Write essay
> Shakespearean Tragedy
> See me Thursday next.

It quoted date and time of issue. Christina was frustrated. She had hoped to retrieve her Comedy essay and had envisaged a great many approving red ticks along the left- and right-hand margins. Even, perhaps, in a whimsical moment, one of Mrs Alfieri's glow-in-the-dark stickers awarded for meritorious effort.

Instead, she returned to her room. She applied her mind, grudgingly, to the business of Shakespeare's Tragedies. First, she reflected upon the fact that almost all the tragic heroes reminded her of her father. All of them severe cases of cancer of the ego. Look at me. See how I fill the stage. Even as I lay down my life. I, Myself and Me.

She began to make some undirected jottings on the backs of her college notices:

Othello [she wrote]. Wife dead. Strangled in her bed. And what is the General doing? He is sitting by the corpse as it stiffens and writing his own testimonials. Putting the best gloss that he can on the strangulation incident for the Council of Elders back in Venice. 'I have done the state some service . . .'

The woman is lying there dead on her wedding sheets and Othello is asking to have his record as Chief Honcho in the Marines taken into account.

Macbeth – ditto. Butchers half the county, including best friend, plus Macduff, plus wife and babes. So how does he spend his last moments? Swaggering, of course. Dying the Real Man. No quiche eater he. No, not he. King Bloodbath himself. Put 'em up, and, POWBASH-BAM!! First man down's a sissy. 'Lay on, Macduff; And damned be him that first cries, "Hold, enough!"'

Here Christina paused. She chewed upon one of the bike sharer's Staedtler pencils. Then she wrote:

I don't like to quibble, but 'damned be him' doesn't

sound like grammar. Wobbly pronouns from the Thane of Glamis and Cawdor. Still, the circumstances are terrifically extenuating. Burnham Wood is on the march to Dunsinane – cheap trick that it may be – and Capt. Macduff is swanking his gory caul and afterbirth in a piece of pervy one-upmanship.

Christina paused again. 'Untimely ripped' was horrible. Quite disgusting, in fact, like the whole business of childbirth. She hoped that Mrs Macduff the Elder had managed to die in the process, in order to be spared the discomfort of her bizarre, post-parturition equipment. Or was 'untimely ripped' merely a piece of muscular hyperbole? Did Macduff mean no more than that he had been born premature? ('Like me,' Christina wrote. 'Two whole months premature.')

And – something I have never noticed before – [she wrote] Macbeth calls the witches 'juggling friends'. To 'juggle' is to deceive. Classic case of transference. Mr Axe Man himself can murder his way to the throne in the dead of night, but it's *jugglers* who deceive? This does not apply to my juggler. Nor does it apply to Dulcie. She juggles. They both juggle, but neither of them deceives. Others deceive, not they.

She wrote a memo in the margin:

Saw such lovely juggling balls yesterday. Little shop in King's Parade. Everything overpriced. Crochet work from Guatemala. All crunchy in the hand. Fatly stuffed with barley. Dulcie's Christmas present – if only I can save the pennies for them.

Christina put down the Staedtler and sighed. After a while she picked it up again and wrote:

Say which of the following Tragic Persons you would like to have sitting beside you at the next college guest night:

1. Macbeth – Occupation: General. Hallucinating all over the vegetarian leekbake. Shake not thy gory locks at me. Embarrassing to a degree.

2. Antony and Cleopatra – Occupation(s): General (and General's General?). One on each side of you. Both drunk and slobbering. Playing footsie across your ankle bones.

3. Julius Caesar – Occupation: General (retired). Come on my right ear for this ear is deaf. Oh boy. So left ear he can't hear you and right ear he isn't listening. He's giving you the wall-to-wall boy's talk until the cheese board comes round. Politics and Promotion. Musket, Fife and Drum. Rumpatum. Campaigns accomplished. Conferences attended.

4. Coriolanus – Occupation: General. Don't even think about it. Next thing you know he's followed you home and he's got his foot in the door. Then your body is found floating down the Cam in segments.

5. Othello – Occupation: General. Polishing his assonance in your ear and pulling you with his tales of Darkest Africa. The headless Anthropophagae and men whose heads do grow beneath their shoulders. Ninety-eight per cent crap artist. The litmus test is language. Look at Hamlet's language and what do you see? It's all built on the ordinary small details of life – shoes and cakes and sparrows and moles. But Othello's language is forever banging on about the hills whose heads touch heaven and the steep down gulfs of liquid fire. He's so busy getting drunk on his own cosmic verbiage that he can't tell the nutshell from the infinite space. (Sort of like the difference between my father and Roland Dent?)

Then she wrote:

6. Hamlet – Occupation: Philosophy Student . . . aaah!

At this point, Christina luxuriated pleasantly in the idea of skipping the guest night and of taking the slow train back with Hamlet to his university in Wittenberg. She imagined herself blissfully footloose with Hamlet and his friend Horatio. Two men and a girl – like Kate in *Jules et Jim*. They would hang out, fancy-free, in the coffee houses and in the fleapits to wisecrack and talk philosophy.

Then the cold reality of the play began to intrude. Hamlet was in love with Ophelia. Like the phantom bike sharer, he was committed to another.

Christina got up. With a heavy sigh, she took her lined A4 pad off the shelf and she grabbed a few ballpoint pens. Then she sat down and, for want of inspiration, she gave her mind once more, to the idea of the Objective Correlative.

'So,' said Hugo, making the effort of speech. 'Since you suffer so direly from partiality for the Dane, you might as well tell me about *Hamlet*.'

It was early afternoon on Thursday – Thursday two weeks later. On the Thursday following the first Post-It, Hugo had not been available. A second Post-It had suggested that she return at the later hour of five. At five, when she returned, Hugo was still not there. Nor was there any Post-It, this time, to help her live on in hope.

When Hugo had still not materialized on the morning of the Thursday following that, Christina directed her steps towards the lodge, where the porter – while he declined to make available the home address or telephone number of Dr Hugo Campbell – was perfectly willing to assist her through a perusal of the phone book.

She complained to him of a great many Campbells to impede her selection there.

'Myself,' said the porter, wittily. 'I blame the Highland Clearances.'

Christina ignored him. 'I can try under Judith Levin,' she said. She thumbed through the pages of L subscribers, mumbling as she went. 'Lever, Leveritt, Levi, Levick, Levicki, Levin, Group Captain A. C. OBE. Say,' she said, out loud, 'what next?' Then she mumbled on. 'Levin, Dr D. I, Levin, Dr E. A, Levin, Dr J. I, Levin, Dr J. J –' She looked up. 'Sod it,' she said. 'They're all doctors.'

'Now, let's not forget the Group Captain,' said the porter. 'OBE and all.' He paused to hang some keys on a board arranged with rows of cup-hooks before returning to her at the counter. 'Mind, there'll not be too many among that lot who could fix a person's broken leg,' he said. 'Doctors of Philosophy, if you get my drift.'

'Yes,' Christina said.

'Cambridge, see,' he said. 'Now, if you'd broken your leg, for example – well, then, I'd be able to advise you. If you get my drift.'

'I've broken my leg,' Christina said. 'That's exactly why I came.'

'Ah, well now,' said the porter. 'Then I'd go for Dr Levin, J. J. She'll do you a very nice plaster cast. If you get my drift.'

'Thank you,' Christina said, 'Geronimo. I hope you get the DSO and bar.'

Christina made her descent upon the house after she'd completed her noontide hour in the Fish Bar. Even once she had taken that liberty, it appeared that Hugo Campbell was not at home. Nobody answered the doorbell. It was only as she turned to leave that she saw him through the window. He was reclining at the far end of the garden in a setting which provided a suitably arboreal context for his muted green clothing. There were no flowers in Hugo's green garden, only grass and trees. Hugo was enclosed within a delicate iron structure that looked like a giant birdcage with most of the bars removed. He was slumped in one of two matching dark green garden chairs with his feet on a garden table. He was staring into a pastry-board which was once again propped on his knees. This time he had no pen in his hand and his arms were hanging at his sides.

Hugo looked up at Christina only once her body had got between him and the sun. As he did so his expression was such that her unease made her belligerent.

'Excuse me,' she said. 'But I'd like to ask you if it could be that I smell.'

Hugo raised his nose a half-inch and sniffed the air carefully, delicately, like a cat sifting for evidence of salmon pâté stowed somewhere on a high shelf.

'Slightly,' he said. 'Very slightly. You smell of Sarson's Malt Vinegar. I would hazard that you have recently been in the vicinity of a chip shop.'

Christina elected to ignore this remark, since its accuracy wounded her. She rallied to console herself that the moral ground was hers.

'So,' Hugo said, sighing deeply, 'you might as well tell me about *Hamlet*.'

It was difficult, in the event, to talk about Hamlet, with his great burden of paralysis and inertia. To do so in front of the slumped figure of Hugo would have made everything that she wanted to say sound like a personal remark. As a result she said nothing. A pair of pretty speckled brown birds fussed and rustled in the greenery behind Hugo's head as the silence grew large around them.

Then, suddenly, something strange happened. Horatio came to her rescue. Horatio, the prince's friend. She fixed her mind, not upon Prince Hamlet, who was proving quite useless to her, but upon the attendant lord. As she did so, Horatio grew tall. He ceased to stand in Hamlet's shadow. He was standing head and shoulders above all the others in the cast. He was standing lofty perpendicular, in the mire of treachery and betrayal. Horatio had put on the gown of glory; the Merlin cloak; the blanket of authority. Horatio had become the great warrior-poet; the elegiac musician. And there he stood, alone. Like a cathedral. And all around him lay the dead.

And she thought, with no little excitement, of Horatio's 'flights of angels' as the play's only real uplift.

'I'm not in love with the prince. I'm in love with Horatio,' she said, but she said it only to herself. Out loud, she said, 'I've decided that the play is Horatio's tragedy. I think Horatio is the hero. I'm afraid I've changed my mind.'

'Mm,' Hugo said.

'That is what I think,' she said.

'Mm,' Hugo said.

'Well, isn't Tragedy supposed to give us some hope?' she said. 'Really, the only hope here is entirely to do with Horatio. His loyalty. His sacrifice in agreeing to stay alive in such a rat-hole, just to pass on Hamlet's story. Meanwhile Hamlet can go swanning off to heaven with Horatio's flights of angels.'

'You are rather eccentric,' Hugo said, making eccentricity sound like a disease.

They both resumed their silence.

'If it weren't for Horatio,' she said at last, 'then the bad guys would have written up the story. They're always in charge, aren't they? That's because the superior people like Hamlet always hesitate, because they have scruples and integrity, while the mob of boneheads don't. So they're always quicker on the draw. Take Fortinbras of Norway. He can march about through Denmark, with his soldiers banging their drums, and all for what? To lay claim to a little slice of Poland. I mean, *Poland*. God. I mean, what for?'

'Mm,' Hugo said. She thought that he had maybe fallen asleep.

She paused to look around his garden and noted that it was very much in need of weeding. What had evidently once been herbaceous borders had been overcome with ground elder.

'I could do your garden for you if you like,' she said. 'For money, I mean. Maybe even carve out a few flower-beds for you.' When Hugo didn't reply, she went on, 'Nothing rank and gross. I'm not thinking of doing it over with peonies and giant dahlias. But look. Over there. Right now you could be staring at a carpet of autumn-flowering crocuses. There under those trees.' She dwelt wistfully on the sight of Hugo's beautiful old brick walls and envisaged how they would be all shimmering with dew on spiders' webs first thing in the morning.

'I could plant some of those lilies for you,' she said. 'The ones that come so white they're almost green. They're green in the bud. They have green pollen guides, You know the ones I mean? You get them in pictures of the Annunciation.'

Then she passed some time in contriving the floral accessories for Judith and Hugo's wedding. The Green Man and the Scarlet Woman. She toyed with giving Hugo a green carnation in his buttonhole. Then she settled for a sprig of parsley flowers which were prettier, she thought. She gave Judith a bouquet of dark green broccoli florets with an aureole of scarlet ribbon and lace. She seated Hugo in a mahogany invalid's chair like an old-fashioned baby's push-chair.

'What's wrong with Poland?' Hugo said suddenly, like the Dormouse starting up from the teapot. He was speaking with feeling for the first time.

Christina was taken aback by the unexpected challenge. 'Well,' she said, inadequate, defensive. 'Nothing, I suppose –'

'I have been invited to give a paper in Poland,' Hugo said, rather pompously, she thought. 'In December.'

Christina made no remark, not knowing quite what to say.

'In Warsaw,' Hugo said.

'A paper is sort of like an essay, I suppose?' she said at last. 'I expect it's longer and more difficult to write.' When Hugo didn't reply, she said, 'I hope that you liked my essays, by the way.'

'Mm,' Hugo said. She had no way of knowing whether Hugo's 'Mm' denoted approval, or was merely a way of punctuating the gaps in what she said.

'I enjoyed writing the Comedy essay,' she said. 'I hoped that you would like it.'

'Mm,' Hugo said.

Maybe I would like to kill this person, Christina thought. If there be any cunning cruelty which can torment him much and hold him long ... but would even torments open his lips, or should she dispatch him outright? Instead she made ready to leave.

'Perhaps I could recite both my essays to you, standing on my head?' she said. She saw Hugo sigh and glance at his watch. She took a last look at his garden.

'Excuse me,' Hugo said.

'What?' Christina said.

'My pen,' he said. 'I dropped it just before you came. It's lying to the left of your foot.'

'Oh,' Christina said. She bent to pick it up. It was the same pen as he had used before in the greenish rooms by the river. It was mottled, green and black. On the pocket clip it said 'Waterman'. She handed it to him.

'Thank you,' Hugo said. He uncapped it and began to write.

'I'll tell you something about your Tragedy essay,' he said. 'You failed to mention *King Lear*.'

'Yes,' she said. 'I'm sorry. Frankly, it's because the story always makes me queasy. What I mean is – take the demon offspring. Well, that's just all of us, isn't it? What I mean is, don't we *all* want to get the parents off our backs? Heave them out of doors; get them out of our lives before they nobble us for good? Don't we *all* want to treat the house like a hotel . . .?'

'Instead,' Hugo said, ignoring her, 'you have wasted your time on the idea of the Objective Correlative. A dead horse, if ever there was one.'

'Yes,' Christina said humbly. 'Excuse me, but about my Comedy essay. Could I have it back, do you think?'

'Ah,' Hugo said, 'Ahem. Now, that could be a little bit of a problem. The fact is that I seem to have mislaid it.'

For 'mislaid', read lost, Christina thought. There was a pause. 'Was that before or after you'd read it?' she said.

Hugo sighed. 'I can't remember,' he said and he kept on writing.

The Scarlet Woman, the Green Rabbit and the Very Telling Cranium

On her way back through the house Christina saw that Judith had come home. She was in the kitchen with five children, all of whom were female. A younger trio sat at a breakfast counter, raucous and assertive, while a pair of quieter, older girls stood about holding dinner plates. The older two were probably about twelve years old, Christina thought. One was thin and fair, while the other was fat and dark.

Judith was, once again, dressed in scarlet. Her jacket, slim-waisted and multi-panelled, was tapered at the front into two elongated points. She wore it with wide silk trousers gathered into elegant silk folds. These radiated from the crotch, creating a second elongated V to reflect, almost exactly, the angle of the inverted V, made between the points of her jacket.

The sight of Judith at once lifted Christina's spirits from despondency. She wondered whether, means permitting, she might ever become anything like as dressy. She considered it unlikely. But if she were to, then Judith would be her model; Judith her inspiration. Judith's clothes were not only sexy, she considered, but they had the effect of equating sexiness with efficiency.

And yet, she reminded herself, Judith had married Hugo. Why? How on earth had that come about? Wasn't marriage about exchange? Yet to attempt even verbal exchange with Hugo was like talking into a distorting mirror. It made you panic and doubt yourself. It gave back nothing, except your own self reduced in dignity and self-esteem. So how did Judith stand it? Or did she, like Bottom the Weaver, like to play all the parts herself?

At that moment, Judith, though she looked undeniably sexy, appeared anything but efficient. This, Christina decided, was because her context was unsuitable. A kitchen was not Judith's landscape.

She was attempting to serve basic foodstuffs to the five hungry children. The three youngest were drumming loudly with their feet against the doors of the cupboards beneath the counter. At the same time they were banging rhythmically with their cutlery and chanting as they did so.

'Hi,' Judith called out to Christina, cupping a hand around her ear against the din. 'How are you?'

'Fine,' Christina said, still from beyond the threshold. 'Except that your husband has lost my Comedy essay.'

Judith failed to respond to this. Or was she, perhaps, too preoccupied to assimilate Christina's intelligence?

'This person is Miffy,' she said, her voice still raised. She indicated the fat, dark-haired, older girl, who had begun to gather up plates. 'Mercifully,' Judith said, 'only Miffy is mine.'

Miffy's friend was Rose. And the oldest of the three younger children was Patience. Her voice was consistently raised above others. Right then, Patience was raucously defying the implications of her name as she orchestrated an ear-splitting demand for pudding.

'Why are we WAY-ting,' the little ones chanted, taking their lead from her. 'We are suffo-CAY-ting.' The pile of discarded supper plates – which Miffy had meanwhile quietly removed and dumped beside the sink – contained the unattractive remnants of boarding-house food. Chunky edges of institution piecrust tinged with dark brown gravy besmirched all the plates, along with some soggy-looking vegetables.

'And do you know what Mrs Spencer has made for your pudding?' Judith was saying. She spoke rather too enticingly, Christina considered. She sounded like a childless aunt who had been left in charge to mime the parental role.

'Jelly-rabbit, jelly-rabbit, JELL-EE-RABB-IT,' chanted the little ones, who were evidently way ahead of her. 'We want jell-ee-rabbit.'

'And we want choc-late sauce,' Patience chanted, assertively, with an instinct for upping the stakes.

'Choc-late sauce, choc-late sauce, CHOC-LATE-SAUCE,' chanted the trio, like sheep.

Miffy had already approached the fridge. She drew from it a quivering, lime-green bunny rabbit that had previously been turned out on to an oval serving plate. She now placed it on the workboard under the children's eager eyes, while her friend Rose went to get the chocolate sauce. This came ready-made in a brown aerosol canister, its plastic cap, a gnome's hat, swirled to a crazy point.

'Well, I'm not having the rabbit's ass,' Patience said. 'Holly can have his ass.'

'But I'm not having his ass,' said a younger sister, shrill with indignation.

'Yes, you are,' Patience said.

'No, I'm not,' said the younger sister. 'I'm a visitor.'

'So am I,' said Patience. 'Dummy.'

'Visitors,' Judith said, 'do not abuse the cutlery. And in England, an "ass" means a donkey, okay? The word you are looking for is "bum".'

'Mum,' Miffy said reproachfully. 'Don't.'

'Holly licks his bum and says yum-yum,' Patience said.

'I don't,' Holly said. 'Judith, I don't lick his bum. Tell Patience I don't.'

'You've only started them now,' Miffy said, wishing to educate her mother into the manner of managing small children. 'They're fine, you see, and then you always have to start them off, don't you?'

'Sorry,' Judith said. She looked up at Christina across the children's heads, 'Hang on in there,' she said, 'if you can stand it for another moment. Miff is about to rescue me. She'll cart the whole mob off next door. That's where they belong. The pay-off is she gets to spend the night.' She rolled her eyes somewhat meaningfully. 'She loves it in there,' she said.

Miffy, meanwhile, had applied the knife to the rabbit's controversial physiognomy. She had quietly resolved the problem by dissecting the creature along the spine from the region of its cerebral cortex to the last of its lumbar vertebrae. Then she lopped off the offending nether parts and served the remainder, in equal portions, on pudding plates which she placed before the children.

'Miff,' Judith said. 'You're a genius.'

Patience, having seized first rights to the aerosol canister, had projected a coiled snake of chocolate foam, first, directly into her mouth and then all over her jelly.

'Hurry UP,' said one of her sisters. 'I'm WAY-ting.'

'Me too,' said the other.

'I'm writing my NAYm,' Patience said.

'Me next. Me next,' Holly said, agitating. 'I want to write my NAYm. Huh, Oh, Luh, Luh, Yuh,' she elaborated phonetically.

'You say "Yuh",' Patience said, with nauseating smugness. 'But I say "Wye". I say "Aitch, Oh, Ell, Ell, Wye".'

'Stop it,' Miffy said firmly. And she removed the canister from Patience. In the moments of silence that followed, spoons were gouged into portions of jelly until Holly's produced a small, explosive, suction plop as jelly was parted from jelly.

Patience, primadonna-wise, at once threw down her spoon. 'Urgh!' she said. 'This jelly is farting!'

'Urgh!' said the sisters and they threw down their spoons in emulation. 'This jelly is farting!'

'We'll go,' Miffy said quickly. She was on the ball with diplomacy. 'Thanks, Mum,' she said. In a moment of scuffling and chair scraping, the five of them were at the back door.

Miffy had brought up the rear with Rose. She kissed her mother good-naturedly and spoke with resignation.

'You've got them all wound up,' she said. 'But they'll be fine in a minute, don't you worry.'

The sound of children's departing feet was heard crunching briefly on gravel. A neighbouring door opened to admit them. Then it closed and all was silence.

Christina ceased to hover. She came forward and entered the kitchen. On the counter, brown and green substances lay smashed together in pudding bowls, while coils of spilled chocolate foam were detumescing on the wooden surface.

'Bliss,' Judith said, and she sat down. 'Peace,' she said. 'The kids' parents are here on sabbatical. The family's from Vancouver. Lovely people. Six daughters. Quite wonderful for my Miff.'

Christina began, without thinking, to make inroads into the mess. She dumped the bowls on the draining-board and brought a cloth to wipe up the spillage.

'Miff and Rose have become very close,' Judith continued. 'Best bosom buddies. Poor Miff has begun to imagine that she'd like six children one day.'

'She seems very capable,' Christina said. 'Very domesticated.'

'Ah, she's my Little Nell,' Judith said. 'Far more Little Nell than Miffy.'

Christina wiped up and rinsed and wiped. 'Isn't Miffy a rabbit?' she said. 'I thought Miffy was a rabbit.'

Judith smiled. 'My little brother,' she said. 'He gave her a book when she was born. *Miffy Goes Flying*. It was always her favourite. She took it with her everywhere until she lost it somewhere in North London on a visit to my parents. Her real name is Zuleika.'

'I know that book,' Christina said with a sudden, regressive enthusiasm. She remembered it, oddly, as one of the few books that Dulcie had legitimately owned. All the others on Dulcie's shelf had been the property of libraries. Miffy had had a cross-stitch nose. Her ears had poked up through her flying hat. She had gone off in an aeroplane with her favourite Uncle Bob. They had sat in the cockpit manifesting identical noses and ears.

'"Zuleika"?' she said, thinking it extreme. 'And why Zuleika?'

Judith got up and filled the kettle. She reached for a jar of instant coffee. 'My little brother again,' she said. 'I wanted her to have his name. Unfortunately Zachariah is not of the easiest to match. There were not too many girlish equivalents that scored with me at the time.'

Zachariah, Christina thought. Some name to give your baby. The penultimate book of the Old Testament. Not the last. The second to last. Judith had made a mistake there. I am alpha and not quite omega. Why had Judith got that wrong? Was she a little bit stuck on her brother? By the sound of it, she was. Still, he had to be an improvement on the recumbent green Hugo, she thought.

'Zuleika,' Judith said, musing. 'That was pretty well as close as I could get.' She scooped heaped teaspoons of Blend 37 into two large mugs. 'My parents, of course, are Jewish,' she said. 'They don't terribly care to have the newborn named after the living like that.' She poured boiling water into the mugs and brought them to the breakfast counter. Then she fetched sugar and milk. 'Sit down, Christina, please,' she said. 'Coffee time. Come on.'

Christina sat down. She took a sip from her mug. As she did so, she surveyed the rump of slaughtered green rabbit which, all alone, still lay on its plate on the counter. Hunger rose within her. She discovered an urge to sink her teaspoon into its quivering flank.

'Doctors let their children eat anything,' she said, hoping that stern judgment would obliterate the shameful need.

Judith sussed her at once, however. 'What's the matter, little

Chrissie?' she said. 'Are you pining for a bowl of jelly rabbit?'

Christina dropped her guard and smiled. 'Well, I wouldn't say no,' she said. 'That's if it's going begging. I didn't have time for any lunch today. But please don't bother with chocolate sauce.'

Judith rose and approached the oven from which she drew forth a large pie dish. It contained a substantial half of the children's institution meat pie. A daunting aroma of school dinner promptly assailed Christina's nostrils.

'But have some pie first,' Judith said hospitably. 'Go on. Please. If you didn't have lunch.'

'No, thanks,' Christina said quickly. 'The pudding will do me just fine.'

Judith put down the pie dish. She found a bowl and scooped the bunny's rump into it from the serving plate. Then she handed it over, along with a pudding spoon. She watched Christina dig in with relish.

'So you'll eat synthetic lime jelly,' she said smugly. 'But you won't eat Mrs Spencer's homemade pie. Why aren't you eating properly?'

'I am,' Christina said. 'I do.'

'Ever had an eating disorder?' Judith said, as though she enjoyed the idea.

'Of course not,' Christina said. 'That's ridiculous.'

'So what's the matter with you, then?' Judith said. 'You'll eat junk, but you won't eat food.'

'Nothing's the matter,' Christina said, 'except that your husband has lost my essay.'

'It's very common in these parts,' Judith said.

'Losing people's essays?'

'Eating disorders,' Judith said. 'Binge on junk food. Throw it up down the washbasin. That's till your hair starts falling out in tufts.' She paused to glance quickly at Christina's fine blonde hair which was none the better for its recent sluice in cut-price washing-up liquid.

'My hair is always like this,' Christina said. Judith, for some reason, was going at the theme with gusto.

'And how about your teeth?' she said. 'How are your teeth?'

'My teeth are fine,' Christina said, and she continued to spoon up jelly.

Judith narrowed her eyes, watching Christina closely. 'Stomach acid is detrimental to the tooth enamel,' she said. 'Eats it away pretty quick.'

'My teeth are fine,' Christina said, and she put down the bowl. 'You don't have to lecture me.' She wondered whether Judith had been given a brief from the college to snoop into aberrant eating habits. It was true that the residential corridors did reek, here and there, of people's vomit.

Meanwhile, Judith appeared to be enjoying her tenacious inquisition. 'So why don't you eat when you're hungry?' she said. 'Little Chrissie Angeletti?'

'But I do eat,' Christina said. 'I don't eat meat, that's all.'

'Ah,' Judith said, only partially appeased. 'And fish? You eat fish?'

'Sometimes,' Christina said. 'Look. What *is* all this? I work in a chippy for heaven's sake.' She wondered, as she spoke, why Judith's own catering was so unspeakably dreadful. Gristle pie and green packet jelly. Jesus Christ, what next? It was as if she had gone and raided the local NHS canteen. 'Your husband has just told me that I smell of Sarson's Malt Vinegar,' she said. 'It would be all right with him, I expect, if I'd smelled of the balsamic variety.'

'Come again?' Judith said.

'Balsamic vinegar,' Christina said. 'You know. The miracle of Modena.' Seeing the stuff on foodstore shelves always reminded her of her father. Matured in oak casks since the quattrocento. The Precious Blood of the foodie sect. And why was it that Judith always reduced her to thoughts of her father? Last time, after the party, it had been those camels, had it not?

'I've never learnt how to cook,' Judith was saying, as though this were her proudest boast. 'Learn how to cook and you never stop cooking. People expect it of you. It's the expense of spirit in a waste of shame. Lust in action is nothing to it. Don't ever cook, Christina. I tell you, it's politically incorrect.'

Christina laughed. 'My father has always cooked like a crazy man,' she said. 'Does it all the time. Worships food. Says he's a Catholic, but what he really worships is food.' It occurred to her that, after all, this was not altogether surprising – given how much the ritual centred on the elevation of food.

But Judith was there, waiting to pounce. 'Aha!' she said. 'And now I know why you don't eat, little Chrissie. Your father is a gourmet cook.'

'I don't eat meat,' Christina corrected. 'I eat. I always have.' Green tomato relish and six canned lima beans, eaten slowly, one by one, with a fork. She could not remember what motivating force had lain behind that intransigent childhood stance. Whatever it had been was buried far too deep. And then, of course, there was Pam, who had always eaten meat; had dutifully forked up all that exquisitely tortured veal. Presumably still did. Pam, who had taken such trouble over the nursing of wounded fledglings; had worried so tenderly over the squirrels' tree-houses during wind storms. But, damn it, Christina thought. Now Judith had tricked her into brooding upon her sister.

'As it happens,' she said, 'my older sister always ate meat like anything.' She paused, to reflect rather irritably upon all those star turns of yore that had appeared on her parents' dining-table. Images flashed poisonously upon the inward eye. Images of the dolls' little plates of *crostini*, served with tiny fillets of chicken liver and golden truffle butter.

'He was forever messing about with it,' she said. 'With meat, I mean. Boning it, pounding it, grinding it, wrapping it up in vine leaves, stuffing it with artichoke paste, dredging it

243

in crushed green peppercorns. Jesus, he could even do disgusting things with halved goats' heads.'

Judith was smiling broadly. '*He?*' she said. 'The cat's dad?'

'My father, of course,' Christina said. 'I'm not joking. Really. He wooed my mother with the pancreas of newborn calves.'

'Sexual jealousy,' Judith said, and she paused to gulp her coffee. 'Little Chrissie, I love you. You're so adorably transparent.'

Christina felt both provoked and patronized. Yet, for all that, she loved it that Judith loved her. Most of all, she felt confused. Somehow Judith possessed the power, simultaneously, to raise up and to cast down.

'My eating habits,' she said primly, 'are all to do with my DNA. Some people have genetic arrangements that are best suited for beans and grains.'

'And lime-green jelly, of course,' Judith said, looking at her sceptically. 'Your big sister shares your DNA, little Chrissie, so that doesn't wash, I'm afraid.'

'But my sister was always very compliant,' Christina said. 'She was always very sweet and good.'

In response, Judith delivered a lecture. Christina thought it pedantic. She used a great deal of professional terminology but, all the same, it sounded to Christina as though she had a personal axe or two to grind. It had to do with siblings and with sibling rivalry. Older siblings, she established, were inclined to align themselves with adults. They were, most of them, possessed, by dint of their primacy, of techniques for delegating transgression. Younger siblings, Judith explained, were thus unconsciously co-opted to commit all necessary acts of subversion. And necessary acts they were. That way, Judith pointed out, older siblings could transgress by proxy, while maintaining their unspotted reputations.

'But not my sister,' Christina said, who knew that Pam was different. Judith wasn't listening to her. She had lost herself in stereotypes. Then she got up rather suddenly and found cause to fidget amongst a row of tins and jars that sat on one of her shelves. When she turned and faced Christina, the colour was higher in her cheeks. 'I tell you,' she said. 'Your Miss Goody-Two-Shoes will have been contriving to wrong-foot you.'

Then, suddenly, Judith told her story. It was not a happy one and, like Judith herself, it was something larger than life. It left Christina shattered. She wished that Judith hadn't told it.

Her parents were émigré South Africans who, since the mid-seventies, had managed a small food shop on the fringe of Islington. They had decided – after spending their lives as activists in anti-racist politics – that enough was finally enough. Personal bereavement had affected their stamina and they had simply run out of steam.

Fate had never given Judith's parents a particularly smooth ride. Throughout their lives, they had experienced waves of loss as friends were victimized, imprisoned, or, towards the end, picked off by anonymous hit squads. Yet none of these things had caused them to lose heart as did the death of their older daughter, Sandra.

When Judith, aged eleven, had managed, by misadventure, to drown her sister, it was Zak, her nine-year-old brother, who had taken on the guilt. Judith, by that haunting act of sibling struggle, had ceased, at once, to occupy the place of middle child and had become the older sister. She saw herself become, in consequence, a sort of Tiresias figure, who could walk in the shoes of either. She knew the devious strategies of both.

It had not been an easy childhood for them, being three children of activist parents whose time for family life was inevitably limited and whose safety from the arm of the state was always conspicuously in jeopardy. Jostling and mutual resentment had been intense among the girls. In the event of open conflict, Judith and her younger brother had always stood together. This alliance had been skilfully contrived and artfully maintained by Judith, who was sharper than her older sister and verbally more persuasive. It had meant that Zak was not infrequently the butt of Sandra's physical assaults.

Sandra had come to grief at the close of a long, hot day during a seaside vacation. The children were alone on the beach. The evening was drawing on and all other holiday-makers had returned, by then, to their various seafront hotel rooms. It was Judith who had suggested a burial in sand, though Zak had wanted to linger over a castle for which he was right then contriving crenellated ramparts. It was Judith, too, who – innocently enough – had proposed that unfortunate variation upon the more usual mode of horizontal, beach sand burial. She had set her little brother to digging a prodigious, perpendicular trough.

The work was so arduously accomplished and so impressive that a degree of competition had then ensued between the sisters for the privilege of being buried first. Sandra had only won the day because she was bigger and stronger. She had duly been buried right up to the neck by the time that she and Judith had begun, as usual, to fall out.

'Well, I'm going,' Judith said. She kicked up a little shower of sand. 'Come on, Zak,' she said. 'We're going.'

Her brother was wont to follow her lead but, on this occasion, he had hung back, though not through any foreknowledge, nor special instinct for danger. He had simply, right then, felt sorry for Sandra, who was a pig to him in general, and a thumper into the bargain. But she had seemed to him, suddenly, the more vulnerable of his two sisters. As a result, he had hesitated and had mumbled his reservations.

'But Jude . . .' he said. 'But Jude . . . Say, Jude . . .'

Judith had grabbed his arm. 'Come on!' she said. 'Just leave her. She can jolly well get back on her own. Let's you and me go and buy ice-creams.'

Judith had swept on purposefully, making wide, yeti footprints in the wet, densely packed band of sand nearest the waterline. Zak's footprints had appeared alongside hers, smaller and more frequent, as she had lugged him along by the hand. Her sister's plaintive whinings were, right then, music to her ears.

'But Jude . . .' Zak had objected, as Judith yanked him on. She pulled him by the hand towards that final ridge of sand, where a line of succulent plants appeared as a prelude to the roadway. And then their thoughts were all for the kiosk that sold choc ices and cones.

'Funny thing,' Judith said, pausing to glance up at Christina. 'They were known in my childhood as "Eskimo pies". That's what we always called choc ices. We called them Eskimo pies.'

Judith's parents had, that day, been taking tea with friends. By the time they had returned to their hotel, it was to find the police were on the threshold. And – while this was for them a perfectly familiar occurrence – it seemed that on this occasion, the police required their presence in a matter more personal than political. They were needed to identify the body of a drowned, twelve-year-old girl.

Judith had subsequently been most articulate with the authorities. They had commented favourably upon her clarity, poise and helpfulness. She had explained to them that her little brother had dug a hole and had buried their sister and had filled it up all round with sand.

She explained, now to Christina, that, as she had told her story, it was as though she had seen her own bodily person observing from the opposite side of the room. Her voice, her brain and all her being were working, somehow, without her. It had made her feel curiously elated. It was maybe like speaking in tongues. And Zak – who had wanted so much to finish his castle – Zak had stood by, trance-like, dreamy and silent. He had allowed her to indict him and to damage his reputation. He had gone along with her in that, as he had always done in everything. Zak had simply allowed her to delegate transgression.

Judith paused. She licked her lips and ran a hand over her hair. She turned to face Christina, who was seated at the counter, white and trembling, not wanting to believe Judith's story; wanting to run it through, like a dream, with an alternative ending.

'I stood there and let them blame him,' Judith said. 'The parents worshipped Sandra. They terribly wanted the solace of having someone to blame. They were appalled and they believed me. Can you beat that? Both of them. The stigma hung about his neck for years. They were decent types, my parents. You could tell they tried to wrestle with their burgeoning negative feelings. For quite a while they felt a perceptible aversion to his presence. It pretty well eroded Zakky's childhood.'

Soon, Judith explained, her parents had acted to dispatch the boy to boarding school. A Catholic boarding school, Judith said. A hell-hole.

She spread her hands for emphasis. 'Can you believe it?' she said, a sort of flamboyant bitterness drenching her voice. 'They were Jews, for Christ's sake. Left-wing Jews. This place. It was staffed by brigade of bloody sadists. Celibate imports in long black frocks. Spare the rod and spoil the child. And there was my darling brother – a fat, dozy little Jewish boy with pebble specs and a lisp. Un-physical, Chrissie. Terrified of cold water. Never could catch a ball. Worst of all, he was brainy as hell. It's my belief they loathed him for it.'

Judith stood there as Christina watched, transfixed – a tall, stunning figure of great, troubled beauty. Yet suddenly, having tormented herself with the exhumation of this macabre, appalling vignette, Judith abruptly resumed her bright, brittle manner.

'A serious case of nature imitating the sick joke,' she said.
'You'll know that joke, of course, Chrissie? About Goldberg
and the Catholic school?'

Christina shook her head. She did not feel much in the mood
for jokes, whether sick or otherwise. She swallowed against a
sudden surge of nausea as the contemplation of Judith's
disclosures began to interact with the lingering, faint odour of
meat that still hung upon the air. She began quite suddenly to
panic at the idea that her own dear sister could possibly have
come to grief without her knowing. She resolved to make a
telephone call just as soon as she possibly could. Or did she dare?

Judith's joke had something to do with Goldberg minor
being in need of discipline and the Catholic school having a
boy nailed up to the classroom wall.

'Yeah,' Christina said, sighing heavily. 'Listen, Judith. I
suppose I ought to go. I – I suppose I –'

'You and your sister very close?' Judith said, catching her
unawares.

Christina wiped the back of her hand briefly across her eyes.
Playing for time, she contrived a small cough. 'I guess,' she
said. 'Well, yes. We were sort of like each other's best friend.
See, we were born seven months apart. She was adopted and I
was premature.'

'Chrissie,' Judith said. 'My God. The *older* sister and
adopted, eh? Well, then, it's hardly any wonder that she was
always so sweet and good. She'll have felt her presence in the
family to have been conditional upon perfection.'

Christina stared at Judith, thinking her quite mad.

'You, Chrissie dear, were the lucky one,' Judith said. 'You
were the natural child. You were the one who enjoyed the
licence to be as imperfect as you liked. Besides, by your mere existence, you will have destroyed your sister's *raison d'être*.' When
Christina failed to respond to this, Judith continued all the
same. 'Happens all the time,' she said. 'People adopt a baby.

249

They've no sooner done so than the natural child comes along. They stop trying quite so hard and it facilitates conception. Well, the poor parents are only human. They like the natural child better – much as they may strive against such a disconcerting emotion. They try too hard from then on to do it all perfectly right. Ace parents. Number One Dad. Four-star Mum. They play Happy Families. But it isn't natural, of course. The anxiety is there and the children pick it up – some to play goodie-goodie and some to make trouble. No need to ask which kind you are. Who said families were supposed to be happy? Christ, Chrissie, they are something to be endured, I tell you. Survived if at all possible. And haven't I just illustrated for you that it can be a fight to the death?'

Christina felt more drained than she could ever remember feeling before.

'By the way,' Judith said. She spoke quietly, for once. 'There's no way that you were premature.'

Judith, Christina noticed, was looking at her hard. Not so much at her face but at her cranium; at her whole person from top to toe. Christina sat, transfixed, under Judith's gaze and scrutiny.

'I'm speaking, now, as a medic,' Judith said. 'I really do know what I'm talking about. The shape of your head; your body proportions. Everything dictates against it.'

Christina continued to sit without moving, though she felt her pulse-rate suddenly accelerate. She wondered whether Judith was quite aware of the significance of what she was saying. And was there possibly anything else that Judith was preparing to throw at her?

'That's got to be rubbish,' Christina said. 'My parents only met each other seven months before I was born.'

'Oh dear,' Judith said. 'Oh dear oh dear.' And then they both fell silent.

PART V
Landing

Set Notation and the Holy Trinity

Christina made it for five o'clock. She'd changed trains in London. From the station she took a taxi. She thought speed was of the essence. The weather had deteriorated and it was now raining heavily. Her mind was so preoccupied that it was only as the car wound through the preambling woodland of Roland's school, that she started to an awareness of the driver's conversation.

'You can call me old-fashioned if you like,' he was saying, 'but I don't approve of mixed relationships.'

'Uh-huh,' Christina said, thinking this a novel point of view.

'It's the children I feel sorry for,' he said.

'Which children?' Christina said, puzzled.

'Like what are they then, eh?' he said. 'What are they?'

Christina hesitated, doubtful.

'Are they children?' she ventured.

'Yeah,' the driver said. 'But what are they? Are they black or white?'

'Oh, I *see*,' Christina said. 'Mixed relationships. Black and white. Right. Now I'm with you. I thought you meant men and women.'

She reflected that for her paternal grandmother a mixed relationship had always meant getting it together with a Protestant. For her mother's generation it had meant getting it together with a black person. But that too was now old hat. A mixed relationship for someone as young as the taxi driver ought surely to mean getting it together with someone of the opposite sex.

'You taking the mick?' said the taxi driver, and he swung through the school gate, determined to make no compromise

253

with the series of speed-retarding humps. He stopped outside the main entrance.

'You one of "them"?' he said. 'That'll be two pounds, thirty-five.'

Christina made a dash for the main entrance of the school. Apprehension, combined with the heavy rain, and the taxi driver's bigotry, and the absence of food since Judith's lime-green jelly, and the stresses of the afternoon, was doing something unfamiliar to her supply of oxygenated blood as she deftly skirted the secretary's office and made her way to the maths block. She was lucky in that, though the hour was five, Roland was still there tutoring additional maths. All Saints' Day had come and gone, and once again the mock exams were looming. Through the windows that gave on to the corridor, Alice could see that on the blackboard Roland had drawn the Trinity. Mrs del Nevo's Trinity. Three intersecting circles were there before her eyes, though Roland had not coloured the overlapping centres in gold. He had denoted, instead, the various areas of intersect by a code of differentiated stripes, and underneath he had written a column of set notation. The image was one that inspired Christina and provided her with insight.

'I'm giving up English literature,' she said to herself inside her head. 'What I must do is switch to maths.' She thanked the Trinity for its help and she advanced upon the classroom door. Roland paused mid-sentence. He was holding chalk in his hand.

'Christina,' he said. 'Good Lord. Whatever are you doing here?'

Christina spoke as boldly as she could. 'I've come to see you,' she said, 'on an important personal matter.'

'Ah', Roland said, and he glanced at his watch. It was a tribute to his considerable control that the children, who were grinning and nudging among themselves, were doing so under cover.

'Take a seat, Christina,' Roland said. 'I'm sure it can wait five minutes.'

Christina stood there, dripping. She was making a pool, like

Jeremy Fisher. The oxygenated blood was now coursing through her head.

'It's been waiting for nineteen years,' she said. 'I've come to tell you that I know you are my father.'

In Roland's bathroom, to which he had directed her, she took a bath and washed her hair. Then she put on a pair of Peter's old jeans along with one of Peter's sweaters and a pair of Peter's socks. When she emerged into the living-room she saw that Roland had made a wood fire. A log was glowing and cracking in the grate, sending up small firework showers, bright in the darkened room. Two large bowls of soup were waiting and a few rough chunks of bread. Gentille and the girls were mercifully not there. Gentille, it seemed, had business abroad and on the way she was visiting Roland's sister, so that the girls could have time with their cousins.

'I hope this soup has not got "bits" in it,' Christina said. 'Chicken entrails and things like that.'

Roland peered, unoffended, into the bowls. 'It's leek and potato, I would imagine,' he said. 'My wife made it before she left.'

'I never liked your wife,' Christina said. And then they ate their soup and bread in silence.

Finally Roland put down his bowl and coughed and began politely: 'If you are sitting comfortably, there are things that I need to explain. My dear, I was very much in love with your mother, I was very determined to marry her, so much so that I could not see that the feeling was all one-way. She had kept me most effectively at a distance – a thing I attributed to her shyness. She was very shy, you know, and she had a bad stammer.' He paused, looking rather rueful, 'That is, she stammered with me,' he said. Then he looked straight into her eyes. 'I never made it with your mother, Christina, much as I longed to and stubbornly believed that I would. Ours was not a friendship that was ever sexually consummated.'

Christina sat silent, staring into her empty bowl. The soup

had had no leeks in it, it was just that Roland couldn't tell. It tasted divinely of fresh potatoes, but the other tastes were more those of wild mushrooms and wild sorrel. She found now that her eyes had begun to drip compromising tears on to the empty surface of the bowl.

'I don't believe you,' she said. 'Grown-ups lie. They lie all the time. There's nothing that is what it seems.'

Then Roland told her, as lightly as he could, the story of his unsuccessful propositioning of her mother on the bridge in Northumberland. He told her how her mother had panicked, and rather than have him make love to her had swung the wheel of his beautiful old Citroën so that it crashed over the parapet of a bridge and landed them both in the river. He went on to tell her how, after duly administering first aid to her mother, he had commandeered a man, a personable young Geordie who had been driving a small white van at the time which had coincided with them on the bridge.

'He drove us to the hospital,' Roland said. 'He was local, and thank God he knew the way. Your mother was concussed, you see, and she had several fractured ribs. I confess I did not hang about much after that. I may have been tenacious, Christina, but I had a degree of pride. I stayed only to get my arm bandaged up and to assure myself that your mother was all right. After that I contacted your grandparents, and I said my goodbyes and I left.

'We coincided only once more after that occasion. It was very briefly and entirely by accident in the house of your mother's Oxford landlord. I was giving some extra coaching to one of the children of the family. It was some months after the accident. Your mother appeared with your father and also with her dead friend's baby: the baby, of course, was your sister.

'It is really not for me to say what had become of your mother in the interim. I know that she had gone home after the accident to recuperate in her parents' house, and that some

256

time towards the end of the summer she had coincided with your father. I did hear tell from your mother's landlord that she had for a brief time been engaged to marry the Geordie boy from the hospital. Some sort of science graduate student he was, as I remember – engineering, perhaps. She had taken time out after the accident and your grandparents were very fond of him. I was told that your grandfather had given him a little job – a part-time job, to do concurrently with his studies and help to make ends meet. Your grandfather, I believe, had also agreed to house him, rent-free, for the same reason.'

Christina sniffed and wiped her eyes. 'Mummy's Nice Young Man,' she said. 'Your Grampy let him live in it because we were all so fond of him.' She sniffed again and wiped her nose on the back of her hand. 'Fuckinell,' she said. 'And all the time I thought it was you.'

She looked up at Roland. 'Well, she *had* said he was "nice", Roland, and that he lived in a "very grand house". The Nice Young Man, she told me, had done "very well for himself".'

'Why, thank you, Christina,' Roland said. 'I'm flattered by the association. I'm sorry to tell you, however, that your grandmother never cared for me, nor did she regard teaching school as an up-and-coming career.'

Christina sighed. 'Yes,' she said, 'I can see now that that would be true. I don't know if it's any comfort to you, but she's always detested my father – that is to say, the man who has always chosen to mime that role in my life. Well, at least you weren't a show-off, Roland; nor were you a serious Catholic. So where do you suppose he is now, my father, the personable Geordie? Do you suppose he is engineering somewhere, or will he have taken a step sideways and joined the managerial class? I mean, what sort of person does well for himself? By my grandmother's lights, is what I mean.'

Roland smiled at her gently. 'Dear girl,' he said, 'is it possible that you could try not to let this prey upon your mind? I'm aware

257

of how things stand with you and your parents, but may I even in spite of that suggest that you talk this over with your mother?'

'What was he like?' Christina said. 'Come on, Roland, I want to know.'

Roland sighed. 'Oh, gosh,' he said. He was thinking to himself, 'On the make, little swine. Garrulous. Insinuating. Taking advantage of Alice's parents at the time when they were most vulnerable. God in heaven, I remember how I loathed the idea of the man.'

He was overcome suddenly with sadness as they sat there in the lamp-light. 'You will believe me when I say,' he said, 'I was rather preoccupied at the time. I had a half-drowned girl lying in my lap. I would say that he was "chippy", Christina. A cheerful type. Talkative.'

Christina eyed him suspiciously. 'He was a schmuck,' she said. 'Now I want you to tell me what he looked like.'

'Dark,' Roland said, 'and of medium height. What else can I say?'

'Any distinguishing marks?' Christina said.

Roland took the question seriously. He sat thoughtfully for a while. 'Most of the time,' he said, 'I could see the back of his head. He turned it to the left much of the time – he was throwing his voice to the back of the car. I do remember noticing a curious gristly bump on the lobe of his left ear.'

Christina held forth her lobe in triumph. 'My Born Lump,' she said. 'Do you remember his name?'

'Riley,' Roland said. 'That's one thing I do remember. His name was Matthew Riley.'

Christina got up. 'I must go,' she said, 'I've taken up your time for too long.'

In the car as he drove her to the station Christina spoke with remorse. 'I'm sorry,' she said, 'I embarrassed you in front of your pupils. That was pretty bad.'

'That's perfectly all right,' Roland said. 'I ought to be getting used to it by now. Your family does make a habit of bursting in on me.'

Christina looked up, she opened her eyes wide. 'Why?' she said. 'Has my father been in to duff you up?'

Roland acknowledged her terminology with a smile. 'He came by with your sister,' Roland said, 'almost three years ago now. There was a matter of some gravity that needed to be cleared up. As I remember, they seemed a little worried about your whereabouts. And if I may say so, I was worried about you myself.'

'Sorry,' Christina said again. 'Look, Roland, I scarpered. I haven't seen them since. I know all about the little "matter", by the way: it was because of that that I walked out. I had arranged for Pam to have a termination, you see. I'd sort of hoped to pull the wool over her eyes. I'd found this gynae bloke who was prepared to delude her. Well, anyway, it all went wrong. The parents turned up early – they walked into my grandmother's house two days before they were expected.'

'Blame me,' Roland said. 'I'd summoned them and with some difficulty. I believe – could I have been hearing correctly – that they'd been bicycling through the Western Highlands.'

'You heard correctly,' Christina said. 'Only by the time you got them they must have just about made it back as far as the New Forest. They appeared in a flash, clothed head to toe in lycra and with their favourite priest in tow.'

'I remember that I was concerned about Pam,' Roland said. 'I'd been alerted by her exam results and it did seem to me that she was becoming rather withdrawn.' He paused. 'I could tell that something was bothering her,' he said. 'I'm afraid I drew the conclusion that it might be a form of religious mania. She'd given up the singing, which worried Vanessa. It was the impression of one of my staff that she was not eating properly. I began to fear that she would fly off and take the veil.'

Christina made a sort of spluttery noise. 'So it's all right to get raped by some puking slob at sixteen and find yourself pregnant,' she said. 'Just so long as you don't go and "take the veil". Is that what being a Protestant can do for your brain?'

Roland did not respond to this. 'I had happened, the evening before your father and sister burst in,' he said, 'to have been talking to Vanessa. Once I'd expressed my anxieties to her, she remembered a rather strange letter – it was one your sister had written her on the evening of All Saints'. It mentioned the names of three of her classmates. Putting two and two together, I summoned them immediately. It took a little persuading to get your sister to confront them, but having once done so she was splendid. I wish you had been there to see her, Christina.'

Christina felt a knot form in her stomach. 'All Saints'?' she said. 'Hallowe'en? Three of them? Sort of dressed like cripples?'

'Why, yes,' Roland said.

'So which one of them was it?' she said. 'Stet Gregory, I'll bet. Or maybe it was all three.'

Roland sighed. 'That is something you are going to have to ask her yourself,' he said. 'Given that she did not wish to pursue the matter with the police.'

'And how about the fourth?' Christina said, sarcastic, tense. 'How about Jago Rutherford?'

'Well, this is where you might have helped, Christina,' Roland said, and he looked at her. 'Jago, when I called him in, had a perfect alibi. He had spent the evening sweet-talking you in a pub. You had been wearing a rather unusual mask. The publican remembered the two of you.'

Christina had become quite agitated. 'But that evening,' she said, 'that evening Jago *did* leave me – he was gone for ages and ages. And when he came back he seemed so – well – so different, so shaken. After that he was altogether changed; subdued. He gave up those smart-ass friends. He took up with me, do you remember? I was in a state of bliss about it. I thought he was in love with me. I had been in love with him for years.'

'Oh, my dear,' Roland said.

'I was wild about him,' Christina said. 'He was one of the very few people to whom I'd given my address, yet I never heard from him again.'

There was a longish silence. 'As to your sister's assailant,' Roland said, 'I think we established his identity beyond all possible doubt. Also that the party had numbered three. Three, Christina. Not four. It may be from what you've just told me that Jago Rutherford knew something more than he led me to believe at the time.'

He was silent again, for quite a while. 'I heard from your sister quite recently,' he said. 'The boy is almost two.'

'Boy?' Christina said.

'Your nephew,' Roland said. 'How silly of me. I ought to have shown you the photographs. She's gone back to school, as they say over there, and she's working hard at the singing.'

Then he said, 'But what about you, Christina? Tell me, what have you been doing with yourself since you ran from your grandmother's house?'

Christina shook herself slightly. 'I'd met this girl,' she said. 'Dulcie. I'd met her in the lavatory at the Barbican Theatre. She's great. She's the best. I went to live with her. Her mother helped me fix it so I could join her Sixth Form somewhere in Tottenham. Inner city comp – it was a heap really. It was great. I loved it. It was life. It was education, Roland.'

Roland was smiling a knowing sort of smile. 'I taught in Hackney for a time,' he said. 'When I was young. Well, it's certainly one sort of life, Christina. I'm not entirely sure that I'd go so far as to call it education.'

'It was great,' Christina repeated. 'You ought to try it again, Roland. I mean, why do you waste yourself teaching all these pampered snots?'

Roland laughed. 'Never mind me,' he said. 'I thought we were talking about you.'

'Oh, well,' she said. 'While I was there this geezer came along, you see. This sort of charley from Cambridge, touting for applicants for his college.'

'One of the dons?' Roland said.

'Yeah,' Christina said. 'Total weirdo. Worzel Gummidge sort of person.'

'Well?' Roland said.

'Well, four of us got sent to case the joint.'

'The "joint",' Roland said, 'being a Cambridge college?'

'Yeah,' Christina said again. 'And then they all dropped out, except me.'

Roland beamed at her suddenly with unqualified admiration. 'Can I take it, Christina,' he said, 'that you are in point of fact not a street child but a Cambridge undergraduate?'

'Sure thing,' Christina said, 'English literature. Only my supervisor has a problem. He's one of life's professional truants. I'll tell you something that's going to happen when I get back. I've got plans to switch to maths.'

'Really?' Roland said, sounding pleased.

'Yeah,' Christina said. 'I've got A-Level maths, why not? It didn't occur to me before today. It was only when I saw what you'd put up on the blackboard. I was peeking in through the windows and I saw that you'd drawn the Trinity.'

'The Trinity?' Roland said.

'Yeah,' Christina said. 'The Trinity. I'd been having problems with the Objective Correlative and then your Venn diagram swung me.'

At the barrier she hugged him and gave him a kiss on the cheek.

'I hope you're proud of me,' she said. 'I hope you wish you *were* my father.'

When Christina approached her room that night she was still wearing Peter's clothes. She entered the room and then she gasped, because right there lying on her bed was Peter, and he was fast asleep. To say that he was on her bed was not altogether accurate. Peter appeared to be suspended on a cushion of air above the bed. Christina blinked and stared at him. She removed her shoes, then, very cautiously, she approached the bed and peered at Peter from close up. She went on tiptoes all round the bed on its three accessible sides. It left her with not a shred of doubt that Peter's slight but less pale body was indeed raised horizontally some three centimetres above the covers. She sat down for a while to watch him. He was in all respects quite simply asleep. As she began to get used to his presence, it occurred to her that Peter would probably be cold. He was lying on top of the covers, after all, and his clothing was not of the warmest. She got up and reached for a pair of spare blankets that were stowed on the top of her cupboard. Then she opened them out with a shake. As she did so, Peter's nose twitched and he sneezed and blinked and sat up.

'*Salute*,' Christina said. 'I'm sorry. I made you sneeze. These blankets are very dusty.' She observed that as he emerged from sleep Peter's body had floated gently, unobtrusively downwards until it was resting on the mattress.

'Chris,' he said, and he yawned. 'Forgive me. I came to see you. I must have fallen asleep. Crumbs. It's completely dark outside. What a comfortable bed you have – it feels like sleeping on air.'

'Peter,' Christina began cautiously, and she wondered quite how to go on, but Peter was prodding the mattress.

'Oh, fiddlesticks!' he said. 'Oh, fimblefowl! Don't tell me – I've been floating, haven't I?'

'Levitating,' Christina said. 'That's what it's called when saints do it.'

Peter laughed. 'I spent a long time thinking it was some weird form of epileptic seizure,' he said. 'Now I know it's just plain weird. I've always been considered weird, as you will remember, of course. I've only recently stopped letting it bother me.'

'But the floating,' Christina said. 'That's quite a trick. Peter, it's a gift. It's a privilege. You don't sound properly impressed.'

Peter laughed again. 'As gifts go, one might have preferred something else,' he said. 'Maybe to paint like Tiepolo. Air and angels. Heavenly skies. But yes, what the hell, it has its moments.'

He held out his arms to her in friendly invitation. 'How are you, dearest Chris?' he said. 'Come here. I've been longing to see you.'

Christina moved over and went to him. They hugged each other warmly. They were so curiously the same size, the same colour. They could have twinned at a birth. She was intrigued by how much she loved to have him there, even at the end of such a day.

'I went to see your step-father,' she said. 'And now I'm wearing your jeans.'

'So I see,' Peter said. 'From the M & S children's department. Let it never be said that the parents have had to fork out for VAT on my clothes.'

'So how did you get in?' she said. 'Or do you glide through locked doors?'

'Some woman let me in,' Peter said. 'Bustling type. She

produced a master key – and, before I forget, she's left you a message.' He indicated a yellow Post-It that was stuck to the glass over the wash basin. It had on it the silhouette of a black telephone and it requested, after stating date and time, that Christina feed the neutered beige feline on Saturday and on Sunday, since 'Judy' (as she had written) had not yet returned as expected.

'Fiona,' Christina said. 'She's the college secretary.'

'She's left me her house keys for you,' Peter said. 'I have such an honest face.'

'Peter,' Christina said firmly, 'you have an angel's face. I've always thought so from that first day we met. You look as if you should be playing a mandolin in the snow at the Nativity. None of those angels quite touches the ground either. Does it happen to you when you're standing up?'

Peter nodded modestly. 'But keep it under your hat,' he said. 'Please, dear Chris. I'd be obliged.'

'So where have you been?' she said. 'Where have you come from?' And to herself she thought, who is this marvellous boy, this strange and levitating boy, this boy who is not Prince Hamlet – no, nor was meant to be – he is the attendant lord, and how appropriately he has grown and grown in stature as the others have fallen around him.

'Are you going to tell me your story?' she said.

'You first,' Peter said. 'Please. Go on.'

So Christina, as quickly as possible to get it out of the way, told him about her parents, and about the lycra suits, and about the flight from her grandmother's house, and about Dulcie and the comp, and the Cambridge don, and about Hugo recumbent and Judith perpendicular, and about her most recent mission to Peter's step-father in search of the Nice Young Man who was in fact someone quite other, some schmuck who had done very well for himself and who was probably a wizard with money. She told him about her

265

realization, when face to face with the Trinity in competition with the Objective Correlative, that the way forward was to initiate an immediate switch to maths.

'Now you,' Christina said. 'What's your story, and where have you come from?'

'Most immediately I've come from the dog pound,' Peter said. 'I've been visiting Serious Syrius. That's the Star Dog Two. I brought her back with me from Africa. The Star Dog has changed its gender and acquired much longer legs. She's a mottled yellowy mongrel bitch with a snarl and saggy dugs. She's quite the best little dog in all of history, or perhaps the second best.'

Then he said nothing for a moment. He sat in silence, looking mysterious. 'Chris,' he said, 'after Pam wouldn't talk to me and then she disappeared and so did you, and Jago was in a filthy temper all the time, well, I couldn't see much point to the place. I kept on trying to tell myself, "Go on, enjoy it. Stet and company have left." They'd been chucked out, you see. Sent down with swift dispatch. In the end I stayed to do my GCSE exams and then I went to teach in Uganda. God in heaven, Chris,' he said. 'This place where I went –' He stopped, he sighed. 'I used to meet up with a couple of old priests who talked about it from before. Before Amin, and the war, and the child soldiers, and AIDS, and God knows what.'

He paused again. 'I'd be teaching these people. Lovely people. I'd be taking this class and they'd be any age – say, from twelve to forty – and they'd be leaving the classroom every day to bury the dead. It's all around. They're leaving the school aged twelve and thirteen to go off and head their households. The parents are dead, you see. The children take over and run the farms. There are twelve-year-old farmers drudging through the day to support the infants and the elderly. It's become a society of orphans. Anyway, my story is that in the midst of it I had a rich time. I went there a clueless, unhappy schoolboy with very little to give. I gave what I could and what I got back was – I don't know – infinity.'

'And a dog,' Christina said. 'Why have you come back at all, by the way?'

Peter looked a little sheepish. 'It's silly,' he said, 'but I'd promised the parents when I left that I'd come back and go to university. I did my A-Levels in Africa. There's this outfit. Correspondence outfit. They ship all these course notes to Africa from a Gothic villa in North Oxford. In short, I passed. I did pretty well. Much better than I would have done had I stayed at school. The old priests flung a lot of books my way. It was an extraordinary way to learn. Midnight oil if I was lucky. Otherwise rising at dawn.'

'Tell me about the floatiness,' Christina said. 'Did you learn to float in Uganda?'

'God, no,' Peter said. 'No, that's an affliction that's been with me for years. Discretion is in my nature, Chris. I always kept it under wraps. Pam knew, but I'm proud to say that I never embarrassed her with it in public. There's a couple of other weird things, however, that I only found out about in Africa.'

'Like what?' Christina said.

Peter pulled a face. 'This is embarrassing,' he said. 'For instance, in the school where I taught there was this headmaster. He was mad, as in stark, staring bonkers. Trouble is, people kept dying, you see. Competent people. And sometimes there was nobody half-way decent left to take over. So, in short, the new headmaster was mad. He believed in beating the pupils incessantly. The atmosphere was so fraught that the women students frequently became hysterical.' He paused. 'Possessed, I suppose. You know. Like that man in the Gospel. In the cemetery. "My name is Legion for we number many thousands". Anyway, so the headmaster is always beating people. Girl students are rushing into the fields in hysterics.

It's catchy. The Head rushes out after them, wielding his cane like the Furies to left and right.' He paused. 'I'm talking too much,' he said. 'I'm high. Am I too high? I mean, metaphorically speaking.'

'You're great,' Christina said. 'Carry on.'

'So one evening I'm telling one of the old priests,' Peter said, 'I'm telling him about a particularly hairy incident that day. He says to me, in all seriousness, I must wade in and put a stop to it. I think he's as mad as the Head, of course. I tell him so at once. "Go in there, boy, and stop the man," he says. "Go on. I'll pray for you."'

'And?' Christina said.

'Well,' Peter said modestly, 'I waded in and I stopped him. Funny thing was I did nothing. I touched the headmaster on the shoulders with my hands, that was all. Then I touched a couple of the women. After a while I realized it was enough for me merely to raise my hands and hold them over the crowd.'

'Peter,' Christina said, deeply impressed. 'Hey! Are we talking once or often?'

'Well,' Peter said shyly. 'I'm afraid it was all the time. I feel that I'm blushing, talking about it like this. Well, you know how reticent I am. The worst is I'm not even religious. I used to pretend that I was just to please Roland's father. Also just a little to please your sister.'

'Peter,' Christina said, 'I think it highly probable that you are a very holy person. I think it very likely that even the Queen will come to pay homage to you.'

'Really?' Peter said. He laughed. 'If only I'd known about it earlier,' he said. 'Could it have given me any power over Stetson Gregory? That swine who came along and stole my lovely Jago?'

'If we could keep off Jago,' Christina said. 'Tell me about your dog.'

'Oh, the dog,' Peter said. 'She adopted me. Someone must have drowned all her puppies. She walked in on me one day with horribly swollen teats. I helped her to express some of her milk.'

Christina gawped at him. 'How?' she said.

'With my mouth,' he said. 'How else? Then about a week before I was due to come home she began to hide my shoes. It dawned on me why she was doing it. She could read the signs of my departure. She knew that I couldn't leave the house without my shoes, you see. In those parts you can't walk about barefoot. You get hookworm. It's a parasite that burrows into the soles of your feet. It causes chronic anaemia. I thought, "She's saying we were meant for each other, and she's right." So I got my step-father on to the airline company to fix it for her to come back. Now she's got to be in quarantine for six months. Well, five. She's had one month already. She's been in prison here, while I've been travelling in France.'

'In France?' Christina said.

'Yes,' Peter said. 'In France. Well, I am French, remember? Oh, Chrissie, be happy for me. Will you believe me if I tell you that something wonderful has happened to me in France?'

'Probably,' Christina said. 'Tell.'

'Well,' Peter said. 'Back to the floating. I have recently begun to wonder whether it could have something to do with the stars. You see, as you know perhaps, I used to live alone with my mother in Paris. *J'ai habité une fois à Paris.*'

'Pardon me?' Christina said. 'I never learnt to speak that language.'

'Ah well,' Peter said, 'I lived in a skyloft in St-Germain. I was often alone. I day-dreamed out of the window. I relished the stars, not quite as my friends, but I relished their isolation. Then my mother's marriage to Roland – well, it was quite dreadful, I remember. It was like being ripped from my necessary element.'

'Untimely ripped,' Christina said. 'Yes, how awful for you.'

'It was as though the gases in the air were different. Not the ones I needed to breathe. I've always felt like that, all my life, Chris, not quite properly adapted. Then Jago made friends with me when I was eight. For five years he sort of bound me to the earth. Then, after Jago, I was lucky. I found your sister. She picked me up like a wounded bird. And then, after she vanished – well – there was Africa.'

'Maybe I love you,' Christina said. 'Or are you much too flaky?'

Peter spread his hands. 'It's so wonderful not to be afraid of you,' he said. 'I was always rather frightened by your confidence, by your sharpness, but now after France I'm afraid of nothing.'

'Well, get on with it,' Christina said. 'What is it about France?'

'I went there,' Peter said, 'to find out who I was. I started from the skyloft off the Rue du Bac, and then I combed the place. I kept criss-crossing the country on the TGV.'

'What's the *tayjayvay*?' Christina said. 'Is that proper French?'

'It's the railway,' Peter said. 'I found the house of my Polish grandmother, with a rusted lock-up shop on the ground floor.'

'Polish?' Christina said. 'Well, never mind Polish. Let her pass. Can we please come to the good bit?'

'Well,' Peter said, 'I went south. Way beyond Toulouse. Near the Spanish border. I was pretty tired by then. I walked and walked. I think I was in a trance. I must have forgotten to eat. I remember that I felt rather floaty.'

'"Hieronymo's mad againe",' Christina said. 'Please go on.'

Peter went on. 'I don't remember falling asleep,' he said. 'But when I woke I was lying in a vineyard and there was Jago. He was leaning over me. He was talking to me in French.'

'A porno dream,' Christina said. 'You were having a faggy porno dream about Jago. I don't think I want to hear this.'

'No,' Peter said. 'No, it wasn't Jago. The point is it was Jago's twin brother.'

'Twin brother?' Christina said.

'Yes,' Peter said. 'They'd got separated as infants. Doesn't that happen somewhere in Shakespeare?'

Christina pulled a face. 'All the time,' she said. 'What a cliché. Maybe that's what Jago is. A cliché.'

'His name is Victor,' Peter said. 'And he's the love of my life.'

'A boy?' Christina said, feeling a little crestfallen. 'So don't you believe in mixed relationships?'

'Dearest,' Peter said. 'I've brought him back with me to Cambridge. I've left him with Jago for the moment, so that they can be reunited. I want you to be happy for me.'

'I'm happy for you,' Christina said. 'Maybe I'm a bit sad for myself.'

Peter kissed her cheek. 'Jago is desperate to see you, by the way,' he said. 'He's been sweetening you up, he tells me, by writing you silly letters.'

'What?' Christina said.

'He's been writing to you,' Peter said. 'Leaving messages for you in your bicycle basket. He's written them with his left hand in order to conceal his identity. He's all remorse, you see. He says he treated you very badly.'

'And so he did,' she said. 'The swine.'

'He hid behind you,' Peter said, 'in order to distance himself from your sister's assailants. But it was not as cynical as you think. He saw your sister being raped – that is, he witnessed a rape in the woods. Once he'd found out it was your sister – well, he clung to you in the aftermath – not in order to make use of you. I think you seemed somehow spiritually close to her.'

He paused, then he said, 'I'm afraid he loves your sister madly, and all the while he was tormented.'

'Thanks,' Christina said. 'This gets better and better.'

'I spoke to your sister on the phone yesterday,' Peter said. 'I've arranged for us to meet her in a café.'

'When?' Christina said. 'Where?'

'In ten minutes,' Peter said. 'Round the corner. You won't pull out on me, will you? Chris, you wouldn't dare.'

In the pizza joint where Pam was waiting Christina embraced her sister.

'Oh, Pam,' she said. 'Oh, Pam.' The boy was dark-haired and olive-skinned, and he slept beside his mother in a stroller. Pam looked thinner and older. Her clothes were much the same.

'So you *were* pregnant?' Christina said, trying her hand at irony.

'Of course I was,' Pam said. 'Can you forgive me, Chrissie? I put you to all that trouble and expense when the whole thing so went against my nature.'

Peter meanwhile had addressed the waiter. 'Four seasons,' he said. 'Bring us a big one to share between us. And a bottle of house red, please.'

'How's our mother?' Christina said awkwardly. 'How are the oldies, then?'

Quite a lot, it seemed, had changed. 'Mama walked out pretty well when you did,' Pam said. 'I was left sort of high and dry between them.'

'*What?*' Christina said.

'Look,' Pam said, 'both of them loved me; heaped care and attention on me. It was just a bit like being one of those little joint-custody kids. I had a bedroom in each of their apartments. I was expected to shuttle between them. Now Mama has come back to England.'

Christina gawped at her but said nothing. She left Pam to go on.

'There had always been all that emphasis on how I had

brought them together,' Pam said. 'Quite a burden for me, incidentally. But Chrissie, it was you who had held them together. Once you'd gone Mama saw no reason to stay. She shipped out almost immediately and turned herself into somebody else. She gave up her teaching and became a book-keeper. Right now she's retraining as an accountant. She gave up the Church and became an agnostic. In short, she got a new job, new apartment, new friends, new furniture, new beliefs. Or perhaps they were just all the old ones but they'd been lying there dormant for years.'

'Pam,' Chrissie said earnestly. 'Why did nobody tell me all this?'

'Because,' Pam said. 'You had made it pretty clear that if we did you would stop communicating with us and we'd lose touch with you altogether.'

Then she said, 'The air was poison between them. Papa was sure that she'd taken a lover – I had to stop him from setting spies on her. She suspected him of laying siege to me for the sake of the male grandchild. I'd had to have some tests, you see, for reasons that I won't go into. They'd happened to reveal that Bruno was male. In the midst of it all I fled, Chrissie – for a few months, anyway. It was mean of me but that's what I did.'

What Pam had done, as she now explained, was to come to England and find the hospital where her natural mother had died. She had given birth to little Bruno with the assistance of an elderly nun who had nursed her dying mother. It had been very good for her, she said, to get an accurate picture of her mother.

'The problem for me, Chrissie,' Pam said, 'was always that, because Mama had been so besotted with my mother, she was never in a position to give me any accurate idea. My mother had been larger than life for her. My mother was Wonder Woman. I also found out that they stole me, by the way. Papa, did so, at any rate.'

'*What?*' Christina said.

The hospital, Pam explained, had already begun discussion with her mother before she died. The process of having the baby adopted had already been talked over. Nobody had mentioned her old schoolfriend, Alice, who was, after all, not even a Catholic. Then suddenly on the day that she died, Joe had 'found' a letter, signed by the dead woman.

'He said that he'd found it in her locker,' Pam said. 'In among her effects.' She paused. 'Well,' she said, 'when I went back home I searched for it, naturally, and I found it. For anyone who is as familiar as I am with Papa's handwriting, the letter is not bad, but he's faked it.'

She looked Christina in the eye. 'I don't mind,' she said. 'I want you to know that. It's what I have tried to assure him. In fact, I'm rather pleased, now, that he went to all that trouble. Well, it *was* a terrific childhood we had, wasn't it, Chrissie? All that love and richness; all that Venice and Paris and singing lessons and birthday treats. I've found my real father, by the way – or, rather, the Sally Army found him. He's a mechanic in Rome. He's perfectly nice.'

Christina picked up on Pam's modified tone. 'But he watches TV in his undershirt?' she said. 'I'm on the way to finding mine, by the way. I believe that he's a Geordie schmuck with a Born Lump like mine. Bloody hell, though, why did he do it, Pam? Why did he go to all that trouble?'

'Because he's infertile,' Pam said. 'Haven't you always known that? It's people like you, Chrissie, who talk so much, you never notice anything. I want you to be nice to him, by the way. He's gotten kind of old. He has the gout.'

Christina at this point burst out laughing. '*Gout?*' she said. 'People don't get gout. Not in the twentieth century.' The sound of her laughter caused her sister's baby to stir and open his eyes. She became aware suddenly that Pam's two-year-old son was staring at her, unblinking, through large, velvety brown eyes. 'Hello,' she said. 'I'm the aunt. I tried to put a stop to you.'

Jago and Victor had spent the evening falling over each other. They had encountered a problem with simultaneous move-ment. Each would begin by giving way to the other, after which both would step forward in unison. It happened yet again as they entered the pizza joint, which was blessed with revolving doors. The upshot was that Jago and his brother, tightly wedged together in a segment intended for one, found themselves rotating twice.

'Bloody hell,'
'*Sacré bleu,*' they said.

Jago on the first rotation saw that Pam was sitting very upright on one of those very shiny cheap pine chairs that has its legs screwed to the floor, and that the child was in her lap reaching out for pizza. Behind her, over her head, was a photographic blow-up of Cornetto-ad palazzi. Pam was flanked by Peter and Christina, whom he perceived now as his two redeeming angels. As he rotated for the second time, Jago's mind engaged once again with those two lines of verse that had taunted him in the art room, three years earlier.

> That the topless towers be burnt
> And men recall that face –

And suddenly, out loud, he said, 'Yeats!' and his brother Victor said, '*Qu'est-ce que c'est que ça?*' to which he gave no answer, though he remembered that the verse went on with an exhortation to move gently in the holy place, and he thought with wonder that he was just about to cross that wide, unbridgeable plain in the form of the pizza joint's patterned vinyl floor. And with that they tumbled out through the revolving doors and crossed to where the party sat.

What Christina saw was two Jagos and that both were

276

dressed in black. Both wore their hair close-cropped, almost shaved, and both were astonishingly beautiful. The two Jagos came to a stop in front of the table.

'This is my brother from France,' *'Je suis le frère qui vient de France,'* they said.

They paused and looked at each other. Then they looked back at the company.

'His name is Victor,' 'We lost each other long ago.' they said.

'Je m'appelle Victor,' *'Nous nous sommes perdus il y a longtemps.*

Christina swallowed hard. Then she held out her hand. The two Jagos hesitated before their hands crashed together along the flight path towards her grasp. Afterwards they repeated the routine with Pam. Then they sat down. Jago seated himself beside Christina, Victor alongside Peter.

Jago withdrew a key from his trouser pocket and placed it on the table in front of Christina. 'I'm sorry,' he said, 'I took advantage of you. I'd happened to notice that your padlock was the one from the gardener's wheelbarrow.'

'Chris is a thrifty soul,' Peter said. 'She has become a most efficient recycler.'

'God in heaven,' Christina said. 'Well, of course.' And she rapped her knuckles against her head. She was staring with interest at Jago and deciding that she did not want him; that Jago Rutherford belonged to her salad days when she was green in reason.

Jago meanwhile had turned to Pam. He had been scrutinizing the baby. 'He likes pizza,' he said.

'Yes,' Pam said.

'He looks like you,' Jago said.

'Yes,' Pam said.

'Well, God be praised,' Christina said, 'that he doesn't look like Stetson Gregory.'

The remark was a shock, and it silenced them. Jago looked at his feet. When he looked up, he fixed his eyes firmly upon Pam.

'Pam,' he said, 'I love you. I loved you then. I have always loved you. I have loved you since before the world began.'

'I think I'm going to be sick,' Christina said. 'Peter, can you shut him up, please?'

'I love you too,' Pam said. 'Jago, I always have. I have loved you from the first moment I met you.'

Christina dropped her fork. 'Oh, puke,' she said. 'Oh, Peter, stop them.' Then she said, 'This is degenerating and I have work to do.' She got up.

'Dearest,' Peter said, 'before you go, may I ask you a little favour? May Victor and I please sleep on your floor? That's just for tonight, I mean.'

Christina glanced uncertainly at Pam. 'But what about Pam and the baby?' she said. 'Aren't you staying over, Pam?'

The four of them looked at each other. She felt suddenly terribly naive.

'Pam will come with me,'   'Of course.'
                  Jago and Victor said.
'*Pam ira avec mon frère*,'   '*Naturellement.*'
'Of course,' Peter said.
'I'll go with Jago,' Pam said.

'Of course,' Christina said. 'Well, don't any of you worry about me. I've got the secretary's house keys. I'll sleep over at Fiona's. Peter and Victor can have my bed. I'll double up with the feline eunuch.'

'Dearest,' Peter said. 'Chris, how all of us love you. I say, over Christmas – when I'm away in France with Victor – will you please visit my dog?'

Fiona Campbell's was the top-floor flat in a three-storey Victorian brick villa. It was no more than two streets away from where Judith and Hugo lived. The key in Christina's possession was labelled 'back door', which meant access was through the garden. Fiona's back door was approached picturesquely but somewhat hazardously via a Victorian cast-iron fire-escape staircase that spiralled up the full height of the back exterior wall. Christina made her way through the garden in almost complete darkness. One gently lit upper window was throwing a parallelogram of light on to the end of the communal lawn. She groped her way with difficulty to the treads of the iron staircase. Up and up and up she went, until finally she came level with the top.

It was then that it occurred to her that the light was coming from Fiona Campbell's bedroom. The back sash-windows of the house had been replaced by larger panels of plate glass which came almost to the floor. Fiona had curtained these panels of glass with fine undyed muslin. As Christina stood on the upper platform, her heart leapt into her mouth. She saw through the curtain that the room was occupied by two female figures, and that the effect, through muslin and muted light, was to cast the figures in silhouette in a kind of shadow-theatre. The shadow-women were slim and lovely. One was tall and one was short. The tall shadow-woman was unzipping the garment of the smaller shadow-woman, so that the garment soon fell to the floor. The smaller shadow-woman stepped from it and half turned towards the other, then the taller shadow-woman stretched forth a long, slim shadow-arm with its curving shadow-hand like an opening lotus flower. She placed the hand on the cheek of the smaller shadow-woman and they moved closer towards each other until their shadow-bodies met and they held each other, merged in a sort of partial eclipse.

It was beautiful, Christina thought, quite lovely, like a strange, slow dance. She leaned sideways to press her nose to the pane and saw then that Judith Levin, in a narrow, knitted tube of a dress reaching almost to her stockinged feet, had bent her head to kiss the blonde hair of the smaller woman, who wore a one-piece moss-green under-tunic like an Edwardian male bathing suit. They they kissed each other on the mouth. At the same time Judith ran her hands down the line of the smaller shadow-woman's body, down the slope of her shoulders, down the line of her torso, down the curve of her slight, slender hips. Then the smaller woman turned her head to the window and Christina saw that the woman was none other than her own mother. Alice, seeing the figure at the window, tensed and clutched at Judith and screamed. Christina gasped and stepped backwards, and lost her balance and fell through the air.

Insects and Oedipus

When Christina came round in hospital it was like being on a carousel that was coming very gradually to a stop. Even before she opened her eyes she knew that Judith and her mother were still there and that one of her legs appeared to be encased, from mid-thigh to ankle, in a concrete sewer pipe.

'Insects,' Judith was saying. 'Not only murder but insects. So now you know everything about me.'

'Judy,' Alice said, 'stop doing this to me. Stop doing it to yourself. In the first case, you were a ten-year-old child and the thing was an accident. In the second, you were a confused adolescent who was fooling about with drugs. That was the norm not the exception at the time. Anyway, it's history. Now is now. Dear one, look at your strengths. You are magnificent.'

'I was nineteen, for Christ's sake,' Judith said, 'I was already a medical student. I have told this to nobody but you, by the way, absolutely nobody. And now I suppose you'll go running back to that bald shit of a husband. That's what you'll do, I know it.'

'Judy,' Alice said, 'please don't. In the first place he's not a shit, you know, and in the second you can't know what I will do because I do not know myself.'

'But I know,' Judith said. 'And that's because you, my love, are a wimp and I am a Machiavel.'

Then they were quiet for quite a long time and during the pause Christina dreamed. She dreamed again that mime sequence of the two beautiful women, like ballet dancers, their shadow-limbs curving like pliant plant stems, like swan's

281

necks, like silk, like lilies so white they were almost green.

'The catatonic Scotsman has absolutely no idea,' Judith was saying. 'He has no more idea than my dear brother.'

'You seem very sure,' Alice said.

Judith spoke with her usual assurance. 'Dear one,' she said, 'the boy was stoned. I'm telling you, he knew nothing. The very next week he announced his conversion. Picture it, if you will. Rosh Hashanah. Even in my memory the incident pales in the bigger splash. Parents freaking on all sides. The boy hates his mother. He wants to kill his mother. My son the Jesuit. Oedipus Schmoedipus. Jesus Christ. The boy will nail his parents to the wall.'

It was then that Christina's brain began to talk inside her head. Insects, Oedipus. Oedipus, insects. Insects, Oedipus – *Holy Mary, Mother of God* – Oedipus, *incest!* And could it be that Judith's brother was none other than the fat priest? Zak Levine Zachariah. The penultimate book of the Old Testament.

'And ever since,' Judith said, 'there has been, for my sins, the catatonic Scotsman and his sister Fiona. Oh, Alice, my dear Alice, can I say in mitigation that when I married him he was, at least, divinely beautiful.'

'Judy,' Alice said, 'it's late. Don't you need to get some sleep?'

'He was really clever, you know, once upon a time,' Judith said, in that snotty, irrelevant sort of way. In that stupid, public-schoolish, smart-arse way. And he wanted me well enough. I had some idea that he would "do", you know, and I didn't have that much time. One had these ideas – this pathetic idea – that men were necessary to the raising of children. Were we as mad as hatters, Alice, that we should have thought like that?'

'Probably,' Christina heard her mother say. 'Don't ask me, Judy. What do I know?'

'I was so certain,' Judith went on, 'that I could turn him

into something that would suit me. And look at him, after my efforts. What is he now? Mr Volpone? A blob in the custody of his sister and his wife? The kilted bridegroom? The young Lochinvar? He has become ever more emotionally paralysed and recumbent. That's almost exclusively thanks to my managerial influence.'

'Ground elder,' Christina mumbled. 'In the garden.'

Her mother bent an ear to her, anxiously. 'My angel,' she said. 'Chrissie dear –'

'Down-a-down,' Christina said. 'The unweeded garden. Everything goes down. But not Peter.'

'Peter?' Alice said.

'Horatio,' Christina said. 'And flights of angels hymn thee to thy rest.'

'She's delirious,' Judith said. 'There's something else I ought to tell you, Alice. Then we will get some sleep. He's getting to his Polish conference on the back of your Chrissie's essay.'

'Good God,' Alice said. 'What do you mean?'

'Chrissie wrote an essay,' Judith said. 'An essay on Shakespeare Comedy. Oh, he's elaborated it and expanded it, of course. It bears all the stamp, now, of his own intellectual suavity. But the germ of the thing is hers, Alice. It's Chrissie's and make no mistake.'

Christina opened her eyes for a moment. She blinked twice and looked at the two women before she closed them again. She felt a searing pain in the concrete leg.

'Anyway,' she mumbled, 'I'm switching to maths.'

Though Judith left at midnight, Alice chose to stay. She spent the night beside Christina's bed and watched her as she slept. In the morning Christina felt much better. She woke to see that the concrete sewer pipe was a two-foot length of rigid plaster.

'Hello, Mama,' she said. The two of them hugged and

kissed. 'I expect that I've messed up your love life,' Christina said. 'I've also messed up your marriage.'

Alice felt that there was so much to be said, but because she had no wish to tire her daughter she merely smiled and apologized in her turn and saved her explanations for later.

'Last night I shocked you, my sweetness,' she said. 'And I put your life in danger. Dear Chrissie, thank God that you are all right. You have always been the light of my life.'

Christina bashed at her pillows. 'Mama,' she said. 'But, Mama, it was all so beautiful, what I saw. You. Judith. You were both so amazingly beautiful. I think I was jealous, that's all.' And she said, 'I'm so confused, Mama, I don't think I know who I am.'

Her mother kissed her and squeezed her arm and said that that had to do with being young, though, even as she said it, Alice knew that it wasn't quite the truth because she felt so utterly confused herself and needed someone to lean on. So, after she'd watched Christina have her breakfast, she got up to take her leave.

'I have to see someone in London,' she said. 'I'll come back tomorrow. All right? And right now,' she said, 'I'd like to make way for your Papa. He's coming to see you, Chrissie, and he won't want me in the way. You'll be discharged in an hour or two and he'll drive you back to your digs.'

When Christina pulled a face, she said, 'Now, don't you run out on him, Chrissie. Please, dearest Chrissie, I beg you.'

Christina groaned, she pulled the sheet over her face. 'Fat chance,' she said, her voice coming muffled through the cloth. 'Oh, boy,' she said. 'Is he going to love this? Me with a wheel clamp on my leg.'

Alice took the tube to Seven Sisters Road. She walked much the same route that her daughter Christina had walked when she had first gone home with Dulcie. She walked from the main road, where plastic bags danced in the front gardens and tethered dogs in studded collars barked above the roar of traffic.

Then she made a left turn into the pleasanter, quieter streets. She passed the tall terraces interspersed with rows of small shops – hairdressers mostly, offering Afro styles, though some, for the lank-haired of the species, still offered the five-pound perm. Newsagents' windows offered faded plastic toys and nylon fishnet Christmas stockings full of chocolate bars. The greengrocers sold yams and okra. The second-hand furniture shops were depressingly overstocked with vinyl-seated typist's chairs and buttoned velour headboards.

When the drainpipes got less rusty and the stone front steps less cracked, Alice came upon a second row of shops, among which was the delicatessen run by Zak and Judith's parents. After making her inquiries, she made her way through to the back. The passage was hung with pungent cheeses and strings of garlic and dark red smoked sausage.

Zak Levine was standing at a workboard wearing a sleeveless T-shirt and the largest apron she had ever seen. It descended almost to his feet. The apron strings were crossed at the back and tied at the front over his belly. Zak was doing something purposeful with a sharp pointed knife and a plastic basin full of herrings.

'Father Zak,' she said. 'Hello, I'm intruding on you.'

'Alice,' he said. 'Come on. Intrude.' He held up his hands by way of apology for appearing standoffish in the manner of his greeting. 'How are you?' he said.

'I'm fine,' she said. 'Gosh, this is really some shop. I'd call this my kind of pornography.'

'Mine too,' he said. 'But, Alice dear, you manage to keep your figure.' He crossed, then, to a large stone sink where he vigorously washed his hands.

'Please,' she said. 'Don't stop. You mustn't. I'm sorry to

barge in like this. I felt that I needed to talk to you. I have things to confess – not "confess" confess, you understand, I always found that horrendously difficult. Truth to tell, it goes against my nature and I gave it up over four years ago. I gave up the whole bang shoot.' She turned and stared out of the window at a yard of wintry shrubs and trees. Then, once again, she faced him. 'Are you shocked?' she said.

'Alice,' he said. 'I spend my life these days with cut-throats and diseased prostitutes.' He paused. 'So yes,' he said, 'I'm a bit shocked. Carry on.'

'I fell in love with religion when I fell in love with Joe,' she said. 'And then I fell out of love with Joe. I woke up one morning and the magic wasn't there. Does this sound as though I should be writing to the agony aunt? I've been feeling cheap ever since. I'm troubled – have been for years now – by the idea that neither was ever genuine – neither of my loves.'

'That,' Zak said, 'is exactly when you most need to hang on and wait. Wait for the higher thing. When it comes, you will have shed all the dross. You will be left with something more durable. Perhaps it will be something like the difference between Absolute and Historic truth.'

'I thought that was Karl Marx,' Alice said.

'And so it may be,' Zak said. 'I grew up with Marxist parents.'

'But,' Alice said, 'what if the reality is that twenty years of my life has been completely bogus? A delusion. A dream. And now I've woken up? Well, let us suppose that some malignant demon has been deliberately confusing my sight, etcetera.'

'I think that is highly probable,' Zak said.

'What?' she said.

'The malignant demon,' he said. 'But maybe it is precisely now that the demon is doing his worst.'

'I simply find that kind of talk embarrassing,' she said. 'Any minute now you will start to tell me that my daughter was

286

raped by malignant demons.' She shrugged. 'Schoolboys in fancy dress,' she said. 'I believe that we make our own demons.'

Zak simply indicated a stool, where she sat down.

'I suppose I want to "unpack", as they say,' she said. 'You might say that I need a psychiatrist. I will tell you that I've tried that already, but I find on the whole they are rather lacking in depth and complexity. They have these checklists for human behaviour. I find them like the cruder sort of literary critic. The finer nuance of character evades them. Perhaps we could go to a café? That's if your fish can really wait.'

'Sure,' he said, 'I'll get dressed.'

When she emerged into the street with him, Alice felt that Father Zak was like a ship in full sail. She felt like Scuffy the Tugboat alongside him.

'They're rather good, those Jesuit sleeves,' she said. 'Do people ever join up just for the uniform?'

'The sleeves are okay,' Father Zak said. 'But the shoulders show up dandruff.' Then he said, 'As to the joining, well, after what the Marist brothers did to me at school, I suppose I was not very likely to sign up with them.'

In a café they ordered tea and toast. 'What happened to me was like this,' Alice said. 'It was like a drug wearing off. Like a midsummer dream. Like Titania waking to find that she was in bed with an ass. Excuse me, I do know that my husband is not an ass.'

'No,' Zak said. 'No, he isn't.'

'My life was changed for me overnight,' she said. 'Everything was suddenly a hollow sham – that is, except for my violent love for my stroppy little Chrissie. Then my father-in-law died. That was exactly when I ought to have been supportive.' She paused. 'I believe it's the reason why Joe was so determined to send the girls away to school. He has always wanted them in fairyland. Nothing but the best and most pure. That was yet another thing that began to deter me about him. The way that he believes you simply throw money at any problem. Basically, he's a fixer. I think he dazzled me in the first place by his techniques of manipulation and his bizarre extravagance. Take that crazy bike trip we went on. Those millionaire bicycles. That was merely one of his schemes. Of course, it has to be admitted, he looks mighty good in black skin-fit lycra.'

Zak Levine said nothing. He sipped his coffee and let her talk. She went on to explain Joe's courtship to him. She talked about her dear, dead friend and the newborn, orphaned baby. She told him about that first year of intermittent separation while she was at university in Oxford and Joe ran a business in America. She described for him how her new involvement with Joe's Church had been like being in love twice over; how she had not only been dazzled by Joe, she had been dazzled by his Church. How she had counted the days until she could go again to Mass, to fulfil her Sunday obligation. It had seemed to her really strange that such a thing should be called an 'obligation' when it had beckoned to her so seductively. Everything had delighted her.

For a start, the Church had been so full of people. There was standing-room only if you were more than one minute late. That had been the first surprise. She had expected churches in these days to contain three old ladies and a vicar. Or she had expected that the churches would have all been turned into cafés, with piped Vivaldi and William Morris wallpaper, selling chocolate brownies from the high altar.

She had expected that she would go along and be subjected to the embarrassment of having to say the responses on her own. But not there. Not in Joe's Church, where the congregation was not only sizeable but was also, roughly speaking, half male. And it had cut effectively across age. There were not only the greybeards looking towards heaven, but the young men too. Hunky young men in leather jackets with girlfriends in tow. There were the gum-chewing teenagers examining their finger-nails, along with the lady dons in tweed, and the pale, pious undergraduates, and the phlegmy, homeless old men, and the children colouring in their pictures of Jesus and dropping their fibre pens. Alice, as she spied out the family from the doner kebab van and the lady from the launderette, had decided firmly that Joe's Church was the only institution left in England that effectively crossed the barriers of social class.

And the ritual, of course, had been so dazzling – the incense and the vestments; the litanies and the Eucharistic prayers. She had adored the way people would shuffle up to the altar, just as though they were in a self-service tea-shop in the rush hour. Such an ordinary miracle; an ordinary nosh-up; the Lord's feast. The shared cup, so levelling. And then afterwards, Alice had watched fixedly as the priests had wiped the vessels and had put them away in a cupboard.

'It was the first time I had ever seen men washing up,' Alice told Zak. 'And, of course, they were doing it in public.'

It had bothered her at first, she told him, that the whole thing had not been a bit more foodie. Because Joe himself was so divinely foodie. She had felt impelled to offer her services to the clergy – to make fancier lace tablecloths and nicer bread; bread made with olive oil; bread to munch, like the sort one munched with falafel and kofta. 'Ask me,' she had wanted to say, eager-beaver convert. Teacher's pet. 'Ask me, Father. Ask me.'

Zak's laugh was most satisfactory. It had a nice, deep bass pitch.

'I remember Joe telling me that the wafery stuff was made by Carmelite nuns and that it was their livelihood,' she said.

'And that it wasn't for me to rush in and try to replace it with the likes of what I could buy in the baker's shop next to the halal butchery up the Cowley Road.'

'Bloody converts,' Zak said.

'Excuse me?' Alice said.

'Bloody nuisance,' he said. 'People like you and me. Swing high; swing low. It's people like your Joe are the lucky ones.'

'He's not "my Joe",' Alice said. 'That's the point. You do know that we no longer live together?'

'Yes I know that,' Zak said. 'I have the ear of both your husband and my sister.'

Alice looked at him. 'I'm sorry,' she said. 'But once I'd woken up, then I suddenly saw the whole of Joe's *Weltanschauung* as a trick to rob me of myself. And all that dazzling Catholic stuff had to do with men claiming a monopoly on the best in tabards and hats. I have become very nostalgic. I long again for my girlhood and for the company of Pam's brilliant mother – my first love, I suppose. What a good thing that priests don't go prescribing HRT.'

Zak was now frowning into the table top and refusing to be entertained. 'You talk a lot, not only about "waking up", but about being being "dazzled",' he said. Pam's mother was "dazzling", Joe was "dazzling", the Church was "dazzling".' He paused. 'My sister is also "dazzling". May I suggest that you start to wear dark glasses? You seem to me not so much awake, Alice, as seriously hung over.'

Alice pulled a wry face. 'Oh, dear,' she said. 'Point taken.'

'I too adore my sister,' Zak said. 'But my advice there is to fear Greeks bearing gifts.'

When Alice finally turned to call for the bill, she saw that the waitress was marvellously tall and black. She wore skin-fit blue jeans and high-heeled shoes and a plum-coloured lip gloss. She crossed the floor to them immediately and stood alongside the table.

'Blimey,' she said as she ripped the bill from her pad. 'Excuse me, but you don't half remind me of someone.'

'Me?' Alice said.

'Yeah,' said the waitress. 'I reckon there's no one else you could be. You've got to be Chris's muvver.'

Orphans, Jugglers and Tall Hats

It was evident when Papa entered the general ward that he had acquired a slight stiffness in the gait. But, for all that, he was wearing a soft wool jacket the colour of mango ice-cream and he was carrying a bunch of orangey freesias. Christina, as she watched him, found that she had forgotten quite how effectively he could always cut a dash.

She was all ready and waiting for him. She had her crutch within easy reach.

'Before you utter a word to me,' she said, 'I'd like to point out that you limp. I expect that's on account of the gout.' Then, without pausing for long enough to allow him opportunity for reply, she said, 'And I got myself into this condition through watching your wife who was being sexually active with another woman at the time.'

Papa stopped three feet in front of her. He fixed her with a straight look. He threw the bunch of freesias so that it landed in her lap. Then he folded his arms and uttered one brief, sardonic laugh.

'Congratulations, Chrissie,' he said. 'I'm delighted to see that you are in shape.'

'If you call this being in shape,' she said.

Papa came forward. He bent and kissed the top of her head. Then he straightened up. He held a hand flat against his lumbar region as he did so.

'So what were you doing on a fire-escape staircase forty feet in the air?' he said.

'Me?' she said. 'Well, I suppose I was escaping the stench of sinful humanity. You may carry my bag, if you like.'

Then, refusing any further assistance, she struggled to her

feet. 'If you're planning on taking me out to lunch,' she said, 'it better be pretty damn good.'

Papa said that lunch would be his pleasure, so long as they could go some place where the food came low both in salt and in saturated animal fat.

'Hah!' she said. 'You? If you prefer we can go to the supermarket and grab a few cans of lima beans off the shelf and maybe a jar or two of green tomato relish.'

Over the low-fat, purplish Venetian artichoke salad, Papa diplomatically kept off the subject of Pam's beautiful baby and of Pam's recent annexing of the beautiful and brilliant Jago Rutherford. Instead, he offered to buy Christina the juggling balls for Dulcie's Christmas present. Over the low-fat sea bass and the red and yellow pimentos, he avoided the anticipated post-mortem quiz and offered instead to buy her a house. She had mentioned the need to find herself digs for the following year. She wanted somewhere where she would be able, intermittently, to house Peter's dog, since Peter himself would be forever flitting to France when vacations came along.

'But, crumbs, Papa,' Christina said. 'You don't have to do this, you know. I mean it's not as though you were my father.'

Papa merely nodded his acknowledgement of the jibe and observed, pleasantly, that her 'edge' was alive and well. He ordered, when the waiter came, 'Just two small espressos, please.' Then he caught Christina's eye and he said, 'Oh, what the hell', and he ordered – after some consultation – almond cakes and chestnuts simmered in marsala.

Christina rolled her eyes in reproach. 'Trust you to have the gout,' she said. 'Isn't it just a shade picturesque? I mean, didn't it go out with Samuel Pepys and Doctor Johnson? I mean, couldn't you just have contented yourself with arthritis? Or are you too much of a show-off?'

*

It was the nicest day that Christina could remember for quite a long time. Papa, because he was impulsive and ridiculous and he believed in striking with hot irons, was all in favour of tackling the real estate question without further delay.

'If you're okay to hobble, Chrissie,' he said, 'then I'm okay to limp.'

They flew, dot-and-carry-one, shrieking and laughing from A to B all afternoon. She had forgotten how funny he could be.

'If you don't stop this,' she said, 'I'm going to piddle in my undies.' She marvelled to discover that he could even be funny about Mama and Judith.

'The girlfriend is a great lady,' he said. 'I have a little thing for her myself.'

'And me,' Christina said. 'Me too.'

They decided, within the space of two hours, on a tiny renovated terrace house that overlooked Fenner's Cricket Ground. The idea was that she could share the house with two undergraduate lodgers and that way recoup on the running costs. Christina stood in the empty back bedroom and stared out at the wintry pitch and at the little pavilion beyond.

'I hope you're not planning to buy me,' she said. 'I mean, along with the house. I hope you're not planning to move yourself and your gout in with me?'

'For sure,' Papa said. 'And especially for all that cricket in the summer months. Now there's an exciting game, Chrissie. That's the real big draw for me.' Then he said, 'We'll buy it – what do you think? Would you like it gift-wrapped?'

In the car, after a rare, pensive silence, she said, 'There's that poster you can get – you know – of Stalin with that little girl. She's telling him, "Thank you for my Happy Childhood." I might buy you that for Christmas. Or maybe I'll get you a *Madeleine* book.' After another silence, she went on, 'I read

Robert Louis Stevenson. He says the children of lovers are orphans. Papa – Pam and me – we would have felt like that whatever.'

'Speaking of Christmas,' Papa said. 'Tell me. Do you have plans?'

'I have a prior commitment,' she said. 'I'm committed to Peter's dog.'

When evening had almost fallen, she got Papa to drop her off at the college lodge. He got out of the car and came round and opened the door and helped her to her feet. He handed her the crutch.

'I ought to come in with you,' he said. 'You can't manage with the bag.'

'I'm fine,' she said. 'Don't come. I need to do this on my own.'

Then she allowed him to kiss her. 'So long, Papa,' she said. 'I wish I could've seen more of you.'

He laughed. 'Don't capitulate, Chrissie,' he said. 'Just you keep on sharpening that edge.'

'I will,' she said. 'Now, shove off. I don't want you to watch me.' Then she turned and hobbled down the path.

She had wanted so much to reveal herself in triumph to her friend the porter and to call out, 'Look! See! I've broken my leg for real.' But the porter was talking busily to a man in a pin-striped suit. In his hand the man carried a briefcase. It was not one of the bashed-up leather variety, but a rigid black fibre-glass item for containing product promotions and confer-ence presentations. Reluctantly, she hobbled past them and on into the court.

It was all shimmering with a delicate mist, and there, incredibly, standing on the stepped stone base of the sundial, silhouetted grey in the winter twilight, stood the juggler, her juggler. He stood as lofty perpendicular as ever in his tall witch's hat, his long unbuttoned overcoat hanging down to

295

the floor. He was making balls turn in circles through the air so that they surrounded his head like the stars around the head of the Queen of Heaven.

Christina drew in her breath. She blinked and stared. Then, dropping her bag where she stood, she hobbled towards the juggler as fast as she could across the grass. The foot of the crutch made small tell-tale bore-holes as she went.

'Hello, Chris,' said the juggler, who kept on juggling. 'I've been waiting for you for ages. But aren't you supposed to be Keeping Off of that Grass what you're standing on right now?'

'Dulce!' Christina said. 'God in heaven. It's you. But what are you doing here – juggling on the grass?'

'Well, I'm not actually *on* the grass,' Dulcie said, and all the while she kept on juggling. 'I'm on the steps, then, aren't I? So why don't you come up and join me?'

By the time that Christina had hobbled up alongside, she had taken note that Dulcie's hat was no more than a red and white plastic traffic cone.

'If it's only your leg that's broke,' Dulcie said, 'if it's not your fuckin arms as well – then catch.'

They worked the balls in tandem, as they had used to do, speeding up as the rhythm began to establish itself.

'Andy, pandy, sugar and candy, salt, almond, rock,' Dulcie chanted.

'Alack, I am worn to a ravelling,' Christina said. 'But I have my twist.'

'Methinks I am a prophet, new inspired,' Dulcie said. 'Yet I myself am in want of a feather bed.'

'I like your hat,' Christina said.

'Thanks,' Dulcie said. 'I nicked it off of that pile of sand back there by the cathedral.'

'That cathedral's the college chapel,' Christina said. 'So where d'you buy your coat, then? Tramps' Outfitters?'

'Yeah,' Dulcie said. 'And don't I look a fuckin freak? I give a tenner for it up the Oxfam. Got to have the clothes, then, haven't I? All the bourgeois clothes. That's if I'm coming to join you here.' And the two of them kept on juggling.

'Coming here?' Christina said. And her heart leapt, rejoicing. 'What do you mean, coming here? Anyway, you don't like it here – the whole sodding place looks like churches.'

'Well, it might be a dump,' Dulcie said. 'But it's a damn sight better than stuffing jam in them cakes down the bakery all day long. That's what I've been doing, Chris. That and working in the caff.'

'Our caff?' Christina said.

'Yeah,' Dulcie said. 'That's where I met your mum. She come in with a fat priest.'

'Father Zachary Levine,' Christina said. 'God in heaven, how weird.'

'Chris,' Dulcie said. 'She's great, your mum. She's fantastic, I reckon. Anyway, she persuaded me to think again – about this place, I mean. So I come along this afternoon to bung in the application forms. Today's the last day, you see. D'you reckon they'll have me?'

All the while, as she spoke, Dulcie kept on juggling.

'Are you joking?' Christina said. 'With your grades and your background? Dulce, they'll practically club you over the head and drag you in by the hair. But what about all that choirboy stuff? And all the gargoyles and the cycle clips and that? I thought all that stuff scared you.'

'So why do you think I'm standing here in the middle of the quad?' Dulcie said. 'Pardon me, "court". In the middle of the *court*, like a charley, with a traffic cone on my head? Why d'you think I'm juggling, then, with five oranges what I just nicked from the dining hall over there?'

'You're proving that you're not scared?' Christina said.

'Right,' Dulcie said. 'Right, as usual, Hunca Munca, only

mustard isn't a bird. Gawd, but I've missed you, Chris, I tell you. So, how did you break your leg?'

'I fell off a fire-escape staircase,' Christina said. 'I was watching two women kissing.'

'Fuckin lezzies,' Dulcie said, and all the while she kept on juggling. After a longish silence, she said, 'So how about it? How about us, then, Chris? What I mean is, do you fancy blokes?'

'I thought I did,' Christina said. 'I used to think that I loved Jago, but now I know that I don't. Yesterday I discovered that I loved Peter, but that's more like the love people bear towards their guardian angel, I suppose. I've also discovered – embarrassingly – that I really do love my father. By which I mean to say that I adore my mother's estranged husband.' She sighed. 'What about you?' she said.

'Me?' Dulcie said. 'Blokes? Not bloody likely. But then I never have. It's just them forever going after me – always trying for a grope on the fuckin Underground. It's just like my bum's not my own private property. They're all like fuckin Wayne. Else they're like that charley with the sandals and the posh, squeaky voice. Remember him? I'd much rather be with you, Chris. I've always liked you, haven't I? D'you remember when you first walked into the john? In the coat and the shoes and all? And poor old Trace with her big tits, teasing up her hair? Anyway, aren't fags supposed to meet each other in the john?'

Christina blinked. 'Dulce,' she said. 'Crumbs. I don't think so, but maybe it's too sudden. I don't think it's *me*, to tell you the truth. I think I was aware of that yesterday when I fell off that fire-escape staircase. Not that you aren't this life's most beautiful creature. Not that I don't passionately wish that I was you.' Then she said, 'But excuse me for just a moment. There's a bloke that's coming straight for us.'

She spoke in haste, because she had noticed that the man in

the pin-striped suit with the fibre-glass briefcase had left the porter's lodge and was now striding across the grass. He was gesticulating angrily. When he spoke, it was with quite a strong northern accent.

'Off the *gruss*, off the *gruss*!' he said. '*Cun't* you read?'

'Who is he, do you suppose?' Christina said.

Dulcie shrugged. She kept on juggling. 'Dunno,' she said. 'Bobby Shaftoe? One of the low on whom assurance sits as a silk hat on a Bradford millionaire.'

'*Cun't* you read?' said the man, '*Cun't* you read? What does the notice say?'

'I can read,' Dulcie said. 'It says "Keep Off of the Grass". And who are you calling cunt? Anyway, we're not *on* the grass. We're on the step, aren't we? You're the one who's on the grass, mister. Mister Whatsyourname. Lord Muck.'

'I'm Doctor Riley to you,' he said. 'I'm the new college fundraiser. So don't you trifle with me.'

'Trifle with you?' Dulcie said. 'Trifle as in jelly and ice-cream?' And the girls kept on juggling.

'Do you know what trifle's called in Italian, Dulce?' Christina said. 'It's called *zuppa inglese*. That means English soup.'

'Soup?' Dulcie said, and she kept on juggling. 'You kidding?'

The fundraiser paused. He was fast considering discretion to be the better part of valour. 'You'll not have heard the *lust* of this, you two,' he said, and he turned on his heels to go.

'Lust?' Dulcie said.

As he turned, somebody in the east wing switched on a light. It threw a beam across the court and illumined the fundraiser's ear, upon which Christina noticed that the Born Lump was small but unmistakable.

She faltered. She dropped the balls.

'Now look what you've gone and done,' Dulcie said.

'Sorry,' Christina said. 'It's that man. The thing is, I know who he is.'

Dulcie took the traffic cone off her head. She began to collect the fallen oranges. She stowed them inside the inverted cone. 'So who is he, then?' she said. 'And anyway, who the hell cares?'

Christina shrugged. She laughed. 'Yeah,' she said. 'Who cares?' She picked out one of the oranges and threw it high in the air. It travelled first through the beam of light, then disappeared for a moment into the moonless dark. After that, it fell to the ground with a soft, bursting thud. It landed at Dulcie's feet.

'So who is he, then?' Dulcie said again.

'Second son of old Sir Rowland de Boys,' Christina said. 'I don't know. Just someone. Some schmuck. As you say, Dulce, who the hell cares?'

Epilogue; or, What You Will

So what has happened to them? Did the frame freeze? Did the balance hold? No, of course not. Well, yes and no. Let us take a look at them all, three years on.

Pam and Jago are married. They were married in France by Jago's second cousin, the once so youthful rugby priest. The wedding itself was big and splashy and had to do, Christina considers, with Jago's dubious romanticism about her sister – and with Joe's equally dubious compulsion to control both bride and groom with largesse. It also had to do with Jago's need to act out his own self-consciously reconstructed past.

Jago's mother, Mireille, was delighted by the turn of events and immediately took Pam to her heart. Jago's father, Charles Rutherford – who had advised his son in dastardly manner to 'screw the girl, if you must, Jamie', but 'in Christ's name' not to go marrying her – Charles Rutherford had aptly got his comeuppance and had died suddenly at the wheel of his car before the invitations went out.

Pam, Jago and little Bruno are together now in Italy, where Pam pursues her career as a singer and Jago, for the moment, has taken a break from mathematics to complete a Foundation Course in Art and Design in Florence. For Pam's sake, he is determinedly cultivating the Whole Man. A big mistake this, Christina considers, who is of the opinion that there is quite enough of him already.

Peter Rusconi is still very happy with Victor, whom he loves dearly. Peter was never marked out for Christina, for all that symmetry, colour-coding and all the physical correlatives seemed to point so conveniently in that direction. Colour-coding is, after all, not necessarily a highly successful basis for permanent living-together relationships, and sometimes, as in *Twelfth Night*, for example, it is employed merely to mark out links between siblings, especially twins. Peter and Christina are profoundly infused with a reciprocal brotherly love. They are also, in one sense, related and both, of course, have appeared at crucial moments as Jago Rutherford's angels. Oddly enough, they have recently discovered that they also share a birthday.

Roland and his wife are no longer an item. This was the work of Gentille, who discovered that her life was suddenly ripe for change. Once that time had come, she managed the change magnificently, and Roland at a stroke became a part of her past – and the past by its very nature was history. It simply wasn't there. Gentille, on the day that Christina had burst in on Roland to claim him as her father, had been visiting the people who lived next door to Judith and Hugo Campbell. It was Roland's sister's family, of course, who were on sabbatical from Vancouver. The two little girls mentioned earlier in the story were none other than Roland's sister's daughters, who had in the interim become six. The two older girls were away at school, while Miffy's friend Rose was the third child of the family, and strident Patience the fourth.

Gentille, in short, has struck up with Hugo. It was on the cards from the start. Hugo and Judith were disastrously matched and had brought out all the worst in each other. So the Mermaid Woman, as Christina puts it, has run off with the Watery Green Man.

It was Miffy who brought them together. Roland's daughters, Ellen and Lydia, who were visiting next door, had caused some uncomfortable realignments from Miffy's point of view. Her dear friend Rose, for the course of her cousins' visit, had had eyes only for Lydia, and Miffy, tired of playing gooseberry, had announced that she would return home.

'Well, why don't you go by the rope ladder?' was all that Lydia said. 'That way, with a bit of luck, you'll break it.' This unpleasant personal remark had been too much for fat little Miffy. Though always apprehensive about heights, she had announced at once that she would return by no other means. The rope ladder hung in Rose's garden, but from a branch attached to one of Hugo's trees; it was the work of Roland's brother-in-law, who had made it for the diversion of his two youngest daughters. Miffy and Rose had always gone by the gate, but on this particular occasion, Miffy mounted the ladder and began determinedly to climb.

She made it up to the top of the ladder and on to the horizontal branch. She was already well beyond the Vancouver family's airspace when she looked down, lost her nerve, and froze.

'I'm going to fall,' she called out. 'Help! I'm going to fall.'

To these cries Gentille responded by entering Hugo's garden. This was how Gentille first saw Hugo and how Hugo first saw Gentille. Her effect on him was extraordinary. Hugo put down the pen and the pastry-board and then he rose from his chair, staring at Gentille fixedly. He stepped out through the iron bars of the gazebo and walked, enchanted, towards her. As he proceeded, she began to move forward. Their eyes were fixed on each other. They met half-way between the house and Miffy's tree, their raised arms held out until their four hands met, two and two, fingers touching.

'Help!' Miffy cried. 'I'm going to fall!'

It was then that Judith's brother came flying out of the kitchen. The whole dense mass of him broke through the arch made by the enchanted lovers' limbs and caught the child as she fell. Miffy fell horizontal, belly upwards, into his outstretched arms. It was the first successful acrobatical act of Zak's life.

'In one hour,' Gentille was murmuring on a sigh, 'I must leave for Poland.'

'*Poland?*' Hugo said, incredulous. 'But I too am leaving for Poland. Conference,' he added. 'Humour and Anarchy.'

'Ah,' Gentille said. 'Then it is a miracle.' After that, they kissed.

'Zak,' Miffy said. 'Thank you *so* much. I didn't even know that you'd come.'

Their noses and ears as they hugged were identical, as was most of their physiognomy. As to Zak, Miffy's fall was terrible: it was an occasion for revelation, because in the moment that Zuleika landed in his arms the scales dropped from his eyes. He knew all at once that she was his daughter and that all those curious dreams he had had for twelve years now in which he was falling, falling, always falling into his sister's arms had suddenly taken on a local habitation and name. The habitation was Gordon Square. A party. Student party. Lots of medics. Something very strange about the drink, so that the night was like a dream. And the name of the dream, as he realized now, was incest. Zak blinked. He thought about his sister. He said, talking sadly to himself, '*Timeo Danaos et dona ferentis.*'

'What did you say?' Miffy said. She had swivelled herself upright in his arms and had fixed her stout legs, scissorwise, around his ample waist.

'Oh, my dear,' Zak said. 'I merely said that I feared Greeks, bearing gifts.'

Miffy laughed. 'Greeks?' she said. 'Zakky, hug me, please.'

And Christina? Is she with Dulcie?

No, she isn't, because Dulcie has taken up with Christina's mother. They are living together in Cambridge in that nice

304

little house that Papa had so kindly bought for Christina. Dulcie has just written her finals and she has drafted her research proposal. She has been invited to stay on and do graduate work by the department which, Hugo Campbell notwithstanding, is quite capable of knowing a very good thing when it sees one. She has decided to research the cult of the Black Madonna in Southern France. Alice is working in London with a firm of chartered accountants. Her professional life is matter-of-fact. She saves romance for home and for Dulcie.

Dulcie has become the great love of her life; a miracle, a second chance, because long ago, as a twelve-year-old school-girl, Alice fell in love. She fell in love with Jem McCrail, who subsequently became Pam's mother. Jem had been the tallest, the brightest, the most creative schoolgirl; humbly born, dazzling, and besotted with English literature. And now, miraculously, here was Dulcie – Chrissie's dearest friend – the tallest, the brightest, the most creative schoolgirl; humbly born, dazzling, and besotted with English literature.

And the best thing is that Dulcie loves her back with an infinite and tender conviction. So that, when Alice cries and worries about the difference in their ages, Dulcie is always able to be completely sincere in reassurance.

'Don't be so soft in the head, Alice Springs,' she says. 'Don't be such a dafty. You're thirty-nine, aren't you? That's young. That's nothing. And who gives a fuck? By the look of you, my loveliness, you could be Chrissie's baby sister.'

Dulcie wakes Alice early and brings her tea in bed. She has persuaded Alice to work out with her. They run together on early summer mornings before Alice takes the train. Over weekends they sometimes run the country path from Newnham Croft to Grantchester, passing the cows that helped Christina to formulate her essay. They hold hands in quiet cafés and thank God for the miracle of each other's XX chromosomes. They can hardly believe their own good luck.

It is not that Joe wasn't lots of fun, but Alice can almost not believe, now, that her marriage really happened. Incredible Joe, her mother's *bête noire*, her children's stand-in father, her personal bald, provoking lover, and chef, and hound of hell. It had all been an experience not to be missed. But the energy that it had consumed! All that constant hammering of oneself into something which one was not.

And then, just as she was close to despair, she had found lovely Dulcie in that café off Seven Sisters Road. And then, in the whorl of that perfect exposed female umbilicus, and in that beautiful recessed ropy column of exposed female spine, Alice's mind had at once put to bed the idea of Judith Levin – Judith, who was destructive and manipulating and herself too unhappy and angry to help – and it came to rest and to drown in Dulcie.

So what, then, has become of Judith? Judith has gone with Joe. Their story is as follows. Joe sold out the small, independent publishing house. He sold out to a large multinational corporation that had made its money in biscuits. He has bought the food shop off Seven Sisters Road. He has gone into business with his friend Zak Levine, who is a one-time Jesuit priest. Judith's parents sold up the shop and returned to Johannesburg. There they fell into joyful reunion with many elderly, once-banned, returning exiles, and rediscovered a multitude of modest, well-deserved pleasures, like the beauty, for instance, of bougainvillaea rampant over small suburban bungalows on quarter-acre lots.

Joe lives with Judith and Zak and Zuleika in the sizeable upstairs flat above the shop which expands over the top two floors and has a fire-escape staircase running down the back – 'so Chrissie can visit', as he says. He has touched the flat with his genius for bright extravagance, so that the apartment now looks like a well-lit Aladdin's cave.

Miffy is fifteen and is much happier and a bit thinner because her mother is happier and a bit fatter. She thrives on the fact that, in place of one useless, pale green man who behaved as if she were invisible, she now has two dark, distinctly corporeal men who notice her far too much. She has Zak, who indulges her as he always did, and Joe, who scares her, rants at her, excites her, loves her, and looms over her eating habits, her homework, her deportment and her friends, like a captivating tyrant.

Judith has made it clear that she will have nothing to do with the shop. She will absolutely not engage with the preparation or the sale of food. She escapes each morning to work in the neonatal unit of a London teaching hospital now that the Cambridge junior fellowship has mercifully come to an end.

'Christ, Chrissie!' she says when they meet in London cafés for lunch, as they do from time to time. 'If there are three things above all others that drive me up the wall, then those things are small children and food and Catholics. So what do I find that I'm doing with my life? I'm working with other people's substandard babies. Then I come home to two demented Catholics who stink of tahini and aniseed. And if I'm really lucky, then they've been messing with fish that day. Remember how you told me once about the halved goats' heads, Chrissie? Well, I used to think you were joking. One of them is obese and the other one has the gout. Jesus, am I a madwoman, Chrissie? What am I doing with my life?'

Judith and Joe are somewhat extrovert lovers and this can be tiresome for outsiders because they constantly touch each other in public. Judith's rediscovery of her own heterosexual bias has, if anything, intensified her forcefulness. She had found herself going with women most of the time but merely because all the men on offer had always been such wimps. The problem was that, for all she was stunning – had such great

307

legs, such a shape to die for, such a breathtaking voluminous tumble of dark hair, such small, enticing, predatory teeth – she had tended always to scare men away. That was, until Joe, who was not so easily scared. And then, again, women, of course, have always been inclined to fall for her.

Judith, for all that she is lively, is not that much fun to have lunch with, as Chrissie explains afterwards to her partner. This is because she has such unpleasant eating habits. She will pick for an hour at her spaghetti *carbonara* and then she will binge on chocolate mousse. She will repeatedly run her finger round the inside of the bowl and lick it, apparently without noticing. And if the waiter brings those corny chocolate peppermints along with the bill, then Judith will gather them up – her own and other people's – and stuff them into her mouth. She is, of course, an only partially rehabilitated bulimic. She has an undignified, clandestine habit that Joe drags out of the closet. He calls her a 'goddamn disgusting neurotic', and he sniffs like a bloodhound at her toothbrush.

'Just you get yourself in gear, now,' he says. 'Just you find yourself some less unattractive behavioural disturbance. You imagine that I will still want to screw you when all your hair and teeth fall out?'

The eating is a real pain for him, but Judith has lots of pluses. It's fun for him to cohabit with a person who shares his love of clothes. Judith always looks terrific, where Alice's clothes had been a constant source of let-down. Judith always gets it right. She never fails to turn heads. Also her sharp wit and abrasiveness are a lot of fun for him. Both of them can use their quickness, their verbal flair, as a metaphor and a prelude to the felicitous act of sex.

And so at last to Christina. What has become of her? After the anger over Jago and the anger over Judith, who had played her off so reprehensibly like that, against her mother; after her annoyance with her father for his all too assertive existence within her developmental sphere of consciousness, an existence which had so inconveniently printed upon her mind the reality of the male other; after she had become completely sure that she was not going to find herself sexually attracted to Dulcie, Christina simply stopped, and waited, and took refuge in catching up on the maths.

She was at that time still sharing the house that Papa had bought her with Dulcie and Peter and Victor. Serious Syrius, the Star Dog Two, was in there as well, of course – 'the foul witch Sycorax', as Dulcie insisted upon calling her. She was hardly a dog at all, Dulcie thought. She was one of the pampered of the species. 'A burrowing animal, she spent all day under Peter and Victor's duvet. She whimpered when the beds were stripped. When Peter and Victor were doing sex together, Serious Syrius, the Star Dog Two, spent the time licking their ankles and their thighs. They were, in many ways, the nicest foursome in the world, but when darling Dulcie began, increasingly, to take out weekends in London, Christina for one smelled a rat.

'Chris,' Dulcie said one day, 'I can't do this to you. Well, it's like incest, isn't it? I'm carrying on with your mum.'

Then one Monday morning, towards midday, when Dulcie had entered, commuter-smart, off the train from King's Cross and Christina was still in wake-up mode, not yet washed or dressed, there came a knock at the door.

'Oh, bugger,' Dulcie said. 'And we was just going to have ourselves a coffee.'

She got up and pursued a strategy which always drove Christina wild. She lifted the edge of the curtain and peered out at the supplicant who was standing in the street.

'Blimey,' she said. 'It's an old bloke and two snobby schoolgirls in uniform. Anyone for lacrosse?'

'Dulcie,' Christina said. 'Don't *do* that. It's so rude.'

'Why?' Dulcie said. 'Isn't it etiquette? Well, you can't be too careful these days. I reckon we should get one of them spyglass things that helps you to see who's out there.'

Christina made for the bathroom, where she sought to brush her teeth and wash her face. 'For Christ's sake, Dulce!' she said. 'Just go and open the door.'

Dulcie proceeded to do so. Having elected to be confrontational, she stared out boldly at Roland Dent and at his two adolescent schoolgirl daughters in their bottle-green uniforms. It was the last day of the girls' school term, and they were carrying shoe bags and work baskets.

'Yeah?' Dulcie said. She employed a most daunting degree of eye contact and took conspicuous note of the shoe bags, as though these were the defective offerings of hawkers. On the shoe bags, Ellen and Lydia had embroidered their initials in neat looping chain-stitch, as required by the school regulations.

'What you want?' Dulcie said.

'I believe,' Roland said, 'that Christina Angeletti lives here.'

'And what if she does?' Dulcie said, so belligerently that it made Roland smile. The girl was as tall as an Amazon, he thought, and she had her hand pointedly across the access, rather as if she thought he might try and take the place by storm.

'She was a pupil of mine,' he said mildly. 'Is she at home, do you know?'

Dulcie weighed him in the balance. 'Hold on,' she said.

The next thing she did was to close the door. From the front step, Roland could hear that she was calling out to Christina.

'Chris!' she yelled loudly. 'It's some teacher bloke. He says are you at home. D'you reckon it's okay to let him in?'

From the washbasin, Christina cringed and died. 'For

Christ's sake!' she hissed, swilling toothpaste froth through her mouth. 'Dulcie, ask them in!'

Dulcie once again opened the door. 'She says to come in, and wipe your feet,' she said. She added, for good measure, 'She's on the toilet, see.'

Roland ushered his daughters into the hall. Then he entered himself. All three of them wiped their feet prodigiously before Dulcie directed them to the sofa.

When Christina entered the living-room, she saw that Roland was sitting there with his size twelve feet in beige desert boots and his elbows just about to emerge from the sleeves of some classy-looking porridge-coloured home-knit. He was flanked by Ellen and Lydia, whose shoe bags were lying at their feet. All three of them had the facial bones and skin tones so prevalent in the portraits of Sir Joshua Reynolds. Dulcie was eyeing them from the chair opposite, rather as though she had just apprehended them in the act of breaking open the safe.

'Roland!' Christina said with her widest, nicest smile, and the three of them rose to greet her. She and Roland exchanged kisses and the girls allowed themselves to be hugged.

'You've met Dulcie,' Christina said. Then to Dulcie she said, 'Roland is Peter's step-father. Ellen and Lydia are Peter's half-sisters.'

Dulcie got up. She shrugged. 'So why'd he say he was a teacher?' she said. 'Chris, I've got me supervision in twenty minutes.'

Once Dulcie had gone, Christina hovered, standing. Her visitors, in consequence, were all too polite to sit down.

'Peter's in France, I'm afraid,' she said.

'Yes,' Roland said. 'Yes, I know that. My dear, the girls and I – we wondered whether you would join us for lunch?'

They waited while she got dressed and brushed her hair. Then Roland drove them to Brown's.

'But I don't eat meat, remember,' she said when, with one voice, they recommended to her the pork ribs and the pies.

After that he drove to deposit his girls with their mother at Hugo's house. Ellen and Lydia were at a boarding school in Cambridgeshire. This meant that Gentille could have access to her daughters, though Roland, backed by Ellen and Lydia, had insisted that they board. This was in order to minimize necessary contact hours with Hugo. Afterwards Christina and Roland paid a visit to the Fitzwilliam Museum, where Roland, she thought, spent far too much time looking at chainmail and suits of armour. He seemed very taken by a suit of armour that had been made for a very large horse.

'Do you ride, Christina?' he said and, when she shook her head, he said, 'Pity.' Then he took her to tea at Fitzbillies.

'Your friend,' he said, playing mother over the teapot, 'the tall girl –'

'What about her?' Christina said, somehow so pre-emptingly that Roland did not go on. They merely forked up their carrot cake in silence.

'I never liked your wife,' Christina said eventually. 'Do you remember that?'

'More tea there?' Roland said, and once again they both said nothing.

Two weeks later he came again, this time without his daughters. Peter, she told him, was still in France.

'Yes, I know that,' Roland said again.

This time they visited the Kettles Yard Gallery and then they ate supper in a vegetarian restaurant off King's Parade, where Roland's green and yellow peppers and little yellow gourds and tiny corn-cobs came pleasantly shiny, bathed in a sesame sauce. The vegetables lay on a bed of red lettuce leaves interspersed with star fruit and cherries. Christina ate exquisite pastries made of filo and Roquefort cheese: they came shaped like three-leafed clovers. Intersecting circles.

'They're Venn diagrams,' Christina said. 'Look, Roland. Do you think much about the Trinity? Dulcie says that the whole idea is crap. She says it's all to do with the tripartite structure of male parts.'

Roland merely spiked another gourd and smiled and made no reply.

And then he came again. And again. He was always rather silent and stiff and grave. Dulcie refused to warm to him. She refused to address him properly. She either called him 'that teacher bloke', or she called him 'Old Sir Rowland de Boys'. She said he came because he liked the cricket nets he could see from out the back.

Christina began to wait for his visits with a combination of longing and dread. She began to cry herself to sleep at night. Then she began to cry and stay awake. One day Roland came to the door, but his visit was not for her.

'My dear,' he said, with no explanation. 'I believe that Peter is expecting me.' Then the two of them went off together, while she was left at home.

Christina then sat down and cried. 'Look at me,' she said to herself. 'I've begun to cry in the daytime.'

Roland, having collected Peter, had gone on to collect his daughters. They ate lunch in a country pub.

'I have something to say to all of you,' he said, once they had attacked their apple pies. 'It concerns our mutual friend Christina. I have thought about this long and hard, and I'd prefer to have your approval. I intend to ask her to marry me. I have no idea as yet how she will respond.'

Peter and the girls looked awkwardly at each other. Then they looked at their feet. The girls were both deeply embarrassed.

'But why are you asking *us*?' Ellen said. 'Anyway, isn't she gay?'

'Oh, yuck,' Lydia said. 'She isn't!'

'Oh, please,' Ellen said. 'Grow up, Lydia. What's wrong with being gay? Try taking a look at Peter.'

'Peter's a boy,' Lydia said. 'That's different. It's not so disgusting. Anyway, I'll bet you she isn't.'

Ellen uttered a patronizing sigh. 'Then what about that girl?' she said. 'It's written all over her.'

'That coloured girl?' Lydia said. 'Why is it "written all over her"?'

'Say "black", Lydia,' Ellen said. ' "Coloured" is so racist.'

'Why is it racist?' Lydia said. ' "Black" is more coloured than "coloured".'

'Quite,' Ellen said. 'That's precisely the point.'

'You're mad,' Lydia said.

Roland coughed. 'Oh, dear,' he said. 'Oh, dear. Ellen, I must admit that what you say has never occurred to me.'

Peter was hardly listening to them. He was wanting Victor to be there. Victor thought that Peter's sisters were the best entertainment in the world. '*Les jeunes filles anglaises*,' he said, '*sont les plus drôles du monde.*'

When Roland proposed marriage to her, Christina burst into tears. The idea so rudely confronted her own yearnings and dragged them into the daylight. She buried her face in the porridge-coloured sweater and said, 'Um' and 'Hum' and 'Sorry'. Finally she wiped her nose and she said, 'Yes, please. I'd love to.'

'But isn't he too old?' Dulcie said. 'And isn't it a bit like incest?'

'Well, coming from you,' Christina said, 'I consider that a bit rich.'

Pam and Jago were pleased about it, but Papa and Mama were shocked.

'But are you *sure?*' Alice said nervously. 'Chrissie, dear, it hardly seems suitable.'

Alice was finding it hard to understand that her own daughter could wish to espouse a middle-aged man whose youthful embrace she herself had risked drowning to avoid.

Her father was more sanguine. 'He's a thoroughly nice man, Chrissie,' Joe said. 'Excuse me, but isn't he just a bit of a constipated Brit?'

Christina withheld their opinions from Roland, but she poured them out over Peter. Peter had no problem with the idea. If it felt right, he said, she should go for it. It entertained him to think that the person he thought of as his soul sister was about to become his mother.

'The trouble is,' Christina told him irritably, 'the trouble is my parents. Well, just look at them. My father is shacked up in a *ménage à trois* with a demented medic and a defrocked priest. My mother is co-habiting with a woman who happens to be my best friend. So, what is it that shocks them? Me, wanting to make a conventional marriage with a dependable Anglican headmaster.' She had not even begun to tell her grandmothers.

Roland was not in favour of waiting long, or of sweeping Christina abroad. He was always happiest at home. Yet he resisted the idea of taking her back in the holiday to his headmaster's house; of taking her by the hand and leading her upstairs to that wide, white, elegant bedroom with its stucco swans on the ceiling and its nest of white duck-down pillows. He felt, given Gentille's recent sojourn there, that Christina might be distracted from the pleasure of the business in hand.

Since he had always loved English woodland, he took her instead to a small, ancient inn in a Berkshire village that he remembered from years of hiking through beech groves with the Ordnance Survey map in hand.

'"Welcome to Nettlebed"!' Christina said out loud, reading the sign at the entrance to the village as they passed it.

The beamed doorways of the inn were designed for persons of restricted growth. The upstairs floorboards had taken on giddy and varied gradients. Christina spent some time having fun with the kettle and the sachets of Cadbury's Chocolate Break. She had already decided that the cosiest thing to do would be to join Roland and train to become a high-school maths teacher.

'Nettlebed,' she said severely, 'is not a very sexy name.'

'Christina,' Roland said, so that she stopped playing with the sachets and rose and crossed the floor to him. 'Christina,' he said. And then he kissed her.

She thought, what a satisfactory, what an obvious conclusion. He had always been the only person who had consistently called her Christina. For everybody else she had always been merely Chris or Chrissie. And then, because she was slightly on edge, she found it difficult not to chatter.

'I think,' she said, 'that I had better lie down and close my eyes and think of Venn diagrams.'